Cynthia Roberts was born at Tonyrefail, Mid-Glamorgan, and now lives with her husband in Porthcawl, on the Heritage Coast, which provides the setting for her novels. She has been a teacher and a journalist, contributing articles to a variety of magazines and newspapers and also interviews for radio. She is at present working on a new novel of Welsh village life.

Also by Cynthia S Roberts

The Running Tide

Upon Stormy Downs

Cynthia S Roberts

KNIGHT

To my husband, Alan,
this book is lovingly dedicated.

First published in 1988
by HEADLINE BOOK PUBLISHING PLC

First published in paperback in 1989
by HEADLINE BOOK PUBLISHING PLC

This edition published 2000 by
Knight an imprint of Caxton Publishing Group

10 9 8 7 6 5 4 3 2 1

ISBN 1 84067 266 8

Typeset by
Colset Private Limited, Singapore

Printed and bound in Great Britain by
J. H. Haynes & Co. Ltd., Sparkford, Somerset

Caxton Publishing Group
20 Bloomsbury Street
London
WC1B 3QA

Chapter One

The mist that lay upon the tide was dank and chill. Like some sleeping grey reptile it curled itself into the hollows of the waves until, cast upon the shore, it awoke to slither reluctantly inland.

The stagecoach making for the 'Crown Inn' from the Vale of Glamorgan lurched and swung alarmingly and its passengers, hitherto aloof, were flung together in unwanted intimacy with every new cart-hole and rut. The straw heaped upon their feet in a vain effort to provide warmth sent up a cloud of chaff. It caught in their nostrils and throats with the stench of sweat, damp leather and stale perfume and powder; a mixture barely less cloying than the animal excretions of the horses.

The coachman, familiar as he was with the road, grew anxious. The whale-oil lamps were useless against the swirling fog. It dampened the spirits as rawly as the exposed flesh of his face. The horses, even the experienced leader, stumbled and fretted as though blind, trapped in a grey landscape without feature or sound.

The guard, seated upon his box at the rear of the coach, knew the steep hill to the village must be near, and wondered how in the name of circumstance he could be expected to leap off and apply the drag to the wheels, or, if by some miracle he succeeded, how he could hope to climb back. As for sounding his keyed bugle to warn of their coming, the horn would surely freeze to his lips and the notes hang in icicles upon the muffled air. He would be glad of his hot toddy and milk-sopped bread, and a dry bed in the hayloft, despite the vermin . . .

The coachman yelled a warning and fought to wrench the horses to a stop as a figure on horseback loomed out of the fog. The startled horses slithered and ran into each other, reins tangling, as the luggage jolted into the restraining net, then tore away. For an instant it seemed that the coach must topple and overturn. Then it suddenly steadied itself and drew to a shuddering halt as the guard reached, with the force of old habit, for his blunderbuss. 'Hold hard! Highwayman!' cautioned the coachman as the rider came forward to the carriage and lifted his lantern to identify himself.

'I am no highwayman!' His face showed gaunt in the thin light. 'I ride to the village. Murder has been done – I seek Joshua Stradling, Constable.'

The passengers inside had recovered their wits, and their parcels, and were peering apprehensively through the windows. A plump clergyman, who had been praying most devoutly, seemed astonished that his prayers were so swiftly answered. An old country-woman, trusting in earthly wisdom, was retrieving her wedding ring from the dead beak of a trussed cock-pheasant upon her knee, when the carriage door swung violently open and a young gentleman descended in haste. The horseman's lantern swung towards him to

2

reveal that he was a little above six feet three inches in height, broad shouldered and fair-skinned. His clothes were unusually elegant and his boots, save for the sprinkling of straw, well burnished and of fine leather. Over all he wore a tiered coat of warm cloth and a high silk hat of good quality. Despite his youth, there was about him an air of authority. The lantern quivered in the horseman's hands, then steadied.

'Constable Stradling! Upon my oath!' There was no mistaking the relief in his voice, ''Tis you, sir. Thank God! I had not thought to see you here! I was on my way to –'

The young man cut short his explanation. 'A murder you say? Where?'

''Tis Jem Crocutt, sir, over at Grove Farm . . . Stabbed to death not an hour since. I rode out as soon as I was able, for I was in a mind whether to leave his wife and children alone there. Dafydd, their young lad, ran to my cottage to fetch me over, us being neighbours.'

'You know the killer?'

'No, that I do not! Nor any who might wish Jem dead, for a milder, kinder man God never gave breath to. But,' he said, 'you will want to be on your way. Take my horse and lantern, for what they are worth, and I will find my way as best I can on foot.'

Joshua, refusing the lantern, swung himself into the saddle and, with a word of thanks, was away and swallowed up almost at once in the mist. The coachman gathered up his reins, the guard retrieved the spilt luggage and applied the drag, and the carriage continued on its way downhill.

3

He who had borne the news, James Ploughman, bereft of horse and bearing his lantern, turned back to the lane he had travelled. He was ill-equipped for the weather, for his coat was threadbare and his boot soles worn, although the uppers were well greased with mutton fat. He would keep to the dry-stone walls and hedges for guidance, and have a care for strangers should he meet them. Of one thing he was sure, the murder was not the work of any man from the three hamlets, so violent and bloody it was, and without motive. Jem had neither wealth nor property, saving the soil he worked. Some lunatic stranger, then, or escaped prisoner. He shivered, more from the memory of what he had found than the fog. He had no fear for the safe return of his horse. It would be well treated, he knew. It was a poor beast, winded and broken from its days as a carriage horse, not a fine mare like the constable's grey. Still, it was all he owned. He would have been glad of it now.

Joshua meanwhile, following the track over Newton Downs, felt the mist damp upon his face and beading his eyelashes and hair. There was a coldness about it, a dankness that seemed to penetrate through flesh into bone, and he found himself shivering despite the warmth of his coat.

The mare was a sorry, winded thing, her breathing harsh. Joshua felt the gauntness of her ribs beneath her skin, and in the silent, swirling mist could have believed it to be a skeleton he rode, in some mad dream.

'Behold a pale horse,' he said aloud, 'its rider was death . . .' His voice came back to him, blurred and lost.

The feeling of strangeness and melancholy stayed with

him as the mist thinned and paled to show him veiled hedgerows, and then curled again into a dense, impenetrable fog, muffling the mare's hoofbeats. Yet the good creature never faltered nor slowed her pace, although Joshua judged her heart to be racing, breathing raw. Like a blind man, forced to put his trust in others, he allowed her to lead him until they reached the safety of her master's poor cottage and barn. Then praising her warmly for her good sense and spirit, he set her on the rough track to Grove Farm.

His urgent knocking upon the farmhouse door brought a child to open it, warily. In the wedge of light from the oil-lamp he carried, the boy's face was rough with tears and finger rubbings. Like most of the village children, he was ill-clothed and shoeless. Joshua judged him to be perhaps eight years of age.

'I am Constable Joshua Stradling.'

The boy said nothing but stood aside to let him enter.

'Will you tether my horse?' Joshua asked gently.

The boy nodded and, steadying the lamp, went into the yard. The door closed behind him. Joshua had to bend low to enter, his six feet three inches hunched between the raised doorstep and deep lintel. Even after he stepped down to the flagstones and straightened himself, his head barely cleared the oak ceiling beams. The long room was poorly lighted with but one oil-lamp and two mutton-fat candles in chambersticks, guttering and throwing a thin light which served to deepen the shadows about them.

A woman sat at the fireside, the babe at her breast swaddled in a woven shawl, one end wrapped tight around her back and shoulders, binding the infant so close that he rose and fell rhythmically with her breathing, secure as a heartbeat. At her feet, another babe crawled, raising his head to look at the stranger with dark enquiring eyes. A third child, a girl, who looked but little older, sat upon a stool in the chimney nook, sucking a thumb for comfort, some plaything clasped tight in her fist. Firelight made patterns upon the bare flesh of legs and face, but she stayed grave and unmoving, as if it were the flame and not she which had life.

Joshua, clutching his silk hat to him and feeling the runnels of damp from his hairline, damned the chance that had brought him here in his elegant town clothes. In these austere working surroundings he felt alien and absurd, totally inadequate for the task before him.

'Ma'am,' he began awkwardly, 'James Ploughman told me of the matter . . .'

He could not bring himself to say 'murder'.

She nodded, rocking the baby steadily.

'Where will I find him?' Joshua asked.

'The barn, sir.' The gentle movement continued.

'I will seek it.'

'No, Dafydd will take you. 'Twas he who found him.'

The boy with the oil-lamp had come back into the room and stood waiting. Without being asked, he took a candle lantern from the farmhouse dresser and lit it with a wooden spill from the oil-lamp he had replaced there.

'If you will go with him, sir.'

Joshua followed him into the yard, the lantern bob-

6

bing and weaving before them, splintering the darkness.

When the child threw open the barn door, he stood, then lifted the lantern high. Joshua's cry was torn from his throat as he saw the dead man, chest pinned to the massive oak beam by the bloodied tines of a pitchfork. The body hung grotesquely, limbs askew, the face above caught and frozen in shock painful as Joshua's own.

In the reflected light the child's face dissolved and grew formless, ugly with pain. Joshua drew him close, feeling the small stiff body racked with sobs, and the wetness of his tears upon his shirt front. With awkward clumsiness he touched the thick hair, then forced him away.

'Now, Dafydd, you must hold the lantern while I get him down.'

Joshua was determined upon the task, however fierce and bloody it proved. He would not let the nightmare of the scene drive into the child's brain, so that his last and only memory of the man should be impaled as cruelly as he.

When finally Crocutt was secure upon a bed of straw, and the pounding and aching in Joshua's breast had eased, and the sweat was wiped from his face, he took the child's hand and together they walked back to the house. Joshua's body burned with pain in every muscle and nerve, but he had done what he wanted.

The woman was still seated at the fire as if she had not moved. The younger child had pulled himself precariously upright and was clutching at his mother's skirt for support. The little girl was grizzling hopelessly with tiredness and bewilderment, like a puppy whimpering under its breath. Dafydd set the lantern upon the dresser and went to comfort her.

'I will take them to their bed, ma'am.'

His mother nodded.

He unhooked the smaller child's finger from his mother's skirt and, carrying both him and the lantern, and clutching the other's hand, mounted the staircase. The little girl, still sobbing, let fall a plaything from her hand and Joshua moved to retrieve it and call after her.

In the light of the oil-lamp upon the scrubbed table, the abandoned toy lay upon his palm – a heavy gold cross, some three inches long, studded with blood-red stones which glowed incandescently, the colour deepening and changing as though alive. Joshua thought of the eyes of some startled wild creature caught in the beams of a lantern. He turned the crucifix over and read the inscription:

In Hac Cruce Salus

'In this crucifix lies salvation,' he translated in his mind, observing for the first time the smaller, incised lettering, 'Perugia, 1601'. He took it to the woman at the fireside.

'This is yours, ma'am?' he asked sharply.

She shook her head. 'Some worthless thing Jem . . .' She faltered over the name, 'That he brought home. It is of no value, but Marged liked it and wanted it for her own. He gave it to pacify her . . .'

'You do not know how he came by it?'

'No. When ploughing, perhaps.' In the firelight her

eyes were bleak with remembrance, and she had stopped rocking the babe.

'You will allow me to take it with me?' Joshua demanded.

'Why? What has it to do with Jem's death?'

'That I do not know . . . I should like to find if it has value – a reward perhaps.'

'If you believe it to be of value then I shall be glad if you will restore it to he who has lost it. It will be reward enough,' she said with dignity.

Joshua, seeing the bleak room with its bare white-washed walls, its beams and chimney breast darkened with smoke, the few pieces of rough-hewn furniture, was chastened and moved despite himself. Remarking the paleness of her face and the strain and tiredness about her mouth and eyes, he asked, 'Is there someone you would like me to send for, ma'am? Some neighbour . . . or family?'

'No. There is no one.'

From the stairway Dafydd said, 'I am here . . .'

'Yes,' his mother said. 'You are the man of the family, now. You will take care of us.'

'You will need help with the animals,' Joshua reminded her.

'James Ploughman has offered. He will be glad of work.'

Joshua nodded.

'Dafydd, will you fetch the constable's horse?'

The boy left, taking the lantern.

'I will send someone to see about the burial . . . arrange things, ma'am.'

'I would be grateful for that.'

'I will bring you news of the crucifix.'

'It does not matter, sir.' Her voice said that after tonight nothing could ever matter again.

He hesitated awkwardly before promising, 'I will return as soon as it is light, ma'am, to see what I may learn. I will be bringing Dr Mansel with me to assist with – my work.'

'Yes, that is understood, Constable.' Her mouth twisted painfully. 'Life goes on. It must, whether we want it to or not . . .' She closed her eyes and he saw the tears squeezed beneath her lashes, then falling, although she made no sound. 'It is one thing a farm teaches you, Constable; that, and the closeness of life and death. But not so violent and bloody a death, without reason or gain . . .'

He left her still rocking the babe and he did not know if she sought to bring herself or the child comfort, for it seemed as if she embraced only grief.

The boy brought his mount to the door, then held out his hand, and Joshua took it gravely.

'I thank you for your help, sir,' said the boy with dignity.

'And I, sir, for yours.'

The memory of the barn and the child's weeping lay heavily between them. Dafydd watched the constable mount then ride away and, straightening himself, took the lantern and went into the house.

Already he wore the mantle of a man.

The journey home to Newton was hazardous and chill and Joshua's mind was burdened with thoughts of that young family bereft, and of Jem Crocutt himself, impaled upon the great oak beam like some monstrous insect upon a pin.

He shuddered from the dankness of fog, and memory.

It was with relief and a feeling of deep weariness that he finally rode under the archway of the 'Crown Inn' and into the cobbled yard.

Ossie, the little bow-legged ostler, immediately came forth, holding a lantern which cast flickering shadows upon his creased face and over Joshua and his mount.

'Poor beast, a sorry bag of bones . . .' Ossie shook his head regretfully. ''Tis a miracle she carried you this far, Constable.'

Joshua nodded. 'Yet she is a good creature, Ossie. Sure-footed and brave.'

'Indeed, as she has needed to be to survive the ill use of the past. I fear she is all but blind, sir.'

Joshua felt an ache of pity. 'Look after her, Ossie. I shall pay whatever is needed. She has served me well tonight.'

'I will see to it. And the murder?'

'You have heard?'

'The coachman and guard were arattle with it, and the passengers speak of nothing else, but I grieve for Jem Crocutt and his family.'

'You knew him, Ossie?'

'From childhood, for I once laboured briefly upon his father's farm.'

'A good man?' Joshua demanded.

Ossie steadied the mare and hesitated, as if choosing his words with care, 'Good? Now that I cannot rightly say. Indulgent, certainly, to his wife and kin. Gentle, inoffensive enough. If I were to think of him as some animal, I would say a sheep – docile, willing, easily led . . .'

'Weak, perhaps?'

'If led upon the wrong way.'

Joshua, who had cause to value the ostler's good sense and powers of observation, asked, 'What animal am I, then?'

'Oh, a lion,' said Ossie, smiling his gap-toothed smile. 'Fierce, proud, courageous. A veritable king among beasts – though for the moment you put me more in mind of a drowned rat.' He patted the mare and, whistling tunelessly, led her away.

The next morning Joshua, who had slept ill, arose early, splashed himself icily at the well in the yard, and in his uniform with the wide leather belt and the splendid helmet designed by the parish vestrymen, walked to the 'Crown Inn' to saddle his mare.

The fog of the night had cleared but the air stayed cold and charged with moisture. As he rode out, past the deserted village green and the square-towered church of grey stone, Joshua thought how bleak and wintry was the landscape 'neath the leaden sky. The cottage gardens were empty of colour, save for a few late blooms, their petals browning and mildewed. The trees and shrubs had shed their leaves, rising stark as dead twigs above the bare earth, with no promise of life to come.

It was scarcely six months since he had come to the three hamlets as the first appointed constable. Like the changing seasons he had moved through greenness and the warm quickening of growth to this arid landscape of winter and loss. Rebecca, whom he loved, had gone, the changes in her life a wider gulf than the miles between them. He loved her dearly, but as the proud, independent cottage-girl he had known and not the granddaughter of Sir Matthew de Breos, respected, influential and rich. Upon Joshua's stubborn insistence they had vowed to test their affection: neither meeting nor writing until a year had passed. He knew only that his longing for her grew deeper with the pain of her absence; it could not be eased by work or the deliberate distraction of play.

He was thinking of her dark vitality, her warmth, and the clear blue brilliance of her eyes as he rode through the griffin-topped gateway into Tythegston Court, the house of the justice, the Reverend Robert Knight.

His grey was swiftly stabled by a groom and the door opened by Leyshon, the justice's manservant, who greeted him affably, taking his helmet as respectfully as if it were the royal orb and securing it upon a liveried servants' chair. It was not always so, Joshua reflected humorously. He had thought him a taciturn, ill-tempered fellow until apprised of the poor wretch's rotting teeth and the painfully disordered spine, propped by a wooden splint. This had been the reason for his stiff unyielding manner, which Joshua had interpreted as contempt. It had been a salutary lesson against making rash judgements, and one from which he had duly profited.

'The Reverend Robert Knight bids you await him in the library, Constable Stradling. He will not be long delayed.'

Joshua being seated, Leyshon went upon his way and the constable turned his attention to the curious doors of the 'shadow' library. Skilfully crafted to imitate the surrounding bookshelves they were, in reality, nothing more than simple veneers. Try as he might, Joshua could not relate them to their owner. Deception, desire to impress, or spurious artistry were hardly embodiments of that erudite cleric and justice, the Reverend Robert Knight!

Almost as if Joshua had conjured him from the air by thinking of him, the justice entered, murmuring apologies. He seated himself at his desk, and turned to face Joshua, his plump, benign face shadowed with darkness at jowls and chin, although it was but early morning.

'Well, Stradling, you have news?'

'Bad news, I fear, sir. Jem Crocutt of Grove Farm, murdered last eve . . .'

'Murdered, you say! How?'

'Bloodily impaled upon an upright in his barn.'

'By what instrument? Crossbow? There has been some poaching, I know.'

'No, sir . . . his own pitchfork!'

The justice stared at him in astonishment and disbelief, and Joshua was reminded briefly of the expression upon the face of the dead man, Crocutt.

The justice's protuberant brown eyes were concerned, anxious. 'A disgruntled farmhand then? Or someone slighted and seeking vengeance?'

'No, it would seem not. By reputation he was mild, inoffensive, with no known enemies.'

'Is there such a man? People will wreak havoc and death for reasons which appear too trivial and flimsy to merit notice.'

Joshua did not reply.

'If not that, then a lunatic, or escaped prisoner?'

'I shall make enquiries, sir, but none has been reported hereabouts. I return to the farm directly with Dr Mansel as pathologist.'

'Good. There are children, I believe?'

'Four, sir. The elder boy found him.'

'It is a sight that will be difficult to expunge, although the young are claimed to be resilient. I will go at once and see what comfort I can offer in God's name.'

'I am sure they would be glad of that.' Joshua hesitated before confessing, 'There was something I found there, sir. I should be grateful for your opinion upon it.' He took the crucifix from his pocket, carefully unwrapping the silk handkerchief which protected it. The justice took his gold-rimmed eyeglasses from the shagreen case and fastened them over his ears, the better to inspect it. His eyes behind the lenses were intent, assessing. He looked up.

'A treasure, Stradling! A veritable jewel of both intrinsic and historical value. I would dearly love to own such a rare and lovely thing. How did you come by it?'

'An infant at the farm had taken it for a plaything, the mother believing it to be worthless.'

'How did it come into Crocutt's possession?'

'His widow did not know, but suggested he might have unearthed it when ploughing.'

'No. It is not possible! Remark the condition of it,

15

Stradling! It has been worn and cherished over many centuries . . . It has never lain buried, of that I am convinced! You agree?'

'Yes, sir, that was my thought upon the matter.'

'A treasure such as this, lost, and not reported? No general outcry and reward? It does not ring true. We must turn to some villainy, then. I would hazard wreckers . . .'

'Yes, I fear it is the most likely and devilish explanation.'

'Dear God!' said the justice feelingly. 'It grieves me to think of it wrenched from the neck of one dead, or worse, dying and having need of its comfort.' He studied it upon his palm, eyes dark and compassionate.

'Will you keep it near you, sir, until enquiries have established its provenance? I would hesitate to keep so valuable a thing,' Joshua protested.

'Unlike Jem Crocutt,' said the justice, 'who, not appreciating its worth in life, might well have died for it.'

'That, or turning renegade?'

'Perhaps, for once enmeshed in such a web, he could never struggle free.'

'Yet, if he were innocent?' said Joshua.

'Then the judgement of man is cruelly irreversible. We must look to the comfort of God and His ultimate vengeance.'

'Indeed, sir,' responded Joshua dutifully, thinking that to Crocutt, his relict, and four grieving children, it would bring neither bread, warm flesh, nor comfort.

Joshua made his way back to the village, skirting the lush greenness of Newton Downs. The flocks of plumply contented sheep ceased grazing as the mare galloped by, their protuberant brown eyes wide with curiosity, and so absurdly like the justice's that Joshua was forced to smile.

Through the wide swathe of woodland that bordered Dan-y-Graig Hill he rode, the shapes of sycamore, beech, oak and ash stark against the sky, and in the lee of them the long, low house of grey stone. As he passed, there flashed upon Joshua's inner eye the image of the wild, red-haired youth who had so often ridden out of its gateway. He saw him that last time, atop the cliffs, smiling, taunting, deliberately turning the mare . . . Then the sight of the man and beast silhouetted against the moon as they rode the air to crash upon the rocks below . . . Joshua wondered if he would ever rid himself of the memory, for it seemed burnt deep into his brain. Smuggler, villain, murderer as Crandle had been, Joshua, though hunting him down mercilessly, could not but recognise his reckless abandon. In some other age, some other place, the bloodiness of battle, perhaps, his fearless disregard might have served him well – so thin was the dividing line between evil and good . . . But now there was another murder, as brutal and senseless as the violence Crandle had wrought. Mary Devereaux, that gentle, innocent girl; Jem Crocutt, docile and inoffensive as she – natural victims perhaps, their simple lack of guile the catalyst of their own destruction.

Still musing upon it, he breasted the Clevis Hill and rode the grey through the imposing wrought-iron gateway of Dr Mansel's house. The summer garden, lush with full-blown roses, lilies and the brash exuberance of scarlet geraniums and petunias was no more. The beds were stark, geometric shapes; the statues cold stone. Deprived of their arbours of creepers and mantled ivy, they looked awkward and out of place, as if they had wandered unthinkingly from bathtub into a drawing room of unexpected guests and were trying to make themselves invisible. In contrast, the exotic abundance of the conservatory seemed showy, vulgar, an alien jungle, foreign and unpredictable. Like Madeleine Mansel who had given it birth, and died so violently upon the cold grey shore she had hated, all her thoughts of her beloved France . . .

Strange that Mansel tended it. Would he tame it as he had never tamed her, clipping it into ordered respectability? Or would he care for it as he had cared for Madeleine, allowing it to grow wild and free, expecting and receiving nothing in return? Joshua knew that Madeleine Mansel had never shown anything but contempt for her husband, using him as a shield for her villainy, and believing him to be weak and pliable. What Mansel had felt for her, Joshua could not be sure. Hatred? Pity? Regret? Whatever the truth, Mansel had borne with her in life, and now, in death, could not, or would not, cut himself free.

He saw Joshua coming as he made his way from the stables and along the gravel pathway to the house. He came out to welcome him, busy, corpulent, fly-away wisps of white hair a corolla about his pink scalp. Beneath the overhanging bushes of eyebrows, the eyes were sea-green, opaque.

'Ah, Stradling, an unexpected pleasure.' He thrust out a hand and shook Joshua's warmly. 'Business?'

'I fear so. A death at Grove Farm.'

'Murder?'

'I leave that to your superior judgement, sir,' he smiled. 'I have long learnt the folly of conjecture!'

'Have I been so hard?' His eyes were kind. 'I have been too long probing fact, and dead bodies. I forget the warmth of live human contact – as indeed, I forget my manners! Forgive me. I bid you come inside, sir.'

'If you will excuse me,' said Joshua, 'there is much to do. I had hoped to persuade you to attend me at the farm?'

Mansel nodded. 'The body?'

'Impaled upon a beam by the tines of a pitchfork.'

'Indeed?' Mansel's eyes sharpened, came alive. 'I think that even I might concede it an unlikely accident!'

'I am afraid, sir, that I was forced to move the body – lift it down. I did not want the child who found him – his son – to remember him so.'

'You did right, Stradling. Living humanity is more easily damaged than the dead, although I hope you will not take this as a precedent for strewing corpses about willy-nilly!'

'Nothing was further from my mind, sir,' answered Joshua truthfully.

'I will see you at Grove Farm directly,' said Mansel, turning to go indoors. 'Oh, should you see that odious little undertaker, Evans, tell him that I shall require the body to be brought to me before the inquest and burial.'

'I go there now, sir, and will give him your message.'

Mansel nodded. 'I suppose I should be grateful to him

19

for making good my depredations, restoring them to order. I presume it pays him well.'

Not much joy in restoring them to death, Joshua thought as he went to fetch his grey. If he could restore them to life, would they not give him all they possessed, and the promise of more to come? How gracelessly we accept life. Yet it is all we have.

Chapter Two

After Joshua had visited the undertaker, Ezra the Box, in his cluttered workshop strewn with curled wood-shavings and sawdust, and sharp with the scent of pine-resin and the oils and unguents of the woodworker's craft, he returned to the 'Crown Inn' so that he might stable his mare and make a modest breakfast before the day's work intruded.

At the archway to the inn he encountered James Ploughman, the farmworker who had intercepted the coach and warned him of the murder.

'I thank you for your kindness, sir,' Joshua greeted him, noting the threadbare coat and the patched thinness of his shoes. 'You have come perhaps to claim your mare? She is a good, reliable creature, and served me well.'

'Then I am grateful to have been of aid. It is a small enough sacrifice for a neighbour, although I would have chosen to help him alive, rather than dead.'

Joshua nodded. 'And your mare?'

'Sold, sir.'

'Sold? To whom?' Joshua demanded, surprised.

'I have delivered her into the keeping of Ossie the

Ostler. He paid me well, although I protested that I would have given her willingly for the privilege of a good home and dry stable. I bought her only because she was so ill-used and worthless as a coach horse, and near blind. I could not see her so abused, or slaughtered. I shall miss her sorely,' he confessed, 'for I live alone, and she was friend to me, and company. Yet, having no work, I could not feed her well, or care for her as I ought.' The man's eyes filled with tears. He blinked, and wiped them away roughly with his knuckles, saying, 'I believe pity for Jem's widow, and the violence of his murder, unmans me, sir. You will forgive me?'

'It is a sad business.'

'I go now to help upon the farm. Strange, sir, I have longed to work, and sought it until I could walk no more . . . Now that I have found it, it brings me no pleasure.'

Joshua's return to Grove Farm upon his spirited grey was swift and effortless, with man and beast in perfect harmony. The mare, relishing her freedom, moved smoothly, muscles rippling under flesh, mane and tail streaming in the cool morning air. Joshua, remembering Ploughman's poor winded skeleton of a mount carrying him blindly through the misted darkness, felt a surge of warm affection for the ostler and wondered how many such outcasts had he given food and home. He supposed that no one would ever know, for Ossie would never speak of it. He simply counted it a privilege to share with them what shelter and small comforts he could provide, knowing too well the evils of neglect and poverty.

Like Ossie, Joshua thought as he rode, the countryside about him had an austere, wintry honesty, a spareness of flesh reduced to bone. He saw it in the starkness of tree and ploughed furrow. Even colour was shared – the brownness of skin, earth, fern and fallen leaf. As he entered the farmyard he saw rooks clustered like blackened leaves upon the branches of a long-dead tree, and did not know why the sight grieved him.

Dafydd came forward at once to take his mare. She towered above him, neck arched, nostrils flaring arrogantly, a beautiful, proud creature. Joshua swung himself from the stirrup, smiling to see the open admiration upon the boy's face.

'Dr Mansel has arrived?'

'Yes, sir. In the barn. I am not to go there, he says.'

'No. I will find my way.' Joshua had forgotten how young the child was; he seemed to have shrunk overnight, grown frailer. Joshua realised that it was because the clothes he wore hung loose upon him, cut down from those of an adult.

'If you will stable the mare and return at once, I have a task for you.'

The boy did as he was bid. Joshua watched them go: the horse stepping delicately upon the compacted dirt, the boy bare-footed, scattering the hens in a blur of noise and feathers. When Dafydd returned, running and breathless, Joshua removed his helmet with the splendid badge and handed it to him.

'This is my badge of office, my authority,' he said. 'For now, I invest it in you. You are my helper.'

The child nodded solemnly.

'Do not let it out of your hands, you understand? You must promise.'

'I promise.'

Joshua took a sixpence from his pocket.

'No, sir! I cannot take money!' The denial was swift, emphatic.

'I do not give it to you. You must earn it, as I earn mine!' Joshua consulted his pocket watch, a gold half-hunter, then replaced it. 'I shall be perhaps half an hour. Stay here at the house, as guard. Tell me who comes and goes while I am absent. Protect my helmet with your life, should need arise.'

'Oh, I will, sir! I will, indeed!'

When Joshua entered the barn, Mansel was heaving himself awkwardly up from beside the body, using the huge upright beams as support. His face was flushed, and the fly-away hair wispy about his pink scalp. The pale boiled-gooseberry eyes stared at Joshua for a moment, unseeing, then drew him into focus.

'Oh, it is you, Stradling. I was afraid the boy . . .'

'No. He is occupied. You have examined the dead man?'

'As you say, a bloody enough murder, and one that needed strength and violence. I have never seen its like.' He shook his head. 'But that is not all.'

'No, sir?'

'There were severe bruises, lacerations.'

'An accident upon the farm? Some animal, perhaps?'

'No accident, Stradling! Sustained and deliberate beatings. Even a burn with a branding iron.'

'Recent?'

24

'Some within the past few days, and others from earlier violence not yet healed.'

'Someone who sought to threaten him into silence?' hazarded Joshua.

'Or to extract information.' Mansel smiled ruefully and wiped his hands upon the hem of his Albert frockcoat. 'You see, Stradling, how you corrupt me? Luring me from the hard groundwork of fact to the dangerous quicksands of speculation!'

'Quicksands, certainly!' agreed Joshua, 'but I could hope that all is not irretrievably lost.'

Mansel looked assessingly at the cadaver which, Joshua saw, had locked stiffly into rigor mortis.

'Lost for him,' Mansel said, 'whatever the outcome.' He bent down to his black leather case and extracted a white linen sheet. Silently he set it to cover the body, then straightened up. 'You saw the undertaker, Evans?'

'Yes. I bade him be circumspect – for the sake of the widow and the boy.'

'A wise precaution. He is as incapable of feeling as those poor wretches he deals with! I recall once he actually brought a pauper's body to me upon a handcart! A handcart, if you please! I do not think he will repeat his error.' He broke off to demand awkwardly, 'I suppose you think my attitude strange, knowing the work I choose?'

'No, sir. Humanity, or the lack of it, is born in a man, not his occupation.'

Mansel nodded, satisfied. 'If you will return to my house this evening, I shall have more information for you, I hope. You ride back to Newton with me?'

'No, sir. I regret that there is work I must do here, questions to ask.'

'Well, goodbye, Stradling.' He offered his hand, and Joshua took it, seeing in his mind the cold imprint of the blue-tinged skin and the dead man transfixed upon the wooden beam.

He was surprised to find it warm.

After Dr Mansel had left, Joshua inspected the barn minutely for any evidence he might find, examining beams, implements, every corner of the floor. Finally he lifted the edge of the sheet to search, then resolutely moved the body that he might look underneath, but he found nothing. Nor, he conceded, was he likely to. His real hope lay in questioning, and that must be done patiently and with sensitive regard to feelings, unlike Dr Mansel's quick, incisive scalpel-strokes; but the aim of both must be to open and lay bare.

Dafydd came forward eagerly to greet Joshua as he left the barn, carrying the helmet before him, clasped in both hands.

'There have been comings and goings?' asked Joshua, taking it from him.

'Dr Mansel rode out, sir. Two ladies rode in upon a cart driven by a gentleman with a beard.'

'You know them?'

'I have seen the ladies before, but I do not remember their names. The gentleman I do not know, but he is tall, and must be old, for his beard and hair are grey.'

'Well observed! We shall make a constable of you yet.'

'No, sir. My work will be upon the farm.'

Joshua, remembering his own father's farm, and the anguish his choice had wrought, said simply, 'It is as well to know where your duty lies.'

'If there are questions you must ask, sir,' Dafydd said gravely, 'I will try to answer them truthfully, for I would have my mother spared. She has worry enough with the children and the farm.'

'I shall be grateful for your help. Tell me, did you hear noises last night? See anything suspicious?'

'No, sir, I have thought about it hard. The milking was done and my father had taken the lantern to see the animals settled, and to inspect the barns for fear of intruders.'

'Intruders?' Joshua asked sharply.

'Only those wayfarers who come seeking warm hay, a place for shelter. We do not turn them away,' Dafydd said with dignity, 'we ask only that they respect our property, and do no damage to gates and stock.' The words, Joshua realised, had been the boy's father's, but were now his own.

'Yet there was someone?'

'Yes.'

The memory of it lay between them, making them silent.

'You did not go with your father?' Joshua asked after a while.

'No. I had taken the lantern earlier to lock up the hens and the roosters – there are foxes, you see. I would have gone with him but he bade me stay, saying the fog was damp and I had best look to the fire.'

'You heard no cry, no struggle? You are sure?'

'I am, sir, but the fog was thick and muffled sound, and the barn is away from the house. If the door were closed –'

'And was it?'

'Yes, and barred without – that is why, when he did not return, I took the lantern to search for him but did not, at first, go inside.' His voice trembled and rose uncertainly, then he blinked hard and steadied himself saying, 'I know of none who would have wanted him dead, sir. He was a good man.'

'As you are, and brave,' said Joshua gently. 'I would not persist in my questioning if it were not necessary, you understand?'

'I understand, sir. I would not want whoever did it to go unpunished, for it was a wicked mean act!'

'There have been callers at the farm of late? One man or several, returning, perhaps?'

'No, sir,' he said puzzled. 'We have few callers, save those like James Ploughman or the paupers, who labour as needed.'

'Your father has bought much stock of late?'

'Two bacons – pigs, sir, for our own use – although they are special, for they have ginger hair like a squirrel's, long snouts and little pricked ears! Tamworth pigs they are called. You would like to see them?' he asked eagerly.

'I will return and do so,' promised Joshua, 'and you shall tell me where he bought them, and from whom. But one last thing before we go within – has your father been leaving the farm late at night, or even in the early hours of the morning? Do you recall?'

The child hesitated, and Joshua saw the bones of his knuckles showing white as he clenched them. 'He would never do anything wrong! He was honest, sir! Everyone will tell you he was honest!'

'As he would want you to be, Dafydd.'

'He does not go now – not for a long time!'

'When last? Do you remember?'

'Three months ago. I sleep in the wall-bed in the inglenook, for it stays warm from the fire. I saw the light from a lantern shining upon the window, and got out of my bed to look. I do not know the hour it was, but I recall it was a dark night, and stormy, for the rain beat upon the panes, and the wind was high and whistling down the chimney.'

'He did not see you?'

'No, sir. I thought he was going to make sure that the beasts were secure, for the storm can sometimes alarm them, and they kick out, causing damage, but it was not for that.'

'You are sure?'

'I stayed up at the window, keeping watch to see him home safe, but he did not come, although the storm grew so wild that I was afraid. It was dawn before he came. I could see by the light of the lantern that he was drenched through, and cold, and he shivered as with some fever. I would have called out to him but he looked so angry and tired, and as I was not abed, I feared he might leather me. So I said nothing then, or after.'

'Can you recall the time of month?'

'The very day, sir! It was the last day of September.'

'You are sure of the date?'

'Yes, for it was the eve of Marged's birthday. I remember well, for the next day, when she was three years old, he gave her that plaything for a present – the pretty golden cross with the red glass.'

'He did not say how he came by it?'

'No, sir, for it was then that James Ploughman came upon his mare, urging my father to ride with him. There was a ship wrecked upon Sker rocks, he said, so all else was forgot.'

Joshua stood aside to let Dafydd open the door to the farmhouse. He saw the child tug at the ill-fitting jacket, smoothing it and setting the buttons straight, then he lifted his head and looked at Joshua who put a hand firmly upon his shoulder before handing the boy the helmet. No word passed between them.

By daylight the room was lighter, less oppressed with shadows. The whitewashed stone of the walls and smoke-blackened beams gave it an air of solidity and permanence. The log fire under the great curved beam of the inglenook glowed brightly, and a hanging chain suspended from it supported an iron kettle which was steaming busily. There was a baking oven set into the wall beside the fire, and Joshua could smell the warm yeastiness of crisping bread.

He had barely time to acknowledge the widow seated in a wheelbacked chair, her young babe cocooned in a shawl, and glimpse another woman nursing a sleeping infant, its lips curved open, eyelids fringed with dark lashes, before a large, bearded man leapt up from the inglenook settle.

'Joshua, my boy! How good it is to see you!'

'Jeremiah? I had no thought of you being here.'

They shook hands firmly, and with pleasure, clasping each other in awkward embrace.

'You see, Hannah is here,' Jeremiah said.

The woman cradling the sleeping child to her beamed at him delightedly, plump face under the frill of the cotton house-bonnet flushed from the closeness of the fire and the warm flesh of the babe.

'You will forgive me, sir, if I do not greet you as I ought.'

'Your kind face and goodwill are greeting enough, ma'am.'

'There is another friend.' Jeremiah inclined his head to the far corner of the room. Joshua turned to see a slender, grave-faced woman dressed in softest grey. Her hair was drawn into curved wings at her cheeks, and fastened softly at the nape of her neck.

'Mistress Randall, your servant, ma'am.'

'Constable Stradling,' she acknowledged with a graceful bow of her head. 'It is I, sir, who am your servant, for the kindness you have rendered me.' The company grew quiet for each knew how he had delivered her from the aridness of the poorhouse. Joshua flushed awkwardly, but she went serenely on, taking pewter plates from the vast oaken dresser, handing them to the dark-eyed child, Marged, to place upon the scrubbed table flanked with rough benches.

'Well,' cried Jeremiah loudly upon seeing the helmet. 'A constable, is it? I did not know the vestry had appointed another.'

'I am Dafydd,' the child explained gravely, 'but I guard it for the constable.'

'An honour, indeed.'

'He has proved a fine aide,' approved Joshua, 'and worked well for me.'

'And I have earned a sixpence!'

'A sixpence! What will you do with such a fortune?'

'I will use it to feed the animals, sir, but with some I will buy my mother a ribbon for her hair – a red one, and everyone will look at her and think how pretty she is, and how gay.'

There was a shocked silence in the room, and his mother put a hand involuntarily to her hair, then her composure crumpled and broke and she sobbed hopelessly, without check. Dafydd, bewildered and afraid, began to sob too, and Marged, and soon the three women were comforting and being comforted, telling Dafydd that he was a good, kind boy and there was no call to reproach himself, or weep.

Joshua and Jeremiah availed themselves of the opportunity to slip outside under cover of the commotion.

'Bedlam!' said Jeremiah. 'Sheer bedlam! I swear that women prize a good cry above laughter!'

'There is little enough to laugh at in this,' said Joshua.

'You are right, my friend,' agreed Jeremiah, his eyes grave. 'It is not the crime of a vagrant, or a passing stranger, disturbed, who would reach for the protection of some weapon. This is violent, bloody and remorseless. The coldness of it freezes the blood. There is something deeper behind it.'

'You have heard nothing of any feud? No rumour?' Joshua probed.

'None – neither in tavern, nor at my fishing upon the shore, nor in shop or market place . . . but I will listen hard and question where I may.'

'You have news of Rebecca?' Joshua asked hesitantly.

'That which Mistress Randall reads out from the letters which the little maid sends to me . . . They come from all corners of the earth,' Jeremiah marvelled, 'winging like pigeons come to roost! It is a miracle, is it not, that what is thought can come to you across an ocean, unchanged?'

'She is well, Jeremiah?'

'It would seem so. She is full of the marvels of things she has seen – paintings, figures carved and such. Places, too, like churches and gardens. So many that I grow confused, and mix them in my head. Mistress Randall would read them to you, I am sure, or I would lend them, gladly.'

'No,' said Joshua, 'it is better not, for we were agreed.'

'Does your friend, and her tutor, Dr Peate, give you no news of her?'

'He would not break a confidence, and I –' Joshua broke off as Dafydd came to the door of the farm, still clutching the constable's helmet.

'If you would take some tea . . .' the boy said, 'it is set out upon the table. My mother bids you come. There is cake! Two kinds.' His face still bore traces of recent tears, but his eyes were bright and unclouded.

So easily, Joshua thought, is a child's pain turned to joy. He wished he held the secret, still.

*   *   *

The two men returned within obediently and took refreshment, thanking the good ladies for their hospitality and marvelling at the victuals which could be so effortlessly stored beneath Dafydd's and Marged's small bones.

'You have seen the rector?' Joshua asked of the widow. 'He has visited you, ma'am?'

'Indeed, he came as soon as he heard, sir. A great comfort, for he spoke of Jem most kindly, and with respect. He would not hear of my paying for the funeral, although I told him how I had saved threepence a week lest one of us – lest it be needed. He vowed he would bear all expense himself, and conduct the funeral service.' Her eyes were bright with unshed tears. 'Do you not think it was a good Christian gesture, and kind?'

'I do, ma'am,' said Joshua.

After making their goodbyes, Jeremiah went to fetch his cart, and Dafydd with him to saddle Joshua's mare. As Joshua stood waiting, he glimpsed upon a small table through the open door of the kitchen platters bearing Jeremiah's sea-bass and pouting, and bottles of elderberry and parsnip wine, and sweetmeats that Hannah and Mistress Randall had brought for the children, and was warmed by their concern.

The child in Hannah's arms still lay asleep, soft lips open, dark lashes lying thickly upon his cheeks. His eyelids, blue-veined and translucent, reminded Joshua cruelly of the blue-tinged flesh upon the floor of the barn. He looked up to see Hannah's eyes upon him, pained and compassionate, as Dafydd called out to him from the door. He lifted the boy up before him and they rode together to the farmyard gate where he set Dafydd down.

'We will meet again,' Joshua said, 'as friends. In kinder times.' He raised his helmet and rode away. Where the track reached the highway he paused, hearing the familiar rattle of Jeremiah's cart. He turned, and for a moment saw again that first picture of Rebecca holding the reins, and Jeremiah's face upturned in the lamplight, as he gazed from his bedroom window high in the deep stone wall. Oh, Rebecca, he thought in anguish, how simple life seemed then. Without you, life goes on, but without meaning or joy. Like the widow at Grove Farm, he had suffered a grief and there was no way to ease it.

Jeremiah, flicking the reins upon the little Welsh cob, was troubled. He called out to Joshua in greeting, and Joshua turned and raised his hand in salute, then rode on.

Jeremiah was old and had suffered the deaths of those he had loved, but never the death of love itself, so he could not say which was the harder to bear.

Chapter Three

Rebecca de Breos, had Joshua but known it, was seated at her desk in her writing room at Southerndown Court, and she was thinking of him. It is true that ostensibly she was engaged upon reading a letter from her dear friend Jeremiah, but penned for him by Mistress Randall for, like most of the cottagers, he could neither read nor write. It should have brought her pleasure, for with it came an invitation to attend the wedding of her good friend, Rosa, to the ebullient Irishman, Cavan Doonan. Instead it brought back the sadness and pain of parting from Joshua, a hurt which neither travel nor the warm undemanding affection of her grandfather, Sir Matthew, nor the privileges of her new life could ease. She loved Joshua dearly, of that she was sure, but she respected the pledge they had made to remain apart for a full year, neither seeing each other nor communicating.

She left the letter upon the desk and went to gaze from the window, seeing the woodlands and park flowing bare and wintry to the white-flecked sea beyond.

She was as unaware of the elegance of her surroundings as of the appealing picture she made in her rose-silk gown, softly muted as the colour of lips and cheek.

Against the light, her sloe-coloured hair seemed tinged with blue, dark as the lashes which fringed the remarkably clear blue eyes.

She wondered if she would ever reconcile the two cultures and the two separate worlds which made up her life . . . It was a curious dichotomy. Sometimes, she thought wryly, she scarcely knew herself which was the true Rebecca. The chasm between the poor, hard-working cockle-maid and the privileged gentlewoman had seemed unbridgeable, and yet this life no longer seemed so alien, so strange. It was as though, unconsciously, she had been preparing for it all of her life and its coming had somehow been both inevitable and expected.

She left the window and paused for a moment at her desk, fingering Jeremiah's letter uncertainly, then walked through her small dressing room and into her bedroom.

She brushed her hair quickly at the pretty muslin-draped dressing table, its embroidered skirt and bows echoing the deep mulberry-coloured silk upon the walls. She loved this room, so carefully planned for her by her grandfather, and furnished with the small treasures he had chosen with such loving thought to make her feel that she belonged, was a de Breos born. He had forgotten nothing which might bring her comfort or pleasure: from the silver-topped crystal bottles and fragile ornaments to the books from his own library. Always a warm fire glowed in the grate, its chimneypiece of marble subtly veined with pink and topped by a girandole looking glass of gilded wood. Her bed had become not a hard, ill-tempered thing to bruise and pierce the flesh with straw, but a warm, enclosed place of comfort, its delicate draperies and hangings a special joy.

She picked up her books from the small, rosewood table and glanced with pleasure at the painting which hung above it, suspended by chains from a slender brass pole. It was a Dutch still life of everyday things – vegetables, fruit and full-blown flowers shedding silky petals, the drops of dew upon them so real that she had once, unthinkingly, stretched out a hand to feel their wetness. Best of all she liked the fragile butterfly, its jewelled wings seeming to quiver with life and yearning to fly beyond the confines of its gilded frame.

And if you could, she thought, would you, like me, take wing restlessly, aimlessly, longing to return, and yet unable . . .? What would her tutor, Dr Peate, make of such wild illogical imaginings? Was he not the most meticulous and logical of men?

She went now to join him in the study which had once been a schoolroom and day nursery. He stood up to greet her, stooped, slender-boned. His smile was warmly affectionate.

'You have benefited from your travels in Europe, Rebecca?'

'I enjoyed them, sir, although overwhelmed by so much beauty and antiquity.'

'And now so much beauty has returned to yet another antiquity!' he said mischievously. 'Well, Rebecca, *revenons à nos moutons* – let us return to our sheep,' he translated.

'Do you think it possible, Dr Peate?' she asked, her eyes serious.

He paused, puzzled for a moment. 'To return, you mean?'

'Yes. I have an invitation to go back to Newton. A wedding.'

'I see. And what is it that you would have me say?'

'The truth, sir.'

'Then the weight of experience reminds me that it is a mistake. Nothing stays the same, my dear. Neither places nor people.' The candid eyes regarded her shrewdly. 'But you will go, anyway.'

'I have not decided.'

'Then have no care for what I say, Rebecca. If we lived only through the experiences of others, then we would not live at all.'

She nodded.

'I may say, truthfully, that I would not have you hurt . . .'

'I thank you for that, sir.'

'Do you? Taken to its logical conclusion, you would therefore do nothing, say nothing, be nothing.'

'Then you will give me no advice, sir?'

'I thought, my dear, that I had given it to you,' he said innocently.

Jeremiah Fleet, seated upon Rebecca's old cart with the bull terrier, Charity, ensconced upon a clean sack beside him, was crossing the cart-track through the dunes which led to the bay. Upon the crisp, cold air of early morning, the cob's breath spurted in small clouds of vapour, and the iodine smell of the sea was sharply astringent. From the dunes the smell of the sand rose, salty and wet as the fish which he sold for his living. In his ears was the soft, rhythmic drag of waves over pebbles. Jeremiah let fall a sigh of pure contentment, and the dog thrashed its tail in agreement, pink-rimmed eyes bright. Suddenly its spine bristled and a growl of warning broke low in its throat. Jeremiah glanced about him to see a small piebald pony cresting a hill from Plover's Plain, the rider all but hidden by the steep banks of sand atop with marram grass.

'Upon my soul, Illtyd,' Jeremiah exclaimed in delight, 'what brings you here?'

'I seek those sheep which might have wandered from the commons and downs.'

'Well. Now you have found me! A poor lost lamb . . .'

'A ram?' said Illtyd, pretending to mishear. 'The description fits you well, Jeremiah, for you are indeed stubborn, argumentative and a horned beast when ladies venture near!' They laughed together, warmly at ease as befitted friends, and the dog trembled and jumped upon the cart for sheer pleasure.

'You have news of Rebecca?' Illtyd asked.

'Yes. She will attend the wedding. Rosa and Doonan will be glad to have her there . . .'

'And Joshua, our constable?'

Jeremiah shook his head. 'I have not told him.'

'But you will?'

'I do not know what I should do for the best.'

Illtyd's fine intelligent eyes were grave. 'He has trouble enough with Jem Crocutt's murder, and I fear I might be about to cause him more.'

'How so? You are not threatened?' Jeremiah's voice

was sharp, anxious, for he loved the little man.

'There is talk of sheep-stealing. Already there have been losses in Kenfig, I hear. A band of ruffians, rumour has it. They style themselves drovers, and will steal a flock, forcing them along the drovers' roads to Hereford or London.'

'Take care, Illtyd!' Jeremiah warned. 'I would not see you harmed, and such men are ruthless, dangerous. You are armed?'

'There has never been need,' he answered simply. 'The people of the three hamlets are my neighbours, friends. Those from outside the parish who would reclaim their sheep are free to do so. They might bluster and swear when forced to pay a fine, or when their beasts are impounded, but they mean no real harm . . .'

Jeremiah was not convinced. 'Arm yourself for your own protection, Illtyd, my boy. Speak to Joshua, I beg of you, and if you wish it, Doonan, Emrys and I will take turn to ride with you until the danger is past.'

Illtyd said gently, 'I am poor in stature and stunted in body, Jeremiah, but rich in friends! I count myself lucky indeed, and I thank you for it.' Holding his ungainly head awkwardly upon the wry neck, he rode away. Jeremiah and the dog watched him go, swift and sure upon the piebald, Faith. Illtyd turned and raised an arm in salute above the ugly curve of spine and shoulder.

'A brave little knight!' confided Jeremiah to Charity, 'so convinced that he and his Faith can move mountains.'

The bull terrier cocked its wedge of a head, slanted eyes enquiring.

'And so he might . . . with just a little help from his friends.'

Joshua walked out of his cottage overlooking the village green and the small Norman church of St John the Baptist, its crenellated tower neat and precise as a child's toy fortress. The sky was empty of clouds but silvered with cold light so that church, air, stone walls, and even the trees which rose above them seemed to blur and dissolve into one.

The smell of the brewhouse, yeasty and hop-filled, permeated the air. Joshua sometimes thought that had they not promised companionship and games, the 'Crown Inn' and 'Ancient Briton', which flanked it, would have been superfluous. The villagers could have become intoxicated upon the brewhouse fumes alone.

Last night he had skirted the inns on his way to Dr Obadiah Mansel's house and paused, seeing the truckle of pale lamplight from their windows and hearing the warm sounds of laughter, conversation and song. He might have been tempted within, to become a part of it, and the company of friends, had not duty forbidden it. Instead he had been admitted by the timid, pinched little housemaid, called Lily, into the pathologist's house. Joshua could not be sure, but he fancied that since Madeleine Mansel's death the child had grown less nervous of him, yet she still resembled nothing as much as a shy, twitching little shrew. As he followed her thin, darting figure along the passageway to the library, he half expected to see a slender grey tail peeping from under the hem of her dress, before she scampered away.

Mansel motioned him to a chair. He was seated at his desk, studying the notes he had written, and above them a crystal chandelier, wax candles already aflame, threw glittering splinters of light, fragile and sharp as broken ice. Beneath it, Mansel's pink scalp wore its circlet of hair like an illuminated halo.

'So,' he explained, 'apart from the burn, the branding I mentioned at the farm, there is little of real value to add – although, of course, I have made a copy of my findings for you.'

Joshua thanked him civilly.

'It is a curious brand-mark, Stradling. You would care to see it? The flesh was not healed, so it remains perfectly clear. Quite exceptional . . .'

Joshua, remembering the surprised, disbelieving face of Jem Crocutt, and the cyanosed flesh, refused, adding, 'Could you not sketch the shape for me? Your trained eye is more exact, more perceptive.'

Mansel, not deceived, smiled, and taking a piece of paper and a quill from a drawer, proceeded to do so, sanding it carefully, then pushing the finished drawing towards him.

'You recognise it, Stradling?'

'No. It is new to me, sir, although it is certainly not the cattle brand of Jem Crocutt's few beasts . . .'

'How will you determine it?' Mansel asked. 'Since you will not wish to forewarn the perpetrators of your knowledge?'

'The blacksmith, Ben Clatworthy, is discreet, sir, and will know all upon the farms, for he visits them to repair their tools and ploughshares. My friend, Illtyd the hayward, who impounds both straying sheep and cattle, will doubtless know their marks.'

Mansel arose from his chair and fetched two drinking glasses from a cupboard upon the wall and, taking a decanter from the silver salver upon his desk, poured twin measures of cognac. He solemnly handed one to Joshua saying, 'Shall we not drink to the death of crime?'

They raised their glasses in unison.

'To the death of crime, sir,' responded Joshua obediently. 'Although I would be satisfied, in the short term, to solve the crime of death – Jem Crocutt's!'

'Then we will drink to that, too,' agreed Dr Mansel, smiling and reaching again for the decanter.

The smell of the brewhouse mercifully receding with distance, Joshua made his way into Newton village and to the workshop of the undertaker, Ezra the Box. The appellation had been bestowed upon him by the cottagers, and he was rarely known as anything else, although Joshua had once heard him referred to as Ezra the Fox! Cunning and sly he certainly was, yet he lacked that animal's devil-may-care bravado. He resembled more a sleek, mean-tempered little ferret.

With his hand upon the latch of Ezra's door, which opened directly from the street, Joshua thought, not without humour, that when he and Dr Mansel had drunk a toast to 'the death of crime' it might well have embraced the unspeakable Mr Ezra Evans!

As Joshua entered, the smells of resin and woods and the oils and unguents of the woodworker's craft caught in his nostrils and throat with a warm, sensuous pleasure, and he breathed them in gratefully. It always surprised him that Ezra was so unlike the evocative, romantic scents which surrounded him. He should have absorbed their warmth through his pores and into his flesh, yet a colder, bleaker, more colourless creature never breathed. Joshua suddenly thought of the dead flesh of Jem Crocutt and its marbled blueness, and felt a stirring of sympathy for the undertaker, and the loneliness of his bleak task . . .

It was immediately dispelled when Ezra came out of the rear of the shop whistling cheerfully, spokeshave in hand, scattering sawdust and curled shavings. 'Well, Constable, and to what do I owe the rare honour of your visit?'

'Business . . .'

Ezra's narrow ferret face brightened. 'Indeed?'

'Official business.'

'Oh . . .' Memory of the undertaker's past skirmishes with the law kept him silent.

'In fact, I have come to ask your advice, Mr Evans.'

'What about?'

'Is there somewhere we may speak in confidence, in privacy? Our conversation must not be overheard!'

Ezra looked alarmed.

'It is your opportunity to be public-spirited, Mr Evans. To help authority.'

'I am sure I know my duty, sir,' Ezra said stiffly. 'I have often been tested, and never found wanting . . .'

Or found out! thought Joshua, suppressing a smile.

'You had best come through, then,' invited Ezra ungraciously.

Joshua followed him into the cluttered workshop,

strewn with tools, half-finished furniture, coffins and trestles, and into his living quarters. It seemed to Joshua that these were even more chaotic and crowded than the shop, with clothing, food, tools and discarded rubbish piled upon every available surface. Ezra cleared a dozing tom cat from a ladderback chair near the fire and bade the constable be seated, then installed himself upon a stool.

'How can I help you?'

'With information.'

'What information? I haven't done anything!'

'Of course not,' agreed Joshua innocently. 'I was thinking of you more in an advisory capacity.'

'Well . . .' Ezra looked mollified, but not completely reassured. 'I am sure that any advice I can offer you will be honest, unbiased, and given freely, without thought of financial reward or gain.'

'Of course. That was understood.'

Ezra looked disappointed.

'I seek information about wreckers . . .'

'Wreckers!' Ezra leapt up in consternation, overturning the stool. 'I have no dealings with that ungodly trade! You insult me, sir! I would not stoop to such filth!'

Joshua believed him, for Ezra's indignation left him spluttering and impotent, unable to continue. He wiped saliva from the corners of his mouth, leaving small flecks of sawdust upon his blue-shadowed skin.

'Do not distress yourself, Mr Evans. I merely wished to ask you about their victims, the dead.'

'Ah!' Ezra righted the stool and reseated himself. 'Now, that I can tell you . . .'

'The wreck of the *San Lorenzo*, holed off Sker sands three months ago – you must have dealt with the bodies?'

'I did, sir, and a grisly and bloody business it was. I tell you, Constable, it fair turned my stomach, used as I am to violent accident and death.' He shook his head.

'The rocks, perhaps, and the violence of the sea?' Joshua prompted.

'No! The violence of men, more like!' Ezra's little ferret face sharpened, grew more animated. 'The scars and wounds of nature are terrible, but clean. They do not chop off fingers from the living to get at rings, suffocate and choke women and babes, throw the bloodied and barely alive back to the mercy of the rocks and sea . . .'

'You have seen all this?'

'Aye, and tried to hide its ravages. I know that you do not like me overmuch, Constable, for we have often disagreed, been upon opposing sides, so to speak. I swear to you, sir, upon my most sacred oath, that I have wept for these people, ministering to them with tears wetting my cheeks, and hatred and vengeance in my heart towards those who wrought such viciousness! They are filth! Carrion not fitted to be called men!'

Joshua was strangely moved by his outburst.

'I admit to you, sir,' Ezra continued, 'I am not a brave man. Not to put too fine a point upon it, I am sometimes cowardly and not to be trusted, for I fear pain, and the thought of falling foul of these men and being tortured . . . as I admit I have been threatened.'

'Then you would know the wreckers?'

'No, sir, for they came at night to mock and threaten

me to silence, never by day. Their faces were covered . . .'

'But you witnessed the wreckers at Sker House? Saw their depredations, the evil they wrought?'

'Only upon dead flesh, sir . . . for the bodies were laid upon the floor of an outhouse, guarded by a servant, or so I supposed him to be. No, it was another wrecking I witnessed, unseen, many years ago when I was but a child, and I am still haunted . . . possessed by the horror and bloodiness of it, for then, as now, I was afeared to speak of it.'

'But surely you did not work alone at Sker? There was a doctor present?' Joshua's voice was sharp.

'No. I saw none. Not then nor afterwards . . . Save at the inquest. You understand, I would have begged carts from the villagers to fetch the bodies, for they would willingly have done all they could . . .'

'Why did you not do so?' demanded Joshua, puzzled.

'I was forbidden either to return to my home or call upon others. All I needed was brought to me. Farm carts were used to convey the dead. They were buried as paupers are, sir, in winding sheets, uncoffined, and in one grave. I beg that you will believe me, sir, that I ministered to them after death with compassion and dignity . . .' His thin face grew pale, mouth pinched. 'Well, I have told you about them and I am glad.'

Joshua rose and shook Ezra's hand, feeling it cold and trembling in his own.

'I thank you for your help, sir,' Joshua said. 'It is not a cowardly thing to fear pain or torture; only a stupid or insensitive man would not know fear. But it is a brave act indeed to fear such torment, and act in the right way, as you have done.'

Ezra's little ferret face twitched, and a slow flush spread from his neck, suffusing his skin, as he escorted Joshua to the door of his workshop. He glanced anxiously along the deserted street.

'You will not repeat what I have told you, Constable?' he asked nervously.

'No. You have my word upon it.'

Tomorrow, Joshua knew, they would be enemies. Ezra, wily, unreliable, would be up to his old tricks, and very likely learning new. In this, at least, they were united. Joshua's step was lighter, demeanour relaxed, optimistic even, as he went upon his way. The smell of the brewhouse was quite inviting.

Chapter Four

Sir Matthew de Breos was seated at his desk in the library at Southerndown Court meshed in thought. Rebecca had asked if she might speak to him there, after luncheon, on 'a matter of some importance'.

He was a tall austere man. Some even declared him to be grave and forbidding, but never Rebecca. If she had been asked to describe him, she would have studied him with a critical, painter's eye, and declared his essential quality to be 'a spare elegance'. Indeed, it fitted both character and appearance: upon his person he wore neither spare flesh nor ornament; in his manner, movement, speech, as in his dealings, there was the same economy and directness, a stripping away of inessentials.

Perhaps that was why the library was his special refuge. Apart from its intricately vaulted and painted ceiling and the high mullioned windows, for neither of which he could be held accountable, all was purely functional. He enjoyed the smell of it – that strangely masculine smell of old leather, ink, and the familiar mustiness of long-closed books, mingling with tobacco and dampness. Even the shapes of things pleased him, and their textures: the mellowness of waxed mahogany, the vast atlases upon the reading stands, the terrestrial and celestial spheres, the brass astrolobe, the patterned rows of books . . .

His thoughts were interrupted by the arrival of Rebecca, whom he welcomed warmly and bade be seated that she might tell him how he could be of aid.

'It is simply that I should value your advice, Grandfather.'

'Something which concerns the estate, my dear? The tenants?'

'No, sir, a personal problem – one which you might consider trivial, of no real importance.'

He smiled. 'Everything which concerns you is of the utmost importance to me, Rebecca, for I have not long had the pleasure of having you near me, and I have much to learn.'

She rose and went to him at the desk, putting her arms about his shoulders and kissing him tenderly upon his head. He held her hand to his cheek for a moment, and smiled. 'Well, and what is this dilemma, that only a grandfather is fitted to solve?'

'I wish to return to Newton, Grandfather, for the wedding of my friend Rosa and Cavan Doonan.'

'So you have told me, my dear. There is some difficulty of which I am unaware?'

'No, although I am not sure of Joshua Stradling's reactions in the matter.'

'You wish me to speak to the young man? Explain the situation.'

'No, sir. That is something I must settle in my own mind, before seeking your help and involvement.'

'But you will promise to ask me, should the need arise?'

'At once, Grandfather, for you are all of my family, and I respect your judgement, love you dearly.'

He nodded, satisfied. 'Well?'

'It is to do with Rosa and Doonan. I should like to give them a present. Something special which they would not otherwise have.'

'Yet not so great that they feel beholden to you, and that makes the offerings of others seem paltry and insignificant?' he asked shrewdly.

She nodded. 'I had thought of giving Rosa a sum of money, so that she might feel secure, independent.'

'Not a good idea, Rebecca. From what you have told me of Doonan, he is proud of working hard, providing for Rosa. You would not wish to diminish him, make him feel unmanly?'

'No.'

'Something personal to Rosa, perhaps? Her dress?'

'Her mother is a widow, sir. She has saved over many years and the village dressmaker will stitch it for her.'

'I see. Some jewellery, then?'

'Cavan is buying her a ring, so Jeremiah tells me, of gold, with true lovers' knots. I would not usurp him, Grandfather, or lessen his offering.'

'He has family here? Close relations?'

'No. I think they are all in Ireland, sir.'

'Then there is your answer, my dear. If it could be done tactfully, and without offence, would it not be a kind gesture to bring them from Ireland, and pay for their accommodation at the inns? I do not recollect the names.'

'The "Crown" and the "Ancient Briton". Oh, Grandfather,' she rushed around the desk and threw her arms impulsively around his neck, 'you are a genius! It is perfect! I do love you.' She kissed him hard. 'But how can it be done?'

'Come, child!' he said delighted. 'It is merely the modest suggestion of an old man, requiring no great intelligence or judgement. If you will leave it to me, I will see that it is done circumspectly and without giving hurt or offence.'

'Oh, Grandfather, I am so glad I have you.'

'And I you, my dear,' he said, eyes twinkling. 'For before you came, I was taken up with the trivia of the estate, our farms, tenants, my duties as justice – not decisions of such world-stopping complexity! However, if you would consider another suggestion?'

'Yes, Grandfather?'

'When your friend Rosa is married, and they are settled, would it not then be a pleasant idea to offer them a visit to Ireland, if they so choose, that Doonan might show off his bride to those of his kinsmen too old or infirm to attend the wedding?'

'Why, Grandfather, I believe you are a true romantic!' exclaimed Rebecca.

'Nonsense, my dear!' he said testily. 'I have a logical mind. I do not like untidiness, loose ends – that is all!'

'Of course, Grandfather. You are perfectly right.' She curtseyed to him at the door. 'I offer you my apologies. I completely misunderstood.'

After she had left, he thought how much the lives of both had changed since he had found her after Dr Peate's researches. He had always known that she was brave and

54

independent, but now he was also aware of her quick intelligence, warmth and compassion.

He remembered how she had come to him, when she had lived with him but a month, to say, 'Grandfather, I have a favour to beg of you.'

'Well, my dear, you have but to ask.'

'You will recall that I told you of the man, Crandle, he who was involved in the smuggling and murder?'

'He who rode to his death from the cliff top?'

'Yes. Jeremiah tells me in a letter that his sister and mother are dispossessed, in a sorry state, for the ship involved has been confiscated and there is no money.'

'Indeed?'

'They remain at Dan-y-Graig House solely by the charity of the justice, the Reverend Robert Knight, who owns it.'

'What is it that you wish me to do, Rebecca?'

'You have told me that I should have a companion, sir, someone well used to the mores of society who will act as a friend and chaperone.'

'This young woman is such a person?'

'Joshua believes her to be intelligent, honest and kind.'

'I see – then she comes highly recommended! Do you think that she and her mother might be made comfortable at the East Gate lodge? They may furnish it with whatever is required from the house. The housekeeper will be pleased to assist you, and whatever fabrics you desire will be brought to the Court, so that you may make your choice and give instruction . . .'

Crandle's widow and the girl, Elizabeth, had proved

excellent mentors and companions to the child. He had welcomed Mrs Crandle's role as chaperone and governess upon Rebecca's travels in Europe, and Miss Crandle had been an ideal companion: intelligent and reliable, despite her youth and ill-fortune. Rebecca had promised him that Elizabeth would accompany her upon her visit to Newton. He had made enquiries and learnt that the young constable, Joshua Stradling, was honest and well educated. He hoped that their meeting would not bring Rebecca grief.

Her life had become full since her arrival at Southerndown. Despite her reservations, she had mastered 'the polite arts' and her lessons, painting and music proved her more intelligent and accomplished than any of her peers – although, he smiled, she had never become proficient at her needlework, vowing that she was 'as stabbed with needles as a hedgehog's spine'!

Her duties to the tenants and the sick and poor she carried out with a willingness and sincere concern for their needs which made her visits deeply valued. She used much of her own money, as he knew from the attorney at Newton, to help paupers, lunatic parishioners and those in need in practical ways, which helped to give them independence and self-respect.

She was a kind, loving child, loyal and good-natured. How much of it was due to the cruel deprivation of her past life, he could not be sure, or how much to the bloodline of the de Breos family. About her beauty there could be no argument.

It pleased him to think that he had some part in it.

* * *

Jeremiah Fleet steadied the Welsh cob and guided it down the steep, pebbled ramp which led to the sea. Its small hooves slithered and rang, the cart bumping at its fat rump, Jeremiah and the lobster pots jostling with it, and the bull terrier standing four-square upon its sturdy legs, eyes watering, jowls flopping with every lurch and sway.

'How is that for an old bone-rattler?' said Jeremiah when they were safely delivered upon firm sand. 'I swear it sends the blood rushing to the head, swift as a pretty maid in spring! 'Tis worth more than all the apothecary's fancy pills and potions!'

The dog leapt down from the cart, its paws sinking in the edge of the wet sand, as he, Jeremiah and the pony sniffed the air and surveyed their domain with the pride of common ownership.

The bay curved about them, a wide sickle blade set in a hollow backed by the drifted sand of the dunes and edged by tapering outcrops of rock. Before them, wet sand shimmered to the water's edge, pristine, untrod.

Charity, seeing a gull cooling its feet in the shallows, rushed forward, barking, paws scattering petalled imprints. The bird briefly held its ground, raising its curved beak in a hiss of contempt, then arose, shrieking. The dog made a few half-hearted forays at the pink-scaled feet, then deserted it for a wild chase through the clear ripples; foam and spray showered about it as it ran, abandoning itself to the sheer joy of being alive. Jeremiah watched indulgently, smiled and shook his head, seeing the cur stop and shake itself furiously, slanting eyes seeking approval.

'A born actor!' he said patting the cob, and felt it

stiffen and prick up its ears, straining its neck towards the Burrows. Jeremiah turned to look. Six men on horseback were halted in a curve of the dunes, carefully scanning the coastline and bay. Jeremiah hoped that they had not observed his interest and pretended an absorption with the reins and then the lobster pots, removing them from the cart and stacking them methodically upon the sand. The bull terrier had run back, unnoticed, to stand beside him; now its hackles rose threateningly and a growl rippled the muscles of its throat. Jeremiah's eyes and raised hand signalled it to silence and, taking the cob's reins, he led them deliberately to the small creek where his lobster pots lay beached and waiting. When they had reached it he turned, on the pretext of halting the cob, but the horsemen had gone. Jeremiah was alarmed; they were strangers, he was sure. Why would they come to this lonely place? What was their business upon the shore? Smuggling, perhaps? Or were they in some way implicated in the murder of Jem Crocutt of Grove Farm? That, or more like, as Illtyd feared, sheep thieves, scouring the coast for a small inlet or safe bay from which to sail their stolen beasts . . .

He went about his work of gathering the lobster pots and setting new, but with little enthusiasm, for his mind was occupied. Even the dog, sensing his unease, stayed by him, forsaking its exploration of rock pool and shore, and its playful darting and snapping about the pony's fetters.

Finally, fish gathered from his night-lines and set in the frails upon his cart, Jeremiah took up the last of his pumpkin-shaped lobster pots. Beneath its woven ribs was a lobster as plump and fierce as any he had ever seen. A veritable Goliath of a shellfish! Its great serrated claws menaced the cane bars of its cell as if it would snap them through. Its feelers thrashed the air. Even the eyes, set upon quivering stalks, blazed with rage and fury at its impotence.

'What a beauty!' Jeremiah breathed aloud. 'I shall take it to Hannah and she will prepare it for Jem Crocutt's funeral meats. Yes, that is what I shall do. What is more, I shall tell Joshua that the boy, Dafydd, may come fishing with me upon my cart, and he shall ride with Charity, and hold the reins. He is but a child, and will be crushed all too soon by duty and with grief . . .' Being resolved, he climbed upon the cart, with the dog beside him and, flicking the pony into life, they made their way across the sand.

As they took the pebbled slope to the dunes, the lobster pots bounced and bobbed, slithering helplessly. The terrified lobster reached out a claw and nipped the bull terrier upon its splayed rump, trying to gain some hold. Charity yelped aloud, and shot upright upon the cart.

'Be quiet!' said Jeremiah severely. 'What have you got to shout about? 'Tis the cob and I do all the work! You are neither use nor ornament.'

The dog settled its burning backside upon the wetness of a sack and sighed with pleasure.

Joshua, having returned from his encounter with Ezra the Box, and musing upon what he had been told about the cruelties suffered by those shipwrecked upon the *San Lorenzo*, determined to speak to Dr Mansel upon the matter. It was inconceivable, surely, that he would not have examined the dead. But why then had he not told Joshua of the fact for, like Joshua, he must surely believe that the ship had been deliberately lured aground?

He was admitted at once; Dr Mansel, seeing him dismount from the grey and lead it upon the curved carriageway, had come to greet him, calling a groom to take his mount.

'Good morning, Stradling. Not another errand for me, I hope?'

'No, sir. I wished to speak to you upon a matter arising from a case.'

'Jem Crocutt's death?'

'No, sir. The deaths of many more – those shipwrecked upon the *San Lorenzo*, the vessel driven on to the rocks at Sker, you recall.'

'You had best come inside,' Mansel instructed, and Joshua followed him within the house.

Mansel waved Joshua to a chair and seated himself behind his desk, elbows resting upon it, fingertips pressed together. He regarded him enquiringly from under the thick overhanging brows. 'What exactly did you wish to know?'

'Your findings upon the injuries sustained, and conclusions.'

'There, I regret, I cannot help you.'

'There is some ethical or legal barrier which forbids it?'

Mansel smiled. 'Indeed, no. I simply mean that I was not involved in the affair.'

'But you are the Home Office pathologist, are you not?'

'I am, but you may recall, perhaps, that I was engaged upon business for a week or more at the time. I had travelled by coach to London. There was discussion with solicitors concerning Madeleine's estate . . .'

Joshua made apology, but Mansel waved it down, saying, 'How are you involved in this affair? How does it concern you?'

Joshua told him of Ezra's confidences, counselling the need for discretion upon the matter lest it lead to vengeance.

Mansel nodded, saying, 'It was Dr Elfed Thomas, of Pyle, who took my place at the request of the justice.'

'You know him, sir?'

'Yes, though not well, for I believe no one knows him well. He is insular and unsociable, wrapped up in his work. In fact, not unlike me!' he admitted wryly. 'My judgement is purely that of a colleague and acquaintance.'

'His reputation?'

'Come, Stradling, you know better than that! It would be unprofessional of me to pass judgement.'

Joshua flushed, and acknowledged it.

'I would never, under any circumstances, pass a comment upon his skill or character, you understand. It would be unethical and impertinent. However,' Mansel smiled, 'in conversation upon general topics, between friends, without names or particulars, I would merely say that there are those to whom money does not merely talk, it screams aloud! Just as there are those who, allegedly honouring the Hippocratic oath, do more honour to themselves. If I were sick, I would sooner be treated by a veterinary doctor, sucking medicine through a holed shoe like a fevered pig!' He paused. 'An interesting custom, do you not think, Stradling?'

'As interesting as our conversation, sir, and as ingenious . . .'

'Of course, much depends upon its application. The more enraged the animal becomes and the more reckless, the greater its intake of medicine.' Mansel looked up, innocently, pale opaque eyes amused. 'Is there any subject other than the treatment of swine upon which you seek my opinion?'

'No, sir. I think you have dealt with a difficult subject quite admirably.'

They surveyed each other for a moment, then Mansel's mouth twitched and he broke into laughter. 'As for my colleagues, Stradling, be warned, I will not discuss them!'

Jeremiah had delivered the lobster to Hannah at once, bidding her tell Daniel, her husband, to 'see to the particulars'. He knew that the cartwright had a strong stomach and the nerve to toss the creature into a boiling pot. A barbarous practice, Jeremiah agreed, and one which Hannah would scarcely relish, clothing her great sow, Jemimah, in a frilled bonnet to keep off the sun, and refusing to have it killed – 'for eating her,' she had oft confided, 'would be like feasting upon my Daniel there, so dear is the old sow to me'. Over the years the animal, cosseted and indulged, had grown so fat that she scarce could move, her engorged teats trailing the mud like dangling medals upon a hero's breast. She regarded Jeremiah from the fence of her sty, snout wrinkling, small eyes buried in slits of flesh.

'You will agree she has a knowing look about her,' said Hannah. 'I swear, Jeremiah, she listens to every word and, what's more, understands.'

'Very likely,' returned Jeremiah, unimpressed, 'but what good is she? She is not company or watchdog. You will never eat her, for she would be tougher than my old fishing boots! She is nothing but a massive bladder of lard, and more useless!' Seeing that his teasing had made Hannah vexed, he added, contritely, 'I see you have sent to a thatcher to roof her sty – a fine job he has made of it, too. It will be cooler for her in the summer, and warm in wintertime. Indeed, Hannah, there *is* something appealing about her, some intelligence in the eye. She is certainly the biggest sow I have ever seen. I have brought her a few turnip ends and a swede upon my cart.'

Hannah, mollified, bade him come in and take some oatcakes crushed in buttermilk.

'And how is the old rooster?' he asked while they fed.

'Need you ask? Arrogant and argumentative as ever, and leading the hens a pretty dance with his . . . appetites!'

When they went out to the cart to collect the pig food and the lobster, plus a good fat cod, Jeremiah said, 'You know that I will give my cart and the cob to be hearse-carriage for Jem Crocutt's burying?'

Hannah nodded. 'It is good of you, Jeremiah, for you will forfeit a day's fishing, I know, and winter is a poor time.'

''Tis poorer for the widow.'

'Yes, that is a fact. I cannot dispute it. I have a black cloth here, from time past; I will take it with me that the coffin may be decently draped. It will give it dignity.'

'There was little enough dignity about his dying,' Jeremiah said harshly. 'I hope that Joshua will bring the murderer to justice.'

'Indeed, for we are not safe in our homes and beds while such lunatics roam.'

He handed her the lobster, secure in its wooden cage.

'What a monster!' she cried admiringly. The dog leapt from the cart and rushed at it belligerently, barking and threatening from a safe distance, showing off.

'Whatever has got into the old dog, Jeremiah? I have never seen him do that before.'

'From the yelp he gave upon the cart as we drove here, I fancy he got his backside pinched.'

'Aye. Like many another in your presence, Jeremiah!' observed Hannah, laughing, and carrying the lobster with arm safely outstretched.

'You confuse me with some other!' said Jeremiah indignantly, climbing upon his cart. Yet there was a smile upon his lips as he drove the cob home.

Joshua waited in the small front garden of Jeremiah's cottage upon the sandy edges of the Burrows, setting the time of his expected return by the turn of the tide.

To Jeremiah, he knew, it would always be Rebecca's cottage. 'I am only the gate-keeper,' he would say, smiling, fine grey eyes warm above the roughly grizzled beard. 'I simply keep a place prepared for the little maid . . .' For a time the incorrigible Doonan had dubbed him 'St Peter' but now even the hell-raising Irishman teased him no more. Jeremiah, with the rest of them, was beginning to accept that Rebecca de Breos was unlikely to return . . .

He had tethered the grey to a thick iron ring, which Jeremiah had instructed the blacksmith to fashion upon his anvil and then hammered through the springy turf into the sand and rock beneath. The mare cropped contentedly at the short grass and Joshua, seeing no sign of Jeremiah's coming, seated himself upon a portion of the stone wall within the wicket fence.

It seemed to him that the few months he had known Rebecca were the happiest in his life. Childhood, and his growing days upon the farm, even the work which he had fought so long and hard to achieve, were as nothing beside their affection. All else had become shadowy, unreal against a love which flared naked and all-consuming as a flame. Joshua sighed. Rebecca had brought light and warmth to the dark places within him . . . To be without her was to live always in darkness.

It was thus Jeremiah came upon him, so enmeshed in self-pity and regret that he did not even hear the jangle of the reins and the familiar clatter of hooves and cart.

'Joshua,' Jeremiah said, dismounting and taking the young constable's hand warmly, 'what a pleasure it is to see you. Go in, I beg you, and make yourself at ease. I will unload my baskets and see to the cob and cart.'

When he returned with Charity, Joshua had regained control of himself and was standing in welcome, fussing the bull terrier and teasing him in his usual affectionate manner.

'You will take food with me, Joshua, or a drink to take away the chill?'

Joshua shook his head. 'No, I thank you, Jeremiah, but the business of Jem Crocutt lies heavily upon me. There is much to do . . .'

Jeremiah nodded in understanding. 'Illtyd said that very thing.'

'He is well, the little man?' Joshua, as all the people in the three hamlets, held Illtyd in true affection.

'He has heard rumour of sheep-stealing in Kenfig.'

'Indeed? I have been so wrapped up in the murder . . . You think there is substance in this, Jeremiah?'

'I fear so. This morning, upon the shore, I saw six horsemen in a cleft in the dunes, scanning the coast.'

'Strangers to you?'

'Yes, and reluctant to be seen.'

'Smugglers, you think?'

'That, or Jem Crocutt's murderers. But more like the sheep-stealers whom Illtyd fears! Brave though he is, he would have little protection against their unholy violence, God help him!'

'And so must we!' responded Joshua determinedly. 'I will organise all those I can to watch over him and tell me of sightings that we may raise a small army should the need arise to go to his aid.'

'Then best have a care, for if he hazarded we thought him weak or incompetent, it would wound him more deeply than the blows!'

'Yes, we must be circumspect. You are with me in this?'

'As every man, woman and child in the three hamlets! Illtyd is more than our hayward, he is our inspiration.' Jeremiah's voice was rough with feeling.

'It is agreed, then?'

Jeremiah nodded. 'I had thought to take Jem Crocutt's boy with me to the shore, when all is over, for the weight of death lies heavily upon small shoulders.'

'I will tell him, Jeremiah,' said Joshua gratefully, 'and convince his mother of the wisdom of it, for I believe too much is expected of the child.'

'Yes, child he is. He wears but the clothes of a man, and those chafing and ill fitting.'

'Is it not true of all of us?'

Jeremiah looked at him hard, and with concern. 'It is not duty which makes you speak thus, but Rebecca . . .'

Joshua rose to take his leave, smiling and protesting.

'Pay no heed to me, Jeremiah. It is nothing! A winter discontent. What news of Rosa and Doonan? Their cottage is finished? By all accounts, he has been labouring upon it as if by a fiend possessed, and the innkeepers grow thin for lack of his bounty! I am to be his supporter, and stand beside him on the day, you have heard?'

'Yes, and that Rebecca comes, too.' Joshua had turned pale, and Jeremiah grieved at the pain in the young constable's eyes.

'Well,' Joshua said, keeping the smile firm upon his lips, 'it will indeed be a meeting of old friends. Rosa will be glad.'

As he rode away upon his grey, so consuming were his exultation and despair that he forgot to turn and salute his old friend, although Jeremiah stood there, waiting until he could see him no more.

Chapter Five

When Joshua returned to Grove Farm, as well as being the bearer of messages and offers of help to the bereaved family from the cottagers of the three hamlets, he had other intentions in mind. He would seek the opportunity to question James Ploughman about his part in the affair, or, at least, his knowledge of it. He had also promised Dafydd that he would look at his squirrel-red Tamworth pigs – a strange and exotic choice, surely, for an impoverished farmer, trying to wrest a meagre living from rented soil. Who had supplied him with them? More pertinently, who or what had provided him with the money to buy them?

Joshua had spent some time in the village deciding upon small offerings for the children which would neither embarrass the widow nor make her feel that he sought to buy either information or their trust. He had been lucky enough, when returning from Jeremiah's house, to chance upon a travelling pedlar crossing the village green, his tray a-clutter with pretty frivolities and useless gewgaws. The seller, a lean, cadaverous man with but one leg, and balancing upon a wooden crutch, had been pleased to wait patiently while Joshua made his choice. Joshua supposed the man to be a survivor from the war with the French, for there were many so mutilated and unfitted for other work. Despite the deep planed hollows of his cheeks and his physical impediment, he was a cheerful fellow and moved assuredly, yet with awkwardness, not unlike the scuttling sideways motion of a crab.

'You buy for a lady, sir? Some pretty trinket for her hair?'

'One lady,' said Joshua, smiling. 'No, I correct myself, pedlar, two! Though one is but three years old.'

He made his two purchases, choosing a strung necklace of coloured beads for the child, Marged, sparkling with colour as a rainbow. For the babe a little bonnet, trimmed with frills of lace, and for the child who clung still at his mother's skirts, a carved wooden horse, some two inches high, dappled grey, and like enough to fit into his small fist. He paid the pedlar what he asked, which was but a few pence, and gave him a sixpence, bidding him refresh himself at the 'Crown Inn', and to enquire there for the ostler, who would very likely warm him at his fire or offer him some warm hay for the night, for later it would grow chill. The pedlar thanked him handsomely for his courtesy and both continued on their ways well satisfied – the pedlar to slake his thirst, Joshua to the village whence, his final purchase made, he rode out upon his quest.

Dafydd, scattering feed to the hens in the yard, ran immediately to greet him, laying aside his basket, and taking the grey to stable her. When he returned, smiling and breathless with hurrying, Joshua silently handed him two parcels.

The child looked at him questioningly, thinking it ill-mannered to ask if they were his by right.

'One I have bought for you, one from you . . .'

The child opened the small packet and saw it was a scarlet ribbon. He said gravely, 'I thank you for your kindness, sir. You will allow me to pay for it, for I have a penny saved for this from the sixpence I earned.'

'Of course,' returned Joshua, 'and I will give you one halfpenny in return.'

The transaction completed, Dafydd opened the large parcel and produced a pair of wooden-soled clogs.

'Will you not try them on?' asked Joshua. 'For if they are not a good fit I may return them, and bring you others.' The boy wiped his bare feet carefully with his hands and put them on, running and clattering upon the cobblestones, scattering the chickens and one vagrant duck from the farmyard pond.

'When shall I wear them, sir?'

'Now, and every day. Jeremiah Fleet has hopes that you will go fishing with him. You may drive his cart and set the lobster pots. They will be exactly what is needed for that.'

Dafydd removed them carefully and replaced them in their wrapping.

'They do not pinch?' asked Joshua anxiously.

'No, sir. But I would not wish to wear them out by overuse,' he said simply. 'I shall keep them for special days – the funeral, and my outing with Mr Jeremiah Fleet.'

'You have others?'

'No, sir, we do not have shoes! The babes have no use for them, and Marged, being a girl . . .'

Joshua nodded. 'We shall ask Jeremiah to take you to see how they are fashioned. Cut from wood by an axe, its edge so sharpened on a stone that it could split a hair from your head. The soles are left to dry outdoors, stacked one upon the other like a monstrous egg-shaped beehive.'

'I should like to see that, sir.'

'Will you, in turn, show me your Tamworth pigs?'

'Willingly, sir.'

The strange long-snouted creatures being admired and remarked upon, Joshua asked idly, it seemed, 'You feed them and care for them yourself?'

'Since – ' and Joshua feared he was going to say 'since my father's death'. He said instead, 'Since Elwyn Morris left, ran away, I have helped with all the animals.'

'Morris? I do not think I have heard the name,' Joshua said carefully.

'He is a pauper labourer, sir, from the workhouse at Bridgend.'

'He lived here, at the farm?'

'No, sir. He walked each morning from Bridgend, and back again by night.'

'Where did he go? You have news of him?'

'Nothing, sir. He went the morning after the storm . . . after James Ploughman came with news of the ship-wreck at Sker. I recall it, for my father was tired and raged and grew cross, bidding me see to the stock, for he was too weary . . .'

'Where did your father buy the Tamworths?'

'I do not rightly know, sir, for when I asked him he said it made no matter, I would not know the place. He went alone upon the journey, bidding me have a care for my mother and the farm. He said it was too far for me to walk; that I was slow and would be a burden to him. But it could not have been too far, sir, for the next day he drove the Tamworths home along the byways . . .' Dafydd's voice was tight with hurt. 'I would have liked to walk with him, sir.'

'Did James Ploughman, your neighbour, know this man Morris?'

'Yes, sir. Well, they would go poach – ' He broke off, embarrassed, and clutching his parcel awkwardly. 'They would work together if they could. Friends.'

'I see,' Joshua nodded. 'You have been carrying on your work as my aide? I bade you tell me of strangers who visit the farm . . .'

'There have been many who have come to pay their respects,' Dafydd said with dignity, 'for my father was greatly liked.'

'No one else?'

'Yes, sir. I do not think my mother wished me to mention it, for it upset her, causing her to become unnerved and weep, although I told her that there was no need.'

'Someone threatened her, or you?'

'No, sir. It was of no importance, scarce worth the mention. A man on horseback came offering to buy trinkets, things of small worth, knowing, perhaps, that my father was dead and we might be in need of the money for the burial. But the rector –'

'Yes, your mother has told me of that. This stranger, was there something special he sought?'

'He asked if we had jewellery to mend, or sell,

however worthless it seemed. A necklace, bracelet or a crucifix, he said, for they are worn by both men and women. My mother answered, "No, there was nothing. We are poor farming folk." She said, "We would have no use for such things, nor the means to buy them." I started to say about the one my father had found, but she bade me hold my tongue, for I knew nothing of such matters and if I persisted, she would be forced to leather me and send me to my bed.'

'She is tired,' said Joshua, 'and grieved.'

'Yes, that is what I thought, sir, so did not pay it mind. And when he was gone, she gave me some warmed buttermilk and an oaten cake, then bade me speak of it to no one.'

'You have not spoken of it?'

'Save to you, sir. You are the constable . . .'

Joshua nodded and removed his helmet, offering it to the boy. The constable opened the door, and with his new shoes safely under one arm and Joshua's helmet under the other, Dafydd entered the farm.

The clogs being displayed and tried on again, to clatter most satisfyingly over the flagstones, Joshua produced the rest of the gifts. The wooden horse was received shyly but with obvious pleasure, and its owner would not be parted from it, even for it to be inspected. The babe's bonnet was declared to be 'pretty beyond belief' and 'suited him a rare treat'. Marged at once demanded a looking glass that she might see herself, and ran upstairs, descending vain and flaunting as a peacock. Finally, Dafydd gave the ribbon to his mother, declaring that he had paid for it himself. Above the child's head,

Joshua nodded, and Dafydd's mother thanked him silently.

'James Ploughman is here, Mistress Crocutt? I would speak with him, if he can be spared.'

'He is not here, sir. He has walked to Bridgend market, taking butter, cheese and eggs to be sold, upon a small handcart. Shall I ask him to call upon you when his work is done?'

'If you will, ma'am.'

She nodded and rose from her chair to see him leave, bidding Dafydd fetch his mount.

'He has told you of the stranger?' she asked before the boy had returned.

'Yes. You believe he knew of the crucifix?'

'I am sure of it.'

'You recognised this man?'

'No, he was a stranger to me. Large, heavy-featured, with shadowed jowls, a scar raised and livid on his brow, a man of perhaps forty years. I would hazard him to be a labourer upon some farm, for his shoulders and arms were hard-muscled as by such work and his hands calloused and grained.'

'You make as observant an aide as your son, ma'am.'

Her eyes met his anxiously above the babe's new frilled bonnet and she settled it straight, unnecessarily, to occupy her hands.

'You think he will return? Threaten us, perhaps? Do some mischief?'

'No, but I have men who will keep watch covertly and I will return.'

'We thank you for your kindness, Constable.'

Dafydd appeared with the grey and Joshua again lifted him up beside him and they rode to the farmyard gate.

'You will be coming to the funeral, sir? I am to walk all the way before the cart, to Newton. I will wear my clogs and they will make a fine echo upon the way.' Joshua felt the sting of tears behind his eyes, as he reflected, of such joys and sorrows are childhood memories made.

Doonan's pretty bride-to-be, Rosa, was standing patiently in the living room of her mother's lodging house near the port. She was surrounded by all the clutter and paraphernalia of the travelling seamstress's art – and by the seamstress herself, a small cottage loaf of a woman, black cotton bodice so rigid with pins that she might have worn armour. Beside her, a young apprentice hovered, a small anxious worker bee humming and buzzing at the command of her demanding, over-stuffed queen.

Rosa was unaware of them, for her mind was elsewhere. She was thinking of Cavan Doonan and the coming wedding, and a small affectionate smile curved her lips.

The overworked apprentice thought how beautiful she was, so pale-skinned and delicate, like some classically draped marble statue, timeless and serene. Her little romantic soul was so stirred that a tear came to her eye and she was forced to sniff, and the seamstress turned on her angrily, asking if she had a handkerchief, for it would not do for her nose to drip upon the gown.

Rosa was thinking how cleverly she had dealt with

Cavan, deflecting him from that quick Irish rage which flamed bright as his red hair. It was a rage swift and unpredictable as his moods, and had earned him a reputation for being belligerent and quick with his fists. Rosa, however, he treated as a rare and delicate ornament, to be admired and used with care and respect. Rosa determined that in their bed, at least, it would not always be so!

When news had come that Rebecca wished to pay for the transport and boarding of his family and friends at the local inns, he had been ablaze with fury. He was at pains to bellow his resentment to any who would hear, especially Rosa.

'Why, Cavan,' Rosa had said mildly, 'what a warm, loving gift Rebecca offers you! What a public declaration of her respect for you as a man – indeed, for your whole family, my dear. That the granddaughter of Sir Matthew de Breos holds you in such esteem, and is so desperate to meet your kinsfolk that she bids them travel from Ireland at her own expense! Why, the people of the three hamlets will be agog with it, saying how greatly she admires you.'

'Well, I do not think it fitting that she offers money,' he blustered feebly.

'Not fitting? Why, Cavan, my love, she offers no money! She offers a wedding gift, as is the custom, but one carefully thought out to bring you the deepest pleasure.'

'Well, perhaps you are right,' he said doubtfully, 'if you wish them to come . . .'

'If I wish them to come! Why, they are your own dear

family, and have made you the generous, warm-hearted and loving man that you are. How could I not wish them to come, and be near me upon the happiest and most memorable day in all my life? The day I come to you!' Cavan, touched and reassured upon his manhood and noble disposition, had kissed her and told her that she was the sweetest and cleverest girl in all the world, and she was not inclined to disagree.

'I will go this very week to Bridgend to buy you a ring,' he promised, 'such a ring as will make the quarrymen and cottagers draw in their breaths, and gaze with envy and amazement . . . Emrys will take me upon the cart.'

Rosa nodded and smiled, now, at the thought of him riding upon Emrys's dusty quarry cart with the pot-bellied, winded hack which drew it, and the surprise upon the goldsmith's face when they stopped outside his workshop.

The seamstress, taking her smile and nods as approval, said, 'Indeed, Mistress Rosa, I declare with my hand upon my heart –' it clasped her pin-cushioned bosom – 'that you will be the most beautiful and elegantly dressed bride that has ever been seen in all of the three hamlets!'

Rosa's mother, who had entered the room, wiped a recalcitrant tear from her eye, and nodded agreement, for Rosa did indeed look virginal and fresh as any bride should be. It was a pity about Doonan, lumbering, drunken, hell-raising, with his battered features and missing tooth from some churchyard brawl. Still, it was the bride's day, and Doonan was but a small impediment.

She turned to the seamstress, saying, 'I am sure that

she will look most elegant, for Constable Stradling will be supporter to the groom, and will lend him his own curricle to transport them to the church.'

The seamstress was impressed, her little blackcurrant eyes sparkling behind the lenses of her metal-framed glasses. 'And not a whit too good for her!' she approved.

'Miss Rebecca de Breos, Rosa's dearest friend and granddaughter of Sir Matthew de Breos of Southern-down Court, has personally arranged for Cavan's family to travel here. They will be lodged at the ''Crown Inn'' and the ''Ancient Briton''.'

'Indeed?' The seamstress bristled with importance. 'Miss de Breos once made some drawings of fashion plates for me. In fact, I sewed her very first gown. A true gentlewoman, aristocratic in feature and manners. She was so complimentary about my stitching that I was forced to blush, quite overcome with praise and modesty.'

'Cavan's family, the Doonans, are landed gentry,' countered Rosa's mother, bosom swelling and making her look like a full-breasted thrush upon thin legs. 'I have heard, although he would deny it most vehemently, that they are direct descendants of the Irish princes.'

Rosa, visualising Doonan's battered, unlovely face, stared at her usually truthful mother in amazement and broke into laughter, which she was almost powerless to control.

'It is some nervous reaction,' explained her mother vexedly. 'She is a delicate creature – has been so from a child.'

The dressmaker nodded knowingly and whispered,

'Sometimes those . . . lewd and carnal expectations have been known to unhinge an innocent bride. Men are but beasts.'

'I fear so,' said the widow, dropping her voice, 'animals at heart, all. I grieve for my dear Rosa, but it was ever thus.'

'At least she will be well dressed.'

Rosa, slipping her pretty gown over her head, was able to pause a moment to hide her mirth. And undressed! she might have added, but of course, did not.

Doonan and Emrys, his friend, their day's work at the limestone quarries at an end, refreshed themselves briefly at the water-buckets filled by the apprentices at the nearby stream, and made themselves ready for their journey to Bridgend to purchase the ring.

Emrys solemnly flicked at the dust upon the cart with an ancient sack. It lay so copious and thick that he had to be content with simply rearranging it from one place to another. The horse he could do nothing to improve. Nor, indeed, did he even consider doing so for, half-blinded as he was with quarry dust and affection, he saw nothing wrong with it.

'Well,' cried Doonan, impatient to be at his task, 'are you fit, Emrys?'

Emrys nodded his grey head. Doonan knew it was grey, for he had seen it washed but, in truth, it was the same dull, powdery colour as the rest of him, so ingrained with limestone were his clothes and skin. Doonan's red hair, too, was powdered as a wig. With the winter light already failing, although it was but late afternoon, their equipage and they might have been mis-taken for some ghostly chariot and crew, had not Doonan been so plainly of this world, and of solid flesh!

As they began to move, one of the apprentice boys, bolder than the rest and agile enough to run out of reach of Doonan's massive fists, handed him a prettily ribbon-tied package, forcing Emrys to halt the cart.

' 'Tis a wedding gift, sir,' he recited, having rehearsed it well, 'a true reflection of our respect and feelings for you.'

The quarrymen, well primed, clapped and made crowing noises, and others more vulgarly distracting, as Doonan carefully unwrapped it. There was a gale of laughter as it appeared.

'A Napoleon chamber pot!' cried Emrys, peering into the bowl from which a raised model of the emperor's face gazed haughtily from under hooded lids. They moved off to a chorus of cheers, jeers and laughter, Doonan waving the chamber pot aloft and bowing from side to side amid shouts of:

'Show him your weapon, Doonan!'

'Wipe the smile off the Frenchy's face!'

'Cover him with glory!'

'Make the froggies hop!'

Doonan tossed the ribbon and its wrappings to the ground, and as they mounted the ramp of stones that led from the quarry floor, he raised the pot and wickedly pretended to drink their health, before placing it solemnly upon his head.

Emrys was almost too overcome with laughter at his antics to drive the cart, and the apprentices and quarrymen were in great good spirits that their jesting had been so kindly received.

As they neared the tollgate upon Three Steps Hill, Doonan still clutching the chamber pot, Emrys slowed the cart, for there seemed to be some fracas ahead.

The tollgate keeper, a thin wizened old man, was being set upon by a band of ruffians seeking to evade their dues. Beaten almost to the ground by staves and fists, he lay with hands over head, trying vainly to ward off their raining blows. Doonan, with no thought for his own safety, leapt from the cart and, laying about him with his mighty fists like a man possessed, beat the ringleader almost senseless, then started upon the rest. Within minutes, they were up on their horses, and swearing and threatening vengeance, riding upon their way. Doonan, with amazing gentleness for such a heavy man, lifted the poor broken wretch up to his feet, dusted him down, and helped him to his chair within the little tollhouse. Emrys, meanwhile, had dismounted, and come to see if he could be of aid, but the old man waved him aside, protesting that he was recovered and not irreparably hurt.

'A few bruises, and they will soon mend. And no bones broken, sir.'

Doonan and Emrys, remarking upon his stamina and courage, returned to the cart to drive through the open tollgate and upon their errand. As they did so, the ancient hobbled out and, running alongside the horse, demanded that they pay him a sixpence at once, or halt! He would not let them cheat him by driving through. He would call upon the toll committee, the justices, the military, if need be!

Doonan, enraged at such base ingratitude, so forgot himself as to raise the precious Napoleon pot and break it upon his head, sending him dazed and bleeding to the roadside.

Emrys turned to Doonan, who sat beside him, the china handle still clutched in his hand, 'And how will you plead before the justice?' he asked, grinning.

'That it was the damned Frenchman clouted him, not I.'

Chapter Six

When he returned from Grove Farm, Joshua had taken the opportunity to ride through Nottage and into Port, making courtesy calls upon the innkeepers and land-lords, and upon the administrators of the docks and the horse-drawn tramroad.

It seemed to him that if there were strangers about, or any signs of incipient unrest or violence, then they would be certain to learn of it. He paused, too, to talk to the farm labourers and villagers he met upon the way, enquiring about their families and day-to-day affairs, and exchanging the pleasantries of neighbours. He was acutely aware that his background as a putative 'gentle-man' alienated him from these good people, a distance exacerbated by his uniform and official status as a con-stable. He knew that he must gain their confidence, so that in time of trouble they would turn to him immedi-ately and instinctively, as to a friend. Yet their trust, like friendship, could not be forced; it must be earned.

When he arrived at his cottage it was late afternoon, and the winter dusk was closing around him, making the air chill. He was forced to light the oil-lamp although it was but four of the clock by his half-hunter, and he set about preparing a modest meal of bread, cheese and ale.

He was about to begin the frugal repast when he was cautioned by the sound of a rider dismounting outside his door. Taking the lamp, he went to investigate, opening the door upon the thin, apologetic face of James Ploughman.

'I have borrowed a horse from Mistress Crocutt of Grove, sir, for she told me you wished to speak with me. I came as soon as I was able.'

'Will you not come in?' invited Joshua. 'For I am about to eat and you are welcome to break bread with me, for I have too little company.'

Ploughman thanked him and, tethering the horse at a ring set in the wall, followed Joshua within.

The meal begun and his guest's awkwardness relaxed, Joshua said quietly, 'I think, sir, that you know why I have sent for you!'

'You wish to know of the day of the shipwreck, when the *San Lorenzo* came aground at Sker.'

Joshua nodded.

'Dafydd told me that . . . of your interest, sir. What do you require to know?'

'First, what did you see? How did you learn of it?'

'From a friend, sir, a labourer on the farms like me, although he has no place of his own, working and making his bed where he may. He had gone to Sker Farm early, hoping to find work, or a crust. He will labour at anything, however filthy or menial, having a terror of the poorhouse.'

'His name?'

'That I do not rightly know. I have never heard

his given name. He goes simply as Dai Bando.'

'Bando?' repeated Joshua. 'It is a strange enough name. How did he come by it? From the game the villagers play, you think?'

'Very likely, sir . . . for he is not unlike the makeshift ball or pebble that is used: rolling, unpredictable, ever moving on . . . and belaboured by life, as the players belabour the ball with rough sticks,' Ploughman said with unexpectedly wry humour.

'What did this . . . Bando see?'

'He begged me to go at once to Sker Farm, taking whatever help I could find, for there had been a ship cast upon the rocks. I asked if there were survivors, or if the family at Sker had offered help . . .'

'What did he answer?'

'He could say nothing, sir. He was unable to speak for he was in a sad state, having run, it seemed, the distance from the bay. He could scarce breathe and was grasping his ribs, so raw was he with pain. I bade him sit awhile and rest, leaving him a pitcher of buttermilk and a crust. I thought to question him when I returned, for I saddled my mare and left at once for Grove to summon Jem Crocutt's aid, thinking there might be some alive and needing our help.'

'And when you got there?'

'Before we got there, sir, Jem began to sweat and shake as if he had the ague, weeping and crying that he could not come. He could not face the horror of it, of what he might see. I begged him to take a hold on himself! In fact, it grieves me now, I admit, I grew quite angry and told him to get himself home, back to the women where he belonged, for he was nothing of a man, fit only to see to puking babes and feed them pap!'

'He went?'

'He did, indeed, without so much as a word, the tears running down his cheeks. I was white with fury and let him go. I am sorry now for things were never the same between us from that day. Although we never spoke of it again, I thought after, fear takes us in different ways. It was not kind of me.'

'And at the wreck?'

'Like me, he would have seen nothing but the broken ship, and what flotsam and wreckage drifted ashore. Those dead who had been recovered were already gone, and there was none living.'

'Gone? Where?'

'It seems the owner of Sker House, a gentleman, had a physician there as guest. He gave what aid he could, but the wind was high and the sea rough and battered them cruelly upon the rocks. Not one soul long survived. The bodies were put upon farm waggons, it appears, and taken almost at once to be buried in a common grave, uncoffined and in winding sheets, or so it was rumoured. A strange thing, sir, yet done upon the orders of the justice, the Reverend Robert Knight, they said, so it must have been right. The Reverend Robert Knight is well known for his honesty in all his dealings.'

'That is so,' agreed Joshua. 'You heard what happened to their valuables, jewellery and such?'

'Left upon them, sir, and returned by the undertaker to the excisemen who later guarded the wreck. Rumour has it that it was worthless stuff. Either the passengers were poor, or their valuables kept in some secure iron safe which was spilt into the sea.'

'And the man, Bando? He could tell you no more?'

'He could tell me nothing, sir, for when I returned he had gone, the food and drink I left him untouched.'

'But you have seen him since?'

'No, sir, not hair nor hide, not this three months and more. It is a strange thing, for that day he was in such a sorry state that I do not think he could walk far.'

'You will tell me should he return?'

'At once, but I do not think it likely, for I have made enquiries all about and he has not been seen. He is living rough, perhaps, and I fear he may have come to grief.'

'The pauper who sometimes worked at Grove, your friend . . .'

'Elwyn Morris.'

'Yes. You know of his whereabouts?'

'No, sir. He left the very same day, with no word of farewell, or explanation. I was so vexed and put about that I rode even to the poorhouse at Bridgend, but they knew no more about him than I.'

'What conclusion did you come to?'

'None, save that it was not in character. He had few friends, and those he valued. He would not have treated me thus from choice.'

'You suspect some mischief, then?'

'I do, sir!' His voice held conviction. 'Some evil is afoot! I have no proof, and it would not be provident to confess it to any but you, sir. Yet something about the shipwreck and the two men gnaws at me, and will not give me peace. And now, Jem's murder . . .'

Joshua said, 'You have answered my questions with honesty, sir, and I thank you for it, and for the help you have given to me today, and the day when you came to intercept me on the coach and lent me your mare. She fares well?'

'Indeed, sir. Ossie bids me visit her as often as I choose, saying he is grateful for my news and company. She has not forgotten me and welcomes me with warmth and pleasure as of old. I believe she understands. She bears me no ill-will, thinking I abandoned her.'

'I do not think you would abandon anyone, or any creature,' said Joshua sincerely.

'But I did, sir. Jem Crocutt,' Ploughman said earnestly, 'and I feel the shame of it every day. It is hard for me to live with.'

Joshua took the man's hand and shook it, saying firmly, 'We cannot live our lives, sir, ruled by the fear of death, another's or our own. It would govern all our actions.'

James Ploughman looked at him steadily, 'And if it did, might we not have fewer regrets?'

The next morning Joshua went early to the 'Crown' to saddle his grey, glimpsing Ossie tossing hay from the hayloft with a pitchfork. The sight of it brought a memory of Jem Crocutt skewered upon the beam, and he was surprised to find his hands trembling upon the mare's reins. Ossie stopped his forking to shout down from the opening to the loft.

'You are well, sir? I have seen little of you of late.'

'No, I fear the affair at Grove possesses me, Ossie. We will meet at the funeral?'

Ossie's seamed face grew strained. 'Yes, although it is not a duty I relish. Respect in life is of more value than in death, sir, of that I am sure. Yet, I would not hurt his widow and kin, if to be there brings them comfort.'

Joshua nodded. 'James Ploughman came last night to see his mare?'

Ossie flushed. 'He has told you, then? I merely keep her here until he is able to repossess her. She is still his.'

Joshua put his hand into his pocket and produced a gold sovereign. 'Since the mare is his, and you board her for him, merely, will you take this small payment for her keep?'

Ossie hesitated, face uncertain, then set down his hay-fork and descended the ladder reluctantly.

'Come,' chivvied Joshua, 'There is no reason to let him know of this! He did me a service. I simply wish to return his kindness in the only way I am able, without causing him humiliation, or me the embarrassment of his refusal.'

'Then I accept for him gratefully,' said Ossie relaxing, a smile showing the gaps in his teeth. 'I swear, Joshua, you have a turn of phrase and persuasion that would . . .'

'Lure an ostler from a loft,' supplied Joshua.

'That, too, although I was going to say, charm a love-bird from a tree,' said Ossie. 'Talking of which, I hear you are to be supporter at the wedding. Rather you than me, my friend, for it would need a dozen pit-props and the Mabsant birch to support Doonan in his cups!'

'But you will be at the wedding?' asked Joshua anxiously.

'Tempest and flood would not prevent me! Rosa, I am sure, will be beauty itself, although Doonan might well play the other part . . . I have been wondering what he will wear.'

'Something neat but not gaudy,' quoted Joshua.

'As the devil said when he painted his tail green!' finished Ossie, grinning.

They considered the prospect in silence, then Joshua said, 'I hear that you are to have some of his family as guests at the "Crown".'

'It seems so. Four here, and four at the "Ancient Briton".'

'Better lock up the village maidens and order two hogs-heads apiece,' suggested Joshua, laughing. 'Or lodge them at the brewhouse to help themselves!'

'Well, at least it will not be dull!' said Ossie cheerfully.

'No. Whatever else it will be, it will not be that,' agreed Joshua, mounting his mare, saluting, and riding out under the arch.

When he reached Nottage he went at once to the small stone workshop of the blacksmith, on the edge of the village, overlooking a copse of sycamore and beech giving shelter to fields and farmland.

Illtyd and his mother, the Widow Cleat, lived in a modest cottage adjoining the forge, and Joshua often called there for they were warm-hearted and kind, and he welcomed the friendship. Today, however, it was business which occupied him as he dismounted and tethered his horse.

The blacksmith, Ben Clatworthy, a massive, thick-muscled giant, was fashioning a horseshoe upon an anvil, brawny arms bare, face flushed from the heat of the fire. His dark hair was wet, springing into curls about his face, and sweat beaded his skin, falling in droplets from hairline, nose and chin. The clang of hammer on metal was so loud and invasive that Joshua felt the smith's blows struck, not upon the anvil but upon the bones of his skull.

He watched silently and with fascination as the young apprentice brought water to cool the metal, and the hiss and spit of steam arose in a grey-white veil.

Clatworthy looked up briefly to say, 'I will be but a moment, Constable Stradling.' Then he returned to his labour and, when he had finished, laid the shoe aside with a grunt of satisfaction, and wiped his face and hands with a cloth.

'Well, sir, and how can I be of help to you? Something for your fine mare, perhaps?'

'No, sir, my business is of an official nature, and confidential.'

The blacksmith looked surprised, but glanced around the cluttered stone shell of his workshop as if hoping to find an empty space to which they might retreat. Finding nothing, for every surface and square inch of the floor was crammed with implements and iron, he bade the apprentice to 'look to the fire' and suggested to Joshua that they walk outside where they could not be overheard.

'Now, sir, how may I be of assistance?' His face shone from the heat of the fire, skin taut and polished as a burn. Joshua took Mansel's drawing from his pocket.

'Have you seen this branding mark, blacksmith?'

Clatworthy studied it briefly.

'Yes, I know it well. There is an iron even now within the forge that I am asked to repair. It is the mark of the Hardees. You see it? An "H" set inside a circle.'

'They live hereabouts? Within the three hamlets? I do not know the name.'

Clatworthy smiled. 'I am not surprised, sir, for the great house and farm are bleak and isolated. Sker House it is called. A gaunt stone place set alone in wild moorland near the sea.'

'How may I ride there?'

The blacksmith ran a hand through the springy, black curls, face intent. 'Now, how may I best explain? It is some miles away, sir, but such a landmark that it cannot be missed! If you follow the track across the common lands, which border the seashore, for a mile or so, you come to that big, curved bay with acres of fine pale sand. The surface is firm, although pitted with small, bubbling springs and shallow streams. You may ride through them with safety, for they will not impede your way. Beyond, there are three more bays divided by spurs of jagged rock, but passable when the tide is at its lowest ebb, one banked with loose pebbles and rocks of the brightest, clearest pink.'

'It is right upon the shore, then?'

'No, sir, set some way back upon flat land, bordered first by rock and sandy dunes. Yet you cannot miss the house, for it stands stark and alone. A grange, it is said, of Margam Abbey from earliest times.'

'And its owner, Hardee, what manner of man?'

'A gentleman like you, sir, but less approachable – not unlike his house,' he said with humour. 'Gaunt, spare in words and gratitude.'

Joshua smiled.

'I warn you, sir,' the blacksmith continued, 'there are great dogs there, some sort of hound left to roam free. They keep watch within the boundary walls. It is best to call out your business, that they may be chained. Your welcome is like to be as bleak as that afforded those poor devils shipwrecked upon the shore.' His eyes met Joshua's steadily. 'I wish you success in finding those who murdered Jem Crocutt, sir, and in any other enquiries you may make. The three hamlets are small, and divided by barriers of nature and occupation. Upon this matter, however, we are united. We know you are an honest man. You will do what needs to be done. We are with you to a man!' He held out his massive, grainy hand, and Joshua's own was grasped firmly, as in a vice. Below Clatworthy's rolled-up shirtsleeves Joshua saw the sinewy curve of muscle and the engorged blue veins, thick as a child's finger.

From the entrance to the smithy, Clatworthy and his apprentice watched in silence as the constable rode away, saluting him gravely as he turned, hand upraised.

The blacksmith's words, recalled, flooded Joshua with pleasure – 'We are with you to a man!'

Clatworthy with you, he thought in rare good humour, would be worth more than seven against!

While Joshua set out upon his lonely ride along the seashore to Sker House, Ezra the Box was engaged in repairing the fitments of a Regency sewing table. A small delicate thing of walnut, cross-banded with rosewood, it demanded, and received, all of his attention. Those who knew him would have been surprised at the gentleness and reverence upon his face and in his gnarled fingers as he set about his intricate task. It was the single great passion of Ezra's life, this swirl and flow of fine wood, its pattern and feel. He would stroke and fondle it as tenderly as any lover caressed flesh, drinking in its smoothness and smell, the living warmth of it. Sometimes, as now, he would even talk to it. So engrossed was he that he did not hear the bell jangle upon the street door, nor the stranger who entered.

'You are the undertaker, Evans?'

Ezra looked up, eyes surprised, unfocusing, then scrambled to his feet.

'I would have words with you. A matter of business.'

'Best come within, sir, where we may discuss it in comfort,' Ezra said.

The stranger, a thickset man with shadowed jowls and deep-set brown eyes 'neath a livid scar, followed Ezra into his living quarters. When they stood alone, Ezra, for some reason which he could not explain, felt a flicker of unease, which he dismissed instantly. The man spoke roughly and his clothes were those of a labourer or artisan, but he appeared respectable enough. Ironically, it was often the poor who spent more upon their dead, striving to give them in death the luxury denied them in living.

'A coffin, sir, was it?' Ezra asked, his eyes gleaming.

'Yes, for someone not yet dead.'

Ezra wondered if the fellow might be drunk, or

deranged, yet he appeared to be sober enough. Perhaps someone was mortally sick, and the man was but provident.

'When will it be needed, sir?'

'At any hour.'

Ezra nodded. 'It will be for a tall man, or short, sir? I ask because it is the custom to take measurements of the deceased and to prepare him. If you will give me some rough estimation, I can begin upon the work now.'

'About your size. Yes, your size exactly!'

Ezra thought he detected an undertone of menace in the stranger's voice, but dismissed the idea as fanciful.

'Now for the price.'

'Yes, but the price for what, shall we say?'

Ezra, by now, was alarmed, but made a brave attempt at a smile, which faltered nervously.

'The price for silence, perhaps?' the man said softly as he slipped behind him and placed an arm about Ezra's neck, gripping him so tightly that he all but lost consciousness. Yet he was painfully aware of the knife-blade at his throat, held in the assailant's other hand.

Ezra tried to scream, but could make no sound.

'Well? Shall we measure you against a coffin as you are? Or shall we slit your throat first, and throw you in? That way, at least, you will talk no more!'

Ezra must have fainted, for when he next looked about him the man had loosened his hold upon his throat, although the blade still pricked him.

'I haven't talked!' gasped Ezra feebly, trying to move his eyes enough to see his tormentor, but failing. 'What should I talk about? I know nothing!'

'You talk of wreckers, you little toad!'

'Wreckers?' Ezra's voice was a squeak. 'What would I know of wreckers? I swear to you, as God is my judge . . .'

'He might be, sooner than you think, you gutless swine!'

Ezra, throat constricted, began to cough, and the knife-blade pricked the flesh, drawing blood. He felt the drops warm upon his skin. Then the grip upon his throat relaxed and the stranger moved away to face him, but Ezra stood transfixed, unwilling even to cough again.

'I give you this warning, Evans! I hear questions are being asked about the wreck. If you so much as open your lips, I shall cut out your tongue and carve the word "Traitor" upon your scrawny chest. You understand?'

Ezra nodded. 'Then you did not want a coffin?' he asked stupidly, not having gathered his wits.

'Your services may be needed sooner than you think!'

Oh, dear Lord, why did I speak? thought Ezra, cursing himself.

'It will serve as a reminder.'

'Of what?'

'That the next coffin needed might well be yours!'

'Thank you, sir,' said Ezra, through the force of long habit, as the stranger walked to the door and into the street.

Ezra took a piece of binding rag and wound it around his neck where the drops had oozed out, darkening his shirt. He knew that his attacker brought only warning, for Joshua would never betray him. If they thought he had spoken, or was likely to, he would be already dead.

He went back to the sewing table, but his hands trembled so much that the delicate pieces would not come together. Neither had he heart for coffins.

Joshua, having cantered the grey across the springing turf of the common lands with its winter drifts of fox-coloured bracken, paused to look back at its sea-washed greenness. The surface was pocked with rabbit craters and scored with eruptions of rock and gorse, its barbed stems still bearing an occasional saffron flower.

Steadying the mare, he then descended the pebbly ridge to the sea's edge. The stones, rounded and sucked clean by the tide, shifted treacherously beneath the animal's hooves, making her falter nervously, ears pulled back, eyes rolling. Once upon hard sand, she relaxed, and Joshua gave her her head and galloped her along the water's edge, seeing the spray rise in transparent sheets, its falling droplets piercing holes through the ripples and making ever widening rings.

The bay stretched about them, its rock a curved grey horseshoe, containing it and separating it from the land. The edge bordering the common lands rose in chiselled steps, each of sheer rock, higher than a man. From the bay it looked smooth, carved, yet its surface was pitted with small rock pools and slashed with crevices and channels from which the sea poured, draining away in white-flecked waterfalls.

From the sea's edge, the sand, its surface clean and untouched, stretched away as far as the eye could see, mile after mile, broken only by spurs of rock extending from the land above and, now, the deep, semi-circular hoofprints of the mare. As the blacksmith had said, there were bubbling springs and outflows of shallow fresh water, clean and transparent as ice. Joshua had never before been to such an isolated place, nor one so desolate, yet his feeling of aloneness was fiercely shattered. The mare suddenly reared, hooves flailing the air, and backed away. Joshua, shaken, searched for the cause of her distress, and saw before him in the shallows the outstretched figure of a man, rigid as the skin of some slaughtered animal left pinned and drying under the sun.

He dismounted and, calming the grey and bidding her stand, walked towards the water's edge. The body was that of a man of middle age, the flesh swollen and disfigured by the ravages of rock and predatory gulls. Joshua braced himself to drag the dead man to the shore, for sickness burned in his throat and fear scrabbled at his ribs like some clawed creature seeking escape.

His grisly task completed, he sat for a time upon the wet sand, regaining control, before summoning the mare for another and more gruesome ritual.

The corpse was of a man scrawny and undernourished, yet the clothes were waterlogged and heavy, affording Joshua little hold. The mare, fidgeting and afraid, was loath to take up so obscene a burden, but Joshua's stern commands and urgency stilled her. Leading her by the reins, he drew her on, retracing her hoofprints along the tide's reach, and then upwards to the ridge. The mare slipped and panicked upon the shifting pebbles and Joshua had to release the reins and hold the body firm, lest it slip away, pushing it and the mare relentlessly towards solid land.

Finally, he left it upon the grass and, reluctantly mounting the saddle where the dead man had lain, set the mare to canter over the common lands, through Picket's Lease, over the dunes and into Newton village, to the workshop of Ezra the Box.

Ezra, his terror eased, but pale still, was at pains to assure Joshua that the bloodied binding cloth upon his neck was nothing at all – 'A stupid accident with a chisel. A splinter flew off and lodged, drawing blood. Scarce worth the bother of a mention, Constable.'

Joshua was not deceived and, at length, prevailed upon him to reveal the truth of it, knowing even as Ezra spoke that his attacker and the man who had visited Grove Farm to barter for the crucifix were one and the same . . . Could it be that the man was Jem Crocutt's murderer, too? That was as yet unproven . . . but it would serve no purpose to remind Evans of the farmer's grisly death, or Joshua's suspicions . . .

'These are vicious and cowardly men,' said Joshua gravely, 'and I fear I can do little, for if they believed you had confided in me, then their vengeance might be even greater!'

Ezra nodded miserably.

'I promise you, upon my oath, Mr Evans, that I will find him and he shall be called to account.'

Ezra looked unconvinced. 'But what is it that you want of me, Constable?'

Joshua explained his errand.

'Then I must get my cart and fetch him, although I expect it will be a pauper's funeral!'

Joshua, pity already turning to irritation, said sharply, 'He is a man! He was alive, and now he is dead. That is all that matters, surely?'

Ezra did not think it worthy of reply, saying grudgingly, 'If you will tell me where you left the body?'

'I will wait until you have prepared the cart and ride with you upon my mare.'

Ezra nodded and sniffed, then went to gird up the cob.

They drove almost in silence to the spot where the drowned man lay, both firmly trapped in thoughts of death. When Ezra had leapt down from the cart and Joshua was standing beside him upon the sea-washed turf, they turned the body over.

'Dear God!' cried Ezra.

'You know him?'

'Bando, Dai Bando!' He looked at Joshua, eyes stricken, a nerve twitching the corner of his mouth. 'The stranger promised I would have need of a coffin sooner than I thought, and after that, my own!'

Chapter Seven

Elizabeth Crandle, Rebecca's companion and friend at Southerndown Court, was also thinking of the dead, but with more compassion for the living. She was about to visit her father in his prison cell and the thought of it brought her as little comfort as it brought him. For her dead brother, Creighton, she had nothing but contempt, knowing him to have been arrogant and selfish, the cause of her father's incarceration and her mother's bewilderment and retreat from the reality of a world she was no longer able to face.

Yes, he had a lot to answer for, and had paid bitterly with his own death. Yet, she was not sure if her father's price would not, eventually, prove the greater. Broken in spirit and body by the loss of his son, he lived in conditions of such filth and squalor as were impossible to describe. No, 'lived' was too vital a word; he existed. She sometimes thought that he existed only in the past, and in his own mind, not aware of the stench and the putrefaction all around him. The prison was a human cesspit, a sewer of rotting flesh and excrement without escape or hope. When she had first entered there, taken in Sir Matthew's carriage and supported by a groom, the smell of urine and excreta, of stale sweat upon unwashed flesh, had made her retch and she had been forced out into the clean air where, to her shame and humiliation, she had vomited. Despite the coachman's pleas, she had bidden him take her back and, pale-faced and trembling, had braved the sullen stares of the inmates to be by her father's side. Now, although the pain of seeing him so degraded and unresponsive remained, she could almost ignore the whining voices and the importunate hands clutching at her basket and skirt as the groom cleared a way for her. She told her mother nothing of this, or the verminous straw-covered floors, and the cells infested with rats and their droppings. Every penny she could spare she gave to the gaoler, a sullen, taciturn creature whom she prevailed upon to see her father fed and given small comforts. She could not know whether her father saw any of these, or if his keeper squandered it upon drunkenness. It was all she could do.

She heard now the clopping of horses' hooves and the rattling of the carriage as it halted outside the door of the lodge. She kissed her mother, who was engaged in stitching some needle-point, its colours delicate and fine. Mrs Crandle looked up at her, eyes tranquil under pink-toned lashes, copper hair faded beneath her lace-frilled cap.

'You will not forget the commissions I gave you, Elizabeth? The sewing threads and the needles for embroidery?'

'No, Mother, I have made a list. I will forget nothing, I promise.'

'Now do not go hurrying from shop to shop, else you will overtire yourself, my dear, and do not linger in the chill air.' She rose, laying down the needlepoint, and walked with her daughter to the door, where she waited to see the coachman salute her, and the groom pull down the steps and assist her into the carriage.

She is much improved, thought Elizabeth. Her spirits and mind are greatly restored, and her prettiness returning to her. She settled the large basket which Rebecca had provided and ordered filled by the servants with delicacies and clean clothing and comforts for her father. For a moment she thought of her childhood friend, Mary Devereaux, the antithesis of Rebecca: pale-skinned and delicately fair, the girl whom her brother, Creighton, had violated and murdered so cruelly. And of Mary's brother, Roland, returned to his duties as an officer at sea. She hoped that they would never meet, for it would break her heart to see his grief, and know that there could never be forgiveness.

She felt the burn of tears behind her eyelids and shook her head impatiently, sitting up straight and erect. The coachman thought what a dignified, composed young lady Miss Crandle was, her dark eyes and hair gleaming beneath her pretty bonnet. Yet she was too grave and joyless for her eighteen years. The groom, who accompanied her to her father's side, was surprised not only by her courage, but that she smiled at all.

Mrs Crandle returned to her sewing after the coach had gone but, unable to concentrate, laid it aside. She had thought that the dark terror which engulfed her when

Creighton died, and Hugo had been trapped in smuggling, was past. Yet, insidious and unexpected, it came drifting back, a black cloud chilling and blocking out the sun, leaving her without warmth or comfort. Yet she was sure that it came less often now, and with less violence. She could even think of Creighton without such bitter desolation and anger, although the loss remained. A son buried and, in all but flesh, a husband with him. She could admit, at last, that Creighton had been a vicious, callous man, over-indulged and made selfish as a child. His excesses with women and at the gaming tables, and his expensive tastes, had ruined him and turned his father to dishonesty. She would not let it destroy Elizabeth's life and her own!

It suited Elizabeth to pretend the excitement of a shopping trip, with commissions one of the servants would, doubtless, undertake. It was a fiction Mrs Crandle must support. Once the truth was spoken, there would be too much pain. She did not know if she had the strength to bear it, or to witness the depth of Hugo's despair. One day, not now . . . She thanked God for Elizabeth's courage and for the kindness of Rebecca and Sir Matthew. Without them she could not have survived. There were good, dependable people in the world, warm and unselfish. Yet, perversely, her longing was still for that wicked boy, with his mocking, heedless ways . . .

Rebecca had grown to admire Elizabeth Crandle for her strength of character and for her warmth and lack of bitterness. They had become firm friends, neither seeing it strange that their positions were reversed. In fact, it was doubtful whether either of them considered it, for the Crandles were treated as members of the family, and thought of as such.

Elizabeth accompanied Rebecca upon her formal calls to the ladies of the neighbourhood and the tenants' cottages and farms, taking with them medicine for the sick, soup and other delicacies for the elderly and infirm, and gifts for new-born infants.

If the courtesy calls at mid-morning sometimes grew tiresome, and the chatter tinkled as emptily as the teacups, Rebecca learnt to hide it well. She played hostess at her grandfather's more formal dinners, enchanting friends and business acquaintances with her sympathy and naturalness and surprising them with her strange, unexpected beauty. If her grandfather occasionally saw fit to introduce the sons of other gentlemen to their table and salon, she was modestly responsive to their attentions, as required, but her love was for Joshua . . .

With Elizabeth, she studied assiduously and with pleasure, welcoming Dr Peate not merely as a tutor, but a dear and valued friend and, although she would not admit it, a tenuous link with Joshua. She was equally proficient at painting and her singing lessons, and persevered obligingly at needlework and tapestry, if with rather less success. Her hands grew smooth and white, the nails buffed and elegant. She read aloud quite beautifully, made modest progress at the pianoforte, and learnt to dance. In fact, her dancing master declared her to be 'as light upon her feet as thistledown, and possessed of a delightful sense of timing and grace'.

All these accomplishments, and her growing confidence in conversation and dress, would soon be put to the test. Rosa's wedding would bring her face to face with Joshua Stradling. Her love for him had not altered, nor would it, of that she was sure. Neither had there been mention of other women in Jeremiah's letters, and surely her old friend would have told her of any? Or Mistress Randall would have penned in some warning of her own? No, all was the same.

It did not occur to Rebecca that Joshua might find her changed.

After Joshua's first abortive ride to Sker House, when he had been deflected by the finding of Dai Bando's body, he once again had to defer his plans. The funeral of Jem Crocutt was to take place the next day, and Joshua was determined upon being there.

He knew Jeremiah was to take turn and turn about with Emrys, Illtyd and James Ploughman, keeping an all-night vigil over the coffin as it lay upon two stools at the farm, Hannah's black mourning cloth draped over it, and surmounted by three lighted candles.

Had not the Reverend Robert Knight paid for a coffin and burial, Jem Crocutt, being poor, might well have been buried in a linen shroud, body carried by kinsmen or upon two very long poles, wrapped with leather or strong sacking, their protruding ends used as shafts, astride two horses – one at either end of the bier. Instead, Jeremiah's cob and cart would act as burial waggon, with the mourners led by Dafydd, as bidder and next of kin.

Following custom, Hannah, Emily Randall and the

Widow Cleat would provide cakes, cold meats and warmed beer for the returning burial party as they had offered tobacco and ale to the vigil men.

Joshua, waiting at the crossroads by the pool, saw the sad little party come into view. Jeremiah had tried to get the boy to ride with him upon the cart, for the child was tired and the way long, but he would not. He came now leading the procession, head held stiffly erect above his too-long clothes, clogs dragging upon the cobbled way. At the crossroads, as was the habit, the village folk came forward to kneel and recite the Lord's Prayer, and Joshua did the same. When he had finished he raised his eyes, and Dafydd bowed in grave acknowledgement, eyes dry. Joshua would have loved dearly to lift him up upon the grey, but knew that he must not.

At the churchyard gate, the Lord's Prayer was recited again, for many, like Ossie, were unable to read, but knew the words by heart, then the body was taken into the care of the church. As they entered, the gravedigger stood beside the porch and Dafydd, as he had been reminded, threw coppers upon his shining spade.

Within the church, near to the altar, a white-draped alms dish was always set to receive offerings of silver as tribute to the priest. Joshua knew, without being told, that the justice meant it for the bereaved, and when all had gone he placed upon it two gold coins, and hid them within a fold of cloth.

He thought he would never forget the simplicity of the burial in that cold earth, sky and trees starkly grey in the December chill, or the forlorn clatter of the child's wooden soles upon the flagstoned floor of the church, and his weeping as the coffin was lowered into the earth.

Afterwards Jeremiah lifted him upon the cart and Joshua watched them drive away.

'You have been a brave man today,' Joshua had told him.

'No, sir, I cried like a girl, although I did not mean to.'

'All men cry,' said Jeremiah, 'when they care enough.'

'Have you ever cried, Constable?' the child asked.

'Often,' said Joshua.

Dafydd nodded gravely. 'Then I suppose it is all right.'

Joshua, avoiding Jeremiah's gaze, turned abruptly to mount the grey, for, to tell the truth, his eyes burned with a man's tears.

Within an hour of arriving with the burial party at Grove Farm, Joshua was riding out upon his errand to Sker House, for James Ploughman had told him of another way to the isolated place and he knew that he must be there and safely home again before dusk fell.

He was glad to be in the cold air, astride the mare, for despite the ladies' hospitality, and the pressing upon all who came of victuals and warmed ale, the farm was a joyless place that day. Jeremiah had said that it was always thus when the coffin had gone, for it was then that realisation came. Bereft now even of that empty flesh, nothing tangible remained. All that was familiar and loved was gone. People spoke of memory bringing comfort, but you could not stretch out your hand to it, and feel its fingers warm within your own, and the voice you heard was but an echo . . . Joshua had gripped the old man's arm, knowing that he spoke of his dead wife and son, and Jeremiah had nodded, but said nothing.

Save for Dafydd, the children were unaware. Marged pirouetted and danced, delighting in her pretty new clothes. The baby slept. The infant who was learning to walk moved unsteadily, clutching at skirts and trousered legs, crowing and chuckling, showering wet kisses upon all. Yet, Jem Crocutt would not return.

With an effort Joshua shook off his feelings of pessimism and regret: 'that black dog who sits upon your shoulder,' the cottagers called it, 'and which bears you down with his weight.' He had best concentrate upon avoiding those flesh-and-bone curs upon Sker Farm as the blacksmith had warned, for they were more persistent and destructive.

The way through narrow lanes with their banked, pleached hedges was long and monotonous, the countryside bare save for occasional fields of grazing beasts. The tracks, mazed and unfamiliar, had a sameness about them, and Joshua hoped that he was not merely doubling back upon himself, losing direction. He eventually recognised the low stone house of Parc Newydd Farm and, taking his bearings from it, turned the mare towards the way that led to the sea.

He thought of Dai Bando as he had come across him, face down, at the water's edge. Then he visualised him running through field and track, breath raw, to give

James Ploughman an alarm about the shipwreck, hoping some might be saved. Yet he had saved neither himself nor them. Why had he not returned to alert the owner of Sker Farm, since that was where he was searching for work? Why had he left James Ploughman's place with food untasted? What circumstances had driven him to the sea, and death?

Even as the thoughts came into his mind he saw before him the distant shape of Sker House, bleak, austere, its bare, grey stone forbidding as a fortress. When he eventually drew up at its boundary walls it looked no more welcoming, and the barking of the great hounds, their snarling mouths and vicious jaws as they leapt against the gate which separated him from the farmyard, did nothing to reassure him. He reached out and tolled the warning bell which was bracketed atop a gatepost, and the mare retreated nervously as the dogs hurled themselves bodily upon the gate, shaking it upon its hinges.

At length an ill-kempt servant, who might have been the kennel-man, whistled to the brutes and they drew towards him reluctantly, cowering and creeping the last few yards upon their bellies, to be chained.

'What is your business here?' he demanded, upon coming forward belligerently.

'It is with the owner of the farm. I come on official business concerning the wreck.'

'Then I fear, sir, that your journey has been wasted. Mr Hardee has left for London, on business, these three days.'

'When will he return?'

'That is not known.'

Joshua, irritated and restive after his long ride and the strain of the burial, commanded with ill-suppressed anger, 'Unbar the gate! I will enter and speak to whoever is left in charge!'

The man hesitated but, aware of Joshua's authority, did as he was bidden. Without a word, Joshua rode past him and the two hounds, jerking and snapping upon their chains, and dismounted at the door of the house.

His knocking brought a manservant to the door and, upon stating his errand, Joshua was led through the great hall, a towering bastion of stone and armorial relics, into a drawing room where a fire burned brightly in the grate, although the room itself was dank and chill and the furniture of heavily carved oak and the thick draperies, designed perhaps to protect against the sea-mists and winter gales, added to its cheerlessness. He was surprised to see a woman seated at the fire, engaged at some embroidery upon a frame. She rose to greet him and he observed that she was young. She wore a gown of deep red velvet, with a collar of white lace, which suited her slenderness and the paleness of her skin and hair, making her seem more delicate against the glowing richness of its colour. As she moved, he saw that it was with difficulty, some ungainliness due to a deformity of leg or hip. An accident perhaps? She bade him be seated, apologising for her husband's absence, and asking how she might assist.

'I seek news about the wreck of the *San Lorenzo*.'

'Then perhaps it would be prudent to interview the exciseman, for he took charge.'

'I seek more human, personal details, ma'am.'

'How can that be so? None survived.'

'Your impressions, ma'am – the noise, the crashing of the ship upon the rocks, the confusion of the rescue . . .'

She looked at him levelly. 'My bedchamber, sir, is in the east wing, set over the courtyard. I heard nothing save the raging of the wind and storm.'

'But your guest, ma'am, Dr Elfed Thomas, was called from his bed to tend to those injured or dying.'

'I heard nothing,' she repeated.

Joshua persisted. 'Surely there was some commotion with the servants, the noise with the fetching of lanterns and ropes and warm clothing, preparing a place for those who survived.'

'None did. But had they done so, my housekeeper would make preparation.'

'She would not summon you?' Joshua asked in disbelief.

'Did not!' Her tone was firm. 'Now, sir, if you will excuse me, I wish to finish my embroidery before the daylight fades. The work is fine and lamplight casts too many shadows.'

'Too many shadows . . .' he repeated. 'Yes, I understand that. Do you not find this place bleak, ma'am, nothing but mists, and the rocky shore and the barren lands?'

'You are impertinent, sir!' She flushed, then controlling herself said carefully, 'This is my home. The lands about are not barren, but rich, productive . . .'

'As the sea,' said Joshua smoothly.

'I do not consider the dead to be productive,' she answered coldly.

'No, you mistake me, ma'am. I had in mind another harvest.'

Silence lay between them, before Joshua continued quietly, 'A harvest of fish, shellfish, living things upon which the villagers exist and earn their bread.'

'I know nothing of these people.' Her tone was dismissive.

'Then you will not have knowledge of a vagrant who came here upon the day of the shipwreck, seeking work or food?'

'That is not my affair. A matter for the kitchen.'

'But your husband, perhaps? His name, although, as you say, it would mean nothing to you, was Bando, Dai Bando.'

She stood up with deliberation, and pulled at the bell rope.

'Yesterday I found him dead upon the shore,' Joshua said.

Her expression did not change from bored impatience as she stood looking at him, waiting for the servant to appear.

When the manservant entered, Joshua glanced at him, then back to her, continuing, 'I have ridden here from a funeral, ma'am, that of your nearest neighbour, a poor farmer by the name of Jem Crocutt. Murdered, leaving a widow and four young children.' He saw out of the corner of his eye that the man had stiffened, biting his lip, and glanced at his mistress.

'Such people live by violence,' she said, 'and very often die by it. They are their own worst enemy and are hard to help, too proud or arrogant to accept charity. They breed like rabbits, wondering why their children die in infancy, or grow sickly and unreliable as they.'

Joshua thought of Dafydd.

'Edwards,' she ordered, 'take the constable to the kitchen, ask the cook to give him a few eggs for the woman, or whatever left-over food can be spared. He will carry it there.'

'I thank you, ma'am, on the widow's behalf, for she is a woman of warmth and courtesy. But as you say, she is too proud or arrogant to accept charity. She has no need of it. She has friends, some as poor as she, who will see that she is never in want of food, or sympathy.'

Joshua bowed stiffly and followed the manservant out into the great hall. The old man put a detaining arm upon him as they reached the door, and looked at him, eyes concerned, then brought out a half sovereign from his pocket, saying awkwardly, 'If you would give this to the widow, sir. I mean it not as charity, you understand, save in the truest sense. I have known Jem's family from early days and I respect them for what they are.'

Joshua held the gold coin upon his palm. 'It is too much,' he said helplessly.

'No, sir, it is not enough,' the old man said as he closed the door quietly.

Joshua crossed the yard to where he had left the grey tethered, beyond the farmyard gate, the dogs straining and snarling as he passed. No sooner was he upon the path and mounted than they came baying and leaping at the gate, the ill-kempt fellow leaning against the wall where they had been chained, face expressionless.

Setting the mare for home, Joshua determined that, come what may, he would return to seek out Hardee, although the meeting would afford him no pleasure.

Chapter Eight

To Joshua, immersed as he was in his hunt for the killer of Jem Crocutt, the wedding of Rosa Howarth and Cavan Doonan seemed to arrive unexpectedly. That is not to say without warning, for as Doonan's supporter, he bore the full brunt of the Irishman's vociferous doubts, insecurities and frequent explosiveness . . . No! he could not marry her! Joshua must tell her so. He was not worthy of such sweetness and dear innocence! He, Cavan Doonan, was naught but a rough quarryman, drunken and loutish! He was not fitted to breathe the same air as his darling, nor to walk upon the earth her dainty feet trod, although he worshipped that blessed ground. No! he would return to Ireland, at once! He was decided upon it. Joshua was not to try to dissuade him! He was firm upon it. Had Joshua arranged for the curricle? The pennies to be thrown to the children? What if Rosa hated the ring he had chosen? What of his family? They would perish in the crossing from Ireland! They would disgrace his own sweet darling by their roistering at the 'Crown'! Would the cottage satisfy her? Would he? Was the wedding-eve party arranged? Finally Joshua was forced to speak to him so sternly that even Doonan was abashed and calmed, although it was but ten minutes before he was demanding the same of Jeremiah, Emrys, Ossie, Illtyd, and any who would listen at the 'Ship Aground' . . .

Rosa, serene and happy, seemed the only one untouched by crisis. Her mother, the Widow Howarth, fretted about the food, the weather, the dress. The rector might die; the church would be struck by lightning; someone would stand up in the service and declare impediment! There would be too many guests, too little food, they would say she was mean! Doonan's family would despise her. His mother would think her too lowly, or giving herself too many airs and graces!

The good woman was alternately warmed and irritated by Rosa's calmness. She had hired the potboy at the 'Ship Aground' to act as chief bidder, to knock upon doors, inviting those living in the three hamlets to be guests at the wedding feast. He could rhyme freely upon the spur of the moment, saying something clever and personal to each. For the few living at a distance and able to read, like Elizabeth and Rebecca, there were invitations delivered by the Penny Post, carefully hand-written by Mistress Randall.

Now, finally, all was arranged for the morrow: the food was baked, the good ladies of the hamlets would serve it; the rooms were prepared at the 'Crown' and the 'Ancient Briton' for the arrival of the Doonans. Cavan would stay there, too, for it was not fitting that he and Rosa leave from the same house, or sleep there overnight. Jeremiah and the dog, Charity, were to remove themselves to Emrys's lodgings, that Rebecca and her companion, Miss Crandle, should stay at his cottage. And the dress had been delivered.

Nothing could possibly go wrong. It would be a wedding that the three hamlets would long remember! the Widow Howarth thought with satisfaction and, being devout and a true believer, she knelt down and prayed most earnestly that it might be so. She could not have realised how spectacularly her prayer would be fulfilled.

Doonan's family were on the last stage of their journey and but a few miles from Newton, and the 'Crown'. The group was charming, boisterous, disarming and reckless as Cavan himself. His four brothers and two male cousins were settled upon a stagecoach, four within and two upon the box, singing lustily, if somewhat discordantly, as the guard played a medley of Irish airs upon his keyed bugle. By singular good fortune the guard could boast an Irish mother, so his repertoire was extensive and his enthusiasm limitless, unlike that of the coachman! The poor man had borne their singing and high spirits with fortitude, for he was a good-humoured fellow and could not fault their generosity when it came to offering him refreshment when they paused at the inns. However, even his forbearance had been overstrained when they called out lewd and indecorous suggestions to a passing trollop upon the way. Nor had he been pleased when the pair upon the box had produced catapults and withered peas, raining them upon a quartet of passing carriage horses until the poor animals took afright, with the coach travelling at such a speed it seemed like to overturn, had not the driver been so skilled. As it was, his ears still burned from the coachman's vigorous oaths and curses. Worst of all, not content with setting their slingshot upon wayside rabbits and unsuspecting sheep, one of them had actually scrambled upon the roof of the coach, borrowing the guard's blunderbuss and discharged it at a passing pheasant, at which outrage he was forced to halt the carriage and read them the Riot Act, and for a good two miles they sat abashed and penitent, leaving him to travel in peace – although they were adamant upon taking the pheasant with them.

Cavan's parents travelled in a chaise behind them, enjoying the scenery and the novelty of their transport, occasionally calling out a reprimand to their sons when their behaviour grew too outrageous, or waving to the startled peasantry, who returned their greetings with pardonable reserve, thinking them to be inmates of some lunatic asylum upon an outing.

In all, it was with relief that the coachman and the driver of the chaise delivered them to their quarters at the 'Crown' and 'Ancient Briton', the coachman confiding to Ossie that he would sooner enter a lion's den, and wrestle with the animal bare-handed, or face a regiment of musketry, unarmed, than return with them! Oh, they were nice enough people no doubt, generous to a fault and high-spirited, but he would be glad to return to conveying old ladies with parrot cages, chained prisoners and their escorts, and even the occasional cadaver, for at least the latter were quiet enough!

Ossie smiled to himself as he heard details of the poor fellow's journey, as he later smiled openly at Cavan's riotous and emotional meeting with his kinsfolk, but he was quick to admit that it was a delight to return to his horses which the good Lord, in His wisdom, had mercifully seen fit to make speechless.

The night's wedding-eve party, to which Ossie had been invited, travelling from inn to inn throughout the three hamlets, promised to be an occasion to remember. But whether any of them would be in a state to remember afterwards was open to doubt. As long as Doonan remembered the wedding, thought Ossie, grinning, and, if he did, proved capable of standing upright through it!

Around the Vale at Southerndown Court, Rebecca's valises and portmanteaux were ready to be packed upon the luggage box of the de Breos carriage, and Elizabeth's smaller ones beside them. As well as her dresses and toilet articles, Rebecca took gifts for her friends, purchased upon her travels in Europe. She had taken infinite pains to choose wisely, not wishing to offend them by seeming ostentatious, yet making them generous enough to please with their modest luxury. She remembered so keenly the rare pleasure of owning a ball of herb-scented soap, a pretty ribbon or handkerchief. For Rosa she had chosen two petticoats of silk, hand-stitched and lace-encrusted, and a nightgown of finest cotton, a deep forget-me-not blue, its pin-tucked bodice embroidered with gentians designed to set off her eyes and pale beauty. For the men there were pipes and tobacco and for Illtyd, her favourite, a pocket watch in silver, inscribed with his name, that he might always know the hour when he was out upon the downs and common lands. Jeremiah was to receive a pair of high fishing boots of special leather, treated to keep out the water, and three pairs of good woollen stockings to keep him warm. For Charity, a collar of leather, well studded with brass, and for Illtyd's mare, Faith, and her old cob, brushes to groom them and rough towels to comfort them after rain.

Mrs Crandle, watching the two girls indulgently as they departed, had remarked that they looked equipped for the Grand Tour rather than for a village wedding not a dozen miles away. Perhaps they had better ask Sir Matthew if they might take the larger coach for their clothes alone! The good lady was light-hearted and pleased, for Elizabeth's face was flushed with excitement and it was a joy to see her daughter so relaxed.

'I am apprehensive, my dear,' Mrs Crandle had confessed to Rebecca in private, 'that Elizabeth will not be welcome there, for they know of her brother's disgrace, and that her father lies in gaol.'

Rebecca had kissed her saying, 'They are the dearest, kindest folk in all the world, save for you and Grandfather, and I love them dearly. It would not even enter their minds to blame Elizabeth for another's sins, and to treat her with anything but warmth and affection, I do assure you, ma'am,' and Mrs Crandle had been convinced of it.

Her grandfather had embraced her, saying gruffly that he would be glad of a day's silence and rest from their incessant, idle chatter, and would very likely invite his good friend, Dr Handel Peate, for luncheon or dinner, that he might share intelligent discourse.

'Of course, Grandfather,' replied Rebecca primly, 'and when you have confounded the philosophers, you may smoke your tobacco and drink your port, and set the world to rights, so that when I return it will be a veritable Garden of Eden.'

'As it was before Woman and The Serpent corrupted it, my dear,' he said, amused. Then, growing serious he continued, 'You will take care, remembering to move gently among your friends, not expecting more than can be fulfilled? I speak kindly, my dear, and out of love for you. You have travelled a great distance, Rebecca, not merely in miles, but experiences which they have not shared. This young man of whom you speak so highly – Joshua Stradling – might he not find that distance difficult to bridge?'

'I am sure that he will see that I am unchanged, Grandfather.'

Only if he has learnt to look not merely with the eyes, but with the heart, the old man thought ruefully, and the young are not always so perceptive – or, indeed, the old!

'Well, my dear,' he said gallantly, 'were I but fifty years younger, it would have given me infinite pleasure to have escorted you both, for you are fresher, and more fragrantly lovely, than early roses – and I, alas, a withered thorn!'

'Well, sir,' responded Rebecca, laughing, 'take care that you do not prick Dr Peate with the sharpness of your wit, or you might find yourself abandoned and eager for even our silly prattling!'

He was smiling as he returned to the house, reflecting that, in truth, he would miss it more than she knew.

Less than an hour after Rebecca's coach had left for Newton, Sir Matthew sent a footman to ask Mrs Crandle if she would attend him in the library, for there was something he wished to discuss with her.

He greeted her warmly and bade her be seated, making polite conversation about the two girls and their journey, and more general comments, before requesting the pleasure of her company at luncheon with Dr Peate, for they would both be honoured by her presence.

She accepted gracefully, thinking this to be the reason for her summons, when Sir Matthew confessed, 'I should be grateful for your advice and your assistance in another matter, ma'am.'

'Then I shall be pleased to help, sir, if it is within my powers.'

'It is Rebecca's nineteenth birthday in a fortnight's time, Mrs Crandle, as you are no doubt aware. I should like to provide some suitable entertainment to meet the occasion. A ball, would you think? Or perhaps I have left it too late for arrangements to be made? I fear that having lived a solitary life for so many years, I know little of the diversions of the young, or the practicalities of such things,' he apologised.

'You would like me to oversee the arrangements, Sir Matthew?'

'Oh no, ma'am, forgive me if I have not made myself clear. I behave clumsily, I fear. In the absence of

Rebecca's mother, and my own dear wife, I should like you to act as hostess for her, and do whatever you consider necessary.' He looked at her expectantly, 'You will, perhaps, need some time to consider?'

'No, Sir Matthew, I accept willingly, and with the greatest delight, for I consider it to be a privilege. I have the greatest affection for Rebecca, as you know, and a respect and gratitude for your kindness to Elizabeth and to me,' she said truthfully.

'I know you to be a woman of taste and discrimination, ma'am, with experience of society, and what is expected in these matters. It would relieve my mind to feel that the affair was in such capable hands as yours.'

'I thank you for your confidence, Sir Matthew, and will not disappoint you, or Rebecca, I promise.'

'Of that, I am convinced. I will leave all the formal arrangements to you, then, ma'am. You may order whatever you choose to make the affair memorable. If you think it desirable, perhaps you would care to accompany Rebecca and Elizabeth to London, to buy their party gowns and other necessities, and, of course, your own! I have a town house, overlooking the park, which will be made ready for you.' He smiled. 'I admit I have little knowledge of frills and furbelows, ma'am, but recall that they, and a great deal of circumstance, were necessary.'

Mrs Crandle's eyes were already sparkling with delight at the prospect, and she looked altogether younger, prettier and more animated.

'I shall set the arrangements in hand at once, Sir Matthew,' she said, rising, 'for time is sorely pressing.

There will be the invitations to be engraved, the flowers and decorations, food, of course. And Rebecca will wish to decide upon the guests immediately she returns.'

He nodded. 'She will have many new friends and acquaintances to invite, as well as those she holds dear from her former life.'

'The young man, Joshua Stradling, perhaps?' Mrs Crandle's face grew thoughtful, grave. 'I can only say, sir, that he is a kind and intelligent young man, a gentleman in the true sense of the word – one who would not, even unintentionally, cause hurt by a cruel or thoughtless action. Elizabeth and I have cause to be grateful to him, for his conduct in – in that tragedy, which it pains me still to speak of. Yet I have to say that, although it grieves me to be reminded of it, no blame attaches to him. I bear him no ill will.'

'You have a kind and generous nature, ma'am, and it does you credit, as does your estimation of young Stradling. We must wait and see if he is mature enough to accept the new Rebecca, and what a life with her would entail.'

She nodded, understanding, then blurted awkwardly, 'I have but one reservation, Sir Matthew, about playing hostess at this affair.'

'Indeed, ma'am?' He looked concerned.

'If you will bear with me, sir, it is difficult to find the exact words. I would not have Rebecca hurt, or you disgraced, sir, by people slighting me or Elizabeth for what my son and husband did. If you think it better that we do not attend . . .'

'Is that all, Mrs Crandle?' His face cleared. 'I feared there was some real difficulty, a serious problem. I will not even consider it! I think I know my granddaughter well enough to say that if you and Elizabeth chose not to attend, then there would be no birthday celebrations.'

'I thank you, sir, for your confidence.'

'Believe me when I say, Mrs Crandle, that I have the greatest respect for you and for Elizabeth, and for the courage and dignity you show in all your actions. My granddaughter is very dear to me, and I gladly surrender her to your instruction and example.'

'You are kind, sir.'

He bowed courteously, 'I am your servant, ma'am.'

She responded with a deep curtsey, and a smile that warmed his spirit.

The family Doonan, comfortably ensconced in the 'Crown Inn' and 'Ancient Briton', were delighted with their surroundings, their journey, the prospect of the wedding, their new relations, and themselves. In fact, they radiated such lively pleasure and appreciation that it was impossible not to be infected by it. Sir Matthew had given instruction that every need was to be catered for and every luxury provided. Should any, or all, need the services of carriage or horses, they might be hired from the stable at the 'Crown' at his expense. The drinks for the entire family, and for Rosa's family and guests were also to be put to his account, along with any additional charge, for whatever reason.

Doonan's parents had immediately ridden out with

him in the 'Crown' carriage, impeccably driven by Ossie, to make the acquaintance of their son's bride-to-be and her mother. The meeting was a great success, so lavish and sincere were they in praise of the arrangements, Mrs Howarth's endeavours, and Rosa's incredible charm and beauty. They declared their son to be heaven-blessed at finding such a darling girl, intelligent, warm-hearted, pure in thought and deed, a very paragon of all the virtues. Such good fortune was almost too exalted to bear!

At the 'Crown' and 'Ancient Briton', the atmosphere was equally auspicious. Doonan had introduced his brothers and cousins to his 'dearest and most loyal friends'. Jeremiah, and Charity, were afforded such praise and hospitality, and so convivial was the occasion, that the dog had to be reprimanded by the landlord for behaving indecorously, Emrys declaring that the excitement had gone quite to his head. In fact, what had gone to his head was a considerable quantity of Finbar Doonan's ale and the poor animal had finally to be carried home upon Emrys's cart, limp and all but unconscious, to sleep it off. Their favourite was Illtyd, for his generous spirit and wit, and indeed his pony, Faith, was so fussed and cosseted that, like Charity, it seemed fit to turn her head. Illtyd loved their high good spirits and sense of fun, for it held no cruelty. Their laughter was always with the one they teased, and never at him, and their generosity unbounded. Unable to pronounce his name, they dubbed him 'our little leprechaun', declaring that he had no need to bring good fortune, for was it not worth a pot of gold to share in his good company? It was with real regret that he saddled Faith for his surveillance upon the downs.

The brothers Doonan and their cousins awaited Cavan's return from Rosa's house with rare good spirits, within and without. They were eager to be started upon the wedding-eve party, although it was but afternoon. The bridegroom-to-be, having left his parents, at Mrs Howarth's command, to be presented to the good ladies of the parish, had walked the long way from the port and, being possessed of a thirst, needed little persuasion. So, the convivial group set out dressed in their wedding finery and, with their vivid blue eyes and curling hair, shaded from burnished copper, through bronze, to flame, they seemed alight with colour and vitality.

Indeed, when they left the 'Ancient Briton' for their first inn stop at the 'Crown', it was almost as though candles, glittering upon a lighted chandelier, had been extinguished one by one, leaving the place and the people to their increasingly sombre reflections. Incredibly, the cottagers found themselves regretting the dullness and quietness which had settled upon them, and the landlord, although exhausted by their demands and wild exuberance, reflected that he mourned less for his profits than their company. Perhaps their flamboyance was what had been lacking in the lives of these sober, industrious people. In any event, their return was pleasurably awaited. The Doonans had been accepted.

Illtyd, meanwhile, was approaching the lane above Dan-y-Graig Hill that led to the windswept wildness of

Stormy Down. As he guided his pony around the steep corner between the high, pleached hedgerows, he glowed with a warm happiness which could not be dispelled by the chill of a winter afternoon. His pocket held the silver pocket watch which Rebecca had given to him, inscribed, she said, with his own name, 'Illtyd Cleat – Hayward'. He thought that his heart must surely burst with the pride of it, as much from the thoughtfulness of Rebecca's choice as the magnificence of the gift. His hand left the rein, briefly, to trace again the outline of his treasure under the coarse cloth. When Rebecca had given it to him, he had taken it from its box, too incredulous and moved to trust himself to speak, fearful that his voice would falter or break with unmanly tears.

'I hope that it will bring you pleasure, Illtyd, over many years.' She had held him close, keeping her soft cheek against his, and he had smelled the fragrance of her hair and skin. 'You are a very special friend . . .'

'As you are, Rebecca, to me.' His voice had been thick, strange-sounding in his own ears. 'It will be a reminder of your kindness to me, every hour of the day. I have never owned anything so beautiful. I thank you for it.'

He had looked at Rebecca, his beautiful, intelligent eyes bright, yet shadowed with secret pain, and Elizabeth Crandle, seeing it, said, 'Rebecca has told me much about you, Illtyd, and says that you are the kindest, bravest and most generous of men. I am privileged to meet you.'

'And I you, Miss Crandle.'

She had taken the small, unformed hand in hers, remarking the beauty and warmth in the incredible eyes. She was filled with pity and rage that he was trapped in this deformed body with the gross head. He had looked at her in understanding.

'I hope that the future will be kinder to you, Miss Crandle. You have suffered much,' he said quietly, for Rebecca had turned and was occupied at some task. 'Our wounds are not always upon the surface, but deeper, and more painful to bear. I admire your courage, ma'am.'

She nodded, unable to speak.

'I would have you believe that if you feel the need of a friend, someone set apart, dispassionate, yet able to understand . . .' The ungainly head lifted upon the wry neck.

'I have this very moment found him, sir.' She touched her hand upon the awkward shoulder and their eyes met in understanding.

'See,' called out Rebecca, who had been engaged with her parcels, 'I have found them at last! I had almost forgot, Illtyd, there are small gifts for Faith.'

The brush and rough cloth to rub the mare down having been inspected and generously received, Illtyd said reluctantly, 'I had best be upon my way, lest Faith believe I have deserted her.' He looked at his watch, smiling. 'I will see you both tomorrow, at the wedding, upon the appointed hour, for now I will have no excuse for arriving late!'

His mind still occupied with the watch, Illtyd drove past one of the barred gates. Then he hesitated, halted the pony and rode back to inspect it. It lay open and leaning drunkenly upon a broken hinge, the grass about it beaten down by the trampling of sheep's hooves. He examined the ground more closely and saw in the soft turf of the field the imprints of not one but many horses. The sight alarmed him, for there was no farmer here, or elsewhere in the three hamlets, who could spare so many men and beasts for so simple a task as moving a flock from one pasture to another. He followed the route which they had taken amidst the scattered black droppings, smeared and trampled upon the way, the tufted sheep wool caught on brambles, and the steaming, still-warm ordure of the horses. He could hear the startled cries of the animals ahead, bleating their confusion, and see the swaying figures of the horsemen driving them.

He urged on the pony as they neared a small beech copse, and she responded to his voice, but too late. Even as he called to her, three men rode out yelling, brandishing staves, and set upon him and the piebald, swinging their staves, and beating man and horse unmercifully. The little mare tried desperately to escape, to take them both out of range of the flailing sticks, but they cut off her way. One mighty blow felled Illtyd to the ground, splitting his head, and Faith, riderless and terrified, took the opportunity to swerve between them, braving their blows and running desperately and fiercely towards freedom.

Illtyd, lying there bleeding and unable to rise, called out Faith's name, but she did not come to him. He cursed his impotence, and the weakness in his limbs which would not allow him to search for her, for she might be cruelly injured, or already dead ... A coldness settled upon him, worse than the pain in his bones or the chill of the day. He could not find strength to wipe the blood which dripped relentlessly from his head, blurring his eyes with redness, and running into the corner of his mouth ...

He tasted the salt of it as he willed himself to raise a hand to his pocket. His watch was gone.

Illtyd Cleat, hayward, lay there and wept.

Chapter Nine

Joshua, walking past the village green to meet the Doonan family at the 'Crown', heard the hoofbeats and rattle of a carriage as it took the corner, and prudently stepped aside. Ossie was upon the box, hands clenched upon the reins, face strangely agitated. Joshua called out a greeting, and the ostler, manoeuvring the coach under the archway, shouted back, 'Quick! Illtyd's mare – she is running wild! Catch her!'

Joshua, hearing the urgency in his cry, ran immediately upon the carriageway to see the little piebald veering towards him, eyes wild, ears laid back, body taut with fear. He called her name, but she was too terrified to hear and continued her stricken flight, small hooves striking upon the cobbles. Joshua put out a hand and caught at the reins as she thundered past, feeling a wrench as if his arm had been torn from its socket, and was drawn with her, stumbling and falling to his knees before he eventually managed to halt her.

The mare's mouth was flecked with foam and her body lathered as Joshua talked her into calmness. Eventually the trembling lessened and died away, and he saw that the lather upon her hide was bloodied from weals and cuts, as if she had been set upon with sticks. He felt such a cold fury, then fear for Illtyd, that at first he was unaware of Ossie standing beside him. Their eyes met above the mare's bruised flesh.

'Dear God!' said Ossie. 'See how she has been treated! What have they done to Illtyd?'

'You know where he was, Ossie? Where he intended to go?'

'Yes, he told me, upon Stormy Downs.' He shook his head in disbelief. 'Who could do such a thing, Joshua?'

'Sheep-stealers, perhaps. He feared they were about – but let us not waste time! Take Faith to the stables at the "Crown". I will get my grey, and as many as I can to help in the search for him.'

Within minutes of his arriving at the 'Crown', it seemed, the whole inn was in a ferment and uproar. Doonan was beside himself with anger, smashing his great fist upon the table in his agitation as he leapt to his feet and making the pots and tankards rattle and dance. The landlord who, with all the cottagers, admired their little hayward, declared that every man capable of riding might take a horse from his stables and 'to hell with the expense'!

'Ossie will drive the carriage and those who have no horses may climb inside, or upon the box,' he cried recklessly. The Doonan brothers and cousins were already at the door, choosing staves and clubs from the landlord's armoury and, led by Cavan and his father, they erupted into the cobbled yard.

Faith being settled with a reliable groom, Ossie apportioned them their mounts, the older men climbing into the carriage, upon the box, and even clinging to the roof and the back. Joshua gave his final directions and they set out, to divide upon their separate ways so that the exit roads from Stormy Downs might be covered.

As they rode beneath the arch they were joined by horsemen from the 'Ancient Briton' and, seeing Jeremiah and Emrys upon the cart, Doonan rode out to them and they, furious and alarmed, left upon the main way that they might take the track that led past the justice's house at Tythegston.

What a scene it was! Every horse that could stand upon four legs was there, even James Ploughman's poor, winded mare who, running with the herd, seemed to have taken on new life, inspired by company and occasion. Behind, Ossie's coach, its passengers jolting and bumping upon every square inch of roof, and packed inside tight as salted herrings in a crock, and following, any and all who, hearing the wild cries and shouts, could find a mount, be it a horse, mule, or even a donkey.

Joshua, at the head of them, upon his grey mare, wondered if any man before had ever marshalled such a ragged motley army, comic and yet filled with purpose and revenge. If Illtyd were dead then he doubted that he could control them, so fierce would be their rage and bloodlust.

Jeremiah and Emrys were silent as the cart took the corner past Tythegston Court, their thoughts upon Illtyd and what they might find. The cob moved steadily, responding to every light touch upon the reins as the two men gazed about them, seeking some sign of the little hayward, or evidence of action.

'There!' cried Emrys. 'Upon the roadway beside the trees!'

Jeremiah drew the cob to a halt and they leapt down from the cart and ran towards the still figure, lying awkwardly.

'Dear God!' cried Emrys. 'They have killed him! Illtyd is dead!'

'No! It cannot be!' The denial was torn from Jeremiah, as he knelt down beside the small twisted body, chafing the cold hands with his own, then tenderly wiping the blood from Illtyd's face with his kerchief. He was filled with such despair that he felt his heart must break within his breast. Then, with a murderous rage which left him cold and shaking, he cried out, 'I will kill them! I swear, Emrys, by all that I hold dear, that I will kill whoever did this.'

'Hush!' said Emrys quietly. 'Our first thought must be to get him away from here, and up on to the cart. We must seek help . . .'

'It is too late!' The tears were streaming from Jeremiah's face, damping the grey beard and falling in unchecked droplets from his cheeks. 'We can do nothing for him now, save bear him home.'

'Stop!' commanded Emrys. 'Stop it, I say! I swear I heard some sound from him! Stop your infernal noise!' He bent to kneel at Illtyd's side, head bent, listening intently.

'Oh, my dear boy! My poor little man! Oh, Illtyd!' Jeremiah was grieving when Illtyd briefly opened his eyes. Emrys had to bend low over his lips to catch the words.

'Jeremiah? Faith?'

'Well and safe,' Emrys said gently. 'Have no fear. Faith is with Ossie at the "Crown". We are going to take you home.'

Illtyd's eyes closed again. Jeremiah took off his jacket and folded it upon the floor of the cart, to pillow the poor bloodied head. Then, with great tenderness, they lifted him upon it. Jeremiah, feeling the awkwardly curved spine and the frailness of bone, began to weep again. Emrys sharply bade him take the reins and, pulling off his own coat, placed it over the inert figure. He was as distressed to see Jeremiah so weak and helpless as he was about Illtyd's plight, but dare not let him see it.

'Ride straight to Dr Mansel's house!' he commanded. 'Do not trouble about the cost, just take him. If need be, I will ask Rebecca for the money, and not feel shame to beg.'

Jeremiah did as he was bid, and Emrys sat in the cart beside Illtyd, searching the blue-tinged lips and eyelids desperately for some sign of life. And all of the way they rode, his own lips moved silently in prayer.

The sheep-stealers who had lain in wait for Illtyd and beaten him and his mare so mercilessly, had ridden to join the others, well pleased with the result of their attack. They had left the little hayward for dead and his strange piebald horse had fled. Injured and exhausted, it could prove no danger to them. It would either lose itself upon the bleak moorland and marshes, wandering panic-stricken until it died of hunger or cold, or fall into some quarry or ravine. Alive, it would prove a danger. They dare not run it with them, for it was too well known, and easily identified. Besides, it was impossible to ride, save by a child. They would have ripped away its saddle of tooled leather and brass, killing the animal, but, like its owner, it had proved stubborn and elusive, clinging tenaciously to life. At least there was a little money, and the watch.

The six horsemen, intent upon herding the plump flock to the creek where the boats lay concealed, had little fear of discovery and capture, although they knew the consequences – whipping, imprisonment, deportation were scarcely hazards they considered, so confident were they of success. There were few people save the occasional shepherd or wayfarer in this isolated place, and those vulnerable, and as easy to deal with as the dead hayward . . . Besides, who was to know that they were not drovers, buying their beasts from the local farmers to add to those herds being driven to Hereford, or onwards to London?

The outriders at the head of the flock heard the distant cries and thudding hooves of Joshua's army as they neared the bottom of Stormy Hill, barring the escape. Startled and uneasy, they shouted a warning, trying vainly to turn the flock. The frightened animals bolted, scrabbling upon each other's backs, panic-stricken, escaping wherever they could find a way. All was confusion and terror, with the riders floundering helplessly in a sea of fleeces. Marshalling what beasts they could control, they herded them back the way they had come, with the pounding horses and wild elated cries of Joshua's band growing ever nearer.

Soon they abandoned the sheep altogether, seeing the fierce club-waving horsemen bearing down upon them, screaming revenge. The sight of that first wave of red-headed savages, faces contorted as they slashed an opening through the bawling ewes, was enough to demoralise them. They fled wildly as the sheep, urging their horses upon the way, desperate for escape.

Even as they reached the copse where Illtyd had fallen, and the way ahead forked into a snake's tongue, they saw it barred by two converging armies of horsemen, carts, and even a stagecoach, its occupants crowding roof and windows threateningly.

They turned to force their way into the copse or leap hedges, but, as Illtyd had learnt, there was no escape. Finally they were forced to stand their ground, and the sound of clashing staves, yells, oaths and the breaking of flesh and bone ruptured the air.

It was, as Joshua admitted afterwards, less a fight than a rout. His most vicious battle was in defending the sheep-thieves from massacre. When eventually the blows ceased and some sort of order was restored, Joshua secured the prisoners within the stagecoach, with Doonan as guard upon the box, beside Ossie. Then, dispatching four willing farm labourers and a shepherd to retrieve the wandering ewes and return them to their pasture, he took stock.

From the sight of the gashed heads, bruises and torn clothing, he could only surmise that his troops had been enthusiastic rather than discriminating, setting about

143

them with complete abandon upon any strange face, or any known to them which barred their way! With the shouting and accusations mingling with the jubilation, the discordant cries of the mules and braying of the donkeys, plus the confusion of the returning sheep, Joshua thought it worse than the battle! His only relief lay in the message that Illtyd had been surrendered to the care of Dr Mansel, wounded but still, miraculously, alive.

As Joshua had herded the offenders into the stage-coach, propelled upon their way by many a sly kick and clout from the onlookers, Doonan had seen one of them toss an object into a clump of bracken and he swiftly retrieved it. He handed the constable the delicate silver pocket-watch, and Joshua read out the inscription – 'Illtyd Cleat – Hayward' – at which the culprit was treated to such a hail of blows that he was pleased to reach the sanctuary of the carriage.

Thanking his helpers for their loyalty and readiness, he dismissed them, beaming, upon their way, save for Ossie, Doonan, his kinsfolk and the miscreants upon the carriage. Then, having begged a word with the shepherd, which set them into peals of unexplained laughter, he set out with his entourage upon the lane to Tythegston Court.

The strange little company halted in the forecourt of the justice's house, to the consternation of the groom and the amusement of Leyshon, who opened the door upon the scene. He could scarce keep a straight face as he escorted Joshua into his master's presence.

'Well?' demanded the justice, rising from behind his desk. 'Perhaps you would care to explain to me the cause of this unlikely invasion?'

Joshua began with the story of Illtyd's beating, and ended with the capture of the sheep-stealers.

'The little hayward, Illtyd Cleat, he is badly hurt?'

'I fear so, sir, he has been taken upon a cart to Dr Mansel's house.'

The justice looked grave, declaring quietly, 'A brave and resourceful young man who has fought hard to overcome his afflictions. I have the greatest respect for him.'

'As I, sir, and all the people of the three hamlets.'

'There will be no charge upon his mother for his treatment, Stradling. His business is official, and he was injured at his work as hayward, defending the flocks. The vestry will certainly bear the costs.'

'Thank you, sir. I am sure that it will be appreciated.'

'Now, Constable, perhaps you will be good enough to explain that ragged and ungodly caravan outside.'

'The coach contains the prisoners, sir, the six felons apprehended for stealing sheep. It is true that we have one cell at the "Crown Inn", but not designed for such a massive and disorderly influx.'

'Then I shall write a note of explanation to the authorities at Pyle, asking for their detention until they can be brought to justice. I suppose that is why you brought them here?'

'Yes, sir. Thank you.'

The justice wrote his request, and handed it to Joshua. 'They will be adequately protected upon the way?'

'Yes, sir, by Cavan Doonan, his father, four brothers, and twin cousins, from Ireland.'

'Indeed!' The justice glanced briefly out of the window. 'It is to be hoped that the marriage will be a little more circumspect than the events of today, and more soberly entered upon.'

'I am sure that it will be conducted so, begging your pardon, sir.'

The justice peered at him sharply through his lenses. 'One thing, Stradling. I am not altogether happy about the lax and desultory way in which some of my tenants care for their flocks, it must not all devolve upon the good offices of the hayward. They must accept responsibility. You concur?'

'Yes, sir.'

'You will make enquiries about the affair. Determine the owner of the animals. He must bear some responsibility in this matter, and be brought to justice. You understand me?'

'Yes, sir,' repeated Joshua, dutifully.

'You will find the culprit and report to me at once, understood?'

'I already know, sir.'

'Well? Come on, man, out with it!'

'They are yours, sir,' said Joshua, straight-faced.

Joshua, Ossie and the Doonan men, to the immense amusement of the justice's household, left the grounds of Tythegston Court to deliver the prisoners to the cells at Pyle. Servants crowded every window, loft and vantage point to see the historic procession move off, Leyshon remarking, when he was able to stifle his laughter, that all it needed was a dancing bear to make a proper circus of it!

Even the Reverend Robert Knight peeped surreptitiously from behind the curtains of the library window,

later confiding to his friend, Dr Handel Peate, in a letter
that 'there could scarcely have been more chaos and
commotion when the walls fell at Jericho!' and 'In truth,
so villainous and disordered were the Irishmen, despite
their fine clothes, that had the gaol-coach been overturned upon the way, it would have been impossible to
tell which were the ruffians!'

Yet, brash and high-spirited as they were, the thoughts
of the Irishmen turned frequently to their 'little
leprechaun', and their silent prayers for his recovery
were no less heartfelt than those of the rector.

Dr Mansel had ministered to Illtyd with great gentleness
and skill, binding his wounds and doing what he could to
ease the hayward's bruised body. Jeremiah and Emrys
waited outside in the cart, apprehensive of what the
physician might say. When he called them in, his face
was grave, as was his prognosis.

'I have done what I can to ease his flesh, but I do not
know how he will withstand the shock and the beating he
has taken, for he is frail and weakened. The blow to his
head alarms me – it was so vicious it might well have
broken his skull, or disordered his brain. We cannot
know what the outcome will be.'

'Is it safe, sir, to take him the distance to his home in
Nottage?' Jeremiah asked.

Dr Mansel nodded. 'Perhaps his journey would be
gentler and less hazardous in my carriage. I will give
instructions to my coachman, and travel with him. My
housekeeper will provide blankets, for he must be kept
warm. A groom shall ride out at once that preparations

may be made. There will be need of a good fire, and straw or bark must be spread upon the road outside to muffle the sound of carriages.'

Jeremiah thought that it would be hard to muffle the noises of the adjoining smithy, with the clanging of iron upon its anvil, but said nothing. As soon as all was prepared Dr Mansel set out, with his patient lying prone upon the seat of the carriage, followed by Jeremiah and Emrys upon the cart.

Having seen Illtyd comfortably delivered to his bed, and declaring that he would return within two hours, the doctor left. Jeremiah took the cob and cart and visited all Illtyd's friends in Newton and the port, begging that the patient be left undisturbed until his condition improved. Emrys went on foot to take the doctor's message to all in Nottage, and the blacksmith, Clatworthy, sent his apprentice home, saying, 'I cannot tell you how grieved I am, Emrys, for the boy is like my own kin. I will not have him disturbed by clamour. Indeed, I could not work. I have no heart for it.'

Illtyd's violent assault seemed set to cast a pall upon the wedding on the morrow, but, distressed as she was, the Widow Cleat still had thought for Rosa's happiness and declared that all must go on as planned, save that she would stay and keep watch over her son. Yet when Jeremiah returned, it was with Elizabeth Crandle upon the de Breos coach, and medicine, comforts and invalid food which Rebecca had procured.

'I have come to stay the night, ma'am, that you may have some rest and company. Tomorrow you shall attend the wedding, for Illtyd would wish it so. It will be my privilege and pleasure to sit with him.'

The Widow Cleat protested that she could not leave him and, kind though she was, Miss Crandle was unknown to him, a stranger.

Elizabeth Crandle took Mistress Cleat's hands in her own, her dark eyes concerned, yet warm with affection. 'No, not a stranger, ma'am, a friend. Your son, this very day, became that to me. Recognising my hurt, he bade me turn to him should I ever have need of a true friend. It touched and heartened me, for I knew that it was truly meant, not empty words. Will you not allow me to offer him that same friendship now?'

The widow paused, then, drawing Elizabeth to her, said, 'Oh, my dear, I accept most willingly. Thank you for your kindness – no, your love, for that is what it is. You are a warm, compassionate girl, seeing Illtyd as he truly is.'

They embraced warmly, and Jeremiah had to gaze through the window at the coach, and clear his throat hard, and shuffle, and wipe his face upon his sleeve, else he seem affected by it.

He left them to return to Rebecca, first fetching Charity from Emrys's house, that his little maid might have their company overnight and receive news. He and the dog being firmly settled in the luxury of the de Breos coach with its gilded coat of arms, Jeremiah turned to the bull terrier. It sat upright, pink eyes imperious, as to the manor born.

'You think yourself a real aristocrat,' said Jeremiah, amused. 'Well, enjoy it while you may, but take a lesson from it. Your next ride will be in a cart!'

* * *

Ossie and the Doonans safely returned to the 'Crown' with news of their adventure, Joshua set out for Dr Mansel's house to seek tidings of his friend, Illtyd, and to talk of official matters, for despite the distraction of the wedding, and Rebecca's nearness, there was much to be done.

With the firm assurance that he would join the Doonans for the evening's partying, he left them being ministered to by Mrs Doonan, who seemed less appalled by their injuries than the outrage to their clothing, and was marshalling every scrap of help available to repair the wedding garments and see them spruced and ironed for the morrow.

Dr Mansel greeted the constable civilly, and for a time they discussed the brutality of the attack upon Illtyd, the seriousness of his condition and the events of the day. Finally, Dr Mansel looked at him questioningly.

'That is not the sole reason for your visit, I think.'

'No, sir. I come to ask about the post-mortem examination upon the man, Bando.'

'You have some reason to fear foul play?' Mansel asked sharply.

'Less a reason than a suspicion,' admitted Joshua. 'There are strange circumstances surrounding his disappearance, few facts.'

'Then let me give you one! He did not die of drowning.'

'How was he killed, sir?'

'A stab wound pierced the heart, but he would already have been helpless, near death. He had been savagely beaten. There is evidence of broken bones in the legs, and also in the hands and lower arms, as if he sought to ward off blows. He was then thrown dead into the sea, for there is no sign of water in the lungs.' Joshua felt sick, remembering the face ravaged by predatory gulls and the force of the waves upon rock. He would not think of Bando's living suffering.

'You do not wish to see the body, Stradling?'

'It is necessary?'

Seeing his conflict, Mansel replied, 'No. It is all there in my report, detailed. There will be a copy for you, and the justice, and for the court inquest.' He paused. 'You acquitted yourself well at the inquest upon Jem Crocutt, Stradling. A foregone conclusion, I fear. The finding: murder by person or persons unknown. You are no nearer a solution?'

'No, sir, to my regret, for he seems to have been an honest man.'

'You have seen my colleague from Pyle, whom we discussed? He who attended the shipwreck victims.'

'Dr Elfed Thomas? No, I have yet to discuss it with the justice, for I must move delicately in this matter, and upon his advice. I fear, this afternoon, other matters were pressing!'

Dr Mansel, visualising the scene in the courtyard as Joshua had described it, was forced to concur. He smiled, shaking his head in amusement. 'I dare say the cottagers upon the way thought it some hellish apparition, come to haunt them for past sins, and retreated to bar their doors and windows!'

'True, I do not know who looked the wilder or more ferocious, the prisoners or we! Certainly they were pleased enough to be delivered into the hands of their gaoler, claiming that they felt safer there than with "those crazed foreign horsemen!".'

Under the lamplight, Mansel's opaque green eyes shone with humour. He ran his fingers through the fine circlet of white hair edging the pinkness of his scalp.

'I should like to have been there to see it, Stradling, not here, engaged in – ' He broke off awkwardly, lightening his tone to suggest pleasantly, 'You will take a measure of cognac with me?'

'No, sir. I thank you, but beg you to excuse me. Tonight there is to be an eve-of-wedding party for Cavan Doonan, with visits to every inn and tavern in the three hamlets! Tomorrow I am to be supporter at the marriage ceremony.'

'Then have a care for your condition,' Mansel jested, 'or I'll wager that the justice will! If he is able to stand at all, the bridegroom might well end up supporting you!'

Chapter Ten

Rosa's mother, Mistress Howarth, awoke to a wedding morn which was cold but had that luminous clarity of air and sky which sometimes marks a December day. She sent up a sincere prayer of gratitude to the Almighty as she set about her manifold tasks.

In a bedroom of the 'Crown Inn', Doonan opened his eyelids to a light that slashed at his eyeballs sharply as a knife-blade. He groaned, and tried to move his head. The pain was so excruciating that he gave up the attempt, lying there fighting nausea and the suspicion that one of the quarrymen had mistaken his skull for limestone, and split it apart with a sledgehammer. Dear Lord! What had happened to him? He was dying – dead even! He remembered the eve-of-wedding party and the afternoon's fight. There was something else he had to remember. What was it? His wedding! Today was his wedding day! Not even the thought of his darling girl, Rosa, could bring him comfort. How could he get to the church? He could not! No, not even if they carried him! They would have to do without him. More than ever he realised that Rosa was too good for him – he was a drunken, shiftless lout, a spineless clod, useless, degenerate, not fit to breathe the same pure air. She was better off without him!

In the other bedrooms of the inn, the Doonan kinsmen lay in disarray, bruised, enervated, only a little less remorseful than the bridegroom. Mistress Doonan was already about her business, apportioning their clothing, ordering their breakfasts, getting them roused. They would not disgrace her! She would get them there on time, and looking as clean and presentable as God would allow – for even she did not look to a miracle! They would be standing there at the altar rail even if she had to carry them upon her back! Diminutive as she was, no one could have doubted her ability and strength of purpose – least of all, the Doonans.

Joshua, in his cottage overlooking the village green, had returned from the well in the bailey where he had sluiced himself with icy water. Aware of his duties as supporter, he had abstained from the grossest of the night's indulgences. There had been no doubt of the Doonans' enjoyment of the celebrations or, indeed, their standing in the three hamlets. They were heroes! Had they not gone immediately, and selflessly, to the aid of Illtyd? Were they not fearless, brave fighters? Could they not ride as if born to the saddle? Were they not good-natured, manly, full of harmless fun and high spirits? The cottagers had taken them to their hearts. Their tankards were never emptied of cwrw da, the local brew, for as soon as they supped it their store was replenished by eager admirers. Joshua did not doubt their capacity, merely their awareness of its potency. It was as well that the landlord of the 'Crown' had dispatched

Ossie with the carriage to bring back those incapable of walking. Ossie himself had imbibed but frugally, yet the horses had set off at such a cracking pace that had any been rash enough, or even able, to sit upon the box, they would undoubtedly have been decapitated at the archway!

Joshua glanced at his wedding finery set out upon the wooden butler, beside his bed. His skin-tight, pale-grey unmentionables, cut to flare above his shiny black boots, the darker coat with its rolled and quilted velvet collar, the frilled shirt which his laundress had crisped so meticulously with the goffering iron. He had worn these very clothes, and the multi-patterned brocade waistcoat, when he had first invited Rebecca and Jeremiah to share a meal . . .

Oh, Rebecca, my love, he thought, I have so longed to see you, to touch you again. Yet, now that you are near, I am afraid! You are no longer that little cockle-maid I knew and learnt to love. You are a woman, with a woman's thoughts, a stranger I do not know. My longing for you has only sharpened, grown stronger, but who is it that I yearn for? Rebecca de Breos or someone who was born of my own need, and no longer exists?

Rebecca was already dressed in a silk gown of softest eau-de-nil, with a tiny matching jacket hugging her small waist, above a skirt which flowed over layers of pretty petticoats, its every movement fluid and elegant. She had chosen it for its simplicity, selecting the fabric, then commissioning it from a travelling seamstress. Her grandfather had understood why she would not travel to London for it, nor would she wear one of the French gowns which Mistress Crandle had helped her to choose during their journeying in Europe. It would have grieved her if her friends had judged her unapproachable, or trying to outshine Rosa. It was a possibility which would never have arisen when she was simply 'Rebecca, the cockle-maid'.

She had fastened at the collar of her gown the pretty silver brooch which Jeremiah had pinned upon her blue cotton gown when she had travelled with Joshua to his parents' farm – a day which had proved as cold and hurtful as their rejection of her. The brooch had been Jeremiah's gift to his young wife upon the birth of his son, who was to die within hours, with the girl who had been delivered of him. Rebecca traced the shape of it with her fingers, wondering how Jeremiah could have borne the pain . . .

'Well, my maid?' He had come to stand beside her. 'Were your thoughts so sad that they grieve you so deeply, even upon a day such as this?'

'No. I was thinking of . . .'

'Illtyd?' he asked gently.

She did not deny it for, indeed, Illtyd had been much in her thoughts.

'He would not have you grieve and spoil Rosa's day, my maid. Besides, he has the spirit and will to survive.'

'Even this, Jeremiah?'

'I have never prayed more fervently, or devoutly, for anything in my life, Rebecca. If there is reason in things, and we must believe that there is, or life would be too much to bear . . .'

'I cannot see the reason for his deformity, and the suffering he endures,' she cried despairingly.

'Or the love he gives? Or the warmth and generosity of his spirit, Rebecca? His example?'

'Oh yes, Jeremiah, but has he not paid a bitter price for our reward?'

'He would not admit so, my dear. He would admit only that today is Rosa's and Doonan's wedding day, and that you are as pretty and fresh as the first flowers upon the blackthorn, and as welcome here.'

'Oh, Jeremiah!' she cried, flinging her arms about him, and resting her cheek against the roughness of his beard. 'I love you so! Don't ever change, for so much has altered, or gone from my life.'

'You vexatious creature,' he blustered to hide his pleasure, 'look what you do to the frills of my poor shirt! They hang down like a flabby coxcomb upon a sick rooster!'

She smiled. 'Jeremiah, do you recall the day when you ran off with Doonan's fighting cocks? Up the quarry ramp, and all the way to Newton, a rooster squawking and pecking beneath each elbow?'

'Yes, and they showed me as little respect and gratitude as you for their deliverance!' They broke into shared laughter at the remembrance of it. 'And the way they plagued poor Charity, leaping upon his back and spurring him with their claws, like devils on horseback?'

'Charity,' she cried, 'I had almost forgot. I must fetch him from the outhouse, and take a sweetmeat to the old cob.'

The three of them, Rebecca in her new bonnet, Jeremiah and Charity, sat in the de Breos coach on the way to collect the Widow Cleat and deliver her to church.

Charity reclined upon a plump cushion, a bow of bright pink ribbon about his neck, 'the colour,' Rebecca declared, 'to exactly match the pinkness around his eyes.'

'Look at him,' Jeremiah said, 'happy as a pig in mud! I swear, Rebecca, he is getting ideas above his station!'

'Then we have much in common,' said Rebecca, laughing, 'for they say the same of me!'

Beside her cottage next to the forge, the Widow Cleat awaited the arrival of the carriage, hoping to deaden its sound for Illtyd by another layer of straw.

Within, Illtyd lay asleep upon his pillow, head swathed in bandages, his face and blue-veined eyelids almost as colourless. Elizabeth Crandle sat in a chair beside his bed, busy at some embroidery.

'Miss Crandle?'

She looked up, startled, and went to him at once. His vivid blue eyes were open wide, but seemed to have difficulty in settling upon her.

'What has happened?' She had to bend low to hear him.

'An accident upon Stormy Downs. You remember? The sheep-stealers?'

His face grew clenched in concentration. 'Yes, I remember . . . Faith? They did not kill her?'

'No. She is safe with Ossie at the "Crown".'

His body relaxed. 'I am glad. I was afraid that –'

She took his hand in hers. 'You would like Ossie to bring her home to you?'

'Please.'

'Then I shall see that it is done.'

He closed his eyes, briefly satisfied, then opened them again. 'They took Rebecca's watch.'

'Joshua brought it back. It is here, under your pillow, unharmed.' She took it out and placed it in his hand, closing his fingers upon it.

'Miss Crandle?'

'Elizabeth.'

He nodded. 'I am glad that you are here,' he said quietly.

'And I. It is comfortable to be with friends, for there is no need for pretence, or reservation. We know each other's true value.'

'Yes, that is so,' he said, voice contented.

'I must tell your mother that you are awake. She will be so pleased, Illtyd. She awaits the carriage to take her to Rosa's wedding.'

Mistress Cleat came in, dressed in a gown and bonnet of lightest grey, looking excited and flushed and absurdly young. She ran to him, and kissed him gently upon his cheek.

'Oh, my dear!' she said. 'My dear boy!'

Illtyd's voice was tired, and his eyelids beginning to droop although he strove to keep them open. 'You are beautiful,' he said, 'like a dove, or a woodland pigeon, all softness and pale light. They will think that you are the bride.' Then his eyes closed, and he did not see the tears upon Elizabeth's dark lashes.

Rosa's uncle, George Evans, the carrier, waited with Rosa in the living room of her mother's small lodging house in the port. He thought he had never seen his niece looking lovelier. In her gown of creamy-white, with its gently fitted sleeves and sculptured bodice flowing into a long graceful skirt, she was 'as pretty a piece of muslin' as he had ever laid eyes on.

George Evans was not an imaginative man, but with Rosa's pale, translucent skin and soft hair the colour of sun-bleached corn, and her frail slenderness, she seemed to him like a cottage garden lily, one of those regal, waxy blooms that made you want to stretch out a hand to touch its silkiness, yet you held back for fear of bruising the delicate petals.

He felt the prick of tears behind his eyelids and, taking out his pocket kerchief which his wife had warned him that he must on no account use, since it was pure ornament, he blew his nose hard.

'My! Rosa, love,' he declared, 'your father would have been a proud man this day! No prouder, though, than your old uncle!'

She kissed him gently upon his plump cheek.

'And you,' she said, 'will be so elegant and distinguished, Uncle, that as we pass in our carriage, they will mistake you for royalty, and very likely bow to you.'

'Go on with you, girl!'

But he was modestly pleased. He knew he looked well, for he wore the clothes he had worn as one of the bidders to the wedding – all save the flower-decked staff he had raised to rap upon the doors. Above his suit of grey and his frilled shirt, he flaunted his bidder's hat of flat-crowned straw, trimmed with a circlet of silken flowers, a spray of ribbons in his buttonhole. There were no fresh garden flowers, it being December.

They heard the clop of the horses' hooves upon the cobbles outside, and the jangle of the harnesses as the curricle drew to a halt.

'Now, my girl,' he said, flustered, 'don't get over-wrought. Try and calm yourself.'

'Yes, Uncle.' She saw how his hands trembled, and that his cheeks shone red as polished apples.

'Don't forget, it is not too late! No, not even at this late hour. If you have changed your mind,' he persisted anxiously, 'don't be afraid to confess it, just tell your old uncle . . .'

'No, Uncle, I am quite sure, as sure as that first day I saw Cavan and decided he would marry me – although he took a little longer to convince.'

Outside, Watkins, the handsome young groom, descended and guided Rosa into the fragile shell-shaped carriage.

A pearl! he thought admiringly. The big Irishman has found himself a real pearl! And, in truth, there was a lustre and milky bloom about her, a sheen of happiness.

The open carriage had brought gasps of delight from the excited onlookers who had gathered to wish Rosa well. The tails of the chestnut horses had been plaited with coloured ribbons, and there were rosettes upon their proudly tossing heads. The carriage itself had been embellished with garlands of bright flowers, lovingly stitched by Hannah, Emily Randall and Mistress Cleat, and with pretty ribboned swags.

As the carriage drove off, with the chestnuts prancing, bedecked and flowered, the bride so beautiful and her portly uncle in his hat of blossom-ringed straw, the watchers raised a spontaneous cheer. It was as though December greyness had burgeoned unexpectedly into spring. Rosa's Uncle George stood up and bowed, and doffed his flower-strewn hat in answer to their acclaim.

'There!' cried Rosa, clapping delightedly as the curricle swayed and jolted him back into his seat, 'didn't I say as much? They will boast to their grandchildren that it was Prince Albert himself they saw, and what is more, he bowed to them!'

He took her hand and squeezed it hard. 'Rosa, my love, I'll swear he never escorted as fair a queen!'

Watkins silently agreed, and even the horses nodded their heads.

Within the small stone church the rector gazed from the rood-loft squint, unseen. It was time for him to descend; the bridegroom and his supporter, the young constable, awaited the arrival of the bride, the congregation neatly separated by the aisle, women upon one side, men upon the other, as custom decreed.

He took one more stolen glance at the male side and his mouth quivered into a smile, and then he felt the laughter bubbling in his chest, although he fought hard to stifle it. He eventually controlled himself, begging God to forgive his lapse as he took a handkerchief to polish the lenses of his gold-rimmed glasses. He was not too greatly troubled by his fall from grace, for he reasoned that God, in creating Man, had most certainly shown a rare and delicate sense of humour.

As he stood before the wedding throng, his parishioners remarked how grave and splendid their rector looked in his embroidered robes. He concentrated his gaze upon Joshua, not daring to look at the bridegroom lest levity again overcome him, and he be disgraced.

Dear heaven! Had there ever been such a gathering? The bridegroom with an eye nearly closed, his right ear shiny and red as a carbuncle. Even his clothes showed signs of distress, however neatly sewn and patched they were. His waistcoat strained upon his massive frame beneath the flame-coloured hair, and the rector was put in mind of a monkey upon a barrel organ, obedient to its grinder, yet ill at ease and wishing to be elsewhere.

Was there a man in the entire congregation, he wondered, who did not bear the scars of battle? Even the verger showed a gash upon his cheek and a nose which seemed to have doubled in size overnight. As for the Doonan men, they would have looked more at home in a travelling fair as bare-knuckled pugilists.

Divided from them by the aisle, their womenfolk looked pristine and innocently free from stain.

The eternal fight between good and evil, the rector reflected, amused. The handmaidens of the Lord and the Devil's horsemen!

The watcher at the door signalled that the bride was near and the rector guiltily recalled himself. The people's voices soared, spontaneously, to the saddleback roof. The service had begun . . .

Everyone said afterwards how beautiful Rosa had looked, her pale cheeks flushed with warm colour, and how touching were the responses.

But Rebecca could not have told you what Rosa wore,

although she followed every word of the marriage service. Her eyes were set fast upon Joshua, and the soft nakedness of his neck beneath the curling gold hair, as he bent forward. Had she not spoken every word of the responses, if not with her lips, then with her soul and flesh, to Joshua Stradling, Constable?

She longed to go to him, say a word that might bridge their long separation, but she was caught up in the excitement and turmoil of meeting old friends, as he was with his duties as supporter.

When they left the church for the wedding feast at Mrs Howarth's house in the port, Jeremiah and Charity and the Widow Cleat climbed into the de Breos coach beside her as they watched the Doonan men and the younger cottagers leap upon their mounts and ride wildly through Newton, for the first at the feast could lay claim to the wedding cake and a kiss from the bride.

''Tis a wonder they could find their horses,' said Jeremiah, laughing at their antics, 'much less the cake! They drank so much cwrw da last night that the rector could set them upon the corners of the roof like gargoyles' spouts. It would be coming out of their mouths, and even their ears, for all eternity!'

There followed the ritual of locking the bride and groom within the churchyard until they paid for their release by throwing halfpennies and pennies to the cottage children. Rebecca and Mistress Cleat laughed aloud to see them dive and scramble, and very often fling a fist in the dispute over ownership, the smallest ones rushing between the legs of the disputants and scooping up the prize. Joshua took the verger's key to unlock the gate, and he looked up, straight into Rebecca's eyes, and turned before she could read the expression upon his face . . .

As their carriage drew away, they saw Ezra the Box leading one of the justice's stray sheep, secured upon a straw rope, and making for the churchyard gate.

'Baaa! Baaa!' called out Jeremiah wickedly as Ezra passed. 'Two little lost lambs, is it? Going to the right place, anyhow!'

Ezra glared, and jerked the loudly protesting sheep after him.

'No doubt which will be the more tender!' said the Widow Cleat, laughing.

'No,' agreed Jeremiah, 'or which one the rector would rather take home!'

The wedding feast was an occasion for the greatest revelry, with food, ale, music and laughter filling the guests with goodwill and the house with merriment.

Indeed, the jubilation flowed over into the inns and taverns, for upon leaving the church after their nuptials, Rosa and Doonan had found the porch barred by a thick rope of horsehair strung through with flowers. The disguised 'ruffians' who held it (all recognised and cheerfully greeted by name by the bridegroom) demanding 'the bride's ale'. Joshua had obligingly supplied the shillings needed and they had departed cheerfully to slake their thirsts, showering blessings and ever more lewd expectations upon the couple, until the arrival of the rector sent them fleeing.

Doonan's brothers and cousins had lodged small sums

of money at each inn and ale-house to be used at the landlord's discretion. Thus, James Ploughman, Clatworthy the blacksmith and his apprentice, and even Ezra the Box, were among those exhorted to 'drink the bride's health, and bless her generosity'.

In Mrs Howarth's little lodging house in the port makeshift tables had been rigged up in several of the rooms, so that the festivities spilled over as freely and convivially as the ale. It was this, and Rosa's clever designing, which caused Rebecca to find herself seated next to Joshua.

His official duties briefly suspended, he took his chair, bowing to her formally, and to the other ladies, before seating himself.

'Miss de Breos, your servant, ma'am!' he said gravely.

'Constable Stradling, sir!' She inclined her head in response.

'Will you permit me to offer you refreshment, ma'am?' he asked.

'I am already well supplied, I thank you, sir. And you?'

'I have been hungry for the sight of you, Rebecca,' he said, so quietly that only she could hear.

'Then, sir, you may look your fill,' she said, her voice demure.

'I fear my appetite could never be sated.'

'Then I suggest, sir, that you start upon the meat and potato cakes as a temporary measure.'

He did as he was bid, laughing, then turning to the others about him to make conversation, enjoying the jests and rough humour and the antics of the Doonan boys, while Rebecca occupied herself with talking to Mistress Cleat about the improvement in Illtyd, and Elizabeth's kindness. After a while, Joshua turned to her again, his face serious.

'Rebecca, we must talk. There is so much I need to say to you, to ask, but not here. Will you see me alone?' He saw her hesitation. 'Please, I beg of you. What I have to discuss must be said in private.'

She would have answered him lightly, as in the past, asking if he wished to compromise her with idle flirtation, but felt unable to do so.

'Yes, I will talk to you, Joshua.'

'It must be somewhere private, where we will remain undisturbed.'

She gave it thought. 'The coach is left here, in the coachyard behind the cottage, for the horses have been stabled with those from the tramroad nearby.'

He nodded. 'And the coachman?'

'I have sent him to seek refreshment at the "Ship Aground". He will return within the hour. I am not sure, Joshua, if this is wise . . .'

'If you do not trust me, or do not wish to come – ' he said stiffly.

'No. I shall be there.'

The atmosphere between them was awkward, strained: she feeling that he had unfairly forced her into a situation beyond her control; he that Rebecca no longer loved him, or had faith in him. Joshua thought, regretfully, that without it there was little to be said between them.

In the hubbub and merriment, the singing, and the

sound of the fiddlers and dancing as the tables were moved away, Rebecca was able to slip away unobserved into the coachyard, then into the de Breos coach, thinking that if she were seen, she could claim the urgent need for fresh air, or a shawl, or some other item left in the carriage.

Joshua had made some convincing excuse for his absence to Mrs Howarth, and explained the truth of the matter to Rosa and Doonan, before opening the door of the coach to climb in beside her.

'You are enjoying the wedding, the festivities?' he asked tentatively.

'Yes, I have been much entertained.'

There was a silence.

'The Doonan family are high-spirited and full of fun, are they not?'

'Most amusing.'

'It was kind of your grandfather, Sir Matthew, to arrange their journey. Cavan was pleased.'

'I am glad.'

They looked at each other helplessly, strangers making clumsy conversation, more aware of the silences between them than the words.

'Oh, damn it, Rebecca,' he burst out angrily, 'we sit here as if there has been nothing between us! What has happened?'

'A parting, Joshua.'

'But now we have come together again, and yet the distance between us lengthens!' he exclaimed in frustration. 'Have we changed so much?'

'No. I have not – at least, not in my deepest feelings

and emotions. Do you find me so different, Joshua?' she appealed anxiously.

'Yes.' He paused, studying her thoughtfully, wondering how to phrase it. 'You are certainly more beautiful, Rebecca, more assured. Yet there is a remoteness I do not recognise. It makes me hesitate to touch you, approach you even. I see no sign of the Rebecca I loved.'

'You speak as if all is past, Joshua.'

'No, neither past, nor ended, although I could wish it so! I love you, Rebecca, believe me.'

She listened in silence.

'I love you more than ever. I swear that every day that we were apart only deepened my love and need for you,' he said truthfully, 'but I am not foolish enough to believe that you could still love me. Your life has changed so much. There have been so many new people, places . . .'

'And if I tell you that whoever I have met, and wherever I have journeyed, my first waking thought has always been of you? I have never ceased thinking of you, or loving you, Joshua. I promise.'

'Oh, Rebecca,' he said despairingly, 'too much has happened! Don't you see? Loving is not enough! It is that very thing I came here to tell you.'

'I do not understand you, Joshua. Will not!'

'Think, Rebecca! Would you marry me? And if you did, could you live with me, here? A village constable's wife . . . Where? My cottage?' he demanded helplessly.

'If necessary. Have you so soon forgotten that it is here that I have spent my life?'

'No, but all is now changed. Damn it, Rebecca, you are changed!'

'It is you who are changed, Joshua!' she returned passionately. 'You take me at the world's estimation, as it sees me now. I had not thought it of you! You should know me better.'

He looked at her intently before saying gravely, 'When I asked if you would marry me, live with me here, you said, "if necessary". What did you mean? Consider before you answer, I beg of you.'

She looked at him, puzzled, not understanding.

'Was it not a reminder that you have the money and power to alter things, to live as you choose?'

'No. I meant that I would live wherever, and however, it is necessary, glad to be with you, whatever the circumstance. Can you doubt it?'

He took her in his arms with a sigh of uncertainty and despair, burying his face in her dark hair, then kissing her eyes, cheeks, lips, pouring out his need for her.

'Oh, Rebecca,' he said helplessly, 'don't ever go away from me again, for I am lost without you. You are the only thing which gives meaning to my life. You are my own darling, my love. I cannot live without you.'

She felt the hardness of bone beneath the firm flesh of his breast, and the strength and leanness of his arms about her, and felt such a surge of love and feeling for him that it was an actual physical pain in her breasts. She felt it flowing as blood to stir the flesh of groin and limbs, and even in the raw nerve-ends of her skin. Then there was the pressure of his hand upon her breast, and the sweetness of his open mouth upon hers, insistent, demanding. More than anything she wanted to be part of his warm young flesh, to feel their bodies joined, fused in loving. It was with real physical effort that she pushed him away, struggling to be free, then a sense of desolation and regret. She heard him groan, and bury his face in his hands.

'I am sorry, Rebecca,' he looked up, face flushed, eyes heavy as with sleep. 'It was unforgivable of me.'

'No, my dear.' She lifted her hand and gently smoothed his cheek. 'It was not unforgivable, for my need was as urgent as yours – more than anything, I wanted to give myself to you, to belong with you.'

'I am sorry, Rebecca. There is no more I can say.'

'Except that you will make an honest woman of me?'

He smiled, despite himself.

'Once, Joshua, a long time ago, you came to me at my cottage, begging to court me.'

'I remember, but I regretted that there was no one to ask for permission, save you.'

She nodded, her mouth curving into an affectionate smile, 'Well, now there is no such barrier. You may make formal application to my grandfather for my hand.'

Joshua took it between his own and held it firm, then examined it carefully.

'But it is so soft and white,' he said with mock seriousness, 'a lady's hand. It would be a crime to coarsen it with common toil!'

'You see it changed from that of Rebecca the shellfish maid?'

'Certainly, for that small hand was raw, flayed by life, roughened with wind and weather.'

'Yet it is the same hand, as I am the same Rebecca!'

He laughed, and raised it to his lips, protesting, 'Do not whip me any more, Rebecca, I beg of you! I admit it freely, you are the same! I am foolish, blind, insensitive. I do not deserve a treasure such as you . . .'

'As I said, nothing has changed,' she murmured as he opened the carriage door and stepped down to lift her to his side.

Chapter Eleven

Jeremiah, replete with good food and ale-house brew, sat with his boot tapping in time to the fiddlers' music for the dance. He usually called such sounds 'caterwauling and scrapings', but so great was his sense of goodwill and well-being that he tentatively stretched out a hand to Mistress Cleat who sat beside him, then rose bowing and formally demanding, 'Would you do me the honour, ma'am, to trip a measure?'

Sophie Cheat arose, blushing prettily and saying with a curtsey, 'Why, sir, it would give me the greatest of pleasure.'

'An honour, ma'am.'

She placed her hand upon his outstretched arm, and together they took the floor. Rather, the three of them took the floor, for Charity, not to be outdone, danced and cavorted beside them, barking, leaping, and showing off alarmingly to the great delight of the company who stood aside to watch the performance. The more they applauded, the more frenzied and outlandish grew his movements, until Jeremiah and Sophie Cleat were so overcome with laughter that they were helpless to continue, and led the cur away lest he do himself some injury, or develop apoplexy.

Joshua and Rebecca had returned to see the end of his spirited exhibition.

'A true thespian,' declared Joshua, laughing and clapping. 'I'll be damned if he did not upstage Jeremiah! He is certainly the better dancer.'

'Let us see, sir, how proficient you are at the polite arts!' replied Rebecca, amused, 'for his performance might well outshine yours!'

''Tis true he has the advantage of four legs, save that it gives him an extra pair to trip over!'

'You have the advantage of taking me for a partner!' Rebecca reminded him.

'Indeed,' he whirled her expertly into the dancing, 'but for more than a dance, I hope, Miss de Breos.'

'Were it only for that, sir, I should pray that the music might never end.'

'Wanton! Hussy!' he said, laughing. 'Have you no modesty? No shame?'

'No, I think I have not, sir, where you are concerned,' she said seriously, and he drew her closer to him, looking into her vivid blue eyes, then gently kissing the top of her dark head as she pressed her face to his breast.

'I fancy, Jeremiah, that it will not be long before we shall have the pleasure of another dance,' said Sophie Cleat with satisfaction, nodding in their direction.

'God willing,' agreed Jeremiah fervently.

'And Sir Matthew,' added Emrys, ever practical, as he passed Jeremiah his ale.

The festivities grew increasingly more relaxed and enthusiastic, and the dancing wilder, until the two fiddlers were so overcome with exhaustion that they had to be rescued by Mrs Howarth and victualled before they collapsed altogether, and their fiddle strings with them. In the hiatus the Doonans kept the company splendidly entertained with their games and frolicking, while the 'wedding plate' was discreetly passed among the guests, that they might pay their tribute to the newlyweds. When all was over, and Mistress Howarth receiving compliments from all sides upon the success of the affair, the bridegroom, at a signal, carried his bride out into the yard, still in her wedding finery, to where Ossie waited with a mount. Then, swinging Rosa on to the saddle, Cavan leapt up behind her and with a shout and a toss of his red head, was off, unruly hair flying. There was a wild scramble for the guests' horses. Joshua, pulling Rebecca by the hand, ran to where a stable lad stood holding his grey, and swung her upon the mare, then mounted before her and bade her cling to his waist, for dear life.

With a shouting and yelling, the riders were off in pursuit of the newlyweds, jostling and swerving, one of the Doonan boys blowing upon a coachman's horn until overcome by lack of puff. Others, overcome by ale, abandoned themselves to ditch or roadside, or the gentler pursuit of village maidens, while the grooms and stable-boys gathered up their mounts. The rest of the company rode resolutely on, chasing Doonan and Rosa up hill and down dale, through sandhills and over village green, until the bridegroom, unable to shake off his pursuers, rode into the yard of his cottage, dismounted and, carrying his bride within, locked and barred the doors.

Sufficient to say that the cock crows and larking, with

the singing and dancing, long continued outside. Then Cavan Doonan, with a gentleness that no one but Rosa would ever see, carried her to their bed.

Joshua, rising early the next morning, was in time to dismount from his grey at the archway to the 'Crown', and to take off his helmet and bow to Rebecca as the de Breos coach took the hill to the Clevis. She waved to him from its window, before blowing him a kiss, her brilliant blue eyes alight with mischief. Immediately afterwards, he had to step smartly aside as the Doonan coach thundered out, its occupants bouncing about inside. Those upon the attic obediently ducked their heads beneath the arch at the guard's shouted command. They yelled good wishes and encouragement to Joshua as he swept them a low bow, helmet to his breast, their bobbing heads glowing flame and copper in the thin, early morning sun. Behind them, Mistress Doonan and her husband followed more sedately in a post chaise, smiling and waving to the constable. Mr Doonan's blazing hair was extinguished under a beaver hat, and his wife's velvet bonnet, with its floating ostrich feather, dusted his nose as she turned and inclined her head, making him gasp and sneeze, before the carriage bore them away, lost in the curve of the hill.

'It is as if a light has gone out,' said Ossie, coming from the stable-yard to stand beside him. 'They carried their own joy with them, a pleasure in living.'

'Yes,' agreed Joshua, thinking of Rebecca.

'It will not be the same without them.'

'No.'

The little ostler's nut-brown face was warm with understanding. 'It is as well we have our work, Joshua.'

'Yes, and I must be off upon it now, although it offers less happy distraction!'

'Now there I have the advantage of you,' Ossie said, smiling, 'for my charges are warm and affectionate, unlike yours, who are dead.'

'Then I had best be about my business,' answered Joshua, smiling in return, 'lest the vestrymen conclude that I am dead, too!'

As he rode the grey over Dan-y-Graig Hill and into Tythegston, Joshua's thoughts had veered from Rebecca and the wedding to concern for Illtyd and the bereaved family at Grove Farm upon whom he still kept a frequent, careful watch, and, finally, the unsolved riddle of Jem Crocutt's murder, and the death of Bando.

He delivered his grey to the justice's groom, and was still so deep in thought when Leyshon opened the door to him, that for a moment the man's words did not pierce his mind.

'I believe congratulations to be in order, sir.'

'Congratulations?' Joshua asked sharply.

'The sheep-stealers, sir.'

'Oh, yes, I thank you, Leyshon,' he said, flushing, 'they are safely under lock and key.'

'And Mr Cleat, the young hayward, sir?'

'Conscious, now, and improving, I am happy to say.'

'Thank God for it! He is a brave fellow, not least for the way he has overcome his disabilities.' Leyshon bent his head forward stiffly and with some effort gently traced the bone at the nape of his neck, atop the spine, saying, 'I can but guess at the pain such deformity gives him.'

Before Joshua had time to reply, Leyshon brought a small pigskin pouch from his pocket, saying awkwardly, 'I hope that you will not consider it impertinent, sir, an intrusion, yet I know you are a friend of his. We – that is the servants here – have collected for a small gift. It would please us if his mother would accept it, with our sympathy and goodwill.'

Pleased and touched, Joshua assured him that he would deliver it, with their message.

The justice looked up from his desk as Joshua entered, protuberant deep brown eyes amused behind his lenses.

'Well, Stradling, there has been a mass exodus of our Irish invaders, I take it?'

'Yes, sir. They left this morning.'

'With the warning beacons aflame upon their route, no doubt,' he observed drily.

'No need, sir, they carry their own upon their heads!' returned Joshua, smiling.

'Well, we shall miss them, not least in the congregation, for their voices were loud enough to awaken the dead, let alone a dozing parishioner! I have no doubt that their fists proved equally impressive.'

'Although to render unconscious rather than to arouse!' agreed Joshua.

The justice enquired about Illtyd's progress, then remarked that Dr Mansel had resolutely refused to accept payment for his services from the vestry, so impressed was he with the hayward's bravery.

'It was about Dr Mansel's findings concerning the dead man, Bando, that I wished to speak to you, sir, and upon other matters touching upon the death of Jem Crocutt.'

Having apprised the justice of his abortive visit to Sker House, and his suspicions regarding Bando's violent death, and the disappearance of the pauper, Elwyn Morris, from Grove Farm, Joshua finished by relating Ezra the Box's confidences about the wreckers, the threats upon his life and his unexpected bravery in the face of it.

'You surprise me, Stradling,' confessed the justice, 'for I admit with some shame that I find his ways irritating. Perhaps, after all, I have misjudged him. Only yesterday, he returned a stray sheep to my keeping.'

'Well, perhaps he has reformed, sir.'

'I could wish that my sermons had that effect,' returned the justice wryly. 'The real purpose of his visit was to enquire about a reward.'

They both laughed, for the undertaker's parsimony was well known.

'You will keep a watch upon him, however?' the justice asked more seriously. 'For I truly believe his life to be in danger. These are ruthless men; another death is of no consequence to them.'

'Of course, sir. I have told no one but you and Dr Mansel of his confession.'

'Good. It is to be hoped that he is as circumspect!'

'There is one other thing, sir, about Dr Elfed Thomas of Pyle.'

'Yes?'

'If Ezra the Box is to be believed, and by his terror and the wound upon his throat it appears that he speaks the truth, then Dr Thomas would seem to be in some way involved, either for gain, or out of fear for his life.'

'It is true that at the time of the inquest upon those shipwrecked, he declared their injuries to be consistent only with drowning, or being battered upon the rocks by the sea,' said the justice thoughtfully. 'He mentioned no other wounds, or possibilities.'

'You think it wise for me to approach him upon the subject, sir?'

The justice considered for a moment before instructing firmly, 'No, leave it with me, Stradling. We do not want to alarm him, for he might then alert others. If need arises, then I will apply for an exhumation order upon the bodies. Yet we will need evidence, not suspicion, you understand?'

'Yes, sir. There is news of the crucifix?'

'No, I fear not, although the ship's owners are investigating, and the British consul is making discreet enquiries of the families involved. It would be cruel and profitless to tell them of the violence and outrage wrought upon those shipwrecked, I feel, for it would serve only to heighten their grief.'

Joshua nodded.

'We shall see,' concluded the justice, his voice tired and strained. 'Meanwhile, about the matter of the stolen sheep; you will be relieved to know that I have seen that my fences and gates are in excellent order, and given my shepherds firm instructions!'

'Indeed, sir, I am relieved to hear it. Perhaps, if you do

not consider it an imposition, I may safely leave the offender to you, as you were so anxious for me to reprimand the culprit?'

'You may be sure that I will speak to him most severely,' said the justice, eyes twinkling.

When Joshua reclaimed his grey, his immediate intention was to ride to Nottage and take Leyshon's gift to the Widow Cleat, and spend some time with Illtyd. However, at the gateway of the court he hesitated, then reluctantly turned the mare towards Bridgend, the flourishing market town some six miles away.

He reasoned that yesterday's wedding had provided diversion enough and, despite his inclination, he had best be about his duties as parish constable.

He would visit the workhouse, newly built beside the river Ewenny, to glean what he could of the missing pauper, Elwyn Morris. The workmaster or fellow inmates might give him some picture of the man's character, or a reason why he should have disappeared so unexpectedly and without trace.

As he neared the bottom of Three Steps Hill, and the tollgate, his progress was halted by a flock of sheep being driven onwards by two farm labourers, while the farmer rode behind them upon his mare, deflecting the stragglers and trying to bring them into some sort of order, to pass through. The chaos was absolute: the sheep bleating, and charging in blind confusion, leaping and scrambling upon the backs of others. One of the labourers had eased through the turnpike to await the flock upon the other side, and the pikeman was alternately berating him for leaving the way open and trying, vainly, to count the animals as they charged through, their heaving bodies a restless sea of fleeces. Joshua waited with increasing irritation as the highway became churned by their skittering hooves, and made foul by their urine, excrement and shed fleece.

The pikeman was old, and his movements agonisingly slow, with the farmer red-faced and irascible, demanding to be gone, for he was losing money – the market would be closed! The ancient would not be hurried and, decrepit though he was, appeared to have an absolute knowledge of what was due to him – a toll fee hotly disputed by the farmer, who was growing ever angrier and more abusive. Had not Joshua ridden forward when he did, they would undoubtedly have come to blows.

'There is some disagreement?' he asked pleasantly.

The farmer blustered, but eventually subsided into resentfulness, and paid what was due. When he was clear of the gate he shouted back contemptuously, 'It is wrong! Others grow fat upon our honest labours, and for doing nothing! The trusts are corrupt, for now they seek powers to block off even our side roads, ways we have ridden freely since time began! There will come a reckoning!'

Joshua, who had some sympathy with him, turned to the pikeman, saying, 'It is a hazardous task you choose, sir!'

'Beggars do not choose!' replied the old man with a wry attempt at humour. 'It is this or the poorhouse, for who else would employ a winded old nag like me?'

Joshua smiled, and handed him his fee, receiving a ticket in return.

'I sometimes feel, sir,' the man added wryly, 'that I might be more respectfully treated as a pauper, but since I value my freedom, I work. Since I work, then I must do it honestly, despite the threats!'

'There are many?'

'Certainly, and increasing. I have been set upon by ruffians, menaced by their curs, threatened with a backside full of lead shot. Why, only a week or so since some madman upon a cart cracked open my head with a chamber pot! You see? I bear the marks still, here.'

Joshua, who had heard of Doonan's part in the affair, resolutely kept his face straight. 'I hope, sir, that you are now recovered.'

'From the onslaught,' agreed the old man, smiling, 'but not the insult. You have not heard the worst of it! It was one of those Napoleon pots, into which you "pay your respects" to the Frenchie. Having been a soldier, and helped him meet his Waterloo, I tell you, sir, I had not bargained upon his striking back!'

Joshua rode on, amused at the old man's resilience and sense of fun. Yet there was an underlying pathos in the fact that at an age when he might expect to be settled in the comfort of a chimney corner, he would suffer abuse and physical hurt rather than enter the place whither Joshua was bound.

As he approached it, riding alongside the river, its water brackish and foul with the detritus of living, he thought how sad it was that wherever men settled, they corrupted all in nature which had first attracted them there. Even their buildings, it seemed, were meant to subdue and dominate nature, rather than live with it in harmony. Certainly, the workhouse could not be ignored! It was bleak, grey and uncompromising as the lives of those within. Small wonder that the old pikeman would choose violence above being buried alive.

One of the paupers came from the stable-yard to take Joshua's mare. He was a lean, attenuated fellow with a darkly shadowed face and deep-set eyes. From his stooped shoulders and hollowed chest, Joshua suspected some aggravation of the lungs. It proved to be so, for his breathing was laboured and shallow. He took the horse, not speaking but merely touching a finger to his forehead in acknowledgement.

'Good day to you,' Joshua greeted him. 'Do you know aught of a man by the name of Elwyn Morris?'

The man paused, his hand upon the bridle, his face expressionless. 'He has gone away. Left here.'

'Do you know where he has gone?'

'No.' The man gripped the bridle tighter, shuffling his feet. 'No, but he has done nothing.'

'I seek him only for his own safety,' Joshua said gently, 'and not for any crime. I fear for his life. Will you not help me?'

The pauper hesitated, glancing about him as if afraid that he might be observed. 'I am not permitted to speak to you, sir, and if I were, I could tell you nothing, save that I fear harm has befallen him.'

His body was shaken by a spasm of coughing, and Joshua retrieved the mare, steadying her, until he had regained control of himself and stood gulping air, redness leaving his face with two spots of burning colour.

'If you will give me your horse, sir . . .'

Joshua studied him compassionately, and handed him the reins.

'You are not the first to enquire, sir. A friend from the farm came asking.'

'James Ploughman?'

'That was his name, but there were two men later. Ruffians, big, blustering fellows, foul-mouthed, one cruelly scarred upon the forehead.'

'You told them nothing?'

'There was nothing to tell, but had there been, I would not have spoken, although they offered me money, and then grew angry and abusive. I would not sell a friend, sir . . .' He began to cough again, but waved Joshua's offer of assistance aside. When he was able to breathe freely and speak, he continued, 'They meant to harm or kill him, sir, of that I am sure, for they made no attempt to see the workmaster, as honest men would do. At least, it leaves me with hope that he is alive.'

He made to move off, but Joshua halted him.

'If you were Elwyn Morris, and in danger of your life, where would you flee?'

'To somewhere I would least be observed, a small farm or stable, for I would need to follow the only trade I know – horses.' He stroked the grey's face.

'And if you needed help?'

'I would seek out someone who knew what it was to be a pauper!' Turning, he led the mare gently away.

When Joshua had been admitted into the workhouse by a woman in the coarse, ill-fitting clothing of the institution, he wondered about the guardians who decided such things. What kind of person would see another reduced to such uniformity? Shapeless, colourless, hair rigidly confined within an ugly mobcap. He thought of Rebecca in her gown of softest eau-de-nil, and Rosa's pride in her wedding finery. Was it not enough for pauper women to lose freedom, family and home? What cruelty of human nature demanded that they also lose their individuality and self-respect, making it a condition of the right to exist?

The workmaster, Littlepage, was a plump, pink-faced fellow with a ring of grey curls which gave him the look of an elderly cherub. A full, petulant mouth added to the picture of other-worldliness, as did the thin locks pulled across his scalp like tightened harpstrings. Joshua, who had dealt with him before, was under no illusions about his disposition; he had reason to recall the insensitivity with which he treated the paupers in his care.

'Ah, Constable Stradling!' Littlepage held out a soft-fleshed hand which Joshua accepted reluctantly. 'And how may I be of assistance, sir?'

'My visit concerns one of your charges, a man by the name of Elwyn Morris.'

'Morris? Morris?' He motioned Joshua to a seat. 'No, he is no longer with us.'

'Dead?' asked Joshua, deliberately obtuse.

'No, absconded.' The workmaster's expression showed that he felt it a personal affront and a slight upon the institution.

'What can you tell me of him?'

'What can I tell you of any of them, save that they are without means, destitute, thriftless. Some, like the man,

Morris, do not avail themselves of the opportunities. We offer them a roof, food, clothing, and a chance to redeem themselves.'

'Where has he gone?'

'It is to be hoped to some place of correction, for a spell upon the treadmill, for that is how we treat those unwilling to work.'

'I was given to understand by those who employed him that he was a good worker, honest and conscientious.'

'Indeed? Then I do not know why you waste your time in asking my opinion, sir, who knew him best!'

'And your opinion, Mr Littlepage?'

'A troublemaker, sir! One ever eager to redress imagined slights upon other paupers. Importunate, aggressive, forever demanding their rights. What rights? I asked him. You have no rights, man! You are here on sufferance, dependent upon the generosity of the guardians. You should be down upon your knees, thanking God for the privilege of being given a chance of a new life, instead of whining and snivelling about your rights! Oh, I tell you, Constable, I was relieved when the man took himself off, always busying himself with the affairs of others, affairs which in no way concerned him!'

'What nature of things?'

Littlepage sniffed and shrugged expressively. 'Discipline, punishments, families being separated, children sent to work in the woollen mills. Practical matters all! Matters of policy and administration, of which he could have no real understanding or knowledge, being uneducated.'

Joshua wisely forbore from comment. 'He has family or close friends hereabouts?'

'I understand that his wife died in the cholera epidemic,' Littlepage replied stiffly. 'It seems there is a girl of some eight or nine years, farmed out, I know not where. But that is of no concern to me, I deal only with the able-bodied paupers living within the workhouse.'

'So you have no idea then of where Morris might be?'

Littlepage stretched out his hand before him, and picked at a hangnail.

'No, nor interest,' he said glancing up. 'One less eases the burden.' Then seeing Joshua's contemptuous face as he scraped back his chair and stood up, 'I mean, of course, that I have no immediate interest since he is now beyond my control, my jurisdiction. But care, yes. I care deeply about them all, for that is my work. I spare no time or effort in their service, as the Board of Guardians will testify. No doubt you will do your best for him.' He faltered and broke off, lamely.

'You may be certain of that.'

'Should you find him alive, then I am not sure that I – we – will be able to take him back!' Littlepage added, defiantly.

'Then it will surely grieve him as deeply as you, sir,' replied Joshua, bowing.

Chapter Twelve

Upon leaving the workhouse, Joshua rode at once to the Widow Cleat's house to take the gift of money which Leyshon and the servants entrusted to his care.

Mistress Cleat greeted him with delight, and grew pinkly tearful with pleasure at the thoughtfulness and generosity of those at Tythegston Court.

'So much kindness everywhere,' she exclaimed, 'and from people we hardly know! It warms the heart to think of it. But will you take refreshment with us, Joshua? I have made a pitcher of shot for the invalid.'

'Gladly, ma'am.' Joshua's pleasure was real, for he was partial to the baked oatmeal, crushed and stirred into buttermilk, which reminded him of the harvest-time drink upon his father's farm. He carried the willow-cane tray, set with jugs and pitcher, and followed her into Illtyd's room.

He was surprised to see Emily Randall seated at Illtyd's bedside, with a slate and crayon in her hand. She looked up, smiling and serene.

'You did not know, sir, that I have a pupil?'

'No,' said Joshua. 'What do you teach him?'

'To read,' said Illtyd happily, from his bed. Joshua

thought how pallid and frail he looked, his head swathed in bandages the colour of his skin. Only the incredible, thick-lashed eyes gave colour, their deep blue lighting the bruises beneath.

'You know your letters?' asked Joshua, astonished.

'More than that,' announced Emily Randall with genuine pride, 'he is able to read well, and with intelligence and feeling. I have been teaching him secretly for several months, at his own request.' She smiled, taking Illtyd's hand in hers. 'I tell you, truthfully, Constable Stradling, that I have never had a more apt and willing pupil. His thirst for knowledge is insatiable!'

'Well, for now,' said Mistress Cleat, practically, 'he will quench it upon shot, and we will join him.'

They all smiled, and complied, the talk turning to the wedding and the excitement and adventures it had provided, with Mistress Cleat taking not a little interest in Rebecca's part in the affair.

Joshua left in warm good spirits, with a promise to return soon, bringing books from the cottage that Illtyd might study and enjoy.

'Although,' Joshua jested, 'I will, doubtless, be making a rod for my own back, for I swear that in no time he will be constable, doctor, priest and justice, all rolled into one!'

'And hayward and undertaker in my spare time!' agreed Illtyd comfortably, taking his watch from under the pillow with an affected flourish and grimace, which set them all to laughing.

While Mistress Cleat gathered up the tray and pitcher, and put her son's pillows to rights, Emily Randall

---

walked with Joshua to the door. There was a quiet dignity and grace about her which always pleased him. He found her presence restful. Perhaps, he thought, because she is at peace within herself; freed from envy and brittle restlessness. He turned to see her regarding him steadily.

'I have just returned from a visit to the workhouse in Bridgend, ma'am.'

'Then I do not envy you, Constable Stradling.'

'It was to enquire about a man, a pauper,' he explained gently.

'Who, sir?'

'Elwyn Morris. You remember the name?'

'And the man. He is not in trouble? Guilty of some crime?' she demanded anxiously.

'No, he has done nothing. I merely seek him for information. What manner of man is he?'

'Gentle, certainly. Honest, beyond all doubt. He was a friend to me, as to all, at that bleak place. I never recall him saying a bitter or cruel word, or treating another without respect, even the most lowly or simple in mind. Yet he would fight for justice, refusing to be intimidated, even by the workmaster!' She broke off. 'Elwyn is not ill?' she asked, concerned. 'Or unable to work? I would wish to help him.'

'He has disappeared without trace.'

'Then something evil has occurred. The sick and broken in spirit depended upon him, for he brought them strength and hope, even at their lowest ebb. He would not desert them. And there was the child . . .'

'You know where she lived. The farm?'

'No,' she said regretfully, 'I know only that the people who took her were old, and lived in some remote place, barren and unrewarding. Once, he met the old man at the market at Bridgend, and gave some ribbons and a sweetmeat for the child.'

'Her name, mistress? Even that might help us.'

Emily's intelligent eyes clouded with concentration. 'If I could remember . . .' she muttered helplessly. 'It was Welsh, I think, and unusual . . . Wait! Haulwen! Yes, that was what he called her, Haulwen. He said it meant "Sunshine", and that was what she was to him.'

They were silent for a time.

'If you should find that he is dead, that some accident has befallen him, you will tell me of it?' she asked anxiously at last. 'The child will be alone, and if the people are old . . .'

'I will tell you,' he promised.

'I would take her willingly. I would not see her live as he . . . as I did.'

He nodded, understanding. 'If he should come seeking your help, Mistress Randall?'

'I will tell him of your concern, sir.'

'Thank you, ma'am.'

Her eyes brightened mischievously as she asked with mock gravity, 'And Mr Littlepage, sir, how did you find him? Overworked? Burdened with caring for the ungrateful and degenerate? Modestly reticent about his achievements?'

'All that,' agreed Joshua drily, 'and glowing with virtue and rude health, more's the pity!' And they parted in perfect accord.

Joshua, leading the grey, halted at the forge to exchange pleasantries with Ben Clatworthy. He was measuring a red-hot shoe against a pony's hoof, the air acrid with smoke and seared horn.

Glancing at the farm labourer who held the beast, Clatworthy took a nail from the pocket of his leather apron and concentrated upon hammering it home, saying obliquely to Joshua, 'That branding iron which needed repair, sir.'

'You wish me to take charge of it?' asked Joshua, puzzled.

'No.' The blacksmith did not look up as he drove in another nail. 'Its owner has collected it. It seems he needed it urgently. He made enquiries about your health.'

'Ah!' said Joshua. 'Then I must pay him a visit as soon as possible, to return the compliment.'

'It would be courteous and neighbourly,' agreed Clatworthy, driving the final nail home, and releasing the pony's hind leg from its grip between his sturdy knees, 'for I confessed that I could not remember the last time I had seen you, so long ago it must have been.' His eyes met Joshua's in implied warning. 'Have a care how you ride, Constable, for the way can sometimes be treacherous in this climate, and the going rough. Should you have need of my services, I am always available. There are few things I am unable to tackle, believe me!'

Joshua thanked him and the blacksmith nodded, his lips twitching with a barely perceptible smile of satisfaction as he returned to his labour.

Joshua rode away reflecting that he would certainly

return to Sker House to interrogate Hardee, but first he must settle the question of Elwyn Morris, for he might have some knowledge of Crocutt's murderer, or Bando's abduction and death. The inquest on Bando was upon the morrow and Joshua had little doubt of what the findings would be in the absence of fresh evidence: 'Wilful murder by a person or persons unknown.' He had seen it written of the farmer from Grove, and very much feared that the pauper, Morris, would earn a similar epitaph.

Outside the 'Lamb Inn', he hesitated briefly, wondering whether to seek out James Ploughman at Grove Farm, then turned the mare, instead, towards Newton.

He dismounted at the small stone cottage of Walter Bevan, the relieving officer for the poor, and tethered his horse to a tree at the wayside, making sure that it was well secured. As he did so, the man came to his door, his sallow, earnest face alight with pleasure, and ushered him inside, bidding him stoop low, for the lintel beam gave little headroom for such as Joshua.

Being seated upon a rush-bottomed chair, and having declined his offer of refreshment, Joshua had a chance to take stock of his surroundings. Though a small fire burned in the grate, the room was clammy and chill, the furniture sparse and of poor quality. There were books and ledgers scattered about, and the remains of a frugal meal of coarse bread and a saucepan half-full of mutton-bone broth, its surface congealed into circles of fat, yellow and unappetising. Bevan arose and put some drift-wood upon the embers, declaring that he had not realised that it had burned so low, 'for I am fortunate in that I do not feel the cold'.

In truth, he looked pinched and raw enough about his lips and nostrils, and the ink-stains upon his fingers and thumb were scarcely as blue as his flesh. Joshua suspected that most of his earnings went to supplement the meagre allowances of his 'out-paupers', those too old and impotent to work and fend for themselves, and so useless to the guardians of the workhouse.

'You have news for me, Constable? Or some request to make, perhaps?'

'Information, rather. It concerns the disappearance of the pauper, Elwyn Morris.'

Bevan nodded, his face grave. 'Yes, I have heard of that. It is a sad business. James Ploughman came to me, begging my help in the matter, but I fear I could give him none. Morris was not in my care, for he was fit and able-bodied, you understand. You had best see Littlepage at the Bridgend workhouse.'

'I have already done so, sir.'

'Then I do not understand.'

'There is a child, a girl of eight or nine years.'

'Indeed? I had no knowledge of it.' Bevan's eyes were dark, concerned. 'There is something you wish me to do for her? Some help I may give?'

'I hoped that you might tell me of her whereabouts.'

'Surely she is a resident at the workhouse, with her mother?'

'The mother is dead, and the child farmed out, but we know not where. We know nothing save that the farm, a cottage, is poor and the people old.'

'This is recent, you think? In the past year or two?' His tone was brighter, his eyes alert and interested. 'I have been appointed but a year, but my predecessor's records might tell me, although, I confess, they are few and incomplete, and his penmanship . . . Well, let us say that I might have less trouble deciphering the hieroglyphics in an Egyptian burial tomb! Still, with patience . . .'

'It seems that she has been there almost from birth – at least since the mother died in the cholera epidemic.'

Bevan's eyes clouded with disappointment as he shook his head. 'Then there will be nothing, and the workhouse itself is but three years old. I am sorry, sir, truly sorry.'

Joshua nodded. 'It was but a chance,' he said, rising to his feet and extending his hand. 'I thank you, sir, for the trouble you have taken, and your readiness to help. I fear for Morris's safety, and thought that by tracing the child we might also find him.'

'Or secure some provision for her future, should he already be dead?' mused Bevan, then: 'Wait! All is not irretrievably lost. My out-paupers are scattered widely throughout the area, and I visit them regularly, and often. They are old and would know of those of a similar age hereabouts, or even in the remotest, outlying areas. Their sons and grandsons often labour casually upon the farms, or upon lanes or highways. I shall make urgent and extensive enquiries, I promise. I shall not rest until the child is found, and Elwyn Morris's fate known.' His sallow face was determined, animated, and Joshua felt a stirring of optimism, so absolute was the man's conviction.

'I am fortunate to have your help,' Joshua said sincerely, 'as are the out-paupers in your care, sir.'

Pleasure and surprise brought unexpected colour to Bevan's face as he shook his head, protesting, 'No, sir, I do only the little which is allowed, counting it a privilege. Yet I cannot tell you what joy it gives me to take my poor people the small luxuries provided by the new fund!'

'The parish provides it? The vestrymen?' asked Joshua, surprised.

'No, sir. It is the gift of Mistress de Breos which I am allowed to spend, unhindered. A fine and generous gift, and giver . . .'

'Indeed,' declared Joshua, with the same warm appreciation.

Jeremiah Fleet, his day's fishing ruled by the tide, had already delivered crabs and lobsters to favoured customers and friends like Hannah and the Widow Cleat, and taken the surplus in his cart to the fish-stall at Bridgend market, it being Wednesday. His catch was eagerly awaited there, for it was always of excellent quality and renowned for its freshness. Indeed, the fishmonger, a plump, jocular, red-faced fellow with a passion for teasing the ladies, had often been heard to declare, 'Fresh, ma'am? Why, it lies upon that marble slab with the twinkle yet in its eye! It could not have got here sooner! No, not if it had swum up the Ewenny and leapt there itself! I swear, upon my oath, that were it any fresher, I would need to summon the tooth-puller, lest it jump down and bite you!'

Jeremiah was smiling to himself at the absurdity of the recollection, the cob trotting rhythmically before the cart, and Charity dozing upon a sack, as they approached Newton village. He glimpsed Joshua's grey tied to a tree in front of Walter Bevan's house and wondered idly what his business could be, before halting the cob outside Ezra the Box's workshop.

He thought that he would ask the carpenter to make him a strong, solid, wheelbacked chair, the kind with a curved back and arms, the seat comfortably polished and shaped to fit a backside. His bones were getting older, with the rest of him, and grew stiff at the end of a day spent in bending and wading through rock pools and shallows. It would welcome him home. Rebecca's chairs were pretty things, there was no denying it, with their shield backs and delicate carvings. Yet he felt awkward upon such paltry gewgaws. They offered a man neither comfort nor support . . . as a well-made chair or wife should. In the absence of a wife, a wheelbacked chair must serve with, perhaps, a three-legged stool to rest his feet upon . . . With the bull terrier warm upon his lap, he could doze in comfort.

He was still rehearsing, in his mind, what he would say to Ezra the Box as he opened the door to the shop. When he was safely inside all he could do was gape in shock and bewilderment, unaware even that he had cried aloud. There could never have been such a scene of devastation. All about, tables, chairs and coffins had been overturned. Everywhere wood lay splintered, tools broken, glues and oils emptied upon the sawdust and shavings, a glutinous, filthy mess. He called Ezra's name, and hurried through to the living quarters. Here the havoc and destruction were, if possible, worse. There was barely a stick of furniture standing intact, with crockery hurled against walls and smashed upon the floor, cushions ripped apart, their feathers scattered over all. Even the food from his overturned table had been trampled underfoot, milk spilling from a broken pitcher. Of Ezra there was no sign.

Jeremiah ran outside, so agitated that Charity leapt from the cart to run beside him towards Joshua's grey. Even as they approached, the constable and Walter Bevan came out upon the doorstep and, seeing Jeremiah's stricken face, hurried towards him. He gasped out his story as they ran, the bull terrier barking and dancing at their heels, but even Charity was rendered silent by the ferociousness of the assault upon Ezra's treasures. It was frenzied, unspeakable.

'Dear Life!' exclaimed Walter Bevan. 'And Ezra?'

'No sign,' said Jeremiah bleakly. He turned to Joshua in appeal. 'Who could have done such a thing? Do you know?'

'I think that perhaps I do.' The constable felt the blood leave his face and sickness churning his stomach. To his mind returned the picture of Dai Bando's mutilated face, and the words Dr Mansel had used about his injuries. He remembered Ezra's confession of his cowardice.

'I pray to God that I am wrong!'

Afterwards, Joshua spent an hour and more calling upon the shopkeepers, craftsmen and cottagers in the village, asking if they had seen anything to make them suspicious, or noted any strangers near at hand. Yet he learnt nothing which could help him in his quest to find the vanished Ezra. He knew that it was not fear, or even dislike of the little undertaker which held them back. They admitted freely that he was a mean, cantankerous fellow, yet they had a certain grudging affection for him, despite his crabbiness, for was he not one of their own?

All that emerged was that none but the usual faces had been seen: Jeremiah with his fish, Rowden the miller upon his cart, Rosa's uncle, George Evans, and all those whose proper business it was to be there. The abductor had come stealthily, his vengeance deliberately wrought. It was unlikely that Ezra himself could have escaped unscathed.

Joshua felt the first chill in the wind as he unfastened the grey. The sky had become ugly and bruised and a breeze shivered the slender, spidery branches of the trees, giving promise of a sudden squall. He mounted, and within minutes, it seemed, the air grew dark and the first hailstones came, stinging his face, striking the mare's flesh with darts of ice, so that she shuddered and grew restive. The seabirds, sensing a storm, had flown inland, seeking shelter, and as Joshua skirted the village green he heard them screaming and wheeling above, their cries forlorn, until they dropped to earth, their whiteness splashing the grass like flung pebbles.

The wind had risen high, with a keen edge, the fierce hail driving into corners and crevices in tiny drifts as frosted snow. Joshua's exposed skin burned from its sting, and he and the mare were glad to ride under the archway of the 'Crown', and reach the haven of the stable-yard. Ossie soon had the grey sheltered and warmly rubbed down, while Joshua thawed himself gratefully before his cottage fire with a mug of warmed ale. His mind was engrossed with the disappearance of Ezra for, perversely, now that the old man was gone, he felt not irritation but a sense of loss. As if a thorn had been plucked away, Joshua thought wryly, leaving a small wound he had not grown used to after the familiarity of a long-felt pain.

The wind sighed and moaned in the chimney with an almost human sound and, strangely disturbed, Joshua arose to busy himself with securing the doors and windows against the force of the storm.

While Joshua had been questioning the villagers, Jeremiah, no less troubled by what he had seen at Ezra's workshop, left to restore himself at the 'Crown', leaving the cob and cart to Ossie's care.

Tom Butler, the landlord, seeing his favourite so dejected and low, cheered him upon the promise of a fishing expedition in his new sailing boat, should Jeremiah be ready and waiting within the hour, when the tide was right. In an instant, Jeremiah's depression had lifted and, pausing only long enough to finish his ale, he was on his way to Grove Farm to pick up Dafydd, the cob travelling, as Ossie reported, 'like a bat out of hell'.

Dafydd's mother had barely time enough to put a wet flannel to the boy's face, and caution him to 'mind your manners', before they were off, with the boy clinging to the cart-side as they rattled away, so filled with laughter and excitement that Marged threw a tantrum because she could not go too. Within the hour they had stabled the cob at Jeremiah's cottage and, leaving Charity behind, had arrived at the 'Crown', raw-ribbed and breathless with running, to clamber aboard the waggon. Then, with Ossie at the reins and Dafydd perched beside him, Jeremiah, Butler and his wife dressed in the newest 'coal scuttle' bonnet, and the potman, took the cart-track to the salt-laden beckoning sea.

It was Jeremiah with his fisherman's respect for weather and tide who first saw signs of a storm in the crying of the seabirds with their disturbed, restless flight, and the gathering clouds.

'We had best be getting back,' he said, 'before it is too late!' The others, immersed in their fishing, paid no heed. They had anchored well out beyond the curve of the bay and the men were busy at their tasks, baiting their hooks with lug-worms, casting, and reeling in small fish, while Dafydd fetched and carried tirelessly, face vivid with excitement. After a time, Jeremiah had given him an old rod and line, and had shown him how to use it, cautioning that should the hooks catch in the flesh, then they would need to be cut away with a knife, for they were cruelly barbed and would pierce deep as the bone. He must have a care, not only for himself but those around him.

Dafydd had listened gravely, and obeyed. Now his own basket held three small pouting, their mouths agape, eyes filmed, silver bodies iridescent with colour as the curve of a bubble. Mrs Butler sat beside him, trailing her fingers in the icy water, revelling in the child's pride and excitement, the ecstasy upon his face bringing her every whit as much pleasure as his catches brought him.

By now Jeremiah was thoroughly alarmed, for the

clouds had darkened ominously and he could hear the rising of the wind. He knew how swiftly the Atlantic gales blew up, whipping the sea to a force and fury nothing could withstand. He began to pull up the anchor unbidden, crying vexedly, 'Will you not take telling? Let us make for the shore while we still have a chance!'

Dafydd, seeing Jeremiah's concern, gathered up his tackle and came to sit beside him, touching a hand upon his arm.

Tom Butler grumbled and muttered that Jeremiah was 'a fussy old woman for taking on so! Anyone with half an eye could see that it was nothing but a squall. It will be over in a second!'

Even as he spoke the surface of the sea grew choppy, as if some giant hand plucked unseen at the waters, and the first icy rain fell. There was a hurried scramble, with the potman taking the rudder. Already the wind grew fierce, bellying, then tearing, at the small sails. It seemed to come from all directions, gathering in strength and ferocity, so that the mast swayed and the boat shuddered violently as though cast upon a rock.

Mrs Butler's plump face, or what little could be seen of it under the coal-scuttle bonnet, was shaded like the sea itself, skin streaked and muted with white and greyish-green. Her stomach echoed its movements; she felt it heaving and churning restlessly. She was going to be sick! No! She would not! What a fool she had been to wear her new dress and coat, and her best bonnet would be torn to shreds, if they didn't all drown first! She looked up to see Dafydd's face, whiter than the sails, and motioned him to come and sit beside her.

The wind was howling now and the sea so violent that, as Dafydd arose, the rocking of the boat sent him staggering unsteadily then falling to his knees, bare hands striking the timbers. Palms stinging, he eased himself forward painfully on all fours, inch by inch, until Mrs Butler was able to reach out and drag him up beside her. They clung together helplessly, lashed by the fierceness of gale and frozen rain.

Jeremiah had moved to the helm to take over the tiller, but was helpless against the pull of the current and the high swirling waves that came crashing against the boat's sides, spewing water. Butler was vainly trying to bail out. His movements grew ever more frenzied and desperate, but faster than he cleared it, it came swelling back.

The seas grew mountainous, the sails ripped by the wind into useless shreds. Above them the mast creaked and swayed ominously, battered by wave and gale until, with a fierce splintering, it cracked to the deck, and with a glancing blow hurled the potman into the sea. Jeremiah, shocked and half-deafened by the noise, let go the tiller and, leaning over the stern, grabbed at the drowning man, arms jerked fiercely in their sockets by the weight of the body in its sea-drenched clothing. He screamed for Butler, who came crawling across the boards to scramble up beside him, and together they managed to heave the potman aboard, spluttering and coughing, to lie shivering beside them.

The boat was trapped in the swirling current, racing and spinning helplessly, Jeremiah's frantic efforts to steady the rudder useless against the relentless tug of the tide.

Mrs Butler and Dafydd sat huddled together, arms wrapped about each other protectively, barely able to open their eyes for the cutting force of the wind and spray, and the lashing hail. And all the time the craft rocked and twisted sickeningly.

'Mr Fleet.' The child's voice reached him, thin and faded by the storm.

'Yes?' His own was ragged with alarm.

'We should have gone home when you said . . .'

Jeremiah, drenched with spray, frozen fist still gripping the tiller, glanced down at Butler who was ministering to the potman. Butler's lips twitched, then Jeremiah's mouth broke in an answering smile, and they began to laugh. They laughed until the tears ran down their cheeks and their cold-numbed bodies shook with mirth. And even the potman, sitting upright now and fighting for breath, began to laugh too, relief and hysteria sharpening his tone. Dafydd and Mrs Butler, bewildered, looked at each other, drawn into the mad spluttering chorus as wind and current bore them relentlessly towards the rocks . . .

Ossie, alarmed by the violence of the storm, had brought the waggon early, thinking they would have come ashore to seek the shelter of the dunes. There was no sight of a boat upon the shore, nor sails upon the water, although the waves were so towering and strong that a small craft might easily be hidden in their troughs. He leapt from the waggon and, struggling up a dune, his eyes made raw by whipped sand and gale, tried to search for them. Finally, with the fall of a wave, he saw them, sail-less and unbelievably small, bobbing like a cork upon the water and held fast in the Black Rocks current.

With a scream raw in his throat, he charged down the sand dune, slipping and grovelling in the soft sand in his effort to reach the waggon. Then uncoupling the horse, he clambered upon it, clinging frantically to its neck, and urged it onwards as he rode bareback through the teeth of the gale to the constable's house.

Chapter Thirteen

As soon as he had recovered breath enough to give the alarm, Ossie ran with Joshua to the 'Crown', where the constable urged the landlord's son to send out a groom with the rocket and line that the justice had provided, then to dispatch someone to Dr Mansel's house, bidding him ride at once to the bay, for there might be those in need of his assistance.

Joshua, meanwhile, rushed to saddle his mare, calling out to all who would help, and thence to the brewhouse to command the services of the draymen and dray. When all was accomplished, the procession hurried upon its way.

Doonan, returning with Emrys upon his cart from the quarries, hearing of the urgency, followed swiftly. Yet not before Rosa, already at the door to greet him, had gathered warm blankets and leapt into the cart beside them, refusing to budge despite Doonan's entreaties and threats.

His ears deafened with the sound of the storm, Joshua turned to see through the slashing rain those on horseback behind him, glimpsing the set face of Butler's son, and following, not a groom, but Ossie himself, driving the cart with the life-saving rocket and line. Behind him came the plodding shapes of the great shires, pulling the brewhouse dray, with its draymen and six good men from the brewhouse. And finally Emrys, Doonan and Rosa upon the small cob and cart.

They were facing into the gale, the wind from the sea stiffening their faces with salt, raw and excoriating, as if skin had been peeled from flesh. Rain soaked them through; hands upon reins grew numbed of pain or feeling; eyes gritted with sand, and all the time the storm threw a fierce, invisible barrier, slowing the way. Once upon the beach, taking the full force of the gale, they were barely able to stand, clinging to the carts and dray for support, and even the plodding shires could make little progress. Their heads had been covered with hessian sacks lest they be blinded by the wind-whipped sand, or their mouths and nostrils clogged, hindering breathing, so adding to their terror.

Ossie had brought the storm-proof lantern and, when the cart and rocket had been positioned, with difficulty, at the water's edge, he handed it to Joshua that he might ignite the fuse. Joshua braced himself against the gusting wind and rain and shielded by a small semi-circle of men, backs bent to the storm, struggled to light it and heard it first splutter and hiss, then a fierce whoosh of sound, as if of wind in a tunnel as the rocket and line exploded into the air. For a moment it seemed that it might succeed, cleaving its way with the flight of a bird, but the force of the gale was a solid barrier. Halted, it hung suspended before the raging wind swept it uselessly to the shore. Three times more Joshua attempted it with increasing desperation, knowing that time was running out, yet it was powerless against the insane forces of the elements.

He felt the tears running down his face with the rain and his body shaken with sobs as he cursed and fumbled with the equipment, willing it to work, his fingers so numbed with cold that they could no longer act, and Doonan had to take over the task.

With time too precious to waste, Doonan snatched up the rope and line, declaring that he would swim out to them. He would not see them drown before his eyes! Rosa tried to struggle forward against the wind and rain, her clothes whipped tight about her, but could not reach him. Already Butler's son had dismounted and faced him, screaming above the gale that it must be his task, for his mother and father were aboard. He would risk no man's life but his own! When it seemed that tension and fear might drive them to blows, Joshua took command, ruling that the heavy rope be first lashed hard to the brewer's dray. This being done, Doonan would wade out, chest deep, bearing the rope's end, then securing it about Reuben Butler's waist, playing it out, that he might swim to those trapped. So it was agreed.

Doonan's huge figure braced against the storm and, trailing the thick rope, took to the sea. Even at the water's edge the force of the waves made him stagger as he hunched himself against its fury, willing himself forward. Once he stumbled and fell to his knees, but arose and struggled on, breathless, and buffeted by the force of wave and wind. Reuben stripped away all that might hamper him and stood ready for the tug upon the rope that would tell him that Doonan stood firm and waiting.

Then he too was splashing and floundering in the huge crashing waves, swept from his feet by its massive force, yet clinging still to the rope and righting himself to stand beside the Irishman.

The draymen held firm to their shires, soothing and easing them as the brewhousemen played out the reel and line. Joshua lost count of the times Reuben fell before Doonan finally tied the rope about him, knowing that even as he fed it out, his hands would be flayed raw by its roughness. At first, Reuben seemed to make no progress, the sea sending him crashing back, sucking him down to spew him out, helpless and without direction. For a while he disappeared altogether, and they feared that the rope had been swept away, but he re-emerged, a small, barely discernible speck between the mountainous waves, and a thin cheer broke from the watchers upon the shore.

Dear God, thought Joshua, what hope is there for him, or them, in this wild seething madness? They are already dead, and now the sea will take him, too. He found himself beating his bare fists against the side of the dray in an agony of pain and frustration. Then suddenly Rosa was beside him, taking his bruised hands in hers and cradling him to her as if he was a child, and she the strong one. Ashamed, he returned to shore, eyes raking the sea for some sign of Reuben but seeing nothing save black seas and flung spray, and through it the dwarfed figure of Doonan, beaten to his knees, but still holding the rope.

There was a cry from the dray, and the storm-lantern was held aloft to signal that a massive tug upon the rope had shown that the boat had been reached. Now the horses must strain every nerve and sinew to wrench the craft from the fierce grasp of the current. Slowly, with grinding painfulness, the dray began to inch its way from the sea's edge and up the sand of the bay.

The wait was slow and agonising and Rosa, fighting against the wind, battled her way to where her husband waded ashore, refusing all offers to be lifted upon horseback. Doonan stumbled in the shallows and collapsed, unable even to drag himself to the wet sand, and two of the horsemen dismounted swiftly and heaved him ashore, Rosa rushing to his side as they lifted him on to Emrys's cart, wrapping him tenderly in a blanket. His palms were raw and bloodied and Rosa, clambering up beside him, bathed them with her tears as she hugged him close, forcing the warmth of her body into his cold flesh.

There was a wild cheer of excitement as the small craft, torn free by the indomitable shires, was seen rising and falling through the turbulent waves . . . The sea still boiled and seethed about it, a restless, foaming cauldron, but for those within, it no longer held terror of death. Each was filled with exhilaration, sadness, a sense of unreality as the helpers strode into the waters and bore Dafydd and Mrs Butler, Reuben and the potman tenderly ashore, as Jeremiah and Butler stumbled awkwardly through the sea, refusing all offers of assistance.

There were cries of delight and gratitude and many warm tears as they were bundled into blankets, for the recriminations would come later. It mattered only that they were safe.

There would be food, warm drink and a roaring fire

awaiting at the 'Crown', for the helped and the helpers, and dry clothing and beds, sheets comforted with hot coals within a warming pan. Jeremiah and Dafydd would stay, too, to be spoilt and cosseted, upon the orders of Dr Mansel, who declared that it was best for them and he would brook no argument!

Then the physician returned to minister to the exhausted Reuben, his body bruised by the sea and rubbed raw by the abrasiveness of the encircling rope, and thence to cover Doonan's bloodied hands and give comfort to the potman . . . riding watchfully aside his patients upon the waggon along the way.

The journey back held no discomfort for those saved, although the gale still blew, fierce and unchecked, for each was painfully sensitive to how it might have been. Mrs Butler had no more thought of her sea-soaked gown, or the coal-scuttle bonnet abandoned to the winds. She sat beside her husband and Jeremiah and Dafydd upon the rocket cart, huddled in a blanket, her arm encircling the boy as upon the boat. She looked back at the windswept bay, the waves crashing in milky whiteness upon the blackness of rock, then turned, thankfully abandoning the blown sand and drifting bubbles of spume.

'You will soon be home, my love,' she promised Dafydd, 'safe and warm.'

The boy put out a hand to touch Jeremiah's arm, his face aglow 'neath the damply plastered hair.

'Oh, Mr Fleet,' he cried sincerely, 'I thank you for a lovely day! I had never thought to have such adventure!'

* * *

Within twenty-four hours life had almost returned to normality for the storm-tossed fishermen, although all in the three hamlets were unstinting in praise for their calmness and the heroism of the rescuers.

It was seriously claimed that not only had the victims been laughing companionably as the craft drifted towards the rocks, but singing hymns upon the way. No doubt about it, it was a miracle! A sign of grace for such abiding faith. One very old cottager, with rheumy eyes and some loss of hearing, spoke of a 'bright light streaming across the sky, and a noise as of a mighty rushing wind'. It might, of course, have been one of the rockets, but who could be sure? In any event, he was convinced of the truth of it, and since he was so deaf, and known to be stubborn, there was little point in reasoning with him. So it was that Jeremiah's outing passed into folklore as 'that day of the great storm when the heavens were illuminated by a fierce light, and there came the sound of a mighty rushing wind, powerful as the wing-beats of guardian angels'.

On a more earthly level, Joshua's powers of command and preparation were lavishly praised, and Reuben and Doonan rightly fêted as heroes. Dr Mansel decreed that the Irishman must not return immediately to the quarries, lest his wounds be aggravated by work and stone-dust. Doonan's employers, inspired by his bravery and the credit it reflected upon them, undertook to pay him his wages, so he and Rosa shared a prolonged and unexpected honeymoon.

Dafydd, too, was royally treated, with a promise that when the boat was repaired he would be at its launching and there would be many expeditions with his good friend, Mr Fleet.

Jeremiah himself was content to be known as 'that fine fisherman and weather prophet who had warned them most strongly of the coming storm'. The potman received an increase in wages, and Mrs Butler a new gown and bonnet, although her new-found passion for sailing declined and never recovered . . . Perhaps that was the only benefit that the landlord of the 'Crown' derived, although some might have counted his daughter-in-law, for the serving maid who served Reuben his meals when he was recovering abed was minded to join him there, and did.

The day following upon the storm, Joshua, feeling as battered in spirit as he had been in body by the gale, rode out to give an account of the affair to the justice. The Reverend Robert Knight was distressed beyond measure by the failure of the life-saving equipment which he had paid for from his own pocket as a defence for the fisher-folk of the three hamlets. It had been tested, he admitted, only during milder summer weather, and clearly was useless against the violence of the Channel gales.

'I believe, sir, that nothing on earth could have braved the ferocity of that storm!' Joshua tried to comfort him.

'Save the two who risked their lives in that raging sea,' the justice replied soberly. 'It fills one with awe and humility to think of it.'

'It does, indeed, sir,' said Joshua, remembering.

'But it should not be necessary, Stradling!' The justice's fist banged down hard upon his desk, making the inkstand upon it rattle and jump. 'We should have some form of rescue craft, a lifeboat of our own! I shall speak to the vestrymen. Yes, that is what I shall do. It could be kept at the port, and launched quickly should the need arise.' His voice had grown firm, confident, his brown eyes animated behind their gold-framed lenses. 'Do you not agree?'

'I think, sir,' said Joshua carefully, 'that no small craft could have put out in yesterday's seas without being as much in peril as the sail-boat, and there are other practical difficulties.'

'Of course, of course!' he replied testily. 'But nothing which cannot be overcome by logic and planning. What "difficulties" had you in mind?'

'The manning of it, sir.'

'Volunteers! Men would do it willingly!'

'Agreed, but the able-bodied like Doonan work some miles away, at the quarries and upon the farms, or in the brickyards. The old, who are no longer able to work, are unfitted for such a task.'

'Hmmm! Then we must secure men from the docks, who are freely available, or pay them!'

Joshua, mindful of the frugality of the vestrymen, was not convinced.

'Damn it, Stradling, we are talking of human life!'

'True, sir, and who can put a value upon even one human life? Speaking of which, I regret to tell you that the undertaker, Evans, has been abducted, kidnapped.'

'Who on earth would want to kidnap *him*, Stradling?' the justice asked irritably. Then recollecting himself,

'You are sure he has not gone away upon some errand? To secure supplies of wood, perhaps?'

'His workshop was ransacked and his furniture smashed. Also there was the previous assault, with the knife-wound upon his neck.'

'Indeed. Well, seek him most diligently, Stradling. Spare no expense in hiring men to help you,' the justice instructed gruffly.

'Yes, sir.'

'I will pray, earnestly, for his well-being.'

Perhaps not too earnestly, thought Joshua.

'Something I have said amuses you, Stradling?'

'No, sir, I was merely hoping that no one in the three hamlets would be careless enough to expire in Ezra's absence!' he improvised, smiling.

It seemed to Joshua that no sooner had he returned to Newton from Tythegston Court than he was setting out again upon his grey, this time to attend the inquest upon the vagrant, Dai Bando. The evidence was bleak and inconclusive; a true reflection of the poor wretch's life, Joshua thought with compassion. It was only death which had distinguished him. Save for his 'murder by person or persons unknown' he would have died as he had lived: without resting place, and neither remarked nor missed . . .

Joshua, uneasily recalling Dai Bando's swollen, mutilated body, could not but be grieved at life's final small irony . . . that Bando had fled, or was lured, from James Ploughman's poor hovel, food and drink untasted . . .

He had scarce entered his cottage and removed his

helmet to brew himself some tea, before enquiring at the
'Crown Inn' about the well-being of the injured, when
there was an urgent knocking upon his door. He was
momentarily tempted not to answer in the hope that the
caller would go away but, mindful of his duty, he strode
into the passageway.

He was surprised to find the stout, squat figure of
Rowden the miller upon the doorstep, still in his sackcloth
apron, hair, skin and clothing powdery with flour. His cob
and rough cart were at the wayside, but empty of sacks.

'I have been about my business, Constable, delivering
flour . . .'

'Yes?' Joshua was puzzled by the man's awkward,
stealthy manner. 'You have some message for me? Need of
my services?'

Rowden glanced about him anxiously. 'Ezra . . .' he
confided, voice low.

'You had best come in and explain!'

Once inside the miller refused to seat himself, begging
Joshua to pardon his workaday clothes, 'for I have sought
to come here unremarked.'

'Ezra?'

'With me, sir, safe at the mill upon Stormy Downs.'

'How so? I feared that he had been abducted, harmed!'

'I have come, sir, upon his stern insistence, to put your
mind at ease. I came yesterday, but you were engaged upon
the rescue.'

Joshua nodded.

'It is true, Constable, that Ezra's workshop has been
wrecked?'

'Yes, I am afraid so.'

'That was what he feared. He claimed knowledge that one who threatened him had vowed to return, seeking to kill him!'

'It would seem that he was right!'

'Hearing of it, I came at once and bade him return with me, hidden under my empty flour sacks. I drove to the rear of his workshop, into the yard, that no one might see him climbing upon it. Elsewhere I am unremarked, and therefore invisible!'

'Certainly your presence in the village caused no comment.'

'Perhaps it is the flour, sir, that renders me wraith-like and ghostly,' he patted his ample stomach, 'for I plainly do not lack substance!' He smiled. 'Well, I will be on my way, for my message is safely delivered.'

'You think Ezra is safe with you? I ask because these men are ruthless.'

Rowden looked startled. 'Ezra would give me no reason. I thought it some pettiness, a debt unpaid, perhaps, or some disagreement with a neighbour, some childishness magnified. I call him friend, but I readily admit him to be mean and contrary as a wayward mule!'

'You saw no one upon your journey here?'

'Naught but a solitary horseman upon Dan-y-Graig Hill, a stranger to me, making perhaps for one of the farms. A labourer for hire, I thought – a big, solid man, ill-dressed and unkempt.' His voice sharpened. 'Why? He is someone you seek, Constable? I did not know –' He broke off, helplessly.

'Quickly!' cried Joshua. 'Turn your cart about and be away! I shall fetch my grey from the "Crown" and follow, for I might need to pursue him swiftly.'

He unlocked a drawer of his bureau and took out his over-and-under pistol and a pouch of shot, with the leather holder to secure it to the saddle of the mare.

Without another word, Rowden went out to his cart, face white as the flour upon it. Had Joshua not been so intent upon his task he might have also observed that the miller's eyes seemed rounder and wider than his own mill stones!

Although Rowden upon his cart had some minutes' start upon the constable, the grey was so fleet and reliable that the clumsy contraption was swiftly overtaken as it laboured up Dan-y-Graig Hill.

'How do I reach your mill?' called back Joshua, without stopping or slackening his speed.

'Part way towards Grove, beyond the copse. Take that small track to the left, by the beech woods.' The miller's words were carried away as Joshua disappeared from sight beyond the curve of the lane to the downs.

Rowden, cursing with frustration, flicked the cob upon its way, but to little effect. The cart was cumbersome and in need of repair, though it served well enough for its purpose. The cob, too, was designed for comfort, rather than speed, but it obligingly set off at a shambling trot to humour the miller, who appeared to be bereaved of his senses.

'Faster!' he yelled. 'Faster I tell you!' And the cob, a good-natured beast, ever eager to please, skittishly kicked up its heels. Once started, its enjoyment grew, until so wild and fierce was its abandon that Rowden became afraid and tried to slow it, but it would not now be halted. The cart rattled and shook, swayed and lurched, until the miller's teeth clattered together and every bone in his body jolted and fused. Then, with a judder and a thunderous crack, the wheel-shaft broke and the cart tilted and tipped to the ground, flinging him into the hedgerow. The cob ran gamely on, the shattered wreck scraping and bumping behind it.

Thus it was that the miller, red with rage and humiliation, could be seen billowing homewards upon a small, unsaddled cob, his boots trailing the ground as he plucked out hawthorn barbs from his backside. His thoughts dwelt less upon Ezra's imagined plight than his own very real discomfort.

Joshua's thoughts, however, were all for the little undertaker, as he urged the grey along the small track skirting the beech wood. Before him, upon a curve of the downs, loomed the stark grey stone of the windmill and granary.

His shouts as he spurred the mare onwards, and the ringing of metal horseshoes upon the stones, must have alerted the assailant, for he came running out from the mill-tower, a pistol clenched in his hand. Before Joshua had a chance to slow the grey, the man had fired, thrown himself clumsily over his own saddle, then dragged himself upright and was away. Joshua had leaned instinctively, lowering his body to the grey's neck, and the shot went wild, although he felt the mare stiffen and stumble briefly beneath him.

His hand went instinctively to the pistol and stock in its holder as if to reassure himself of its presence as the mare regained her rhythm and stride. The horseman was out of sight now, behind the curve of the tower and the ribbed scarecrow sails, and Joshua did not know what awaited him there. Would the man lie in wait, pistol primed? Or would he flee, riding blindly to make good his escape from whatever violence and bloodshed he had wrought? As he rounded the mill, Joshua braced himself against the expected force of the shot, mouth dry, heart pounding with the beat of the horse's hooves. His veins surged with excitement and fear, a wild, unnatural exhilaration.

It was almost with a sense of disappointment that he saw horse and rider disappearing into the tangled bareness of the beech wood. The man turned for an instant and Joshua fired, feeling the pistol's kick-back in a blow upon his chest, tightening his breath. He had not even been aware that the pistol lay in his hand.

As Joshua approached the small beech wood, he slowed the mare, then dismounted at a gap in the drystone wall, the surface crusted with moss and lichens. There was no sight of the man and the only sounds were the shuffle and swish of Joshua's feet and the mare's hooves through the piled dead leaves upon the pathway as he led her. They moved slowly, carefully, the mare picking her way as if she sensed the need for discretion. Joshua's touch was light upon the bridle, his pistol clasped in his free hand as he restlessly glanced about him, not knowing if his adversary watched him, even now, from behind the shelter of some tree, ready to fire. The copse was thinning now and there was a small clearing ahead with piled-up faggots of wood and the scattered ashes of some long-dead fire, and beyond that a small woodcutter's hut. Joshua could see the tracks that led to it and the disordered heaps of leaves, but could not know if they were freshly disturbed. Leaving the mare, he silently signalled her to stay and crept forward stealthily, flinging open the door of the hut. It swung back violently, revealing the startled, bloodless face of a woodcutter, squatting upon a log, his frugal meal set upon a kerchief on his knees. He leapt to his feet, spilling his victuals unheeded, as he stared into the twin barrels of Joshua's pistol.

Joshua muttered his apologies and, without benefit of a reply, ran out to retrieve his mount and be upon his way. The woods had grown sparse again, and changed soon to open country, the undulating fields and pastures of the downs interspersed with small, isolated coppices and hedges and dry-stone walls. Without difficulty, Joshua picked up the trail and soon saw the rider ahead of him, urging his horse desperately in an effort to be clear. The man neither slowed nor looked back at his pursuer, his horse's hooves thundering across meadows and uplands, leaping streams, ditches, and any obstacle which barred its way. Joshua followed relentlessly, mile upon mile, horse flying over walls and thickets, sometimes knee high in ferns, then wading through shallow brooks, or clouded, stagnant water.

Finally Joshua's grey began to gain upon them and he drew close, praying that the man would keep up his desperate flight, too fearful to take aim and fire upon him. It seemed that the grey was inspired, feeling the blood-lust of the hunter for the hunted, for she was almost upon them when the other stumbled and stopped dead, forelegs grazing a fallen tree. The rider, like some lifeless marionette upon a string, was jerked back in the saddle, the movement stilted and unnatural, and then flew forward over the animal's head.

To Joshua it seemed ludicrously unreal as, pistol in hand, he dismounted and passed the trembling horse, still standing where it had halted. With one foot upon the fallen tree, Joshua remained still, frozen, gazing through the tangled brambles and undergrowth to the sheer quarry face beyond.

With a feeling of hollowness and fear he inched his way forward to see the man he had pursued lying like a broken toy upon the rock below. He knew that he could not leave him, even if there was but the merest sign of life. He snapped the stock from his pistol, replacing the two pieces in their holder, and carefully secured the grey to a tree lest she be tempted to follow him. Then, with both hands free, he began his awkward perilous descent to the quarry floor, nails clinging to the narrow fingerholds, the limestone crumbling and flaking 'neath his probing boots.

Safely down, he walked to the still body, seeing by the awkward angle of the head that the man's neck was broken. Hesitantly, he turned him over, remarking the scarred face. The violence of the new injuries forced sickness into his mouth so that he had to turn away, closing his eyes against the faintness which threatened. He was still trembling, his eyes blurred as though with water, as he searched blindly through the man's pockets, first taking and unloading the pistol and securing it within his waistcoat, then wrapping the few pitiful possessions in a kerchief, and placing the bundle in his own pocket, unchecked. Then, slowly, he began his ascent of the quarry face.

He took the bridle of the dead man's horse and it came with him willingly, subdued and without spirit. He rode slowly back upon the grey, leading the riderless horse.

The unknown man's death weighed heavily upon him, with its violence and unexpectedness. It seemed to Joshua that it was a child's game they had been playing – a war with toy bullets and guns which had inexplicably turned to tragedy.

He was glad that it was not his bullet which had caused the death. It would have been a hard thing to live with, that sudden draining of warm flesh to nothingness. He remembered how pleased he had been when the justice had given him permission to carry a firearm and to use it, should need arise. Well, it would arise again, he could not doubt it. He could only hope that he would fire as he had done today, instinctively, without thought. Otherwise, it would be he who would be lying dead! It was a dangerous game. A game for men. There was no second chance.

As he approached the mill, drained and exhausted, he saw Rowden running out to greet him.

'Ezra?' Joshua asked tonelessly.

'Alive, sir, thanks to your swiftness and actions.'

Joshua felt a warm relief flooding through him as he climbed down from the grey. 'He is badly hurt?'

'A broken leg, sir, and many cuts and bruises, for the fellow beat him most savagely with a pistol, threatening to break his fingers and arms, and then to shoot him. A wicked, godless rogue, indeed!' His eyes went to the riderless horse. 'You lost him, sir? He escaped?'

'No, he is dead.' Joshua ventured no other explanation.

The miller nodded, saying quietly, 'I will help you unsaddle his mount.'

Joshua turned aside to remove the gun which he had stowed away within his waistcoat, and to inspect the man's meagre possessions, knotted within the kerchief: a comb, a plain silver ring with the initials FGP, a snuff-box of horn, friction matches, but no letters or documents to identify him.

'Well!' exclaimed Rowden, bending from the weight of the saddle as he lifted it to the ground. 'Well, upon my oath, sir!' His fingers traced the brand mark burned into its loins. 'It seems the horse is from Sker House!'

Joshua nodded, seeing the familiar H bounded by a circle.

There was a strident cry from within.

'Dear Lord! I had forgotten Ezra! If you will go to him, sir, I will stable the horse, and later attend to the wounds upon its forelegs, for I have no doubt that you will wish to return it!' The miller's voice was hard and angry.

Joshua walked into the mill where he found Ezra ashen-faced, lying upon some flour sacks. His face was bruised and swollen, and there was a cut beneath his eye. His leg had been strapped by the miller with two make-shift splints of ashwood, fastened with sacking, and he was evidently in great pain and shocked.

'You will be pleased to know that your assailant is dead, Mr Evans. He will bother you no more.'

'Pleased?' cried Ezra, indignantly. 'Why should I be pleased? My workshop is wrecked, my tools lie useless, my house a pigsty! And my cat . . .' Tears welled up into his eyes.

'Have no fear, he is safe, taken to be cared for by Walter Bevan, the relieving officer for the poor.'

'Well, that is what he is there for!' said Ezra ungratefully. 'What relief will he offer me, that is what I would like to know? Beaten, persecuted, my leg broken and useless . . .'

'I will have a word with him,' promised Joshua, 'and see what can be done to help you.'

Ezra sniffed, wiping a grubby hand across his small, beady eyes.

'At least you are alive,' said Joshua gently.

'No thanks to you!' snapped Ezra. 'Gallivanting about the countryside while I lie dying.'

'Ezra!' cried the miller's shocked voice from the doorway. 'It was Constable Stradling who saved your life!'

'What for?' said Ezra, ungraciously.

Joshua was satisfied that Ezra the Box was on the mend.

Chapter Fourteen

As he rode to the justice's house for the second time that day, Joshua was all too conscious of the irony, as well as the tragedy in the situation. A man was dead. Certainly he was a villain, and there could be few who would not consider his end well merited. Just retribution – although, in Joshua's eyes, far from divine!

True, the discovery of the branding upon his horse forged a tenuous link with Hardee of Sker House, and the wrecking of the *San Lorenzo*, yet his death destroyed so much more in the chain. Had the dead man been responsible for the deaths of Jem Crocutt and Dai Bando? Why? Was he involved in the disappearance of Elwyn Morris? Upon whose instructions did he act? How was he concerned with the wreckers? The answers to the questions had died with him, that was the tragedy.

The irony lay in Joshua's last conversation with the justice, when he had foolishly voiced the hope that no one would be careless enough to die before Ezra had been found. It was Ezra himself who had almost been killed. Now his assailant was dead, and the little undertaker would take little pleasure (or maybe too much!) in laying him out – always assuming that it was possible to do whatever was required, while standing upon his one good leg! He supposed that there must be someone who shared with him the secrets of his insalubrious craft, and could take instruction. Dear heaven, Joshua found himself laughing aloud, I pity any poor pauper lad apprenticed to Ezra, with his mean, ferrety ways and caustic tongue! No doubt, his disability would render him even more bitter and cantankerous . . . And yet, there had been tears in his eyes for his lost cat. What a mass of contradictions the fellow was, irritating, petty, whining, yet in his own way independent and heroic. Perhaps that was what made human nature so fascinating, its unpredictability. Damn it! Could he be actually getting fond of the odious little man?

The justice listened to Joshua's story gravely, protuberant brown eyes alert behind his spectacles. His dark jowls trembled.

'He fired upon you, you say?'

'Yes, sir, and threatened the undertaker, Evans, that he would be shot, after torturing him.'

'The same modus operandi as Bando,' the justice mused, 'torture and death. No ordinary criminal then, but one in the pay of some organisation or individual with power – the power of life and death! The rewards must be incalculable.'

'As is the danger, sir.'

'But not for the leader. He stands aloof, his hands unbloodied, or so he dares to believe.' He shook his head angrily. 'Damn it, Stradling, it must be Hardee. Who else? Everything points to it, and now the branding of the mare . . . You will return it, of course?'

'Yes, I had planned to take it tomorrow, sir, and confront him. You think it wise?'

'Yes, but it must be done circumspectly. All the evidence is circumstantial. Besides, if you reveal too much, your own life will be in danger. There will be others, willing and trained, to take the dead man's place.'

Joshua nodded agreement. 'You have learnt anything of Dr Thomas, sir?'

'Indeed, it seems he is Hardee's cousin. A blood relationship, yet rumour has it that their personal relationship is abrasive, uneasy.'

'The reason?'

'I leave that to you, Stradling.' The justice's mouth twitched humorously. 'With the interesting puzzle of how you intend getting Evans down the quarry face to retrieve the cadaver, bearing in mind the impediment of his broken leg . . .' Then, seeing Joshua's stricken face: 'Forgive me, I forget your exhaustion and the emotional toll the day has extracted. I beg your pardon, Stradling, it was but a weak attempt at humour, and quite unworthy.'

Joshua looked at him, surprised.

'I will summon an undertaker from Pyle, to assist Evans and do what is required. It will be necessary to bring someone from Sker House to identify the body, you understand. I would prefer it to be here, under my jurisdiction as justice and priest.'

'I understand, sir. I have told Evans that since his workshop is wrecked and his tools broken or lost, I will ask the relieving officer for the poor if there is some assistance which can be given.'

'Yes, I am sure that the vestry would agree to that, since his craft is one which touches us all,' his mouth twitched again, 'as, indeed, my own should!'

Joshua smiled dutifully.

'I do not think he will need pressure put upon him to produce a claim, Stradling! Having said which, he will still need constant protection. His ordeal is not yet over. In addition,' the justice added practically, 'he will be needed as a witness.'

'Yes, sir. I will arrange it, although I do not think that I will be overwhelmed with volunteers,' said Joshua drily, 'even paid ones.'

'Come, Stradling,' chivvied the justice, 'let us be charitable. He has suffered abominably, and sustained grievous loss. He has need of friends.'

'Indeed, sir, he professed a positive and urgent desire to see you.'

The justice was nonplussed.

'In your capacity as rector, sir. He claimed it would offer him comfort.'

'Perhaps Mansel's comfort would be more immediate? More practical? I will arrange it.'

'It has already been done, sir.'

'Indeed? I have to congratulate you upon your persistence, Stradling.'

'Then I had best be about my duties, sir.'

'And I,' said the rector, with rather less enthusiasm, 'mine.'

When the constable had returned to his cottage in Newton, jaded in body and spirit, it was to find not one letter awaiting him from Rebecca, but two.

His lassitude was immediately dispelled. Without even bothering to remove his helmet, he seated himself before the embers of the fire to read news of her.

The first one opened contained a formal invitation to a ball to celebrate the nineteeth anniversary of Miss Rebecca de Breos of Southerndown Court. His presence was requested – but to soften its impersonal tone, Rebecca had added in her own hand: 'It is not only requested, Joshua, but begged, implored, entreated, commanded even; for without you it will be dead and comfortless as ashes!'

Joshua smiled indulgently, wishing with all his heart that she could be there beside him, to lighten the day with her affectionate nonsense, and the beauty of her warm compassionate eyes. He would have been glad to turn to her for advice, for she was intelligent and practical, and had been eager to help him in the past. She would not seek to persuade him, but to clarify and crystallise all that was in his own mind, all that was now formless and confused. With Rebecca beside him, what could he not accomplish?

He opened the remaining letter, and was soon absorbed into her new world at Southerndown Court. She would be going to the London house to spend a few days, with Elizabeth and Mrs Crandle as companions. There would be theatres and shopping expeditions, visits to galleries and calls from her grandfather's friends. There would be carriage drives in the park; they would be fitted for ball-gowns, shoes, gloves, new bonnets. There would be so much to do and see! 'Oh, Joshua,' she wrote, 'if only you could be here! It would be perfect. I think of you constantly, and with deepening love and affection. I cannot bear to be parted from you, for though I hold the picture of you in my mind, and the dearness of you, I do not hold the warm flesh. I am glad that Rosa and Doonan are together yet, in thinking of them, I feel pain, my dear, that we do not share a fusing of bodies and blood, that common, life-quickening heartbeat. I share your thoughts and your spirit, Joshua. Yet until I come to you in shared flesh, I will not feel the joy of wholly belonging. You are my whole life, and future promise. I had no existence until you came. The first time that you touched me, stirring me to life, I was born . . .'

Joshua read the letter through to its end, then sat silently for a long time, deep in thought and yearning, the embers of the fire glowing red and dying away before he felt its chill. Then, as he stood up and replaced the letter reluctantly in its envelope, a small piece of paper fluttered to the floor at his feet.

'Joshua, I have told Grandfather of your wish to pay court to me. He bids you address him upon the subject in my absence. He begs that you present yourself at the Court at two o' the clock on Friday, the tenth day of December.'

The lure of the forbidden apple, Joshua thought amused, before the fatal bite! Well, it had to be done. Faint heart never yet won fair lady! Much as he loved Rebecca, the prospect of explaining why he considered himself to be worthy of her, and what prospects he had to offer, attracted him not at all! In fact, he thought as he removed his helmet and made ready to rekindle the fire,

if asked to judge whether his visit to Sker House or
Rebecca's grandfather promised the more trouble, he
would be hard pressed to choose between them.

The following morning, as arranged with Rowden,
Joshua returned to the mill upon Stormy Downs to collect the dead man's mare. The December morning was
crisply raw, and when Joshua had arisen at seven o' the
clock, the small window in the eaves was covered with a
rime of frost, thick enough to gouge with a fingernail.
As a child upon the farm, winter had been a secret pleasure to him. He loved to awaken at dawn and creep out
of bed to where the leaded casement glittered with a
crystallised landscape: a forest of ferny growths and
strange, exotic plants. As he breathed upon it a small,
clear space appeared, round and magical, a telescope to
the day ahead . . .

If the thrill of such childish pleasures had been outgrown, Joshua still enjoyed winter's crispness. Even the
film of ice upon his washstand jug, and the tingling of
splashed water upon his skin, only served to make him
feel alive and filled with heightened awareness.

Now, as he neared the mill, the bare trees and spiked
blackthorn hedges were sheathed in ice, and the grey's
breath a cloud of steam upon the frosted air. In the
silence her metal shoes rang clear upon the stones, dis-
tinct and resonant as the blows upon the anvil which had
shaped them. Joshua was filled with the contentment of
being at one with the mare and the world about him.

Rowden, hearing his approach, came from his living
quarters alongside the granary. His day had long begun,
but he had been ministering to Ezra, now removed from

the mill-tower where he had fled to escape his assailant and safely ensconced in the miller's bed. The miller himself had spent a restless night huddled beneath blankets and sacks on a straw-filled palliasse upon the floor, his sleep fractured with Ezra's groanings, snores and cries for water, or the chamber pot.

'Good morning, Constable. I have the mare saddled and ready for you, sir, and spread a salve upon her forelegs but I fear that they will be painful and stiff and you must needs go slowly.'

Joshua thanked him, asking, 'And Ezra? He is recovering?'

The miller sighed, plump face resigned under its dusting of flour. 'Indeed, sir! Recovering in all but humour and temper.'

Joshua smiled. A look of understanding passed between them, 'I fear that he might still be in some danger, miller . . .'

'It might well be from me if he continues to be so vexatious and provoking!' Then Rowden grew serious. 'You really believe that they will try again, sir?'

'Yes, but I am empowered by the justice to hire a man to guard him. You know of someone?'

The miller looked sceptical. 'It would need a king's ransom, and someone disordered in mind, to consider it, sir! But have no fear, while he is here I will watch over him.'

'Then you must be paid for doing so.'

'No,' Rowden protested, alarmed, 'for if I did, he would be even more unbearable, using me as a paid servant to fetch and carry at every whim! No, sir, I am but in the mill alongside, and will hear any man who approaches. Then there is my apprentice, a great, strapping lad, strong as an ox,' he smiled, 'and needing a hide like one to put up with Ezra! It was but ill-chance which took the boy upon an errand yesterday. It will not happen again, have no fear. Ezra will be protected.'

'You have my gratitude.'

'But very likely none of his!' said the miller, 'and would not expect it, for then I would know that he really was at death's door, instead of swearing it. You would see him, sir? Exchange a greeting?'

Joshua followed him within.

Ezra was propped upright against the pillows, face puffed and bruised eyes swollen. The ginger-coloured cat lay sleeping upon the coverlet.

'Good morning, Mr Evans.'

'For those who have the health and means to enjoy it.'

'I see that your cat has been restored to you, fit and well.'

'Listless enough,' corrected Ezra, 'and thin.'

'No doubt he has been pining for you,' said Joshua innocently, 'missing your congenial company. You have seen the rector?'

'Yes, but he scarce found time to greet me, claiming a need to oversee the recovery of the body. You are lucky the man fell into the quarry!'

'I am most grateful,' said Joshua drily. 'You have heard that an undertaker is to be brought here from Pyle?'

'Yes, but I am to instruct him first, and to be paid accordingly.' He sniffed, 'I dare say it will be most inferior, but no matter! It is what that bullying rogue deserves!'

'I imagine that it will be of supreme indifference to him, given the circumstances,' said Joshua, fighting his irritation, 'besides which, no one will see him!'

'That is not the point,' insisted Ezra, thumping the bed so violently that the cat awoke and sprang up, alarmed. 'If you do a job, do it properly! Don't leave it half done, I always say!'

They looked at each other in silence for a moment.

'I had best be off to . . . get my job done, properly,' said Joshua, lips twitching, 'I wish you a good day, sir.'

'With the pain of a broken leg, and countless other injuries?' muttered Ezra, disgruntled.

Joshua walked to the door, patience exhausted.

'Constable Stradling?'

'What now?' he asked abrasively.

'Only to thank you, sir, and to say that I will testify against the wreckers!'

'I am glad,' said Joshua, outwitted, shamefaced and utterly in the wrong.

With the dead man's horse fastened beside him, its forelegs painful and stiff, Joshua's progress along the icy highway was slow. He fared little better in the lanes and byways, stopping frequently to rest the beast and give it some words of praise and encouragement. The grey, sensing its distress, adapted her pace, and although Joshua was heartened by her intelligence and intuitive kindness, he found the journey tedious. He was relieved to reach the gateway of Sker House, despite its bleak, unwelcoming aspect.

The baying of the two unleashed hounds had both horses fidgeting and nervous, and Joshua was forced to descend to control them. He tugged the warning bell, but it was some minutes before his call was answered by the taciturn, unkempt kennel-man demanding, 'What is your business, sir?'

'I come to interview Mr Hardee. Tell him I return his lost property.'

The man started visibly as he caught sight of the wounded horse, but swiftly recovered himself.

'If you will wait until I have secured the dogs.' He called out to them, commanding them harshly, and they drew back disconsolate, to be chained. He returned almost at once to unbar the gate, bidding the dogs lie still as Joshua skirted them, leading the horses.

A man appeared from the house and Joshua halted, awaiting him. He did not know what he had expected of Hardee, but certainly it was not this girlish, fine-boned figure. He appeared ludicrously out of place in this austere, forbidding setting. It was not merely in the over-refinement of his clothing, but in the delicacy of his features, the turn of his head, even the languid grace of his walk. Epicene, studied, as if he had carefully rehearsed every movement in front of a looking glass before adopting it. His voice was as Joshua expected, thin and expressionless.

'And you are, sir?'

'Joshua Stradling, officially appointed constable to the three hamlets, and you, sir, are Mr Hardee?'

'It seems that you have some stolen property to return.'

'No, sir, not stolen, although I fear that I cannot return its rider!'

A groom emerged from the shadows where he had been standing unobserved and led both mounts away to the stables.

'It is your horse?' persisted Joshua. 'You do not doubt it?'

'No, why should I, sir? It will undoubtedly be plainly branded upon the loins. My mark is an H within a –'

'Yes! I know your mark,' Joshua interrupted briskly. 'I have witnessed it upon another occasion.'

'You had best enter,' said Hardee, ungraciously, 'for I have no wish to continue this conversation here,' he shivered delicately, 'the air is dank and chill, although, perhaps, you do not feel it.'

Joshua, without answering, followed him into the house and through the stone-flagged hall, with its high roof and weaponry, into a smaller, less intimidating library. Hardee seated himself behind a desk spread with ledgers and account books, motioning Joshua peremptorily to a winged leather chair.

'Perhaps, Constable, you will now come to the real point of your visit?'

'I thought I had done so, sir. I came to return your horse.'

'Well, you have returned it. I thank you for it.' He rose dismissively.

'Are you not curious about the circumstances?'

'It is a matter you may discuss with my bailiff. I have neither the time nor the inclination to waste upon so trivial an affair.'

'The man who rode it is dead!'

'Indeed? Then he will at least escape a trial, and the penalty for horse-stealing. Now, if you will excuse me . . .'

'No, sir, I cannot do that, for I come upon the orders of the justice to command – to request you to identify the body.'

'That is absurd! Unnecessary!' he exclaimed petulantly. 'I tell you, I do not know the man!'

'How can you be sure, sir, until you have seen him? It is the merest formality, of course. An inconvenience, certainly, but less so than being called upon to give evidence at an inquest. The justice will doubtless apprise you of the time and place when you will be required.'

Hardee's pale skin was flushed with annoyance, and there was a peevishness about his full, girlish mouth.

'I suppose one must expect such inconveniences, if one has been used to dealing with gentlemen, not inferiors!'

'I cannot but agree,' said Joshua smoothly, 'and the Reverend Robert Knight is most certainly a gentleman. He spoke most highly of your cousin, Dr Elfed Thomas, and his testimony at the inquest upon the wreck. You recall, sir, the *San Lorenzo*?'

'I am unlikely to forget it, since I was involved in the rescue.'

'Not rescue, alas, sir, for not one soul survived!'

'Surely,' said Hardee with ill-suppressed anger, 'that is a matter which does not concern you, but the exciseman?'

'I fancy,' said Joshua innocently, 'that his official concern would be more for the cargo, jewellery, valuables. Although, as all thinking men with a shred of humanity, his true concern would be for those murdered . . . by the sea.'

There was a cold palpable silence before Hardee moved from behind the desk to escort him to the door.

'It is true, I believe, that Sker House was a grange of Margam Abbey, and rumoured to be joined to it, even now, by an underground passageway? Strange how such myths persist, is it not, sir?' Joshua asked blandly.

Hardee did not respond, but as they stepped out into the hall, Joshua saw his wife, pale transparent skin burning with high colour at her cheekbones as she moved awkwardly away. She neither glanced at Joshua, nor acknowledged her husband's presence, but continued her clumsy, ungainly walk, and Joshua recalled it as the sound he had been uneasily aware of during his conversation with Hardee. As they crossed the hallway, Edwards, the liveried manservant who had given Joshua the half-guinea for Jem Crocutt's widow, came into the hall. Hardee waved him irritably away.

Joshua's grey was waiting for him, held by the groom, as they emerged into the yard. At the farthest end, away from the dogs, a swineherd was ushering a small group of sows and a litter of squealing piglets towards a gate and a distant sty.

'Tamworths?' Joshua asked, surprised.

'Yes. You know this breed?'

'My father is a farmer in the Vale.'

'Really?' The thin, effeminate voice was dismissive. 'I should be surprised if he bred them. I have certainly never encountered another such herd in all my travels, sir. I believe myself to be the only breeder in this part of Wales. It is a hobby, a passion one might say.'

The word 'passion' came strangely from him, Joshua thought, for his manner was so controlled and bloodless – a detachment he shared with his wife. Joshua could not imagine them unbending to make love, or even to bestow a chaste kiss.

Hidden fires, he wondered, or was there passion for the warm, blood-red gleam of jewels, like the rubies upon Marged's crucifix? Would it be fierce enough to plunder and wreck for them? To kill, even? Or, the ultimate absurdity, did it merely begin and end with the ginger-haired Tamworth pigs?

Joshua's thoughts, as he rode reflectively back to Newton, were centred upon Hardee. He had not expected him to be such an effete, languid fellow, almost foppish in dress and manner. Surely such affectation and stupid posturings would make him ridiculed by those men he was believed to command? How could he hope to control them? Yet he had controlled the man who had died in the quarry, and persuaded him or others to kill for him . . .

Was it money alone that was the key to their subservience to him? Unlikely. Their contempt for him would make them careless, unreliable. Yet the wrecking, murders and whole organisation had been carried out with the utmost precision and skill. Was Hardee's appearance and manner deliberately cultivated? A cover to divert suspicion? Or had his girlish looks driven him to prove his power and masculinity to others, as well as to himself?

Joshua supposed that his own life must be in danger. Yet at Sker House, he had not considered his probing and questions a risk, believing that his position as constable, and the justice's officer, protected him. His death there would pose too many questions. Yet outside? As the blacksmith had warned him, it was as well to be upon his guard!

He had deliberately refrained from taking the dead man's possessions with him because, in seeing them, Hardee could have once more disclaimed all knowledge of the man. Better that he believed Joshua to be withholding something which might provide a clue to his involvement in the wrecking . . .

If he could ascertain which men were merely servants in Hardee's household, and which concerned with him in the murders and wrecking, it would be an incalculable advantage. It must be done with utmost prudence. One mistake, and Hardee would learn of it; worse, it would bring risk to those innocent. What was Dr Elfed Thomas's involvement in the affair? It might prove profitable, too, to learn what secret bound them so inexorably together, and what disagreement made their relationship so abrasive and uneasy, as the justice had declared . . .

Joshua would have been surprised had he witnessed the scene taking place in the dankly oppressive drawing room at the house he had left; for the controlled fury of which he had been aware during his questioning of Hardee had erupted into violence, all the more ugly for being so unexpected.

There was nothing weak or effeminate about Hardee now, his face contorted with rage as he gripped his wife's wrist, pulling her accusingly towards him. She stumbled awkwardly, and half fell, but he jerked her to face him.

'What the hell were you doing, listening in the hall? Loitering like some wretched scullery maid! What did you hope to hear?'

'Nothing! Nothing! I tell you.' She tried to wrench herself free, but he merely clasped her more strongly with both hands, twisting relentlessly.

'Please! You are hurting me.'

'Damn it! What were you hoping for? Something to use against me? To take to him?'

'I have told you,' her voice was cold, hard with suppressed loathing, 'there is nothing between us! I will not repeat it again, or listen to your insane ramblings!'

'It is you who are insane, madam, if you think you can make a fool of me, a laughing stock!'

'Well, that is what you are! Foolish! Effeminate! A pathetic apology for a man! It would be small wonder if I sought a real one!'

He had released her arm and, without speaking, dealt her a blow to her face which sent her reeling awkwardly, to steady herself upon a corner of the chimneypiece.

'Yes, that is right. Show me what a man you are in the only way you know!' Her voice was thick with contempt. 'It is only what I have learnt to expect. You have no other way.'

'God damn you!' he cried, moving towards her threateningly. 'You are my wife! My property! To do with as I choose. The law allows it.'

'The law allows you to own my property, my money, that which was mine by birthright. It does not allow you to own me! I am a woman in my own right!'

'Are you, indeed? We shall see about that, madam.' His voice was cold now with menace. 'Perhaps there is some way of showing you the truth of it, to remind you of your duties . . .'

'You have given me a reminder,' she said bitterly, 'and I see it every day in the way I move, the scars on my flesh and my spirit. But God help me, I will not be broken! I am not one of your mares to be beaten into submission!' she declared contemptuously. 'Do not raise a hand to me, sir, and allow me to pass in peace. If you do not, I swear, upon my oath, that I will kill you!'

He stood back to let her pass, seeing the weal his hand had made still livid upon her cheek. She moved awkwardly, slowly, and he knew, even as she opened the door, that he had not really touched her.

Chapter Fifteen

After a disturbed, uneasy night, when sleep finally came to Joshua, it was less than restful. He dreamed that he struggled through a tortuous maze of clipped yew hedges at Southerndown Court, vainly seeking escape. At every turn he was menaced by strange creatures and the ghostly shapes of the dead: Bando, his face part eaten away; Jem Crocutt, skewered upon a beam; Ezra's dead assailant rising from the quarry upon his wounded horse. Their fleshless hands reached out to grasp him, and he fled away to where Rebecca stood beckoning, bathed in glowing light. Yet, even as he ran, she grew smaller, retreating further and further away, until he knew that she was for ever beyond his reach.

He awoke with a start, calling her name. His heart was still pounding and his mouth dry until the confusion left him. With his mind clear, the thoughts of the day ahead came crowding in, and he was scarcely more cheered by reality. Today he was to meet Sir Matthew de Breos, to plead his cause.

Meanwhile, there was work to be done. After a hastily eaten, cold breakfast, he took up his helmet and strode to the 'Crown' to collect the mare.

Ossie brought her to him within minutes, saddled and ready. He watched as Joshua mounted, his weathered, nutshell face concerned, for the constable seemed in low spirits. 'I hear that there was an accident at the disused quarry upon Stormy Downs?'

Joshua nodded, leaning forward to smooth the grey's neck, saying wryly, 'Yes. It seems that either death pursues me, Ossie, or I pursue death. Either way, it is a morbid and profitless occupation.'

'No, not profitless,' said the little ostler earnestly, 'for your work is for the victims. The dead or bereaved, sir, without you, would be unavenged, and the three hamlets would be a more violent lawless place.'

'It is good to have friends,' said Joshua warmly. 'You have restored my faith in myself, and others.'

Ossie's face wrinkled, delightedly. 'I would be proud to be counted as such. A friend. And as a friend, I warn you that there is a rumour of meetings, unrest, disorder even.'

'Here? Within the parish?'

'And beyond. Here it is but small, and poorly supported, I suspect. Yet it could easily ignite and flare up, to sweep as fire through a cornfield. Once out of control . . .' He shook his head regretfully.

'The reason, Ossie?'

The ostler hesitated. 'I have said too much already, Joshua. It is all hearsay, you understand. There is anger about the tollgate charges. It grows ugly, menacing. Small farmers, craftsmen, and the fishermen like Jeremiah are grievously taxed, unable to earn a living. They fear that those who own the turnpikes, the trusts, are corrupt, unreasonable. Their anger spreads even to those who lease the land, such as Robert Knight, the justice.'

'But he is not directly involved in setting the tolls,' objected Joshua, 'nor would he do anything dishonest!'

'When there is injustice,' said Ossie ruefully, 'men become blind to reason, feeling only their own hurt. Their leaders see barely more clearly.'

'A case of "the blind leading the blind", then?'

'More a case of "In the kingdom of the blind, a one-eyed man is king!" ' countered Ossie drily.

'And the king of this ill-sighted kingdom?'

'That I do not know, and if I did, then I think he might share my sympathy. I do not condone violence, for I am a peaceable man, as you will testify. Yet, if someone were to ill-treat one of my animals . . .'

'Then you might be stirred to violence on its behalf?'

'As those who see their children in want, or their livelihoods threatened by other men's greed. There is a point at which every man will rebel. We all carry within us the seeds of violence. They need but feeding and watering.'

'I shall check most carefully, lest they grow,' promised Joshua, smiling, and stirring the mare into action.

'Better tackle the root causes,' called Ossie practically, 'then they will wither and die naturally!'

Joshua turned at the archway and saluted him gravely, seeing Ossie, a small twisted figure, shoulders hunched, legs ugly with rickets.

'Goodbye, friend ostler!' he cried.

Ossie smiled and nodded, then returned to succour his beasts.

Joshua rode directly to the port, then to the customs and excise place, an unprepossessing wooden shed which housed its few administrators. The docks were small, and used mainly for summer trade, for the single basin was ruled by the vagaries of the tides and weather. As well as the fierce Atlantic breakers, which battered the shore, the gales were wild, and arose quickly and without warning, as Jeremiah had so lately seen, battering down all which dared to stand in their way.

As Joshua crossed the horse-drawn tramway, with the small trucks bringing coal and minerals from the hinterland, he wondered if the ambitious plans to enlarge the docks, providing a second, well-sheltered harbour for all-the-year-round trading, would reach fruition. It was true that the needs of the new industries must be met, the ironworks and the coalfields which promised to add wealth to the traditional cargoes of limestone, corn, butter, livestock and wool. Yet the creek at Newton lay deserted and useless, its trade, flourishing since the seventeenth century, gone. As the new dock had superseded it, might not it, in turn, be outgrown? Already there was talk of steamship replacing sail. He looked about him at the small cutters and coastal traders already moored, and those standing off-shore in the choppiness of the grey, December seas. There was something to touch the heart and imagination in a fully-rigged ship under sail: mast proud, canvas billowing. There was a grace and fluidity about it; the lure of strange, exotic places with music in their names.

He remembered the wharves heavy with summer heat, the noise, colour and excitement, the evocative, mingled scents of coffee beans, spices, pine resin, the iridescent bolts of silk, vivid and metallic as dragonflies. Pit-props from France and Scandinavia for the coal mines, iron ore from Valparaiso for the foundries.

He pushed his way around the black sugarloaves of coal, shiny and lustrous as jet, a fine dust misting the grey's hooves as he led her through.

Peter Rawlings, the exciseman, saw Joshua coming and, smiling broadly, came out to greet him. They met rarely, save on those few occasions when their duties became interwoven, the threads merging into a pattern, as now. Yet their liking for each other was genuine.

'You have time for refreshment and talk?' asked Joshua.

'Always.' Rawlings smiled. 'What do you say to the "Ship Aground"?'

'That it is uncannily suited to the subject of my questioning!'

'The wreck of the *San Lorenzo*?' Rawlings asked perceptively.

Joshua nodded, as Rawlings took his elbow, guiding him towards the inn, murmuring, 'I heard that you visited Sker House. Let us hope that the tavern affords us a warmer reception, for I swear my own welcome there was as bleak and uncivilised as its surroundings!'

Laughing, deep in conversation, they walked together to the stables to make comfortable Joshua's mare before entering the inn.

Rawlings ordered them ale, while Joshua secured a small table in a secluded corner, where they would not be overheard . . .

'Well?' demanded Rawlings, when they were seated.
'What is your involvement with the *San Lorenzo*?'

Joshua told him of the deaths and his suspicions.

Rawlings listened in silence, face intent. 'I have no
doubt that you are right, just as I am totally convinced
that Hardee is accountable for the wrecking! It was a
bloody, vicious crime, ruthlessly planned and coldly
executed. I tell you, Stradling, the callousness of it chills
my blood!'

'You have hope of trapping him?'

'I wish to God I had! He has covered his tracks so
cunningly, and planned every last detail. You heard that
he actually had a doctor at the scene, and in Mansel's
absence? It was all so quickly done. And Dr Elfed
Thomas's report at the inquest – impeccable, although I
know that he lied!'

'You are aware that there is a blood kinship?' asked
Joshua.

'I am aware that there is little love lost! I fancy that
Hardee has some hold over him, yet Thomas cannot be
shaken from his evidence! It was given upon oath, and
unchallenged.'

'So whatever threatens him is more powerful than his
professional career, or the threat of imprisonment and
disgrace?'

'It would seem so.'

'Money, then?' Joshua hazarded.

'I think not. He lives well, and enjoys the luxuries of
life, as who would not, given opportunity? Yet it seems
that he has a small private fortune.' Then, in response to
Joshua's questioning look, 'No, not wrecker's wages. A

family trust, genuine, and well administered.'

'And Hardee?'

'The property and money are his wife's. It seems that she is heiress to a considerable fortune.'

'But not enough, perhaps?'

Rawlings shook his head. 'Who knows what drives a man to wrecking? Avarice? Excitement? A lust for power, or blood? It is a vile, corrupting trade, Stradling, the murder of innocents. They are mutilated and degraded when barely alive. I have seen the results of such savagery, and it sickens me!' He banged his tankard hard upon the table, jaw set in anger. 'I would give them a taste of what the victims suffer, that they might reflect upon it!'

'You found nothing to incriminate Hardee? Nothing from the wreck?'

'No, although we searched most diligently from attics to cellar, even to the underground passageways and stores, barns and outhouses.'

'You searched the house, you say?' Joshua could not hide his astonishment. 'But how? Upon whose instructions?'

'Hardee's own,' said Rawlings unexpectedly, then, seeing Joshua's confusion, 'No! I pray you do not look so incredulous, my friend! Hardee is no fool. I searched at his express insistence, indeed, he saw fit to accompany me upon the task, affording every help and direction . . . declaring solemnly that if any one of his men was guilty of looting, unbeknown to him, then he would see him damned!'

'As well he might!' exclaimed Joshua. 'So you found nothing?'

'It is not surprising. Hardee would not risk all for what is washed from the wreck: brandy, tobacco, wines, the ship's fittings and furnishings. He left them to the villagers. His only concern was for the jewels and valuables upon the flesh of those wrecked, or held in the ship's safes. His men would not dare to disobey, or withhold treasure, or their lives would be forfeit . . .'

Joshua nodded. 'I have seen the bloodiness of his vengeance. There is little hope, then, of one of the servants informing upon him.'

'As much hope as there is that Hardee will identify Ezra the Box's assailant.'

'Yet, Ezra has offered his help.'

Rawlings's expression was cynical, amused. 'To provide all our coffins at the pauper's rate?'

'No, to give evidence against the wreckers.'

'Then you may be sure that he knows no one involved, and nothing of value. Have you thought that he might even destroy himself? Dr Elfed Thomas would understandably claim that it was Ezra who had wrought the violence, in his greed for the victims' valuables. His word as a physician, and that of Hardee as a landowner in good standing, would certainly be believed, and could send Ezra to the gallows! Besides, you know well enough what an unctuous, ingratiating little toad the man is!'

Joshua was forced to agree, adding truthfully, 'Yet he persists in his offer, even after threats and torture . . .'

'Come! He is as reliable as a weathercock in a gale, blown in every direction and settling to none.'

'True,' admitted Joshua.

'How would he fare at the mercy of a trained advocate? Would you find him impressive? Credible even? Besides, his only contact is now dead, and therefore valueless . . . No, I fear, Stradling, that like me you must admit to Hardee's devilish cunning.'

'Yes, I admit that, but I will not as readily admit defeat.'

'No more will I! I have sworn from the beginning of the affair that he will be brought to justice. Now there are two of us to see that the dead are avenged!'

'Three,' said Joshua wickedly, 'if you count Ezra as ally!'

'I would as soon share my bed with a viper for, in truth, they are both equally slimy and venomous.'

'Yet not, perhaps, as cold-blooded as Hardee's wife?'

'Agreed. I found her detachment infinitely chilling,' admitted Rawlings, 'despite her beauty. I am of the opinion, Stradling, that the owners of Sker House deserve each other . . .'

Upon leaving the docks, Joshua decided that he would vary his route by returning through Nottage, that he might call upon the Widow Cleat and Illtyd and deliver the books which he had chosen for the invalid's pleasure, and stowed within the saddlebag. However, as he drew near to the forge, he saw that Jeremiah's cob and cart were tethered outside, and fearing that too many visitors might tax the little hayward's strength, although Dr Mansel had declared that he was making astonishing progress, he rode on, courteously acknowledging Clatworthy and his apprentice as they looked up enquiringly from their noisy labours at the anvil.

Before Jeremiah had arrived, the Widow Cleat had been worried and depressed, her usual calm good humour deserting her. When her husband, the black-smith, had died, she had looked no further than thanking God that she and her crippled son had a stout roof over their heads, and food enough to sustain them from the small vegetable plot flanking their cottage, beside the forge.

Her husband had been a good man, working long hours, and well respected by all the folk of the three hamlets. He was kind to Illtyd, despite the grief of having a son too frail and misshapen to be of help to him, and he had never reproached her for giving birth to such a child, nor spoken a cruel word to the boy. If he had been taciturn, or undemonstrative, then it was a small price to pay for security and freedom from want.

Perhaps, she reflected, the strength and single-mindedness needed at his craft had left him with little emotion to spare, or perhaps, like the iron he worked upon at his anvil, hammering it into shape in the white heat, he too had been bent and cooled by circumstance, and had grown rigid and set into his ways. Yet she mourned him truly.

Thanks be to God, and the kindness of the constable and his friends, her son now had his work and future assured. Even Rebecca had loved them both enough to give them hope – a nest egg, protected and warm, to ensure a future. But the new blacksmith, Ben Clatworthy, was to be married soon, and would require the little cottage beside the forge to raise a family of his own. He was a good man, gentle and unassuming, despite his size and strength, and would not see her set upon the street or, worse, sent to the poorhouse, should Illtyd cease to work and she become a charge upon the poor rate. She began to weep, softly at first, then desperately, unable to stop, as much for the hurts and disappointments of the past as for what ailed her now.

It was thus Jeremiah discovered her as he called upon her with a fine sea-bass. Knocking and receiving no answer, he entered to find her quite overcome with grief, pretty dark head bent over her folded arms upon the scrubbed table. He was sorely tempted to stroke her thick, dark hair, scarce touched by grey, and even put out a hand to do so, but drew it away.

'Oh, my dear Sophie,' he said, forgetting to call her 'Mistress Cleat', 'whatever has happened? You are sick?'

She shook her head, unable to speak.

'It is Illtyd? He is worse?'

She raised a tear-stained face to his, the hurt in her eyes cutting him raw, as if it were a knife wound.

'Oh, Jeremiah,' she wept, 'what am I to do? The cottage is needed. Where will Illtyd and I go?'

'Is that all? Why, you will come to me, of course. Where else?'

She shook her head. 'Illtyd, perhaps, but how can I, a widow woman? People would talk, gossip can be cruel. I would not have you hurt.'

'Nor I you. You will come as my wife!'

The moment the words were said, he felt not regret but, surprisingly, joy.

She began to cry anew. 'No! I would not force that upon you, kind and gentle as you are . . .'

'Force it upon me? Why, Sophie, my love, it would give me the greatest joy. As for Illtyd, I love him as dearly as the son I lost . . .'

'Oh , Jeremiah, I love you truly,' she confessed, 'there is no man on earth I would rather wed.'

He took her in his arms clumsily, and stroked her hair, kissing her upon her soft cheek and feeling warmly at peace.

'If you think that Illtyd would be hurt –' he began hesitantly.

'No –' said Illtyd from the doorway, awkward head erect upon the wry neck, intelligent eyes bright '– it is the greatest joy in my life, I swear! Greater, even, than being given work as hayward. You are the best man I know, Jeremiah, and the kindest and most true friend. I have nothing but love and respect for you.'

Jeremiah drew the widow and her son to him, feeling the boy's frailness and misshapen bones. He did not care that they saw his tears falling, although he was a private man, for they were his own flesh, as if born, and he would be taking them home.

Unaware of his good friend Jeremiah's commitment, Joshua set his mind and effort steadfastly to his own. Upon his return he had left the grey at the 'Crown' with Ossie, bidding him, 'Polish the mare until she shines like silk, for it would not do for Sir Matthew to think that he is addressed by some rude, ill-favoured barbarian!'

Ossie had laughed, responding tartly, 'Now there, sir,

I fear I cannot help you. It is in your own hands, and God's! But I will willingly ensure that he can find no fault with your beast. Then, at least, one of you must make a good impression!' and, smiling broadly, he had led the mare away.

The constable, having scrubbed himself in the icy well-water in the yard, and dressed himself in the clothes of a gentleman of fashion, had returned to the stables to find his mare saddled and gleaming like a new-minted silver threepence.

'It is almost a crime to ride her,' observed Joshua, 'and disarrange her.'

'Perhaps, when you come to the river, you can carry her over,' suggested Ossie drily, 'although I warrant there is little to choose between you for grooming . . .'

'You think I will do, then, Ossie?'

'It is not my decision to make, and if it were, I think I would choose the mare by a very short head!'

'Well,' said Joshua, mounting, 'if Sir Matthew holds no great opinion of me, then at least he will admit to the superiority of my ostler.'

'That was never in doubt,' said Ossie, as Joshua, elegant from the crown of his shiny hat to the pale grey unmentionables flaring about the ankles of his boots, rode out upon his way.

If Sir Matthew did not judge the young constable to be handsome, elegant, and exceptional in every way, thought Ossie with satisfaction, then he must either be blind, or a candidate for Bedlam! Then whistling tunelessly through the gaps in his teeth, he went to do what little he could to make himself presentable, before taking tea with Miss Emily Randall in the coach-house loft.

With the tide safely out, Joshua decided that the quickest way to Southerndown would lie in taking the track to the Warren, which led between the church and the 'Ancient Briton' and skirted Jeremiah's cottage. He would ride across the acres of soft, dry-sanded dunes, tufted with spears of silver marram grass, and thence to the deserted beaches beyond Newton Point. He would follow the water's edge, cantering the horse across the hard, wet sand for pleasure and exercise.

This he did, the mare's hooves pressing crescents into the dark gold surface, her muscles rippling beneath her gleaming skin, head held proud. There was an arrogance in her freedom, a rightness, mane and tail flowing rhythmically as water. Joshua would have lingered, feeling the breeze cool from the tide, air clotted with the smells of iodine, salt and the abrasiveness of sea-washed sand.

There was a milky rim of foam edging the clear ripples and, above them, black and white oystercatchers skimmed, bodies sleek as fish, and in the shallows gulls waited, scaly pink legs exposed. They looked both comic and dignified, like grey-coated vestrymen surprised when bathing their feet. And when Joshua laughed, they hissed at him crossly, scolding him for an ill-mannered boy taunting his elders.

The pale bleached sand of the Warren had been sculpted into dunes by the wind, surfaces tunnelled by the myriad rabbit holes which occasioned its name.

Between them and the wet sand of the bays lay huge drifts of rounded pebbles, smoothed and faded by the tide, some so large that they could barely be lifted. Their muted colours of grey, pink, lilac and rose were sometimes stippled, or marbled through with crystals of gleaming quartz. Nestling in seaweed and pale driftwood, they might have been the forsaken egg-clutches of some long gone bird.

Joshua had now reached the estuary, where the dunes fell away to tidal mud-flats, then green surfaces pitted with water-filled holes. Cows grazed upon the river banks and roving sheep made pathways through the ferns, close-cropping the grass. Joshua rode the mare through the wide river mouth, divergent streams patterning the sand into a giant hand reaching out to the sea – and all around him gulls screamed, and wading birds dipped long beaks into the mud and clear water.

Up the rock-strewn bank to the narrow track edged with fox-red bracken, and higher still, over wind-stunted turf and rock-face, to where he looked down and saw the green spread of vale and cliffs, dropping sheer to the sea. Then, cradled in a wooded slope, like some natural outcrop, the grey stone of Southerndown Court . . .

Joshua dismounted, stroking the grey, before reaching into the saddlebag for a cloth to wipe the sand from his boots. After this small deference to the man who awaited him, he remounted and rode through the imposing wrought-iron gateway to the parklands and the entrance to the house.

A groom came forward at once to take his mount, and Joshua stepped beneath the pillared porte-cochere, glancing back briefly at the wide sweep of the carriageway between flowers, lawns and shrubberies that seemed to spill their greenness to the edge of the sea. The door opened and a footman relieved him of his hat and outdoor clothing, and the butler courteously escorted him to the library, where Sir Matthew awaited.

To the casual observer it would have appeared a scene both civilised and gracious. The room, and its owner, had a splendid, faded elegance, and the young constable was undeniably handsome in manner and clothing. He stood six feet three inches tall, firm-shouldered and with immaculate bearing. His features, beneath the wealth of corn-coloured hair, were fine, his blue eyes alert and intelligent, skin whipped to fresh colour by the ride upon the mare. Despite the difference in their ages and station, there was a similarity in the two men. It would have been hard to define, for it owed nothing to physical characteristics, rather to some air of authority, natural and quite unconscious. Sir Matthew's was, perhaps, inbred by generations of autocracy, Joshua's newly acquired through his work as constable.

There was immediate sympathy between them, and relief – recognition. To tell the truth, each had been nervous and afraid; Sir Matthew because of all he stood to lose, Joshua because of what he hoped to gain – their common need, Rebecca. Each felt that, yes, after all, he could accept the rights, and presence, of a third.

Chapter Sixteen

So, in a more relaxed and convivial atmosphere, Sir Matthew's lengthy catechism of Joshua began. Afterwards, the essential formalities disposed of, their glasses of Madeira refilled, the old gentleman asked, 'You are aware, I am sure, that the estate and lands will one day pass to Rebecca?'

'Yes, sir, although it has not been discussed between us.'

'Your life, sir, and your future are your own to order, but I must ask, for Rebecca's sake and my own, if you will one day accept them into your own keeping and responsibility? I ask because this inheritance has been all of my life . . .'

Joshua paused, saying carefully, 'I would wish you many years of good health and active life, sir.'

Sir Matthew waved it aside, declaring, 'I thank you for your courtesy, but seek an answer.'

'Then you shall have it, sir. My life, before Rebecca came, was set to but one aim – to become a constable.'

'Yes, Dr Peate has told me of your struggles, your singleness of purpose.' Sir Matthew's voice was tired and low.

'It is still the work which I wish to do, for it gives me a sense of purpose, a satisfaction,' Joshua declared firmly.

Sir Matthew nodded. 'Yes, I can see why that would be so.'

'Now Rebecca will be in my care and protection, as she was in yours, she would not ask me to forgo my work, knowing what it means to me.'

'Yes, I am sure that you are right,' he said heavily.

'Yet this is a birthright Rebecca was almost denied by the selfishness and cruelty of her father. Yes, I think cruelty is not too strong a word, for it hurt and deprived you both. I would not do the same to Rebecca's children, Sir Matthew. I promise you, most earnestly, that when the time comes I shall bring to your lands and estate that same singleness of purpose, holding them in trust, as you have done, for those who come after.'

Sir Matthew looked at Joshua steadily, then nodded, satisfied. He came forward to clasp Joshua's hand in his own, his bearing erect and dignified, voice low. 'I thank you, sir, for your assurance, for I know what it has cost you to give it. There is no way in which I can express the joy and pleasure it affords me.' He turned away abruptly, but not before Joshua had glimpsed tears softening the opaque blueness of his eyes. When he had recovered, he said warmly, 'I hope, sir, that you will forgive the temporary weakness of an old man, setting it against age and emotion.'

'Neither of which demands apology, sir, for they are both to your credit.'

Sir Matthew smiled, placing an arm about Joshua's

shoulders. 'I see, now, the charm which captivated Rebecca. Come, Joshua, my boy, let us call in our good friend and counsellor, Dr Peate, for I fear his suspense and agitation must have exceeded even ours!' Then as they walked, smiling, towards the door, he stopped, saying with awkward brusqueness, 'I would have you know that whatever your answer to my question about the estate, I would not have withheld my consent to your marriage with Rebecca.'

'No, sir, I already knew it. It was one of the reasons which formed my decision.'

Sir Matthew declared, with evident satisfaction, 'I believe that Dr Peate will be almost as pleased as I that Rebecca has chosen you.'

'That we have chosen each other,' corrected Joshua firmly.

'Indeed,' agreed Sir Matthew equably, 'it is as well to be accurate, although I fancy that as a family, we have the advantage, since our choice was unanimous.'

As Joshua returned to Newton after dining with Sir Matthew and his old tutor, Dr Peate, the wine and victuals still filled him with warm good humour, as did the convivial, wide-ranging conversation between the three men. It was a meeting that he had anticipated with reserve and misgivings, but needlessly. Sir Matthew was as generous as Rebecca had insisted, and Joshua in no way regretted the pledge he had made to ensure the estate's future although, as he had confessed to its owner, he could wish, most earnestly, for that gentleman's good health and longevity! There was much to be done in his own work as constable. When the time came for him to redeem his pledge, then his labour upon his father's farm, and his work with the law and the people, would hold him in good stead as landowner and, perhaps, justice.

As they left the library, Sir Matthew had hesitated and, turning to Joshua, confided that Rebecca had been much concerned before she left, fearing that perhaps the magnificence and formality of a grand ball might intimidate her friends from the three hamlets. She would not have them hurt, declaring that they could well be bewildered by the rigid etiquette demanded, or put to expense which they could ill afford. Any attempt to recompense them would certainly add to their humiliation.

'I suggested, Joshua, that we hold a special function for her friends from the three hamlets,' Sir Matthew explained, 'something which we could all enjoy, with drinks and delicacies, a small orchestra, or fiddlers for dancing, entertainers, whatever else would seem best. Rebecca bade me seek your advice.'

As Joshua remained silent, he pleaded, 'Please, sir, do not be afraid to speak frankly. I do assure you that they would be most welcome here, at the ball, as upon any other occasion. I consider only their comfort and happiness.'

'I think, sir, that it is a splendid idea! Sensitively expressed,' exclaimed Joshua.

'Then it shall be arranged when Rebecca returns, and the invitations sent without delay. Early in the new year, perhaps, as a fitting start to the season. I think we might declare it to be a celebration of your engagement, for I fancy that is what our conversation earlier signified?' he added mischievously. 'But here is our good friend, Dr Peate.'

Dr Peate embraced his old pupil with warmth and affection. He seemed to have grown old suddenly, a little more stooped and scholarly. His pale silvery hair was still luxuriant, and his eyes alert in the delicately moulded face, despite his aura of gentle abstraction.

'By your expression and demeanour, Joshua, I deduce that I am to congratulate you,' he remarked.

'Thank you, sir.'

'You were ever an open book to me, Stradling.'

'Then I could wish, sir, that my story has the virtue of a happy ending.'

Dr Peate smiled, declaring gallantly, 'I believe, Joshua, that with Rebecca at your side, it cannot be in doubt.'

'Well said, sir!' applauded Sir Matthew. 'I am delighted that you judge my granddaughter such a rewarding pupil.'

Dr Peate pretended to reflect upon the matter, then turning to Joshua he declared slyly, 'Since you are so newly betrothed, sir, I need not burden you with examples of how intelligent, persuasive and devious young women are . . . I merely confess that in my opinion they are different from men. But perhaps you have already discovered that?' he asked innocently.

'It is the sole reason for my marriage, sir,' said Joshua, straight-faced, as Sir Matthew led them equably into dinner.

* * *

Joshua, riding home in the darkness, was forced to return the longer way, by the dipping bridge across the river, his path lighted beneath overhanging trees and high hedges by the glow of a lantern. Once, he surprised a fox upon its travels, its eyes incandescent as burning coals, and a white barn owl glided silently ahead, movement fluid as the falling of a mist. When he finally rode into the yard of the 'Crown', by the truckle of beams from his lantern, he was both cold and exhausted, the grey's hooves clattering forlornly upon the cobbles.

Ossie was immediately beside him. 'Your journey went well, sir?'

'Tolerably.'

'And your . . . quest?' Ossie added diffidently.

'It seems that Sir Matthew will allow me to marry Rebecca.'

'Oh, Joshua, my friend,' Ossie's face was wreathed in delighted smiles, 'allow me to congratulate you!' He pumped Joshua's hand excitedly. 'I am pleased. Oh, I am pleased,' he kept repeating. His voice sharpened. 'But you will not leave us? You will still be our constable?'

'Yes, you may depend upon it!'

Fearing that he had revealed too much, Ossie nodded, then took the grey's bridle and led her away. 'I dare say the mare convinced him!' he called out jauntily over his shoulder.

'No doubt,' smiled Joshua, understanding.

The following morning, the good folk of the three hamlets were agog with the news that their young constable was to wed Rebecca de Breos. Their delight was genuine. Notwithstanding that she was the granddaughter of Sir Matthew and 'almost nobility', was she not, at heart, a true cottager? She had lived among them, worked as they did, and shared their griefs and small pleasures. Nor did she put on stupid airs and graces. No, it was as plain as a pikestaff, she was an aristocrat born! It was there in the breeding, like with a mare, or a bacon, and it could not be hid! Not, of course, that it made her a whit too good for their constable. He was a true gentleman – who could doubt it? Indeed, one enraptured old lady who had watched him ride out to Southerndown Court so far forgot herself as to assert that 'he was dressed from head to toe finer than any knight upon his charger!'

'More like any boar's head at a banquet!' countered Ossie wickedly – frivolity which did not endear him to the old lady who studied his bow legs, declaring tartly that the remark ill became a man 'unfitted even to stop a pig in an alley!' – upon which Ossie, laughingly admitting defeat, retired from the fray.

When the news of the betrothal of the Widow Cleat and Jeremiah was made known, it too became a matter for congratulations and rejoicing. Everyone pronounced it to be an excellent match, and an eminently sensible arrangement. Strangely enough, Jeremiah felt far from sensible and, indeed, had no desire to be so. He was captivated by Sophie Cleat, besotted as any young lover by the sheer wonder of possessing so rare and cherished a prize. Was she not beautiful, warm, affectionate? His open avowal of it made Sophie all of these things, and more. Happiness spilled from them both, embracing Illtyd and all within their sphere. If any hinted that at their age such passion was unseemly, neither responded. Jeremiah, had he done so, might have declared that the miracle was that love came at all, not to whom, or when, and he thanked God for the privilege.

With this in mind, he set off for the church to see the rector and ask that the banns be read upon the first convenient Sunday, so that the marriage might be solemnised early in the new year, there being no impediment to their union.

He found the rector within the church, kneeling devoutly at the altar, so deep in prayer that he was unaware that anyone had entered. Jeremiah crept quietly into a pew at the rear of the aisle, waiting for an opportune time to address him. It seemed to him that the rector straightened uncertainly, stumbling awkwardly as he did so. Jeremiah sat for a moment, then rose to his feet. The priest, alerted by the movement, turned quickly and Jeremiah saw the raw gash upon his forehead and the smeared blood.

'You are hurt, sir.' He hurried forward, face concerned. 'You struck yourself upon the altar steps?'

'No, it is nothing.' The rector took a kerchief from his pocket and dabbed at the wound ineffectually, and Jeremiah could see that the cloth had already been stained with blood. Without his gold-rimmed spectacles, the rector's eyes were mild, curiously unfocusing.

'It is Fleet, is it not? Jeremiah Fleet?'

'Yes, sir, it is.'

'I am glad to see you. It is a long time since you joined in worship with us, but perhaps you have been coming here to pray unnoticed?'

'No,' admitted Jeremiah honestly, 'I have not. After the grief of my wife and child, I could not bear to return here, for I was angry with God and had no love for Him, myself, or others.'

'Yes,' the rector nodded, 'I can understand. Yet is it not a greater tragedy that we reject God's help when we have need of Him most? I wish you had found it in you to come to me for advice or comfort.'

'No,' said Jeremiah, 'for I would have taken neither! I was full of anger and hatred. My grief was all I had, sir, and I had no wish to share it.'

'I came to your house more than once, but you would not answer.'

'Had I done so, I would have reviled and insulted you, and that would not have been proper.'

'But, perhaps, a starting point,' the rector suggested, smiling. 'Yet now you have come of your own volition. What is it that you ask of me?'

Jeremiah told him of his intention to marry the Widow Cleat, and the rector expressed his pleasure and offered warm congratulations. The formalities discussed and completed satisfactorily, Jeremiah thanked him and arose from the pew where they had been seated, to leave. As he did so he saw the rector tremble as he half rose to his feet, then sit quietly down again, face ashen.

'Some water, sir? Or would you have me fetch Dr Mansel? The shock of the wound to your head . . .'

'No,' he waved Jeremiah's protests aside, 'I am perfectly recovered, but there was shock, certainly. Someone hurled a stone at me as I rode here upon my mare.'

Jeremiah was frankly incredulous. 'A child?' he ventured, 'unthinkingly?'

'No, it was well thought out and not one, but several lay in wait behind the hedgerow.'

'You recognised them, sir?'

'No, but I heard their voices. They were people of this parish.'

Jeremiah was appalled and troubled. 'That they should seek to harm a man of God, sir, is unthinkable!'

'I believe it was meant for the justice,' he said drily, 'but sometimes it is hard to separate the two.'

James Ploughman walked the short distance along the rough track which led from his cottage to the farm at Grove. As was the custom, he had built his dwelling in a day and a night, that he might claim right of tenure upon it. It was little more than a rude hut, a box of split wood and daub, with a single room which served for all his needs. To the passing stranger it was little removed from those bare, functional barns which housed beasts and fodder upon neighbouring farms. Had it been described so, Ploughman would have taken no offence. The needs of man and animal were the same: shelter, security and enough food and drink to sustain life. Having achieved them after a bitter, often humiliating struggle he was content. James Ploughman would have admitted honestly, without rancour, that he was after all of less value than a well-cared-for beast.

Although it was but dawn, and the morning air thin and chill, he did not hesitate to go about his duties, taking upon himself every task that he could to ease the

Crocutt family's burdens after Jem's violent death. He grieved for the young widow; it was not easy to care for a farm and its animals, even one as small and unproductive as this, and when there were five mouths to feed and scant winter income, a family's plight could grow desperate.

There was little to do in these barren, frosty days save attend to the beasts and try to harvest the few turnips and winter crops from the icy fields. He had taken to mending barns and fences, gathering and chopping fuel, providing an occasional hare or bird for the pot, and giving the family his protection, for the deaths of Jem and Dai Bando, and the disappearance of his friend, Elwyn Morris, were raw in his mind . . .

As he approached the dry-stone walling that bounded the farmyard, he saw with consternation that a mare was tethered to the branches of an elm tree, hooves fidgeting upon the frozen grass. His first impulse was to run to the farmhouse to see that the widow and children were safe, but some warning instinct halted him and he stepped back into the concealment of a small copse, whence he could keep watch in safety.

Within minutes a stranger hurried past: slight of build, stooped, and from the locks of grey hair which straggled at the nape, 'neath the brim of his beaver, of advanced years. He had no wish to be recognised, for that was all that could be seen of him, so muffled was he in scarves and clothing. He mounted with difficulty upon the chestnut mare, seeming to have a slight stiffness of limb, and without a glance back, face averted, he rode off.

When he was out of sight, Ploughman ran to the farmhouse, boots clattering upon the cobbles of the yard, determined to awaken them or see if they had been harmed. Upon the doorstep lay a stout leather pouch. He lifted it hesitantly and opened the drawstring upon twenty or more gold guineas. Instead of excitement, he found himself trembling with terror, stomach churning. He would dearly have loved to hurl the money away from him to somewhere whence it could never be recovered.

Payment to Jem Crocutt for past services, he wondered, or to buy the widow's silence?

The bolts upon the farmhouse door rasped back and she stood there, hair dishevelled, eyes still heavy with sleep, her nightgown bodice screwed tight in her hand as she looked apprehensively out. Her voice was thin, frightened. 'Something is amiss, James? I heard you running through the yard. It sounded wrong, urgent, and roused me from my bed.'

He handed her the pouch and, bewildered, she opened it. Her face grew pale as she looked at him, eyes stricken. 'Dear God,' she breathed. 'Why? What is it for? I do not understand!'

Dafydd had come from his bed in the inglenook to stand beside her, face anxious.

'Where did you find it, sir?' The boy's voice was sharp.

'Here, upon the doorstep.'

'You saw no one leave it?' asked the widow, glancing apprehensively about the yard.

James Ploughman hesitated, seeing her distress. 'No,' he said firmly, 'no one.'

'Then we must give it to the constable,' she declared, 'for it is not ours to keep.'

272

'I will tell the constable, certainly,' Ploughman promised, 'but the money was meant for you. It is yours by right, left deliberately upon your property. Perhaps money owed to Jem.'

Dafydd's face had grown tense, and his lip trembled. There was the glint of tears at his lower lids. 'He would not have done anything wrong!' he cried defensively.

'Of course not! What an idea!' his mother said, putting an arm protectively about his shoulders. 'It was never in my mind, or anyone else's! We will keep the money, and spend it on the farm. Now, let that be an end to the matter!'

Dafydd nodded, satisfied.

Over the boy's dark head, James Ploughman saw in the widow's troubled eyes a reflection of his own doubt. She was being paid for something as yet unknown to her. It was not an end, but a beginning.

It was Jeremiah who told the constable of the assault upon the justice, as they sat supping their ale at the 'Crown Inn' in celebration of their forthcoming nuptials, with Charity snoring gently at their feet.

'Pale as a ghost, he was,' declared Jeremiah, 'and his eyes like mud-holes in the snow. I tell you, Joshua, I could scarce believe my eyes when he turned from the altar with that wound raw upon his brow.'

'You are sure that he recognised no one?'

'He heard only voices, it seems, from behind a hedge where they lay in wait for him. To tell the truth, he was still weak and trembling when he spoke to me of it, but would not hear of Dr Mansel being called.'

'It is strange, certainly,' mused Joshua, 'for they are friends, and it would be natural to seek his help. You think, perhaps, that he was too confused and shocked by the blow to think clearly?'

'Indeed not! He spoke most lucidly about the affair, and in all our discussions about the wedding.' He paused. 'There was something about mixing his roles as rector and justice . . .'

'You recall exactly what he said? The words?'

Jeremiah shook his head regretfully. 'No, for I was concerned lest he stumble and fall, and what with that, and the calling of the banns plaguing my head –' He shrugged. 'My old mind is not as spruce as it was,' he apologised. 'But wait, when I protested that it was unthinkable for anyone to harm a man of God, he said that it was as justice he was attacked, and by his own parishioners!'

Joshua's face grew grim. 'Then they are either fools and rogues, or good men driven to desperation!'

'Fools, indeed!' declared Jeremiah. ''Tis but a week since the servant of a Cowbridge magistrate was ordered to gaol for a year for drinking a bottle of his master's wine, and first publicly whipped around the Bridewell. I know it for a fact, for the landlord from the ''Lamb Inn'' took a party in his coach to witness it, and after, to Stalling Downs to see the body of a highwayman rotting upon a gibbet.'

'A charming diversion!' said Joshua sarcastically.

'It would not entertain me,' admitted Jeremiah, 'but it goes to show . . .'

'Show what?'

'That if a man is tempted to steal, it had best not be from a justice!'

They laughed companionably.

'Yet there is a serious side to all this,' reminded Joshua, 'for it shows that they are desperate enough to risk gaol, or being transported to the colonies. If they suspect, then, that he has recognised them, even by their voices, they might be forced to kill him.'

'Perhaps it is a personal grudge?' suggested Jeremiah. 'Some criminal he has ordered to prison, or a disgruntled servant, dismissed?'

'There were many involved,' reminded Joshua, 'and he recognised them as parishioners.'

'I cannot believe it!' declared Jeremiah stoutly. 'They must be sheep-stealers, smugglers even, seeking to divert attention.'

'To draw it, rather!' Joshua exclaimed. 'No. I believe that Ossie is right, and that it involves the turnpike trusts – anger about the tolls.'

'There is anger, certainly. I admit, to my shame, that I have ranted and raved upon occasion, and sworn vengeance, as many another,' said Jeremiah, 'for I am as hard pressed as any, travelling as I do to the market with my fish. But had I seen the rector hurt by a stone hurled blindly, in anger, I swear I would be quickly sobered.'

'As others might be whipped into bloodlust, like those viewing the prisoners at the Bridewell?'

Jeremiah was silent.

'If you are approached to join in this madness, you will tell me, Jeremiah? It is likely that your help will be sought.'

He hesitated. 'I will tell you if there is some violence which can be averted,' he promised reluctantly, 'but I will name no names, for my sympathy is with those forced to near-starvation by the greed of others beyond the three hamlets, whose only interest is in bleeding us white, like the blood-sucking leeches they are!'

Joshua nodded.

'Let us turn to more pleasant subjects,' said Jeremiah, nodding to the potman and tapping his tankard as a signal that it needed to be refilled. When it was accomplished, although Joshua would not take more, he said, 'I am bound now, with Charity, for Sophie's cottage, where she prepares me a meal. I swear that she is the finest cook that the good Lord ever put breath into! You are welcome to come, Joshua, for she would be delighted, I know, and always cooks enough to victual the entire population of Newton and Nottage!'

'There is nothing I would rather do, my friend,' said Joshua, 'but there is a duty I cannot neglect.'

'Something more inviting, perhaps?'

'Infinitely,' said Joshua, rising. 'I go with Hardee and the justice to inspect the corpse.'

Jeremiah wrinkled his nose in disgust. 'I will not offer to think of you when I am supping.'

'No, it is better not,' agreed Joshua, smiling, 'or Mistress Cleat will fear that you are ailing, and reach for the brimstone.'

'I would tell her that I was only faint with love for her, and pining,' said Jeremiah shamelessly, 'and she would offer a second helping!'

As Joshua left the 'Crown' to walk to Ezra the Box's

workshop, he was hailed by Doonan, who was rounding the corner to the village with Emrys upon his cart.

'Your hands are recovered?' asked Joshua.

'And the rest of me!' Doonan grinned irrepressibly. 'I return to the quarries next week, and glad to do so . . . for relaxation! Marriage makes too many demands upon me, I swear. I am but a shadow of the man I was!'

'A substantial one,' grumbled Emrys, 'for when you climbed upon my cart, the cob's belly dropped four inches nearer the ground, like your own great beer pot!' He turned to the constable. 'It was you I came seeking, Joshua.'

'Trouble?'

'It might well be so. Someone has broken into the hut upon the quarry floor, which we keep secured and padlocked . . .'

'You have lost something valuable?'

'Explosives. Enough explosives to blow up the whole of the three hamlets!'

Chapter Seventeen

Joshua had barely arrived at Ezra the Box's small workshop and funeral parlour, to be let in by the borrowed undertaker from Pyle, when he heard the rattle and creak of the justice's small coach arriving in the village.

He returned immediately to the doorstep, to see the coachman dismounting and securing the steps that his master might step down in safety. It seemed then that Robert Knight had taken the assault as seriously as Joshua had hoped, and forsworn making himself an easy target upon his horse, or in an open carriage. His clerical garb showed that he came here in his capacity as rector, although it was hardly enhanced by the bloodless pallor of his face, or the bandage swathing his large head like a shrunken nightcap!

He came forward confidently enough, although Joshua had heard him commanding his coachman to wait, and to be ready and alert to take him in the coach upon an instant, should the need arise.

Joshua greeted him civilly, but was set into a quandary as to whether he should allude to the rector's injury. Indeed, he thought, as his eye was irresistibly drawn towards it, it would be hard to ignore it! Like trying to hold a normal conversation in the presence of an embalmed mummy, without letting one's eyes stray towards it . . .

'You have met the undertaker from Pyle?' Robert Knight demanded curtly.

'Yes, sir. You wish to speak to him?'

'No. I have given him the necessary instructions. He will not be needed when we view the cadaver. It has been made ready and set into a coffin for burial.'

'Dr Mansel has examined the body, sir?'

'Yes, and declared his injuries to be consistent with a fall from his horse into the quarry.'

'And the inquest, sir?'

'Tuesday. You will be expected to give evidence, of course. I foresee no complications, for we both know that the identification is nothing more than play-acting, a farce performed for our benefit.'

Joshua nodded.

'Indeed, Stradling,' Knight declared with a touch of his old spirit, 'I have attended so many inquests of late that I am wondering if I should transfer my entire household to the courthouse, and take up permanent residence there!'

Joshua smiled involuntarily. 'There was a matter of some importance that I wished to inform you of, sir.'

'Not another death, I hope, Stradling? My duties as priest and justice will see me permanently engaged! It would oblige me if you could order them better spaced . . .' As he spoke, they heard the clopping of hooves on the cobbles outside and the jingle of harness, and looked out to see a small, open carriage halt beside the justice's coach, and Hardee descending, immaculately attired.

'Whatever it is, it will have to wait, Stradling!' said the justice sharply, 'for this will need all our attention.'

Joshua introduced the two men, and after a bare exchange of civilities they followed him inside. He thought that he had never before seen two people so ill-matched in build and character, and their antipathy was mutual and undisguised.

'You are both magistrate and rector of this parish, I understand,' observed Hardee languidly. His eyes strayed to the justice's bandage with ill-concealed amusement. 'Do you not find some conflict of duties?'

'None at all!' said Robert Knight tartly. 'I prosecute both with equal vigour!'

If Hardee detected an implied warning in the words, he gave no sign.

'Some conflict in dress, then?' Hardee persisted, glancing carelessly towards the justice's head, mouth twitching.

'None, sir!' The justice's dark jowls trembled. 'I come to view the body in clothes suited to the occasion!' His eyes went pointedly to Hardee's frills and brocade and the slim silver-topped cane. 'That is not to say, sir, that when wearing the clothes of one occupation, I neglect the duties of the other!'

Joshua had difficulty in composing his features to the required gravity as the rector stumped inside, protuberant brown eyes blinking rapidly. Hardee followed looking about him with distaste, Joshua at his elegant heels. They pursued Knight across the small yard, through the high-piled timbers, broken furniture and other impedimenta, to a wooden shed.

'Hardly the most salubrious of resting places,' ventured Hardee mildly.

'It is his ultimate resting place which should concern him more,' rebuked the justice tartly, 'as others who practise violence and infamy!'

'If you will show him to me,' said Hardee, plainly bored, 'I will do what is required. I do not relish spending more time in this place than I am forced to!'

'You attend of your own free will, sir, and "this place", as you call it, is the home of a poor, innocent man, who even now lies wrecked and broken as a result of the dead man's callousness.' Knight's eyes met Joshua's and then he looked away hurriedly, opening the door to the hut with intense concentration.

Joshua glimpsed the dead man in the coffin, and relived the horror of turning over his lifeless body in the quarry to show the torn flesh of his face.

Hardee stepped briefly into the shed, silk handkerchief pressed to nostrils and mouth, and with a swift look of disgust, came back into the air.

'You know him?' Joshua demanded.

'No, I have never seen him in my life.' His translucent skin was stained with unnatural colour, and he looked as if he might vomit. 'Now, if you will allow me to leave – ' he hesitated – 'did you not say there were some possessions of his, papers, personal effects?'

'Yes,' agreed Joshua, 'documents, and items of great help and value to us. However, sir, as the man is unknown to you, they can be of no interest or relevance.'

'Of course.' Hardee sucked his full, girlish underlip in his teeth. 'No doubt someone will come forward to claim them.'

'Then they will be expected to satisfy the constable and the court as to their claim upon them, and their part in this affair,' said the justice coldly.

Joshua noticed that his bandages had begun to unfurl and had slipped awry upon one side of his face, giving him a curiously lop-sided look. Yet it in no way detracted from his air of purpose or authority.

They watched Hardee climb into his carriage, epicene, immaculate, and, with a straightening of his grey high hat and a signal to the groom with his silver-topped cane, the light carriage was upon its way, bouncing delicately upon the coarse cobblestones. Hardee sat, staring about him fastidiously, with never a glance in their direction.

'It was as we anticipated,' said Robert Knight, 'he disclaimed all interest in the dead man.'

'Yet not in his possessions. I think he is convinced that we have some scrap of evidence which links him with the corpse.'

'Let us hope then that it will panic him into some mistake. I admit, Stradling, that I find the fellow effeminate and odious, a comic, posturing little bantam, pretending to be a peacock! Yet that is his greatest asset, for it confuses people into believing that he is as ridiculous and harmless as his appearance.'

'Your defence of Ezra, sir, was masterly,' approved Joshua.

'And unexpected, no doubt?' agreed the justice.

'Beside Hardee, Evans takes on the purity and selflessness of a martyr.'

'As he would be the first to admit,' said Joshua, smiling.

'I fear that I overplayed my role as justice, rather than rector, Stradling. I sometimes feel that I lack that humility and charity needed in a clergyman. Had I extended a welcome to Hardee to the parish church, I doubtless would have found myself thundering from the pulpit, "Take no thought for your raiment, what you shall put on".'

' "Vanity of vanities," saith the preacher, "All is vanity . . ." ' quoted Joshua.

'Indeed,' agreed Robert Knight, looking at him sharply. 'Well, what was it you wished to discuss with me, Stradling?'

'A theft from the quarries, sir.'

'The quarries?'

'Yes, sir. Explosives.'

'What quantity?'

'Enough to blow up the three hamlets in their entirety.'

The justice's hand moved involuntarily to the bandage on his head, and he sat down heavily upon one of Ezra's few remaining chairs. He buried his face in his hands and his shoulders trembled, and then shook convulsively. He looked up, and Joshua saw that he was laughing uncontrollably.

'Well, Stradling,' Knight said, wiping his eyes upon his pocket kerchief, 'I admit that you never do things by halves! But, even for you, is it not rather an excessive solution to all of your problems?'

His initial amusement over, Robert Knight swiftly resumed his magisterial status, and every aspect of the theft, its possible implications, and Joshua's findings in his other enquiries were analysed, commented upon, and discussed copiously.

As he took his leave, the justice said casually, fingering his bandages, 'I dare say that you have noticed my injury, Stradling.'

'Yes, sir,' said Joshua, commendably straight-faced, 'an accident?'

'No, I regret to say a deliberate attack. I have reason to believe that it is because I leased my land to the turnpike trust for a period of twenty-one years. You will know the composition of such trusts?'

'I know only that they are usually men of substance – local dignitaries such as yourself – who undertake to improve the roads and keep them well maintained.'

'Indeed, and at first, I am glad to say, that we did so, scrupulously, using parish labour. Having seen it well established, for reasons I cannot go into, I withdrew my pecuniary interest, you understand?'

'Yes, sir, I understand.'

'It seems that the trust over-committed itself and borrowed lavishly. Perhaps they were ill advised, or merely too greedy,' he admitted. 'In any event, the huge interest rates, the legal fees, the hiring of a surveyor and a tollkeeper, plus the building of the tollhouse itself, proved too expensive. To try and recoup at least part of their losses, and avoid bankruptcy, they were forced to farm out their toll-gathering to a "toll-farmer" from outside the area, for a price. The result you know.'

'That the toll fees grow ever more crippling, and the farmers and traders more incensed . . .'

'And therefore turn their anger and violence to those they hold responsible, such as I.'

'Wrongly, sir,' Joshua insisted.

'It is hard for them to reason otherwise,' said the justice quietly, 'and as a priest, I can but sympathise, and understand their anger. Yet, as a justice, violence against any individual or property cannot be tolerated. There will be no more of it!'

Joshua nodded agreement, asking, 'The wound, sir, is improving?'

'It is but superficial, Stradling. The real wound is to my self-esteem – my belief that as a priest, I was trusted by them, held in affection even. That will take a long time to heal, and when it does, the scar will remain to remind me.'

As the constable watched Robert Knight being assisted into his small coach by the liveried coachman, he thought of the first time Rebecca's grandfather had come to visit her in the tiny cottage in the lee of the Burrows. The image of the white-haired gentleman, sitting erect and dignified in his crested carriage, returned to him vividly, and with it the realisation of the changes his coming had brought to them both . . . He felt a fierce surge of love and longing for Rebecca, wishing that she could be there beside him, as of old, flesh softly fragrant and touched with bloom, as fruit warmed and ripened by the sun.

It was only the sudden rattle and creak of the justice's

coach, and the rumble of its wheels upon the cobbles as it drew away, which recalled Joshua abruptly to the present. He saw the horses' tossing heads and the shining curves of their rumps, then, through the window of the carriage, the justice's plump figure, bandage slack against his grainy jowls. Joshua turned away and entered the workshop to seek the undertaker from Pyle who was being temporarily lodged with the relieving officer, Walter Bevan, in his modest cottage across the way. At least, thought Joshua, he had been spared the additional burden of Ezra's whining and complaining, with his mean, ferrety little face aggrieved. How had Robert Knight described him? 'A poor, innocent cottager.' Full marks to the rector for charity, but none for observation or truthfulness!

Elizabeth Crandle, in the smaller of the de Breos coaches, was, at that moment, being driven over the sheep-dipping bridge of grey stone which straddled the Ewenny. Her mother and Rebecca were closeted in one of the drawing rooms of the Court, deep in their preparations for the ball, and Elizabeth had embraced the opportunity to take a drive into the country at the insistence of Sir Matthew. Her visit to her father's prison cell the day before had been more than ever distressing. For once, his mind had been clear and incisive. Aware of both his daughter's compassion and the pitiful degradation all about them, he had wept like a man broken. She had wept with him, trying to give him comfort as best she could, but he could find none. He was tortured upon a rack of his own making. When Elizabeth was leaving, he had begged her most earnestly not to return. It grieved him sorely, he said, that he had brought her to this foul cesspit of filth and squalor. The responsibility was more than his spirit could endure. She had left him staring after her unseeing, tears wet upon the dirt of his face, the small delicacies and clean clothing she had brought him unopened at his feet. She made her way out into the fresh air, the groom solicitous at her elbow, first pressing some coins into the gaoler's eager palm and begging him to procure for her father any small necessities allowed.

She had been unaware of the straw about her feet, with its cockroaches and rat-droppings, not troubling to lift the hem of her gown clear of it. So familiar had she grown with the omnipresent odour of stale urine and human excreta, and the fetid air of the place, that she had learnt to bear them unflinchingly. After a time, even the wretched prisoners with their unwashed bodies and rapaciously grasping hands no longer menaced her thoughts.

Yet, then as now, as she sat alone in the de Breos coach, the picture in her mind was of the haunted ugly face of her father, sculptured in grief, and she could have wished that it was he who had died and Creighton, her brother, left to rot in that God-forsaken place for his brutal, senseless murder of Mary Devereaux.

Elizabeth was aware of the carriage drawing to a gradual halt in a byway, sky above laced with the slim branches of beech trees, their trunks showing silver in the wintry light. She glanced through the window to see Hillier, the old coachman, already climbing from the box.

'Miss Crandle,' he said diffidently, 'I do not know, mistress, if you wish to return to Southerndown Court, or to proceed.'

'Where are we, Hillier? I do not recognise this place.'

'But a few minutes' drive from the highway to the three hamlets, mistress, by way of the turnpike.'

'Then we will drive on to the stableyard of the "Crown" at Newton. There is a visit I would make.'

Ossie, with pitchfork fast in his horny palms, was spearing bundles of hay from the loft and tossing them down on to the cobbles below. He was whistling cheerfully and tunelessly, seamed face intent. He felt neither the keen edge of the wind from the sea, nor the burning in his arm muscles. Ossie was that rarest of creatures, a contented man.

In her small dwelling, the converted coach-loft, Emily Randall was entertaining a visitor with the keenest interest and enjoyment. To do so, in her own surroundings, was a heightened joy after her sojourn in the workhouse at Bridgend, where she had known neither privacy nor possessions. There was an added reason why she appreciated her visitor's company, although she would have welcomed him for his own sake. He was all that remained to link her with Mary Devereaux, the child she had been governess to and had loved so dearly. Now, Mary was dead, coldly and viciously murdered, her grave in the churchyard of the small Norman church of St John the Baptist, across the village green. Emily went there often to sit and meditate under the trees at the graveside – not from any feeling of morbid loss, but because there was a peace and tranquillity there that had wiped away the horror of it all, the unreality. Sometimes she took with her a favourite book of poems, or fine stitching, and had upon occasion found herself repeating some of Mary's favourite verses aloud, so vivid was the girl's presence. It was as if, spiritually, the child had slipped a trusting hand into hers, as of old, drawing them together in understanding . . .

Roland Devereaux, Mary's brother, had come to the hamlets by chance, seeking news of his sister, and had found instead her grave. Having no home or family, it had seemed natural to return from time to time, and when he did, between his sea voyages, it was to the 'Crown' he came. The landlord, Tom Butler, saw that his room was kept ever prepared, and waiting for him.

At first the villagers had held aloof, fearful of intruding upon his need to grieve, but gradually the young officer had become one of their own, respected for his warmth of manner and courtesy. In turn, he respected these hard-working, reserved people for their generosity in seeing that Mary, a stranger in their midst, had not been buried in a pauper's grave, but one tended with love and even in his absence kept bright with cottage flowers . . . Joshua and Devereaux had become firm friends, and to Ossie and the servants at the 'Crown', his visits were a rare treat. He seldom returned without some well-chosen gift or remembrance of his voyage to delight them.

To Emily Randall he wrote vivid, colourful accounts of the places he visited, so that what had been cold words in a text book became alive and real to her. She lived his life of excitement and adventure vicariously, and he, in turn, entered the tranquillity of smoother waters, finding in her world the peace and serenity denied by his. It was a warm, comfortable relationship they shared, secure as that of mother and child, yet free from all demands of passion, jealousy or duty.

They sat together now in the coach-house loft, engrossed in talk about his journey as ship's officer aboard the clipper bound for Valparaiso, his deep blue eyes animated with enthusiasm, face sun-browned 'neath the thatch of corn-coloured hair. There was the unmistakable sound of wheels and hooves upon the cobblestones below as the coach swung beneath the arch, the opening and slamming of a carriage door, Ossie's voice, and the lighter tones of a female one. Then came light footsteps upon the stone staircase outside. Emily, anticipating the hesitant knock upon the door, was already there to open it.

'Why, Elizabeth, my dear, what a welcome surprise,' she exclaimed with genuine pleasure. 'Please come in. Rebecca is with you?'

'No, I came alone. It was not planned . . . An impulse. I had visited my father in prison and felt the need of a friend, someone set apart –' She broke off in confusion as the young man rose to his feet.

'I beg your pardon, sir – and yours, Emily.' She coloured in embarrassment. 'I did not realise that you had a visitor. Please forgive my intrusion, I was impetuous and rude. I will go at once, for I had planned to visit Illtyd.'

Emily put a restraining hand upon her arm. 'No, please stay.' Her fingers grew firm and supportive upon

Elizabeth's sleeve as she said gently, 'Elizabeth, my dear, I present to you a friend, Mr Roland Devereaux. Roland, I have the honour to present Miss Elizabeth Crandle.'

There was a tense silence. Emily, seeing the colour drain from Elizabeth's anguished face, feared that she would faint. Roland, too, stood awkwardly transfixed, then, recovering himself, lifted a chair and carried it to her. When she was safely seated, Emily hurried to fetch her a glass of cool water from the pitcher upon the floor, while Roland studied her with grave concern. She looked up at him remorsefully.

'I am sorry, sir.' Her voice was low, dignified. 'I know that meeting me must surely cause you pain, and perhaps anger . . .'

'Miss Crandle . . .'

'Believe me, I would have spared you . . . There is nothing that I can say or do which can lessen the revulsion and hatred which you must rightly feel for my family, and for me. I ask you only to believe that my sorrow and distress are as profound as yours. I pity you from the bottom of my heart, sir . . .' She buried her face in her hands and began to weep wretchedly. Emily hurried forward, but Roland lifted a hand and motioned her to stay.

'Miss Crandle . . . Elizabeth,' he said quietly, 'you have nothing in all the world to blame yourself for. You were Mary's dearest friend, and she wrote to me often of your kindness and affection. I have neglected my duty in not seeking you out and telling you of my gratitude sooner, ma'am. I regret it deeply.'

She looked up at him, face tear-stained, but calmer

now. 'I thank you for that, sir,' she said gravely. 'I would tell you that my brother Creighton's death was not payment enough for the vileness and wickedness of what he did. It is my father and I, sir, and my mother, who will go on paying the price, as you . . . If I could take the grief of you all upon my shoulders, I beg you to believe that I would willingly do so.'

'It seems to me, ma'am, that you have already done so, adding a guilt for which you are in no wise culpable,' he said compassionately. 'Rebecca has told Joshua and your friends of the burden you have taken upon yourself in visiting the prison. I admire you, ma'am, for your courage and loyalty to those you love.'

Emily, who had listened to the exchange, came forward discreetly with the water, saying as Elizabeth sipped it, 'You are feeling recovered, Elizabeth?'

'Yes, I thank you for your kindness, and you, sir, for your understanding.'

Roland Devereaux had a feeling of unusual, protective tenderness towards this gentle, dark-eyed girl with her sweet oval face. He would have loved dearly to wipe away the tear marks from the high planes of her cheeks and smooth the black wings of hair beneath her bonnet. There was a strength about her, a gravity, which he found appealing.

She rose now to her feet, saying firmly, 'I will take up no more of your time, for I have imposed upon your kindness enough.' She took Emily's hand. 'Illtyd is improving, I trust?'

'Yes, he is almost returned to health, and his spirit and enthusiasm never falter.'

'I had hoped to see him but perhaps I had best post-
pone the visit. I think that I am not fit company, today. I
beg you will give him my affectionate remembrance,
ma'am.'

'Yes, I will do that most willingly.'

Elizabeth held out her hand to Roland Devereaux.

'I bid you good day, sir.' Her eyes shone with sudden
tears. 'Your warmth and kindness are more than I
deserve. It has been a privilege to make your acquaintance, for Mary's sake, and my own.'

He held the small, delicately boned hand firmly in his
own, and looked into her eyes steadily. 'We will meet
again, Miss Crandle – Elizabeth, but as people in our
own right, owing nothing to the past. Strangers, without
bitterness or regret, for none of it is of our doing.'

'Yes, I should like that, sir,' she said.

As Elizabeth rode back in the coach to Southerndown
Court, she felt drained of emotion, physically enervated,
as if she had begun to recover from a long illness. She
was strangely at peace.

Even as she dwelt on it, her father was walking from
the prison, awkwardly shackled, bewildered by his freedom. He had watched a fellow prisoner smash a pitcher
over his gaoler's skull as he lay in a drunken stupor upon
the straw. Then, without thought or direction, Crandle
had followed him into the clean air . . .

Chapter Eighteen

Cavan Doonan was an extremely worried man. His marriage to Rosa was not the cause. On the contrary, he admitted unblushing, it was the first sensible decision he had taken in all his life. Was she not the very soul and essence of what a good wife should be? There was no better homemaker in the whole of the three hamlets! She could cook and sew to perfection, her beauty was breathtaking, her disposition and character would put a saint to shame! No angel could have been more chaste, pure, or so adoring. To those who felt life with such a paragon must be dull, Doonan might have confided that she was also passionate, unexpected, and her lovemaking an art . . .

For the moment his mind was not upon his young bride but upon the theft from the quarries. His ale lay untasted before him as he discussed the matter with Jeremiah, Ossie and Emrys at their usual table in the 'Crown'.

'One of the quarrymen, do you think?' asked Jeremiah, concerned.

'No, I do not!' said Emrys. 'They know the dangers of it. Besides, they would have come prepared, sawn through the padlocks if they were determined upon it.'

'What did they do, then?'

'Went at the shed with axes, smashing into it like fiends possessed! Then they attacked the safe with the same frenzy. It was a miracle they were not killed! It would have been no more than they deserved, the damned stupid louts!' declared Emrys.

'Yes,' agreed Doonan soberly. 'The pity was that they were not discovered, for a few months upon the treadmill at the house of correction might have given them time to reflect upon their stupidity!'

'Or you could have knocked a bit of sense into their silly heads!' exclaimed Ossie. 'But was there no watchman on duty?'

'Drunk!' said Emrys disgustedly. 'They found him senseless, snoring like a pig! I'd have wrung his worthless neck for him!'

'But there will be an enquiry, surely?' demanded Jeremiah.

'Much good it will do them!'

'Locking the stable door after the horse has bolted!' agreed Ossie. 'But whatever would they want with explosives? It makes no sense. Were they hoping to find something else there? Money, wages perhaps?'

'No,' declared Doonan, 'that is the most frightening part of it. They knew exactly what they were looking for – the dynamite and detonators. Yet they were so reckless, savage almost in their attack, creating havoc for no reason save the excitement of it. If they make use of the explosives in the same spirit, then God help us all!'

'As He undoubtedly will! Over to the other side!'

said Emrys in an attempt to lighten the discussion.

Doonan ignored his levity. 'I tell you, it is no laughing matter,' he rebuked, 'especially for those of us with responsibilities, family to protect.'

'No, indeed,' agreed Jeremiah fervently, thinking of the Widow Cleat and Illtyd.

'Could it be those who are angry about the tolls?' ventured Ossie.

'As we all are!' declared Jeremiah. 'But is there a man in the three hamlets who would be callous enough, or stupid enough, to hazard the lives of women and children with explosives?'

There was an uneasy silence, broken when Emrys glanced out of the window, exclaiming incredulously, 'By heaven and all that's wonderful! Illtyd! I tell you it is Illtyd upon his little piebald!'

The four friends ran outside, greeting the hayward with pleasure. To mark the occasion, Tom Butler refused to hear of Faith, the pony, being housed in the stables, but led them both triumphantly within to rapturous acclaim and congratulations from Mrs Butler and Reuben, the young officer Roland Devereaux, the servants, cottagers, and proudest of all, Jeremiah . . .

There was no doubting that the landlord was a generous man, glad of the diversion. It was not wholly business which prompted his relief that Doonan was supping his ale . . .

Unaware that Hugo Crandle was no longer immured within the walls of his prison, his wife was wholly absorbed in the preparations for the grand ball to celebrate Rebecca's nineteenth birthday. She could scarcely remember a time when she had been so excited and stimulated by a task. Perhaps 'task' was the wrong word, she reflected; in truth, the arranging of the ball, and her designation as Sir Matthew's chosen hostess, made it a positive pleasure. True, the invitations should correctly have been dispatched a full month before the event, but there were few, if any, who would cavil at such a mild breach of social etiquette. Certainly Sir Matthew's standing in the community would ensure that an invitation sent at any time would be most eagerly accepted as a rare, exclusive privilege. The visit to the London house with the two girls had been a great success! It had pleased her to be back upon the familiar, predictable whirligig of society, renewing old acquaintanceships and making new. When Sir Matthew's friends called formally upon Rebecca, she was always presented, not as a servant, a paid companion, but as 'My dear friend, Mrs Crandle' – a distinction which allowed her to believe that her circumstances had not altered irrevocably. Unlike Elizabeth, Mrs Crandle was wholly dependent upon the opinion of others, the brittle dictates of fashion, to determine her own value.

There was so much still to be done! True, the dresses were delivered, and quite exceptionally stylish. She was sure that she would look an elegant and fitting hostess for the occasion. Rebecca would be irresistible with her striking, unusual de Breos beauty, and of course Elizabeth too, in her quieter, more ladylike way . . . But why was she daydreaming here, as if she had not a single care in the world? There was yet another meeting with the caterers to be planned, and she must be quite sure that the candles for the chandeliers, and the decorations, would be exactly as ordered, and delivered in time . . .

Watching her indulgently, Elizabeth thought that often now, she felt as if they had reversed their roles, that she was the older, and her mother growing younger and more carefree by the moment. There was no doubt that this frenetic activity diverted her; it filled the hour with a pattern and purpose she had lacked. She was animated, vibrant as of old, her faded auburn prettiness taking on new colour and depth.

For a moment Elizabeth was reminded of her brother, Creighton, with his flame-bright hair and his mocking, restless ways. Then, in contrast, the grave, compassionate gaze of the young officer, Roland Devereaux, came into her mind. He had been kind enough, certainly. Yet what could she hope for from him, or any man?

Her past, present and future had already been decided by others: the brother who was dead, and the man with the ugly, bewildered face, who had wept and implored her not to return, knowing even as he did so that she would come.

Hugo Crandle had seen his fellow prisoner crashing the water pitcher on to his gaoler's skull and securing his keys, but neither the spilt blood nor the man's violence had meant anything to him. There was a confusion in his mind; if he tried to make sense of it, he could not. There was some cloud, he knew, that seeped into his head, obscuring what was hidden there. And within it a rat with vicious needle teeth which gnawed unceasingly, but to no purpose; as soon as it devoured a corner of the cloud and let in the light, the cloud seeped in again, thicker and more frightening. There was darkness there, and menace, but he did not know if it lay in the cloud, the rat, or what was hidden there. If someone could tell him what it was that frightened him, then he would be able to kill it. Only there was nobody there to ask.

There was someone in front of him. Perhaps, if he asked him, he would know about it . . . Was there something he ought to take with him? Food? A coat? No. If he stopped, the man would disappear and then he would never know. Stumbling awkwardly, for he had long been shackled, he made his way after the man, screaming at him to stop, the weakness in his leg muscles a burning pain. The marshes lay all about them, flat and uninviting, the air heavy with rising dampness. The man had stopped now, alerted by his cries, and Crandle tried to make the words into sense.

'Damn you, you stupid old fool! Are you mad? You will bring them all running!' He hit out at Crandle with his closed fist, striking him hard across the mouth. The blow sent him sprawling into the mud, and he lay there for a time, dazed, unable to summon the energy to get to his feet. When he did there was a trickle of blood from his mouth, and wetness had soaked through the thin cloth of his shirt. The man had gone, but he knew that he must find him. The ground beneath his feet bubbled and sucked, oozing black water. One of his shoes was wrenched away in the spongy marshland, filling with viscous dark slime, but he did not retrieve it. He stumbled on, not knowing what drove him, or why.

*　　*　　*

When the messenger from the prison authorities arrived at Southerndown Court, Sir Matthew read the letter he presented in silence. Then he immediately seated himself at his desk and penned a reply. Having made the impression of his seal upon the soft wax, he bade the messenger deliver it without delay to the governor.

After the man had gone, Sir Matthew remained deep in thought for a while, then ordered a manservant to bid his bailiff attend him at once upon a matter of the utmost urgency. When he arrived, the contents of the letter were disclosed, and thoroughly discussed by the two men, before Sir Matthew issued instructions which the bailiff left to implement.

When Elizabeth, in turn, was summoned to the library, she believed it to be over some detail concerning the ball which so occupied them all, and entered smiling and at ease.

Sir Matthew motioned her to be seated, saying gently, 'My dear Elizabeth, I fear I have some disturbing news to impart.'

'My father?' she exclaimed at once. 'He is ill, sir? I feared so, for he seemed so strange, distressed . . .'

'No, my dear,' his voice was compassionate, 'he has escaped.'

She rose involuntarily, clasping her hands together tightly, face drawn with concern and disbelief. 'How? I do not understand. He is so bewildered, sick. I do not think he will be able to survive.'

He came around to her side and took her hands in his, feeling them cold and lifeless. 'The guard was killed. Struck down.'

301

'My father?' she broke in, horrified.

'No, Elizabeth, another prisoner. A violent creature, detained upon a murder charge. One who had nothing to lose. Your father followed him blindly, it seems, but was in no way implicated.'

'Thank God!' Her relief was so great that she stumbled, and Sir Matthew supported her gently back to her chair.

'What will happen to him?' she asked helplessly. 'It is a wild, comfortless place, set around by marshes. Shackled, how can he hope to survive? He will be hunted like some animal.' She began to weep hopelessly, apologising even as she did so.

'Hush, my dear,' said Sir Matthew, patting her helplessly, 'do not distress yourself so, I beg of you. I have given orders that the bailiff and ten of the estate workers shall go at once, upon horseback, and seek him.'

'But if they find him, sir? What then? He will be punished, and returned to that vile place. He would be better dead! Oh, I do not think that I can bear it, Sir Matthew, for his suffering tears my spirit, as it broke his.' She looked up at him, face anguished.

'Your mother?' Sir Matthew began awkwardly.

'No, sir! I will not have her told . . . It will serve no purpose, save to distress her. She is happy now for the first time in many months – ' She broke off, unable to continue.

'I have ordered the carriage, my dear,' he said compassionately, 'so that when he is found I will be there waiting with my own physician, in case he has need of such help.'

'Then I will come with you, Sir Matthew, if you will allow me.'

'Do you think it wise, my dear? It will be a sad, even bitter, experience . . . For him, too.'

'Then he will have need of my support, sir, and affection.' She wiped the traces of tears roughly from her face with her fingers, and stood up. 'I will get my bonnet and cape, sir.'

'You wish Rebecca to come with you, Elizabeth?'

'No, sir. I would wish to see him alone. He will be pained and humiliated enough. I would not want others to witness his hurt.'

He nodded, understanding. 'He is a fortunate man, my dear.'

'How fortunate, sir? I know that he was punished justly. What he did was wicked and wrong. He has suffered the death of his only son, and a physical and mental degradation beyond belief. It is a punishment that has crippled his mind. No, sir. I cannot think him fortunate.'

Sir Matthew took her hand and led her to the door, pausing there to look down at her ravaged young face. 'He has you, Elizabeth. That is why he is fortunate.'

Hugo Crandle could no longer see the way before him. A pale mist arose from the marshes, swirling, thinning, like some strange emanation that could change at will. There was a numbness in his legs and feet, a heaviness, but no longer any pain. He supposed that whoever it was had shackled him had done so in order to pursue him. The shackles and chains were of iron; he could feel them dragging him down, forcing him deeper into the dank slime. The strange thing was that his head and flesh felt light, disembodied almost, as if he might dissolve away and be absorbed in the mist itself, drifting with it, without texture or form.

A wind had sprung up suddenly, smelling of decaying vegetation, the rottenness of marsh gas, its cutting edge keen. There was a light ahead of him, but like no other light he had ever known. It skimmed and danced, elusive as a firefly, winging for ever out of his reach . . . It seemed to lure him deliberately, tantalising, restless, materialising first in one place, then another, until he grew confused, railing at it to stop. Somewhere beyond an animal was baying – a forsaken sound, as if caught in the teeth of a trap. Crandle did not know why, but the tears were running down his cheeks for a red-haired fox, arrogant, bloodstained, and already dead.

The gaolers from the prison, with their dogs and pistols, had found the prisoner who had murdered the guard. Beaten and exhausted, he had crouched like some wild animal cornered, then sprung at them in his shackles, desperation lending him strength and fury. Even when held to the ground, he had not been subdued, screaming and spitting vengeance at his captors as they led him away. It was the sight of him being dragged back in his chains, amidst the cries of his gaolers, and the frenzied barking of the dogs, which Elizabeth witnessed from the coach where she sat with Sir Matthew. Seeing her pale face at the window, the captive had lunged towards her, screaming obscenities, face contorted to near-madness, to be restrained by his leg irons and the guards, one of whom struck at him with the butt of his pistol. Sir Matthew pulled her gently away, but the sight of it stayed with her, haunting her mind.

Perhaps having recaptured the man who had murdered their companion, the fate of Crandle mattered less to the searchers. They had achieved their aim, each one of them conscious that it might have been his blood spilt upon the prison straw. A few remained, but their purpose had been blunted and their searching was now desultory and disorganised.

It was one of Sir Matthew's men who found Hugo Crandle huddled against the wind, arms wound protectively around his head as if to ward off a blow. He went with them without a sound, allowing himself to be led away like an exhausted animal, too cowed and bewildered to resist.

Despite Sir Matthew's restraining hand and the pleas of the physician, Elizabeth wrenched open the door of the carriage and ran to her father, flinging her arms about him, despite the filthiness of his clothing, feeling the coldness of the flesh beneath the wetness of his shirt. He looked at her in puzzlement, eyes bleak and uncomprehending.

'I do not know you,' he said as she led him to the coach. 'I do not know you.'

The only thing which sustained Elizabeth during that pitiful journey was the insistence of Sir Matthew's physician that her father would not, under any circumstances, be returned to his cell. He would be taken immediately to the prison hospital. It was a grim, dispiriting place, he admitted, and she would not be allowed to enter it, but he would go with the patient and keep watch upon him until he was settled there. He was willing to sign a declaration that Mr Crandle was unfitted to be returned to prison and Sir Matthew, as a justice, would willingly corroborate his findings. There would be no objection, he felt sure, from the prison authorities, and he would petition the governor as a matter of urgency. Elizabeth watched her father go. She was dry-eyed and numbed of feeling, as if it were some stranger she glimpsed, without curiosity, from the window of a coach. She seemed to have no ties of blood, or memory, with that pitiful husk being led away.

Sir Matthew watched her compassionately, seeing the exhaustion upon her young face. 'Elizabeth, my dear,' he said gently, 'there is nothing I can do to ease the cruel anguish which you have felt today, but, believe me, I grieve for you.' He took both her hands into his own, rubbing life into their coldness. 'I promise you that he shall remain in that place only until the papers for committal are signed. I shall see that he is removed, at once, to a private asylum, where he will have care and kindness for all of his life.'

Elizabeth wept then, withdrawing her hands from his and throwing her arms impulsively around his neck, burying her face against his breast. He felt the warmth of her tears and the trembling of her thin shoulders as he turned to comfort her.

'I thank you, sir,' she said, when she was able to speak. 'There are no words warm or loving enough for the gratitude I feel, for it would break my heart to leave him there. We are not deserving of such kindness.'

'Not true,' he said, gravely. 'Your courage and dignity

today have been exceptional. You have done far more than anyone has a right to hope for, even a father. One day, Elizabeth, when his mind is restored, he will recognise the love you feel for him, and bless you for it.'

He lifted his silver-topped stick and bade the coachman drive them home.

After much persuasion upon Rowden the miller's part, and not a little resistance from Ezra, the abrasive little undertaker had been induced to turn his talents to making a new cart for his host. He had approached the task with little enthusiasm, claiming that such exertion would, undoubtedly, see him into an early grave. His friend, the miller, was diplomatic enough not to own that this would be an unlooked-for bonus. He was a good-natured fellow, and quick to admit that Ezra, for all his grumbling and fractious ways, was an excellent craftsman. Ezra was soon so absorbed in his carpentry that he forgot to limp or groan with such harrowing realism. There was no doubt about it, with the addition of the wheels commissioned from Daniel the wheelwright, it was a carriage fit for the Queen of England herself.

If its first passenger was infinitely less noble, his progress into the village was as triumphantly heralded. Ezra the Box was coming home! Upon the instructions of the vestry, two willing paupers had been paid to scour his house from top to bottom. His tools and household artefacts had been replaced or mended, and all was spick-and-span for his arrival.

Conveyed upon the gleaming new cart, injured leg

outstretched before him and the ginger-haired cat clutched in his arms, Ezra nodded from left to right like some revered eastern potentate, acknowledging the bemused peasantry. His injuries and enforced absence had turned him into a legend – a case, perhaps, of absence making the memory grow weaker.

The miller, it must be said, had tears in his eyes at the reception afforded them, for he was a sensitive, kindly man, with a genuine affection for the cantankerous Ezra. He helped him down tenderly from the cart and, setting the key into the lock, escorted his friend into the restored workshop, looking about him with delight and amazement.

'Well, what do you think of it, Ezra?'

'Of what?' said Ezra, releasing the cat and stumping through to the living room, limp as pronounced as his familiar scowl.

Upon the instructions of the justice, Joshua had managed to secure the services of a pauper to act as companion and bodyguard to the irascible undertaker, upon the firm avowal that Ezra would not be expected to supply him with drink or victuals. The constable had ordered that all the newcomer's meals were to be supplied and served from the 'Crown Inn' – a concession which delighted the pauper, but did not endear him to Ezra, whose frugality was outraged by the lavishness of the landlord's fare. To exacerbate matters, the ginger cat spurned Ezra's leftovers as stale and unappetising, its palate having grown refined at the miller's. It attached itself slavishly to the pauper who obligingly fed it with titbits that made Ezra's mouth water with their succulence, and he was hard pressed not to snatch them from the animal's dish.

Tom Butler, hearing with amusement of the damage his meals had wrought, promised to supply Ezra with the same victuals, free of charge, for as long as the pauper was needed to protect him. It is doubtful whether the undertaker realised that the plan was hatched by Joshua. He certainly treated his house guest with new respect and consideration, fearing that any meanness would provoke him into leaving. Against all expectations, the two men became firm friends, the pauper staying on as apprentice in Ezra's undertaking business.

If the outcome was unexpected, it indubitably brought advantage to all concerned – Joshua, Ezra, the pauper, but most of all, the cat.

Chapter Nineteen

With Sir Matthew's commitment to finding an asylum
for her father where he would be safe and kindly treated,
Elizabeth Crandle found a measure of peace and normality returning to her life. Her father's retreat from
reality troubled her greatly, yet it was not surprising that
the loss of a son and his own incarceration in that foul,
inhuman place should cripple his mind. Perhaps it was
merciful; that blotting out of life and memories too painful to bear. It was a relief that Elizabeth would gratefully
have sought in the dark times when she had witnessed his
degradation. She could only pray, most earnestly, that
with compassionate medical care his mind and troubled
spirit would be healed.

To Mrs Crandle nothing of the events of that terrible
day was revealed, upon Elizabeth's insistence. She was
merely told that Sir Matthew had arranged for him to be
treated for minor physical disabilities at a small hospital
of his own choosing. This she apparently accepted
unquestioningly, professing no desire to see him, or
indeed any further interest in his condition or whereabouts. Like Hugo Crandle himself, she seemed to have
the facility for blocking out all those things which were

painful or disagreeable to her. To Elizabeth's relief, she immersed herself in her growing social life in the district and her plans for Rebecca's birthday ball. If Sir Matthew thought it unnatural that she had not remarked her daughter's evident distress and grief, he said nothing. He reasoned that her self-absorption freed Elizabeth from at least one emotional burden, and confided in Rebecca some of the more harrowing details of the escape which he knew that her friend would feel never able to reveal. He saw that there was a real bond of affection between the two girls, and Rebecca would instinctively respond to Elizabeth's need, without being overtly protective. So it proved, and Sir Matthew was pleased when the old, easy bantering and youthful nonsense returned, although he obligingly pretended to be irritated by it. As he confessed to Dr Peate, their tutor, 'It was but a few brief months ago that I thought myself alone in the world, save for the company of good friends like yourself, sir. Now I have discovered the pleasure of not one granddaughter, but two, for Elizabeth has grown as dear to me over the past few weeks as if she were my own flesh and blood.'

Dr Peate was careful to let fall this confession to Elizabeth by the sheerest accident. He was a firm believer in the healing power of love; was not his own philosophy as a priest dependent upon it?

Rebecca, meanwhile, was awaiting the arrival of Joshua at Southerndown Court. It was to be a brief visit, for his duties as constable were pressing. He would ride over the Warren and beaches upon his grey, and then take the carriage to convey Rebecca upon a visit to his parents' farm, at her firm request. Joshua had informed them of the plan, and had no doubt that scrupulous preparations had been made to entertain them. He remembered with pain and humiliation how discourteously she had been treated upon her first and only venture into their world, when she had been dismissed as a poor shellfish gatherer, unworthy of their attention or civility.

If she had any misgivings about returning in her new role as Rebecca de Breos of Southerndown Court, she showed none as she climbed into the curricle beside him, helped by Elizabeth, who had come out to witness their departure.

'Your friends, Mistress Randall and Roland Devereaux, send you their warmest regards. I was to convey them most specifically,' said Joshua, surprised to see the warm colour flood Elizabeth's skin.

'I thank them for it, sir, and would ask you to return their courtesy with' – she paused, before adding '– appropriate greetings of my own.'

Strange, thought Joshua as he stirred the horses into life, it was quite unlike Elizabeth to be so hesitant and indecisive. What in heaven did 'appropriate' mean? Civil? Fond? Affectionate, even? His attention was diverted by the need to negotiate a curve in the carriageway, and he gave the matter no more thought.

'You will have observed, sir,' said Rebecca as soon as the delicate carriage was safely on the highway, 'that my grandfather has allowed me to drive with you unchaperoned, although Mrs Crandle confessed to being mildly scandalised.'

'I believe, ma'am, that there is method in such

madness!' returned Joshua. 'It puts me upon my honour as a gentleman not to become over-familiar in my attentions. Had we a duenna, then I would feel honour-bound to elude her clutches.'

'How?'

'By making the carriage bolt, happily tipping her out. Or by sending her upon some ludicrous errand – a trip to London, perhaps, to retrieve a lost handkerchief?'

'I would not have credited you with such deviousness, sir!' she confessed, laughing.

'Ah, but you are a woman, and gullible,' he said wickedly, 'which explains my success with chaperones. Although, I readily admit that you are the most beautiful woman I have ever seen, also the most elegant, intelligent and . . .'

'Rich?' she supplied slyly.

'That too . . .' They laughed together companionably.

'Rebecca,' he began more seriously, 'I know that last time you came to the farm you were disillusioned, made unhappy, by your treatment. There is no excuse or apology that can suffice. I would not have you hurt again.'

'I am not that young girl, Joshua,' she said gently, 'naïve, expecting more than people can give. I am a woman in my own right. I told you then, as I tell you now, I am not simply Rebecca the cockle-maid, nor Rebecca the granddaughter of Sir Matthew de Breos. They are part of me, certainly, but I hope that I am more.'

He nodded. 'You are everything I desire or need in a woman, Rebecca,' he declared, letting his hand stray from the reins to fasten over hers. 'You were beautiful the first time we made this journey, in your pretty sprigged gown of blue cotton, and the bonnet which matched the colour of your eyes. Today, I swear you are even more beautiful.' He leaned over to kiss the curve of her mouth.

'Unhand me this instant, sir,' commanded Rebecca, laughing, 'or you will have me toppled into a ditch, like your gullible chaperone. My gown will be spoilt and my beauty marred, and I will make no impression at all upon your family! Besides which, my grandfather would be forced to come after you with a blunderbuss for impugning my honour.'

'Would that it were so!' exclaimed Joshua, flicking at the reins.

'Indeed! Would that it were so!' echoed Rebecca, eyes shining mischievously, as they entered upon the carriageway to the farm.

The atmosphere upon Rebecca's first meeting with Joshua's parents had been awkwardly strained, and it might well have been so again had not Rebecca firmly taken the initiative. As it was, the changes in her fortune, and the memory of his rudeness to her, made Joshua's father clumsy and guilty, and his mother defensive. They had anticipated this reunion with the girl whom Joshua had determined to marry with little optimism.

'How pretty you look, and how well your gown becomes you, my dear,' exclaimed Joshua's mother sincerely, regarding her with approval.

'And this one,' said Rebecca, smiling, 'I did not make myself, ma'am!'

Joshua's mother regarded her doubtfully, remembering her indiscretion, but seeing Rebecca's lips twitching with real amusement at the memory, began to laugh too. Then Rebecca bent over without embarrassment and, as if it were the most natural thing in the world, kissed Charlotte Stradling upon her soft cheek, saying, 'Grandfather and I so look forward to seeing you at the ball, ma'am. He bids me tell you that it would give him the greatest pleasure if you would dine with him before then. If it is agreeable to you, he will call and arrange a time most convenient to you.'

Joshua's mother, as elegantly assured as Rebecca remembered her, smiled with real warmth and said that they would be delighted, but his father seemed still ill at ease. He was as unlike Joshua as it was possible to be, both physically and in character. He was thickset, dark in every aspect, by temperament taciturn and brooding.

'Mr Stradling,' said Rebecca, going to stand beside him and putting her hand lightly upon his arm, 'it would make me happy, sir, if you would accept Grandfather's invitation.'

He made the slightest gesture of withdrawal, remaining silent and expressionless.

She looked directly into his dark eyes and said, voice so low that neither Joshua nor his mother would overhear, 'We started off upon the wrong foot, sir, when first we met. I was a foolish, headstrong girl. I admit, now, that my love for Joshua blinded me to all else, and you must have found me irritating and heedless.'

Philip Stradling was surprised into an involuntary shrug of disavowal.

'I confess, sir, that were Joshua my son, I too would have thought it an unlikely alliance doomed to failure. I would have demanded better for him. My reaction would have been as yours.' She was regarding him frankly, clear eyes calm and unwavering. 'We were both concerned solely with Joshua's future happiness, then as now.'

He nodded, hesitating. 'I was rude,' he blurted clumsily, 'I regret it! My wife tells me I have a brisk, abrasive manner, which gives offence!' He flushed awkwardly. 'I lack the social graces.'

'You have the greater advantage of honesty, sir.' Her eyes twinkled.

'Then I had best be honest and admit that when we last met, I was pig-headed and ill-mannered,' he acknowledged gruffly.

'A failing I have oft been charged with, sir. It seems we have more in common than regard for your son.'

'I do not expect to change dramatically,' he warned.

'Nor I, but there is a value in consistency. We shall know where we stand.'

Almost against his will, his mouth twitched, and he smiled broadly. 'We stand nearer, ma'am,' he admitted, 'a step nearer.'

Joshua and his mother had been conversing half-heartedly, their attention straying to the other pair, trying to judge from their expressions the gist of the exchange. Seeing her husband smiling, Charlotte Stradling moved tentatively towards them, to hear her husband declare, 'Yes, Rebecca, I shall certainly look forward to meeting Sir Matthew at the earliest opportunity. As for the ball, I hope that having discharged the necessary courtesies to your grandfather and Joshua, you will grant me the honour and privilege of a dance.'

'I accept with the utmost pleasure, sir.' She sank into a deep curtsey. 'I shall inscribe it upon my card at the very first opportunity!'

He bowed with exquisite formality, straightening to meet his wife's surprised eyes. He frowned. 'I have long thought, Charlotte, that we do not entertain enough,' he declared, testily. 'We are in danger of growing insular, alienated. Perhaps, when the betrothal is officially announced, you might arrange a small celebration for our friends. Nothing too lavish . . .'

'Of course, Philip,' she said faintly.

'Joshua, what are you grinning at?' he demanded. 'I see no cause for levity! Sometimes I wonder if you are bereft of your senses . . .' He turned to Rebecca, quite unabashed, as the parlour maid entered to announce luncheon. 'Miss de Breos, may I have the honour to accompany you?'

She placed her hand formally upon his, bending her head to whisper, 'Where do we stand now, sir?'

'United, my dear,' he said with satisfaction.

The meal was congenial and pleasant, with the four diners agreeably relaxed. Certainly they were all relieved that thanks to Rebecca's diplomacy, the abrasiveness of their last encounter had not been resurrected. Rebecca's only regret was that she had not met Aled, Joshua's brother, who had been so welcoming and gallantly supportive upon that disastrous day when she most had need of a friend. He had been forced to journey to Cardiff upon urgent business, it was explained, and was unlikely to return before nightfall.

With the prospect in mind of riding the grey back to Newton, after escorting Rebecca to Southerndown Court, Joshua was forced to caution them several times about his need to leave without delay. Finally, and with reluctance, his pleas were heeded and Rebecca's pretty coral-pink bonnet was brought with her matching travelling coat. There was a further hiatus while the history of its purchase, in France, was recounted to Charlotte Stradling, who was lavish in her admiration and delight. Rebecca kissed her impulsively upon her fragrant cheek, declaring how fashionable was Mrs Stradling's own dress with its slimmer, less outrageous leg-o'-mutton sleeves and the small, stylish bustle, the colour so subtle and delicate a blue that it perfectly complemented her fair colouring and eyes.

'You have such good taste, ma'am, and natural elegance,' confessed Rebecca truthfully, 'that I would dearly value your help in choosing my wedding gown and trousseau, if you do not consider it too great an imposition upon you. I have no mother or family to whom I may appeal . . .'

Charlotte Stradling was undeniably touched and flattered, declaring that nothing in the world could give her greater pleasure, for she regretted deeply the lack of a daughter, although she dearly loved her boys.

There was more unexpected excitement and delay when Aled arrived, swearing that had the horses flown any quicker, they would have assuredly sprouted wings like Pegasus, and left the byways for the sky! He had been determined upon meeting Joshua's lovely bride-to-be, although it must be plain to anyone with even half an eye that his brother was quite unworthy of such a treasure as Rebecca!

'I take it, ma'am,' he said, smiling, 'that I have no need to invite you, as once before, to remove yourself to the warmer, more salubrious, air of the pigsties?'

They all joined in the laughter, including Philip Stradling. As they left, to step into the curricle, he came forward to help her up beside Joshua.

'Rebecca,' he stated baldly, 'it is not easy for me to say this –' he fidgeted uneasily – 'it is not because your position, your circumstances have changed that I accept you, you understand? It is because you have not changed. It was I who was at fault for not using what little sense God gave me.' He looked at her in puzzlement as she bent to kiss his plump, darkly shadowed cheek. Joshua waved, and they left him standing there, sullen, uncomfortable with himself and others. Then he touched his fingers to his face and, smiling, turned away.

Having returned safely to Southerndown, and his respects paid to Sir Matthew, Mrs Crandle and Elizabeth, Joshua led the grey along the wide carriage drive of the Court, Rebecca at his side.

It was beginning to grow dusk, the December air chilled by a wind from the sea. They saw the Channel spread below them, pewter-coloured, merging into the greyness of sky, identifiable only by plucked feathers of white foam.

Shielded from the house by the curving drive with its

glossy-leaved shrubs and bare woodland, Joshua let the mare crop at the salt-laden grass, reins trailing. Then he drew Rebecca towards him, his back turned to the sea, to afford her shelter from the wind. She had unfastened the strap of her bonnet and held it loosely in her hand, her dark hair streaming swift and flowing as black water. Joshua traced the delicately boned outline of her oval face, with its wide cheekbones and generous mouth. Against her warm, olive skin, the crescents of her brows and her thick, silky lashes gleamed with a bluish-blackness that heightened the vivid clarity of her remarkable blue eyes. She regarded him steadily and with such naked, unmistakable love that Joshua felt it absorbed into his own flesh and feeling, as violently as if they were physically joined. He kissed her gently, then with growing fierceness and passion, feeling her lips part softly as they yielded to the soft thrust of his tongue which explored the depth and sweetness of her mouth. His need for her grew increasingly urgent and demanding, his bones crushing the softness of her flesh, sensing her breasts grow firm and hard as his desire stirred response in her, feeling quickening his blood. Then suddenly, unexpectedly, he thrust her away from him, his face flushed, eyes still softly unfocusing.

'Oh, Rebecca!' he said, 'this is madness.' He buried his face in his hands, trying to control the violence and pain still ripping through him, and the trembling that brought weakness to his limbs, like the aftermath of some long-felt illness. Rebecca's eyes were bright and her bonnet, released, had blown across the grass to nestle against the dark leaves of a laurel, like some wind-scattered blossom.

'I had best go,' he said, 'for I swear, Rebecca, if I stay, I shall be tempted to lift you upon the grey behind me, and take you to some place where I shall make love to you every hour of every day.'

'Then you had best retrieve your mare, sir, for I fancy she is already halfway there of her own volition!'

Horse and bonnet retrieved, Joshua, fingering the bridle, said quickly, 'I will not say that I regret what happened, Rebecca.'

'No, sir. Merely, as I, that you regret its lack of completion, the strictures that forbid it.'

'Not even that,' he said, 'for I would take you gently, tenderly, Rebecca, that first time, and in our own soft bed . . .'

Rebecca looked at him for a long moment, then touched his hand before lifting it tenderly to her cheek and saying, voice low, 'It will grieve me to wait, sir, for I confess, without shame or reserve, that my most urgent desire is to be at one with you, in flesh as in spirit . . .'

Her eyes were unnaturally dark, and Joshua could not doubt that the intensity of her longing was as fierce as his own. Much moved, he took the hand which she held against her cheek, turning it to kiss her soft palm. Looking up, he saw the gleam of tears upon her dark lashes.

'My love for you fills all of my life,' she said simply. 'Now and always . . . but I must offer these few brief months to my grandfather, Joshua, for he has need of me. I owe him the nearness and affection he has been denied . . . although he would never demand them of me . . . I am all that remains for him.'

His fingertips gently wiped away the tears which had spilt, now, upon her cheeks, as she said most earnestly, 'I beg you to believe that it is my duty, and not lack of love or desire for you that keeps us apart . . .'

'Not keeps us apart, but draws us closer, my love . . .' He kissed her with great tenderness, feeling a stirring of warmth and protectiveness as deep as his earlier passion. He touched her chin, uplifting it gently to look steadily into her eyes, saying with honesty, 'I love you, Rebecca, for what you are: warm, loving and constant. I would have it no other way.'

He set his foot into the stirrup and swung himself on to the grey, then bent down to kiss her upturned face. 'The remembrance of holding you in my arms will stay with me, to warm me, in many a cold winter's bleakness. I love you, Rebecca de Breos.'

'As I love you.'

He stirred up the grey and, saluting her gravely, rode away. She watched until he was out of sight, and stayed motionless until the sound of the mare's hoofbeats upon the carriageway had softened into silence. Then, with a smile touching the corners of her mouth, she replaced her bonnet upon her unruly black hair and walked, slowly, back to the house, reluctant to share so personal a happiness.

With the darkness deepening about him, Joshua pulled the collar of his tiered coat closer about his neck to ward off the coldness of the wind. He had foolishly refused the services of a lantern, and now he regretted it, for the winter darkness had fallen swiftly and, but for the muted lightness of the dry-stone boundary walls and the mare's sure-footedness, his progress would have been painfully hindered.

As he approached the hump-backed dipping bridge which crouched across the high, wooded banks of the Ewenny river, he heard men's cries, with the muffled splash of water, then saw the bob and weave of lighted lanterns along its far reaches.

'Poachers!' – he thought, swiftly reining in the grey that he might dismount to investigate. But the offenders, hearing approaching hoofbeats, had already extinguished their lanterns. There was a renewed flurry of noise and splashing as they crashed their way to the bank, slithering and falling as they heaved themselves ashore, then into the woodland, and silence.

Well, Joshua thought ruefully, as he remounted, their thieving has been postponed briefly, at least. Without a lantern he was powerless to identify them, or even pursue them. Besides, it was a matter for the estate bailiffs. He had no jurisdiction here, simply the rights of an ordinary citizen. Yet his immediate reaction had been to accost them, with no thought of the dangers involved, so ingrained had become his sense of duty.

There were urgent duties of his own to perform, as the justice would curtly have reminded him, he reflected as the mare's hooves clattered over the stones of the bridge. Yet he could not feel guilt or regret that today had been time set apart. In Rebecca he found renewal and strength: a cleansing, cool as the river waters which flowed beneath. Today, Rebecca and his family, the people whom he loved best in all the world had drawn closer in understanding. It was more than he had dared to hope.

When the constable finally rode under the lantern-lit archway to the 'Crown', its beams making a rainbow-coloured halo of splintered light, he delivered his mare into the keeping of one of the stable lads.

'Ossie is not here?' Joshua asked, surprised.

'No, sir, he has gone to a wassail party in the village, a celebration by the newlyweds – Doonan, that big, red-headed Irishman who works in the quarries, and his bride. Ossie did not tell you, sir?'

'I had forgotten,' confessed Joshua, as indeed he had, for his presence had been requested some weeks before and events had pushed the invitation, and his acceptance of it, to the back of his mind.

'From all accounts, sir, it will be a night to remember. Or, maybe, not remember,' the lad exclaimed, grinning, 'for I heard that the brewery delivered a hogshead there today! It will be needed; it seems most of the people in the three hamlets are already there!'

Joshua was half tempted to retire to his bed, but knew that his absence would be noted, even in that exuberant throng, and it would have grieved him to hurt Rosa's feelings, or Doonan's, for he was deeply fond of them both. After a brief visit to his cottage to freshen himself at the pump and brush away the dusty ravages of the journey from his boots and clothing, he abandoned his outer coat and, still attired in his elegant finery, walked the short distance to the newlyweds' cottage.

It seemed to Joshua that the stable lad had under-estimated the size of the gathering. From the noisy excitement and general merriment which erupted into the street outside, the entire population of the county appeared to have gathered there! As he stepped over the threshold, bearing his small welcoming gift, as was the custom, Rosa ran to greet him, embracing him affectionately, impulsively demanding news of Rebecca, Elizabeth and the farm. Her transparent skin was vividly lit with colour, and Joshua had never seen her so animated and pretty. She led him into the midst of the celebrations, calling, 'Cavan! Joshua has come to join us! I said he would come!'

Cavan forced his way through the surge of revellers, bearing a massive wassail bowl high above his unruly red hair. His skin shone with heat and scrubbing, and his smile of welcome was as evident as the gap from his missing front tooth. Joshua was immediately proffered a drink of mulled ale from the monstrous crater of the bowl. Were it not for Doonan's strength, he felt sure that the twelve handles sprouting 'neath its rim would have justified the need of a man apiece to lift it. Gripping two of the handles firmly, and steadied by the Irishman, he managed to take a tentative mouthful, re-emerging spluttering and coughing from its depths to the applause of the company. As he smilingly dried his face upon his kerchief, and mopped at his shirt frills and weskit, Jeremiah's unmistakably deep voice called out, 'A toast, now, Joshua! You must declare a toast!'

'To Rosa, and Cavan our host,' cried Joshua, his voice clear in the expectant silence, 'may they be ever richly surrounded by love for each other, and the warmth of friendship.'

Doonan, still bearing the wassail bowl, nodded at him, satisfied, and looked at his Rosa with such naked pride upon his battered, unlovely face that Joshua felt humbled.

'A graceful toast, gracefully expressed,' approved Jeremiah, moving to his side with Sophie Cleat and Illtyd.

'And honestly meant,' responded Joshua, 'for there can be nothing more rewarding than the blessing of true friendship.'

'Save, perhaps, the blessing of a family,' said Jeremiah, putting one arm protectively about the widow's shoulders, and the other about Illtyd.

'Then God has doubly blessed us in granting us both, my dear,' declared Sophie, her eyes bright.

There could be no doubt that the party was a resounding success for all save the innkeepers of the parish, and since Doonan had sensibly invited them, they would have been churlish indeed to have brooded upon their losses. There was an air of informality about the entertainment, spontaneous gaiety which was not due solely to the lavishness of the hospitality. True, the fiddler had dipped so unwisely into the hogshead and wassail bowl that he had to be lifted bodily into the fresh air of the yard to recover his senses, but since his playing had become increasingly wild and discordant, no one minded. In fact, as Emrys reasoned, there was no room to dance – the hubbub drowned the music, and he'd be damned if he could not play better himself upon two cracked bando sticks!

Joshua and the company were accepting rich slices of Rosa's wassail cake, a delicious apple confection, and admiring the great Ewenny pottery wassail bowl, borrowed, she confessed, from Tom Butler, when there was a terrifying commotion from the street outside.

Doonan had rushed to open the door, gigantic fists ready for action, with Joshua, Emrys, Jeremiah and Roland Devereaux at his heels, when they broke into such amused and prolonged laughter that it had the women crowding to see the spectacle – for such it was.

Upon the highway stood a most fearsome beast, a horse's skull upon a long pole covered with a white sheet. Its fierce glass eyes were beer-bottle ends, and it was lavishly decorated with streamers and rosettes of bright ribbon set about its black calico ears. A fiddler and a man with a concertina made music, and the beast swayed and danced grotesquely, its fearsome jaws snapping in time to their rhythm. A nightmare, indeed! The Mari Llwyd! The leader, who held its reins, tried to force it over the threshold and into the house, but Doonan and his band thrust it back, defying it to enter, then slammed the door and retreated into the passageway.

Then began the traditional battle of wits between the Mari Llwyd and those within. The musicians ceased their playing and the little party sang a verse demanding entry, while Doonan's company sang impromptu rhymes in turn denying it, the leader rapping upon the door with his stick more and more urgently, as the competition gathered pace. As the hilarity grew, and the salaciousness of the reasons why the beast could not be conveniently admitted, it capered and snapped alarmingly at the passers-by until, finally, the company within acknowledged defeat, and it was allowed to enter to seek refreshment and coins.

Joshua, trapped in the passageway with the posturing horse and trying to avoid the clashing jaws, was laughing too much to do more than move beyond its reach, for its leader and the musicians were already at the wassail bowl. Suddenly the animal swerved aside and, passing Joshua, drove him back relentlessly towards the closed front door. Joshua had stopped laughing now, for there seemed to be a sense of menacing purpose in the action. He hesitated, alarmed.

'Joshua,' came a whisper from somewhere under the white sheet, 'watch out for tomorrow! Devilment is planned. Have your men ready . . . I can tell you no more.'

'I thank you for your advice, Ossie,' said Joshua, laughing aloud with relief and the absurdity of it all as he led the willing ostler to the wassail bowl.

Chapter Twenty

Long after the other guests had departed, replete and in rare good humour, Joshua and his friends remained. A brief explanation to Rosa and a word to those concerned had secured their eager co-operation. At first Mistress Cleat had cavilled at Illtyd's involvement, declaring that he was not yet recovered enough from his injury to be abroad so late, but Illtyd's obvious pleasure at being included in the company, and Jeremiah's avowal that he would deliver them both home safely afterwards upon his cart, prevailed upon her. In truth, she was delighted to join in the kitchen gossip with Mistress Howarth, Hannah and Emily Randall, as they gallantly tried to bring some order to the chaos wrought by the revelry. There was a minor diversion when Rosa's terrifed screams took Doonan running to the privy midden in the yard where Ossie had thoughtlessly stabled his mount. Its bleached skull and beer-bottle eyes, glowing amber in the candlelight, had filled her with such alarm that she had all but fallen in a swoon. When Doonan had scooped her into his arms, murmuring endearments, she had barely been able to point, babbling incoherently, and burying her pretty head in the comforting curve of his shoulder. Ossie had apologised most abjectly and Doonan had feigned anger, being hard pressed to restrain his hilarity with the rest of them. He had no wish to offend his new bride, and it had given him a chance to embrace her and kiss away the tears, declaring, 'Your Cavan will never let anyone harm a hair of your precious head, my own sweet darling' – a sentiment which he prudently expressed out of earshot of his irreverent friends. He castigated poor Ossie, taunting him that, 'such lewdness was only to be expected from a bachelor!' which so convulsed the rest of the company that it was a full five minutes before Joshua could restore any semblance of order.

Finally Joshua was able to impart the information that there was rumour of trouble erupting in the three hamlets upon the following day, making no mention of his informant. Without exception they volunteered their aid, Jeremiah, Illtyd, Roland Devereaux, Clatworthy and the landlords of the inns promising to be available upon the instant. If necessary, they would bring with them good reliable men to assist. Emrys and Doonan, although needed at the quarries, declared that should a stable lad from the 'Crown' be sent to warn them, then they would come at once, for the question of the lost explosives still burdened the quarry owner and he would make no objection.

Thus agreed, at Doonan's suggestion they disposed of the remaining contents of the hogshead, while the ladies happily refreshed themselves upon tea, wassail cake and scandal. Then those who could be fitted comfortably into Jeremiah's cart left for Nottage, while Ossie, Devereaux, Butler and Joshua escorted Emily Randall to her coach-loft at the 'Crown', where she solemnly bade good night to the little ostler and the Mari Llwyd, declaring that, but for the shape of the head, she saw a remarkable resemblance between the beast and Littlepage, the master of the workhouse.

'There is indeed a likeness,' agreed Joshua, straight-faced. 'Something, perhaps, in the glassiness of the eyes and the empty clacking of the jaw?'

'The horse is a noble beast, do not malign it!' called back Ossie as the friends went, laughing, upon their way.

For a long time that night Joshua lay in his bed in the small whitewashed room under the eaves, mind alert and active. The candle in the chamberstick beside his bed still gut-tered, its sides a frozen waterfall of wax. Against the winter dark which seeped from the high window, its mean flame shed little brightness, flickering as restlessly as his thoughts, a changing pattern of shadows.

Rebecca, his parents, the wassail party, the unsolved murders, the riddle of Elwyn Morris – all came, merged, and disappeared, swift and ephemeral as those shadow-shapes of his childhood, cast from the reach of his own small hands.

Even after he snuffed out the candle flame and slept, the shades danced in his brain. The Mari Llwyd snapped at him, staring with bottle-top eyes, its jaws a bony rictus. But when he tore the sheet aside it was Hardee who stared back at him, foppish, amused, his girlish laughter rising into the squealing of a Tamworth pig. Then he was strug-gling under water, strange hands pushing him deeper and deeper until he burst through into an oblong of light, with Ezra the Box remorselessly nailing down the lid.

When he awoke it was to brittle winter sunlight, and regret that he had indulged himself too richly at the farm, and upon Rosa's apple wassail cake. The frugality of his life as constable, he decided, was poor preparation for such culinary excesses! He washed himself at the jug and bowl upon his washstand, tingling from the coldness of water chilled overnight, then combed his thick, fair hair and dressed carefully in his uniform for whatever rigours the day might bring. He would confine himself to the parish today, leaving word with Ossie at the 'Crown', and its landlord, as arranged, as to where he might be. They, in turn, would send out stable lads and servants to rally his supporters should the need arise, and the volunteer army would converge from all directions, unified by his command. It was by no means an ideal preparation for battle, he thought ruefully, yet it had two inestimable advantages: the shock of surprise, and the resolution of men fighting for their own. He only hoped that whoever their antagonists proved to be, they would mount their attack in daylight, for once it grew dark the difficulties of rallying his men and co-ordinating their efforts would lead to chaos. Should explosives be used, as Doonan feared, the consequences of their mishandling in unskilled hands could prove too horrifying to contemplate.

Joshua was deep in thought as he walked into Newton village, occasionally being forced from his morbid introspection by the greetings of cottagers whom he passed upon his way, always returning their courtesies civilly.

The errand which took him to Ezra's workshop was less

in the course of duty than in pleasure. Lest this seem a contradiction in terms, the pleasure lay not in Ezra's company but in his undeniable skills as a wood carver, and the use to which Joshua hoped to channel them for his personal use. Yet he could justify his visit also by his duty to enquire after the little undertaker's health, and his willingness to act as a witness should the shipwreckers be called to account. This was what Robert Knight demanded.

Joshua opened the door which led from the street into Ezra's restored workshop to reveal not its owner, but the startled face of a stocky, lantern-jawed fellow who was engaged in sweeping the few curled wood shavings and sawdust into a heap with a besom, a shovel positioned precisely beside them. He propped the besom against a coffin stool.

'May I help you, sir?' he asked respectfully. 'Or do you require the services of the proprietor, Mr Evans?'

'If you please,' said Joshua, 'perhaps you will tell him that Constable Stradling has need of his services.'

'With pleasure, sir.'

He disappeared into the living quarters behind the workshop, and Joshua studied with amazement the changes the sturdy pauper had wrought. Small pieces of furniture were set upon display, each fastidiously cared for, polished and positioned to advantage. Even the coffins glowed with mellowness, their surfaces waxed with loving care, as were the stools and biers upon which they rested and even the floor beneath. This was clearly the tribute of a man who cherished beautiful objects to the skill of the artist who created them – Ezra the Box. Joshua found himself absurdly moved that a pauper, whose stark life was spent in the bleakness of a workhouse and judged to be of so little account, should feel such an affinity with beauty. As if to dispel the thought, Ezra came limping in, rudely taciturn.

'If you have come to enquire about my health, Constable, I reply as I always do – it is no better for asking!'

'Then I will not,' said Joshua equably, 'for I have no doubt that should it deteriorate, you will tell me soon enough!'

Ezra sniffed. 'If it is to ask if I will do my duty . . . then the answer is yes, despite my wounds and financial losses, and the dangers to my life and limb. I am proud to say that I am a man of my word, sir!'

'I am delighted to hear it! You are, no doubt, heartened by the services of your bodyguard?' Joshua thought it undiplomatic to allude to the pauper's industry and devotion.

'Heartened?' repeated Ezra indignantly. 'There has never been any question about my stoutness of heart, nor its generosity. You had best come through to the back.'

Joshua followed obediently. If there had been an improvement in the workshop, the change in his living quarters was little more than a miracle, so spick-and-span was everything, and well ordered. Even the ginger cat seemed to have grown sleeker and more comfortable upon the cushion before the blazing fire, and Joshua suspected that Ezra, too, was better victualled, if not tempered.

'You have met my pauper apprentice, Dic Jenkins?' he muttered ungraciously.

'A privilege, sir.' The man rose from his stool in the

corner and bowed his head, broad, ingenuous face warm with pleasure.

'Take yourself off to the workshop,' ordered Ezra, 'the constable and I have important private business to discuss.' Dic Jenkins met Joshua's eye, and smiled without rancour. 'You are right, Mr Evans, sir. Time is money.'

'Now,' said Ezra, 'what do you really want, Constable? I am sure that it is not solely my health which concerns you!' His little ferrety face was slyly intent.

'I had in mind some special gift, sir, something personal, to be treasured for its intrinsic beauty, and your skill.'

Ezra actually smiled with pleasure. 'For a young gentlewoman, sir, would it be?'

'Yes, and one who has possessions of great antiquity and beauty all about her – silver, paintings, family jewellery . . .'

Ezra nodded thoughtfully. 'Yes, but it is only wood which is alive, a real growing thing which breathes, has warmth, always growing more mellow and dignified with age. Like people . . .'

Joshua was impressed with his enthusiasm, if not his accuracy.

'Now tell me, sir,' continued Ezra, 'what have you in mind?'

'Once when I came here, I saw a needlework box upon slender legs, a delicate thing, to be repaired. You could make one, like it?'

Ezra's face lit up with joy and amazement. 'Of course, Constable. With pleasure.' He made no mention of money. 'You will not be disappointed, I promise you, with

337

its design or workmanship. I shall make a start on it at once, leaving all else . . .'

Joshua said hesitantly, 'There was one other thing – a love spoon. You would be able to fashion one to order?' He felt himself colouring, stupidly.

'If you will supply me with the lady's initials, sir, and your own, and the date and occasion to be celebrated, I shall carve it as no other love spoon has ever been carved, with a coat of arms, hearts, a chain, initials, even a ball in a cage, and all from a solid piece of seasoned oak. I shall put my very soul into it!'

There was an urgent clatter of hooves upon the cobblestones outside, and the sound of someone hurriedly dismounting. The door to the workshop flew back upon its hinges as Illtyd entered, flushed and breathless.

'I have seen them, Joshua! Twenty or more, ruffians all! They mean violence, I fear.'

'Where are they now?'

'Marching upon the turnpike house with staves and picks.' His voice was agitated, shocked. 'It is to be hoped the tollkeeper has sense enough to flee.'

'Come, we waste time!' exclaimed Joshua. 'Ride with me. I shall pick up my mare from the "Crown". Ossie has my pistol ready and waiting.' He turned to Jenkins. 'Have a care for Mr Evans, sir! These men are dangerous,' he warned in leaving.

'I will defend him with my life, if need be.'

'Don't talk rubbish!' said Ezra ungratefully, peering through the open door. 'The "Crown", he said? Well, I only hope it doesn't hold our victuals up, that's all!'

*   *   *

The supporting horsemen who rode out with Joshua from the 'Crown' were outwardly grave, yet filled with a strange exhilaration as they set out for the turnpike at Three Steps Hill, unsure of what they might find. They were watched in silence by Mrs Butler, Emily, a sprinkling of the inn's serving maids and those ancients too infirm to heave themselves upon Jeremiah's cart. The stable lads and grooms had reached the other inns and rallying points, and the three hamlets were a maelstrom of activity, currents already swirling and sucking them inescapably towards its vortex.

Emrys, Doonan and half a dozen well-armed quarrymen were leaving Stormy Downs upon Emrys's cart, or following on foot, with Joshua's horsemen converging upon them at the summit of Dan-y-Graig Hill, when the fierce, deafening explosion caught them in its blast. So violent and unexpected was it that, briefly, the little tableau stayed inert, frozen in shock. Then the earth and air seemed to vibrate about them and the horses reared and strained uncontrollably, eyes rolling in terror as they sought blindly to escape. Some of the riders were unseated and had to scramble up to chase their mounts which were running wildly, kicking out at whatever barred their way, so frantic were they to escape. Even Joshua's reliable grey was so startled that it rose up, raking the air, and he was forced to dismount to steady it and stop it trembling.

'Dear God,' cried out Doonan, 'the tollhouse! The lunatics must have blown up the tollhouse!'

With a yell to the cob and a flick of the reins, Emrys was off in the cart, and Jeremiah in his, their startled passengers clinging on for grim death as they careered drunkenly upon their way. Those in possession of their horses followed swiftly with the rest straggling on foot.

Despite the tenseness of the situation, Roland Devereaux, riding abreast of Joshua, could not control his amusement at the rattling frenzy of the waggons as they jolted and swerved upon their way.

'The battle of the Roman chariots!' he exclaimed laughing.

'It is to be hoped,' said Tom Butler drily, 'that the losers do not get fed to the lions!'

'Doonan would prise their jaws asunder, then knock their damned great heads together,' called out Illtyd from his piebald, Faith.

Glancing behind him, Joshua saw that a small troop of horsemen had emerged from the byway which ran past the justice's house. He recognised Rowden the miller, Clatworthy, Daniel the wheelwright and others of the Nottage band, and merging with them from the main highway, labourers, innkeepers and tramroad workers from the port. They looked a fearsome, bellicose crew, wielding their staves and weapons, and Joshua glanced at his pistol and stock, strapped at the mare's side, hoping fervently that their presence would render it superfluous.

As they rounded the bellying curve of the stone wall of the Court they saw, ahead, the drawn-up carts with the men already spilled out and fighting stave-to-stave with the marauders, a tangled mass of flesh, noise, and weapons. Beyond lay the disordered rubble of the tollhouse, broken stones erupting ugly and jarring as stumps of teeth in a ruined jaw.

Suddenly they were in the thick of it, in a wild fervour of

sweating activity without pause or reason. The instinct for survival was all that mattered now, deadening fear and pity, remorseless as death itself. Strike, or be struck down! There was a fierce surge of exhilaration felt in the blood, a sense of being god-like, inviolate, the sudden arbiter of death and destruction. Yet as long as battle raged there would be no consciousness of wounds or pain, no final reckoning, for it held the numbing unreality of a dream . . .

Joshua, upon his grey, stood a little apart from the action, hand upon the stock of his pistol, seeking to determine where the explosives lay hidden. He had searched the ruins of the tollhouse and found nothing, grateful only that the tollkeeper's body was not in the wreckage. As he emerged, he glimpsed between a gap in the hedgerows, in a neighbouring field, a cob and roughly hewn cart, a black mare tethered loosely behind. The cart was laden with stout wooden boxes, and two brutish-looking men stood guard wielding heavy staves. Joshua urged the grey across the highway towards them, only to find that Doonan had pre-empted his movements and was already setting about him dementedly with his flailing staff. One man had been felled to the ground, and Doonan had dismounted to stand threateningly over him, but even as Joshua approached the other assailant had seized something from the cart, unloosed the black mare and was off past him, flying for the gap in the hedgerow, as fierce as a bat out of hell. Calling out to Doonan to guard the cart and what lay upon it, Joshua took off in pursuit, riding furiously through the continuing battle, surprised to find himself unscathed on the other side and with Devereaux and Illtyd at his heels.

The horseman ahead turned his mare abruptly between the griffon-topped pillars of Tythegston Court and Joshua, as he urged the grey up the incline and then on to the carriageway, heard the breaking of glass and the man's frenzied ranting.

He stood obliquely upon the curve of the pathway, wild-eyed, disarranged, a gaping hole in the window behind him. In one hand he held the explosives high above his shoulder, and in the other a half-open box of friction matches, ready to strike. Leyshon had opened the door and made as if to step forward.

'Get back!' the man shouted. 'Get back, I tell you!' His voice was rising uncontrollably and Joshua, aware of the fear and desperation in it, nodded to Leyshon to do as he was bid.

Illtyd had leapt from his pony and had secured the man's mare, saying persuasively, 'Here, give me what you have in your hand. I will bring the mare. You still have time to go unhindered . . .'

The man's face was ugly, bathed in sweat, his hands trembling with terror, and Joshua could not be sure that he was able to comprehend what Illtyd was saying.

'Come, my friend,' coaxed Illtyd, his voice gently soothing, 'give it to me. No harm will come to you, I promise. I believe, as you do, that the tolls are wrong, and would willingly stand beside you in every way, save this!' He took a slow, deliberate step forward, his movements unhurried.

'Stand back!' The man's voice rose shrill, terrified, and Illtyd paused, a small misshapen figure, yet strangely impressive in his calm certainty. He was close enough to the man to reach out a hand and touch him but he made no movement, looking at him compassionately, his fine, intelligent eyes unwavering.

'You have done nothing to regret,' said Illtyd quietly, 'save hurling a stone – or perhaps it was kicked up in a panic by your mare? I beg you, most earnestly, my friend, to do nothing now to hurt yourself or others . . .'

The man, crazed and suspicious, only clutched the explosives tighter, grasping the box in the same hand and wrenching out a friction match with the other in a swift threatening movement.

Joshua had taken the pistol and stock from his leather holder, and held it to him, ready primed, his mouth dry.

'Why should you choose to hurt yourself, my friend?' Illtyd was saying quietly. 'Are they worth it? Will you let them take your life? Would you have them win?'

'They have taken away my livelihood, my family. What is left for me? My life is worth nothing!' There was terrible despair and anguish in the man.

'What of the lives of your family? Are they worth nothing?' Illtyd's voice was deliberately hard and contemptuous. 'Will you let them rot? Leave them to curse you for it?'

There was shock and bewilderment upon the man's face as he hesitated.

'Show them you are a man! Prove to them that you love them. Tell them that you will work at whatever you can, wherever you can, for months, years even, until you are together. Give them hope, man! Something to believe in.'

'Work?' the man's voice was raw. 'What work? Who would take me?'

'Look at me,' Illtyd commanded. 'Well? What do you see? A twisted, pathetic travesty of a man. Could I not say the same a thousand times over? Yet I do a man's work as hayward, asking and receiving no concessions. Crippled as I am, life is good because I believe, and make it so. If I had a family, I swear I would work for them until I dropped. I would rather die for them than the blood-sucking leeches of the turnpike trusts!'

The man's violence had gone out of him and, big and brutish-looking as he was, he seemed shrunk, diminished. His face crumpled like a child's and the tears coursed soundlessly down his cheeks as Illtyd, his eyes dark with pity, took the explosives and matches from his unresisting hands.

'Now,' he said, 'you are a real man again, my friend, as God made you. You can begin anew.'

Joshua and Devereaux had come up beside him, and Devereaux took the explosives from his hands as Joshua, hands trembling almost imperceptibly, replaced his pistol and stock upon his mare.

'You are a brave man, my friend,' said Devereaux warmly.

'No, it is he who has the courage,' said Illtyd, 'to choose the harder way. Prison, and a future made bleak by the carrion who feed upon the flesh of the poor. It would have been so easy to end it!' He looked at Devereaux steadily, his eyes shadowed and unreadable.

'You will be taking me before the justice,' said the man, 'to prison?'

'I will speak out for you,' said Joshua soberly, 'say what I can in your favour.'

The man was wiping his eyes roughly with his knuckles, his face bleak, drained of emotion, as the coach rumbled unexpectedly upon the carriageway and the door of the house opened simultaneously. Robert Knight, in his clerical robes, dismounted stiffly from the coach, helped by his coachman. He looked bewildered and ill at ease.

'What has happened here, Stradling? I heard the explosion as I ministered to a parishioner whom I could not, in all conscience, leave.'

'An explosion at the tollhouse, sir, completely wrecking it.'

'And the tollkeeper?' he demanded, concerned.

'Here, sir, safe and well.' It was Leyshon's voice from the doorway. 'He came seeking shelter when the crowd approached.'

'And this man?' He looked from the prisoner to the shattered glass of the window.

'A stone, sir, kicked up, I believe, by the mare's hooves.' Joshua half turned and looked at Leyshon in appeal.

'You saw this, Leyshon?' the justice demanded sharply.

'I saw nothing, sir. I was within the house, calming the household staff.'

The justice nodded, satisfied. 'I see that you have recovered at least some of the explosives, Stradling,' he said drily. Joshua flushed, unaware that he still held the box and the matches. 'And the rest of the dynamite and detonators, where are they now?'

'Upon a cart near the tollhouse, sir, guarded by Doonan.'

'Then I suggest you check upon it, at once, and remove this prisoner, either to the cell at the "Crown Inn", or to Pyle with the others. There will be others?'

'Indubitably, sir. There has been a pitched battle upon Three Steps Hill.'

Robert Knight's eyes were alert, anxious, behind his gold-rimmed lenses. 'Those who blew up the tollhouse –' he paused '– they are our people? Parishioners?'

'No, sir, strangers from outlying areas, unknown to me.'

There was no doubting the justice's relief. 'You had best clear up the detritus of battle, Stradling, and bring me a detailed report. If I may make a suggestion?'

'Of course, sir.'

'If you are going to make a habit of carrying explosives upon every occasion, it might be politic to keep your matches elsewhere, or to renounce smoking!'

'Yes, sir. I will see to it,' responded Joshua, serious-faced.

'Now, Leyshon,' the justice said, dismissing them and putting a restraining hand upon the old man's shoulder, 'you will explain to me what uncharacteristic quirk of human nature so restrained your curiosity as to make you unaware of what transpired.'

'Fear.'

'Indeed? With your usual concern for the servants, of course, and the absolute truth?'

Joshua was in no doubt that the justice would be able to elicit every detail of what had occurred.

Chapter Twenty-One

With their subdued prisoner remounted upon his mare, Joshua, Illtyd and Devereaux returned soberly to the scene of the conflict at the Three Steps Hill. Realisation of the enormity of the tragedy which had been averted had dulled any sense of triumph which they might have felt. Yet there was a closeness between them, the kinship of survivors bound by the same fragile membrane which so narrowly separates the living and dead.

The battle was already over between the men of the three hamlets and the turnpike protesters. Yet here, too, there seemed an absence of joy, unusual in victory. During the fight no blows had been withheld, for the defenders had been spurred by the violence to the toll-house and the threat of what might follow.

Faced by their unexpected strength and superiority, the attackers had hesitated. Some of the more committed of their number had held their ground staunchly, others had retreated or fled. Disorganised, ill-equipped and denied the threat of their explosives, they had soon lost heart and battle. Yet how could the victors rejoice at their crushing of such a pathetic band? They were nothing but rabble, ill-used and stirred to violence by a few inept agitators who had been swiftly identified and isolated. Now they awaited transportation to prison. For the rest, the cottagers felt pity rather than contempt, knowing that they, too, might as easily have been rallied to serve the same cause. There was not one among them who had not cursed the rapacity of the turnpike trusts and felt the impact of such violation upon their own lives. If they had not actively helped their beaten attackers to escape, then they had made no overt physical effort to restrain them. They were content to prevaricate in the certainty that the ringleaders would be brought to justice and that the explosives remaining had been safely recovered. Later, perhaps, they might boast of how the Court and its occupants had been delivered from disaster, but for the moment it was enough to examine their bruises and return to the ministrations of their families. First they watched Doonan and Emrys load his cart with the explosives and detonators for the quarry with meticulous care, then saw the six prisoners being conveyed to the cells at Pyle upon Jeremiah's fish cart, Charity having been prudently left in the care of the indulgent Widow Cleat. The truculent captives ran the gauntlet of jeers, blows and curses upon their way, spitting and mouthing obscenities in return, as was expected. Yet it was a half-hearted exchange at best; no one could be sorry that the tollhouse lay in ruins. It seemed hypocritical to vilify those who had freed them, however briefly, from its tyranny. Yet they had destroyed only the visible growth upon the people's flesh. The roots and poisons remained and spread, growing ever deeper and more radical. Joshua, riding with Devereaux,

Clatworthy, and Illtyd beside Jeremiah's cart, wondered despairingly how it would end.

Over the following few days, as life gradually returned to a more leisurely pace in the three hamlets, Joshua's time was absorbed by interviews, day-to-day investigations and the inevitable written report for Robert Knight the justice. He was grateful that Illtyd's compassion and sound common sense had averted bloodshed, and pleased, too, with the warm friendship which had been forged between Devereaux and the little hayward. Devereaux was to return to take command of a ship, a trading clipper, bound for Valparaiso upon the thirty-first of December, and together he and Illtyd had charted its course upon an atlas, Roland stirring his imagination with vivid sketches of seafaring life, the thrill of wind upon sail, and of curiously exotic shores and people. He would keep a journal especially for Illtyd, he declared, describing all those things which most intrigued and delighted his senses. Indeed, he would commission the ship's carpenter to make a miniature sea chest to house the samples of spices, grains, the handicrafts and colourful fabrics of which he wrote, that Illtyd might see, smell and actually feel them with his own hands, breathing the atmosphere of heat and excitement. In return, he would ask that Illtyd send him news of his friends in the three hamlets and those beyond at Southerndown Court, for they were all of the life he now had beyond cabin and deck. A man's view of things, he insisted, would add force and vitality to Emily's gently pastoral reflections which so much delighted him. So it was arranged, although only Illtyd knew what effort of mind and physical difficulty it would entail to form the letters, since writing was new to him. Yet it was a challenge and adventure as great as Roland's, and he could scarcely wait to embark upon it.

Joshua was thinking warmly of the two men and all the others who had come so selflessly to his aid when the letter arrived from his father. This in itself was an unusual event since his father was, by nature, taciturn and uncommunicative, leaving matters of correspondence to his wife and arguing that such faradiddles became women better, men, of course, being occupied properly in wresting a living from the land or commerce, and above such frivolities.

Joshua would be pleased to know, he wrote, that the dinner at Southerndown Court had been a quite exceptionally pleasant affair, notwithstanding Joshua's absence upon his duties as constable. Sir Matthew, it seemed, had been an attentive and gracious host and discussed most knowledgeably all aspects of farming and estate management, as well as the usual nonsense about art, books, plays and other such frothy notions more agreeable to the womenfolk. They were to dine together shortly at an all-male gathering which promised to be altogether more congenial, although, to be fair, the ladies had not disgraced themselves by 'simpering, twittering, or putting on high falutin' airs and graces'. His mother had looked well enough in a new gown, a sort of earthy colour, like wet mud, and Rebecca in green. Mrs Louisa Crandle and her daughter had joined them after the port, and Aled seemed unusually taken with Elizabeth, although he was relieved to say that, for once, he had behaved circumspectly and not made an exhibition of himself. The company seemed to enjoy the boy's 'nonsense' and there had been much good-natured laughter and banter throughout. Sir Matthew was eager to join a 'shoot' upon their land and to ask his advice about matters pertaining to the smooth running of the estate. He, in turn, had declared himself willing to offer such help as he was able.

'I had almost forgotten the purpose of this letter, Joshua,' he ended. 'About the Tamworth pigs of which you bade me enquire – I have asked most extensively, and even mentioned them to Sir Matthew, but it seems that they are virtually unknown, save for those at Sker House, beyond the three hamlets. It appears that the Stradlings of St Donat's Castle sought to purchase a brace, but were curtly refused.'

Joshua smilingly replaced his father's letter in its envelope, delighted as much with the harmony he read between the lines as with the written words upon its pages. He was not convinced that his mother would have been flattered by having her new gown described as the colour of 'wet mud' or being told that she 'looked well enough' in it. However, after more than two decades of living with him upon the most intimate terms, her wonder would surely be that he had noticed it at all! Joshua reflected, not for the first time, upon that strange alchemy which brought them together . . . What had induced the sensitive, beautiful young gentlewoman to fall in love with him? Certainly he owned some of the finest farms and land in the Vale, yet there had been others, richer and more eligible, and revelling, as she did, in the social extravagances which he affected to despise. An attraction of opposites, then? Perhaps she saw in him that purpose and virility which so many of her society beaux lacked, while he, in turn, prizing her alien delicacy and refinement, longed to possess them in her . . . There was no doubting that they loved each other, yet it was such an unlikely coupling, like Doonan and Rosa, Jeremiah and the Widow Cleat . . .

Well, thought Joshua in puzzlement, they say that love is blind, yet is it? Perhaps those in love are the only ones who see clearly, and in depth, beyond the surface imperfections and differences. Love was an enigma, a gift. How fortunate then that Rebecca had no surface imperfections, or indeed imperfections of any kind, and there were no differences between them. She was, and always would be, perfect. It was little short of a miracle.

Within the gaunt bleakness of Sker House, overlooking the rocky shore, there was a cold absence of love, and differences and imperfections ran too deep to heal . . .

Sarah Hardee, seated awkwardly at her dressing table, laid aside her hairbrush. She was unaware of the pale face which stared at her from her looking glass, or the hurt which showed in her eyes as darkly as the shadowed bruises beneath, the legacy of sleeplessness and constant pain from her cruelly misshapen leg.

How long, she wondered, could she endure life here in this dank forsaken place? It was more prison than farm; more fortress than home. There had been too many houses like this. So many that she had almost lost count, for they merged into sameness. They were always bleak and forbidding, set upon some rocky, inhospitable shore. Yet not so inhospitable as that cruel, all-devouring sea which, whipped to madness by the gales, battered itself upon the rocks with a power and fury nothing could withstand.

How often had she wished herself sucked into its swirling depths, waters closing over her, blocking out all thought and memory, washing away guilt, easing pain? Yet she would not give him the satisfaction of her dying; the knowledge that he had triumphed and she could bear no more . . . that . . . 'creature' she was forced to call 'husband'.

Dear God! How would she ever exist here without Elfed Thomas and the old manservant, Edwards? How could she survive Hardee's taunts and sneers, the knowledge of his life as wrecker and murderer? He was a man devoid of pity, and without remorse.

The tears blurred her eyes then fell unchecked, splashing from her mouth and chin on to her hands, clenched tightly upon her lap. No, Hardee had broken her body, coldly and deliberately, but he would not break her spirit, for that would be his real victory . . . A tremor ran through her, lightly, almost imperceptibly, and then the old trembling began, fierce, uncontrollable. Help me, God! she cried silently, it begins again, that nightmare without change or end . . . Could she ever expunge from her mind what she had seen, that first time upon the Cornish shore . . . running to him in her innocence, begging him to help those terror-stricken survivors of the wreck?

She had seen the lanterns in his henchmen's hands,

and in his own; heard the screams of the dying, their piteous calls for mercy; the poor, bewildered faces, hands seeking to ward off the blows, the exhausted, the defiled, the dead . . .

She had hurled herself defiantly across the barely living body of a child and he had torn her away, hurling her from him with a blow and a curse . . . his savages laughing as she humbled herself before him, begging him in the name of a pity he did not possess.

She had run into the sea, grasping at a woman's dress, floundering, sucked beneath the waves, yet somehow dragging her ashore to find it was a dead woman's hand she held within her own. It was then that, with a cry of rage and pain, she had torn the lantern from him and struggled across the shifting pebbles of the bay, screaming that she would see him 'hanged', and with cold deliberation, he had set his foot into the stirrups of his horse and raised himself into the saddle, hunting her down.

She lived again now the terror to escape, fear clawing at her ribs, breath raw, as she forced herself on to firm land. She had hurled the lantern away, believing herself safe in the darkness . . . Then there were only sounds, distant ones from the bay and sea and, nearer, the horse's hooves, glancing and slithering upon the pebbles . . . She heard the thud of its leap upon turf and saw the lantern she had thrown raised from the ground where it lay . . . Then Hardee's face, triumphant in the lantern beam as the horse reared wildly above her, hooves flailing, shattering flesh with bone . . .

And now she was imprisoned without escape, as was

Elfed whom she loved, as remorselessly as if they were shackled and locked within a prison cell. Hardee was aware of his cousin's love for her, and it amused him to have it so. He had hated Elfed Thomas from boyhood, for he was all that Hardee was not: clever, admired, rich . . . and Hardee but a poor relation, living upon the crumbs of charity from his cousin's table, feeling them choke and sour him . . .

Now for the first time Hardee possessed something which Elfed Thomas lacked. Was it perhaps why he had chosen to come here? To wreak revenge upon him for the past? Then he had assuredly found it, knowing how dearly their silence was bought . . . If Elfed spoke of what he knew, then her life would be forfeit, for Hardee had nothing then to lose . . . If she informed upon him, then Elfed Thomas would be named accomplice, career ended, his life in ruins . . .

The door was roughly wrenched open, and Hardee accused, peevishly, 'You are not dressed! Make haste, ma'am, I have guests newly arrived. You must be there to entertain them.'

'I think, sir,' she said dully, 'that they would not notice my absence . . . for they are either drunken louts or your foolish, prattling friends who have eyes only for each other.'

He strode across the room, face ugly with rage, and struck her a blow across the mouth. She felt the sharp pain as teeth pierced her lip, and the warm trickle of blood, but she rose unsteadily to her feet, facing him.

'You will come!' he commanded, 'for what you are

worth, a spineless, useless cripple, with neither looks nor spirit . . .'

'I am what you have made me, sir,' she said quietly, 'but I will come.'

He turned upon his heel and left, face flushed and sullen.

Sarah Hardee stared into her looking glass, witnessing for the first time her pallor and the blood which ran from her bruised lip . . . but she was seeing other faces, paler, more bloodied than her own.

'Yes, I will come . . .' she said aloud, 'as surely as retribution, and the judgement of the dead.'

At Southerndown Court, the preparations for the grand ball were completed and even Louisa Crandle, the perfectionist, was forced to declare herself 'well satisfied'. Such a degree of understatement hid the certainty that never before had an event been planned with such exquisite tastefulness and attention to the minutest detail which might bring pleasure and comfort to the guests. The refreshments were a triumph, a masterpiece of culinary art. The tables, with their pristine damask cloths, swagged with fresh foliage and flowers, were delightfully elegant, their surfaces sparkling with crystal and dancing candlelight. The silver punchbowls and ladles gleamed invitingly, and the epergnes, with their cornucopia of flowers, fruits and silver baskets of delicious sweetmeats and bonbons, almost too pretty to disarrange. The orangery, under its domed roof and high-arched windows, was set with small chairs among the greenery for those desiring tranquillity and privacy – although not the young ladies, of course! The long gallery had been cleared for dancing, save for the portraits upon the walls, the small console tables, gilded chairs, and the podium for the musicians. But the guests must first be discreetly gathered in the great hall, that Rebecca might make her entrance down the elegant sweep of staircase in a style fitting to the occasion . . .

Yes, Louisa Crandle thought complacently as she gave a final scrutiny to the arrangements, it is quite satisfactory. She was not, after all, a woman given to hyperbole.

Rebecca's maid had made the final adjustments to her toilette when Sir Matthew knocked quietly upon the door, and was bidden to enter.

He looked austerely elegant in his formal evening wear, spare-fleshed and dignified. Rebecca rose impulsively from the stool at her dressing table and, standing on tip-toe, kissed him affectionately. There was a smile upon his gaunt face as he held her back at arm's length, saying gravely, 'My dear, you are so beautiful that you take my breath away, robbing me of words.'

Indeed, with her blue-black hair falling to her shoulders, and her wide, clear eyes sparkling with excitement, Rebecca was all vitality and pulsing life. Even her gown seemed to alter colour subtly in the flickering light, shades of blue-green fusing, then changing swiftly as the sea.

'You are like a water nymph, Rebecca,' he declared, smiling, 'beautiful and enchanting. Yet, there is something lacking . . .' He regarded her critically, assessing.

'There is something wrong, Grandfather?' she asked anxiously.

'Nothing which cannot be put right, my dear.' He took a slim, rectangular box from his coat, and from it removed a necklace of deep blue sapphires and diamonds, which he fastened carefully about her neck.

'There,' he said, turning her towards the looking glass, 'now my water nymph is perfect. I know, my dear, that your grandmother's jewels were awaiting just such an occasion. They are my birthday gift to you, with my deepest and most grateful love.'

'Oh, Grandfather!' She turned and buried her face in his waistcoat. 'I love you so! You are the dearest, kindest man in all the world. I shall love it and treasure it all the days of my life, because it is so beautiful, and because you gave it to me.' Her eyes were spilling with tears.

'Now, my dear,' he said, mopping them gently with his silk kerchief, his own eyes bright, 'do not cloud such a fine day with tears. Water is an element for nymphs, but not for poor old gentlemen with dry and rheumy bones.'

When he left Rebecca, he went at once to the room which Louisa Crandle had been given in the Court to make it more convenient to supervise the arrangements for the ball, and for her dressing. There, to her surprise and gratification, he presented her with a delicately fashioned brooch of gold and aquamarines, which might be separated into two matching clips, to wear at the neckline of a gown. He thanked her gravely for her kindness and dedication in making Rebecca's birthday such an elegant occasion, repeating what pleasure and benefits her coming, and Elizabeth's, had brought to his granddaughter's life and his own. Mrs Crandle was quite overcome with emotion, declaring that it was they who were eternally in Sir Matthew's debt. Aquamarines, she declared warmly, were the gemstones most suited to her colouring and preference. It was a gift doubly appreciated, both for its beauty and for the kindness of its intention, for all her jewels had long since been sold. She would wear it with pleasure.

Elizabeth, in the boudoir and dressing room which had been apportioned to her, was smoothing her dark hair, her mind dwelling not upon her comely reflection in the looking glass, but upon her father, settled now, most comfortably, in the small private hospital which Sir Matthew had selected for him. His mind remained vague and disordered, but there was no doubting his contentment and the care he was given.

She glanced up in surprise at the knock upon her door, and immediately went to open it, expecting that it might be a servant with some message.

'My dear Elizabeth,' said Sir Matthew, 'how elegant you look, and how well that soft colour becomes you.'

She did indeed look charming in the pale honey-coloured gown of silk with its low neckline, which set off the warm brown of her eyes and her dark hair. Although lacking Rebecca's dramatic, almost theatrical, beauty, there was a dignity and warmth about Elizabeth which lingered in the mind. Rebecca was an orchid, Sir Matthew thought, exotic and rare, and Elizabeth something gentler and less flamboyant, but nonetheless appealing . . . a wild pansy, perhaps, heart's-ease, velvety-brown and graceful, with a quiet serenity of its own.

'I have brought a small gift for you, Elizabeth. I hope that you will wear it for me, to bring me pleasure.'

She surveyed him gravely as he opened the thin jewel case and removed the pretty filigree necklace and pendant of gold and seed pearls.

'Yes,' he said, fastening it gently about her slim throat, 'I was right in my choice, Elizabeth. It is as I thought – you bring it to life. My wife used to say that pearls need to be worn, for the warmth of the skin gives them lustre, without it they fade and grow dull.'

Elizabeth turned and kissed him gently upon his cheek. 'It is truly beautiful, sir, and I thank you most warmly for it, and I shall treasure it as much as I cherish the new life you have given to my father, as to my mother and me. Without your kindness, we too might have grown dull and lacklustre, and my father would certainly have died. If I bring life and warmth to your pearls in wearing them, Sir Matthew, it will serve to remind me of the debt we owe to you.'

'There are no debts between friends, Elizabeth,' he said gently, 'only outright gifts of affection, which reward the giver as much as the one who receives.' He took her hand in his, saying, 'I chose these pearls, Elizabeth, because they were the first gift that I made to my wife. You are as dear as a granddaughter to me, and there is no one I would rather see wearing them. Had Emma known you, my dear, she would respect you for your courage and loyalty, as I do, and be happy to see her pearls so loved and appreciated.'

Elizabeth nodded, her throat too constricted by tears to allow her to speak. She did not envy Rebecca the family jewels which would one day be hers by right of blood. Had she been granted the choice of any, this one piece would have brought her the keenest joy. No matter what the future held, she would never part with it.

The household servants were agog with excitement and curiosity as the first coaches negotiated the long sweep of carriageway to discharge their elegant occupants 'neath the porte-cochere. Only a few of the older retainers remembered those gracious years when Lady Emma had made the Court such a joyous meeting place for social entertainment. They recalled it now, nostalgically, as the liveried coachmen and flunkies came and went, sartorially splendid, their manner infinitely more aristocratic and unbending than any of their masters.

Within the Court, Sir Matthew and Louisa Crandle received the guests in the Great Hall as they were announced, the dignity of the tapestries and portraits softened by the myriad candles of the glittering crystal chandeliers.

Louisa hesitated briefly as Joshua came forward to be greeted, accompanied by a strikingly handsome fair-haired stranger, most elegant and assured in dress and manner. There was something disturbingly familiar about him, and yet she could not quite recall . . . She only knew that Sir Matthew had mentioned a friend whom Joshua begged leave to bring, and whom Sir Matthew had suggested might well be seated near to Elizabeth.

'Captain Devereaux!' said Sir Matthew, bowing, 'it is my pleasure, sir, to welcome you.'

Louisa Crandle lost colour upon hearing his name, and faltered, but Sir Matthew put a reassuring hand to her elbow, nodding almost imperceptibly, and she swiftly regained her composure, taking his hand and murmuring some pleasantry. Roland Devereaux looked steadily and calmly into her eyes, saying, 'I have long waited to thank you for your kindness to my sister, ma'am, and do so now. Your daughter, Elizabeth, and I are already friends.'

He saw her eyes fill with sudden, unshed tears as she thanked him soundlessly and turned to greet the waiting guests, outwardly poised and charming.

When all the guests were assembled the musicians began to play, and Joshua, deep in conversation with his parents, was aware of a sudden quietness, then a murmur of expectation, as Sir Matthew descended the softly curved sweep of the staircase with Rebecca's hand resting gracefully upon his arm. So vividly beautiful was she that Joshua's breath caught in his throat and his eyes pricked with unmanly tears, making the sapphires and diamonds at her slender throat, her bright eyes, and the iridescent colours of her gown blur into points and daggers of light, like sunlight striking water.

Joshua, feeling a pressure upon his shoulder, turned to see Dr Handel Peate smiling at him understandingly, and beside him, Aled and Elizabeth, but her eyes were not for Aled – they were fixed upon Devereaux, and Joshua saw that he was returning her gaze with the same anguished intensity. It was a look which excluded all about them, so intimate and revealing that Joshua felt an intruder, a voyeur happening unexpectedly upon an act of love.

The tension was broken as the company surged forward

to surround Rebecca, leaving Elizabeth and Roland Devereaux isolated.

'Miss Crandle, Elizabeth,' he said hesitantly, 'I hope that my presence here does not distress you.'

'No, sir, on the contrary. But you have spoken to my mother? She realises who you are?'

'Yes, I told her the truth – that I thank her most humbly for the kindness she offered to Mary.'

'Then, sir, as you once said to me at the "Crown", there is no reason why we cannot begin again, as strangers.'

'I would rather not,' he replied gravely, 'since I know so much of you already, ma'am, from Mary, Joshua, Illtyd, and others who love you dearly, recognising your worth. It is you alone I wish to know, no other.'

'And I you, sir,' she said without guile, 'for I too have known you as a brother for many years, from Mary's letters and her stories of your kindness.'

'I would rather it not be as a brother, Miss Crandle.'

She looked at him steadily, her dark eyes compassionate. 'Yes, sir. I can see that there is no going back to those innocent, childish days for any one of us.'

'Yet we may go forward, Elizabeth, if you will allow it?'

'Yes, I should like that .'

'It must be to a different relationship, Elizabeth, deeper, more personal, forgetting that Mary is dead.'

'No, sir, remembering, and knowing that my brother Creighton's viciousness, which might have wrenched us apart, has served to bind us closer in pity and understanding.'

He nodded and, without speaking, thrust his hand

into his pocket and taking out the little silver model of a ship in full sail which had been his sister's greatest treasure from their childhood days set it gently into her hand.

'I have not been separated from it since Mary's death, but if it does not hold too many sad memories, Elizabeth, I would beg you to keep it for Mary's sake, and my own . . . I gave it to her when our parents were dead, and she so bitterly alone, vowing that she held my voyage in her palm and that as long as she possessed it, I would return to her.'

'As you will return to me,' she said directly, without archness.

'Can you doubt it?'

They looked at each other in perfect understanding.

'Today, Roland, I have received the two most precious gifts in my life.' Her hand moved involuntarily towards the necklace of pearls at her throat. 'No,' she said softly, 'there are three gifts. I have you, my dear, beside me. I could not have asked for greater happiness.'

If Elizabeth's happiness that evening was so quietly glowing as to be visible only to those who knew her best, Louisa Crandle's delight was a universal beacon flame. Had she any doubts about Rebecca's party being a success, they were swept away by the evident rapture of the guests. It was unanimously agreed that the whole affair was a triumph. In fact, so lavishly was it praised for the arrangements that a lesser mortal might well have been in danger of having her head turned!

The refreshments were declared to be delectable, the decorations exquisitely tasteful, the musicians excellent.

When Rebecca had taken to the floor to begin the dancing, upon the arm of her grandfather, it was such a gay and elegant sight, and their affection so plain, that a spontaneous ripple of applause broke from the guests as he guided her into a graceful waltz by Strauss.

After that, her card might have been filled fifty times over by friends like Dr Peate, and would-be suitors, had not Joshua taken the precaution of filling in a goodly percentage with his name beforehand. Philip Stradling, however, would not relinquish his claim upon her and, to everyone's amazement, took to the floor with unexpected finesse and flair. Indeed, so great was his enthusiasm thereafter that his wife Charlotte, elegant in her gown of softest lilac, was heard to confide to Joshua that it was a relief to dispatch him in search of refreshment, for if she danced any more she would need to be shod, not by the cordwainer, but the village blacksmith!

Aled seemed always to be at the centre of a delighted coterie of prettily dressed young ladies and their escorts, his presence invariably bringing pleasure and good-humoured laughter. Yet it was to Elizabeth that his eyes strayed most often, and upon the two occasions when his name had been entered upon her card, Rebecca noticed that he was unnaturally subdued, his handsome face serious as he partnered her most formally in the dance. Joshua, who knew him best of all, wondered if he had been wise in arranging with Sir Matthew for Devereaux to be brought here unannounced. They had conspired for Elizabeth's sake, feeling that it might ease her vicarious guilt for her brother's violence. Yet he knew now how deeply Aled felt for Elizabeth and, glancing at the young captain, saw how attentively he watched their progress. Elizabeth, cool and serene in her honey-coloured gown, the pretty gold and pearl necklace at her throat, looked unusually relaxed. There was a warm glow about her which seemed to light her skin and fine eyes and Joshua, seeing the little sailing vessel beside her reticule at the table where she sat, and knowing its history, felt it to have been as binding as an open declaration.

When Dr Peate took the floor with Louisa Crandle, his tutor's lean ascetic figure bowed over his partner's dove-grey, Joshua hid a smile as he thought fleetingly that it was as if a heron unbent to partner a soft-breasted wood pigeon, aloof yet delighting to see her preen and strut. Knowing her to be so pleasurably occupied, he persuaded Rebecca into the concealing greenness of the orangery, where they might be alone.

'Miss de Breos, may I say how delightful you look this evening, upon your anniversary, and how well those sapphires become your eyes. Although, I swear, the latter are the brighter and more beautiful.'

'May I in return, sir, say that I have never seen you look so splendidly elegant.'

'You may, ma'am, for I know it is but the simple truth!'

They laughed companionably.

'I am glad to see that you wear Jeremiah's little brooch at your waist, Rebecca,' he said more seriously. 'It would give him great joy to know that you value it so.'

'I value it for his dear sake, Joshua, remembering that he gave me that which he cherished most. I vowed that I would wear it every day of my life.' She traced its delicate outline with her fingertips, smiling at him.

'The gift which I had planned to give you is not yet completed,' he confessed, 'so I fear it must wait until Christmas, Rebecca, since it is but two weeks or so distant.'

'It makes no matter, Joshua, for I have you here beside me,' she said, kissing him gently upon his cheek.

'Perhaps you will be gracious enough then, Miss de Breos, to accept this small, quite unworthy, bauble in the meantime?'

He removed a slim black jewel case from his pocket and snapped it open, to fasten a slender bracelet of diamonds and exquisitely matched sapphires about her wrist.

'Joshua?' Her voice was puzzled, distressed. 'I do not understand . . .'

'A small conceit of Sir Matthew's,' he admitted, laughing, 'for I confided in him my predicament. He bade me keep one part of his gift to surprise you, seeking to prolong your pleasure no doubt.'

'Oh, Joshua, it is so beautiful,' she said, admiring it by the light of the flickering candles set in the candelabrum upon the table where they sat, in an alcove of greenery. 'As beautiful and memorable as this whole day, and I thank both you and Grandfather for it.'

'I will never be able to buy you a gift as beautiful or valuable as that, Rebecca,' he said gravely, 'but if I could, there is no jewel on earth fine enough, or fair enough, to do you justice. Yet all I am, or ever will be, I offer most willingly to you.' He turned her hand over, clasping it in his own, then looked into her eyes. 'The work I do will never make me rich, or envied, or allow me to offer you the life you deserve, yet it is honest and helpful to those most in need. I make no apologies for it, for without care and protection the lives of the poor would be even more wretched and deprived.'

She removed her hand, and put it gently to his lips. 'You do not need to convince me, Joshua,' she said quietly. 'I was one of the poor of whom you speak. I admire you for your courage. I love you for everything you are.'

He took her into his arms and kissed her fervently, and with the greatest satisfaction, before leading her into the gaiety and the music.

Sir Matthew, remarking their return, smiled, thinking that Joshua escorted her with all the pride of a young man displaying his dearest possession, but the reluctance of one ill-disposed to share it.

Chapter Twenty-Two

Joshua and Devereaux, driving home in the newly acquired cabriolet from the 'Crown Inn', had scarcely exchanged a word. Yet there was no sense of awkwardness between them, rather the ease of those who find a companionship in silence. Neither seemed aware of the chill in the early morning air, although the carriage hood lay folded back and the frail beams from the whale-oil lamps trapped the glitter of hoar frost.

The strong rhythm of the horses' hooves upon the icy ground and the sounds of wheel and jangling harness were agreeably soporific. In the darkness, Joshua forced himself to flick at the reins to alert his senses. Devereaux too felt a gentle inertia, that sense of well-being which comes from wining and dining in the company of friends.

'It will be the first time that I have felt regrets about joining my ship.' He had not realised that he was speaking the words aloud.

'It is not the journey? The ship, itself?'

'No, my regret is at leaving my friends.'

'Then it is for the best of reasons,' said Joshua warmly, 'for your absence will only serve to strengthen the bonds of liking, and there is a special pleasure in the reunion. Do you not agree?'

Devereaux hesitated, and Joshua could not see his expression in the darkness. 'And the bonds of loving? Does it strengthen them?'

'You have in mind Elizabeth?'

'Yes, Joshua. I shall be gone for many months.'

'Then you need have no fear, Roland, for there is none more loyal or constant in all the world, I do assure you. I have seen her loving kindness to that poor, deluded wretch, her father, and witnessed the strength which took her mother's grief upon herself.'

'I do not doubt her constancy, but if I have the right to demand it.'

'It is a question I asked myself a thousand times in my separation from Rebecca,' confessed Joshua, 'and that, perhaps, less bearable because it was self-inflicted. I could have broken my trust and so easily sought her out.'

'Yet, you did not.'

'No, and I believe that our love grew stronger and more resolute for our parting,' he admitted truthfully.

'Yet I feel so strongly that with all that Elizabeth has endured, I should be beside her, giving her strength and purpose, for she has borne so terrible a burden alone. I cannot add to it . . . I know the depth of my own grief for Mary.'

'She is no longer alone,' stated Joshua unemotionally, 'and you add nothing save love and happiness. I believe that if Elizabeth were denied the comfort of that, and you the life which you have chosen, her pain and guilt would be worse than any she has known.' He gathered the reins determinedly as the mares took them beneath the archway to the stable yard of the 'Crown'. 'There,' he said briskly, 'you have sought my opinion and I have given it, for what it is worth!'

Devereaux, seeing Ossie emerging eager and smiling from the shadows to greet them, said, 'As I told you, my regret is at leaving those I have grown to value as true friends.'

Elwyn Morris, in the remote hill farm at Hawksreach, was ready to leave. He was no longer in fear of the wreckers who had killed Jem Crocutt and made his own life furtive and degrading. He was weary of living like a hunted animal. He would have no more of it . . .

He looked about him, seeing the 'farm' for what it really was – a barren, rocky wasteland, barely clawed from nature. Soon even its stone-built dwelling would be a ruined thing, brambles and ferns growing through its empty hollows, a haunt for rats and foxes.

Now that the old woman had died, there was nothing to hold him. She had taken him in, giving him shelter and a bare existence when he had needed it most. In return, he had laboured upon the poor soil, wresting what little he could from it to feed them. The animals had long since gone, as had those few hens which had scratched a living as arid as the earth. Now, she was buried in a pauper's plot in the hamlet beneath, where the soil was richer, and the climate more gentle. He turned to the child at his side.

'Are you ready, my lovely?'

'Yes, Dada, I am ready.' Her small, roughened hand

stole into his, and the dark eyes regarded him trustingly.

'It will be to a big adventure we are going,' he promised as he swung her up on to the cart, feeling the frail bones beneath her thin dress. 'You had best take my coat, Haulwen, for the wind is chill.' He took it off and wrapped it about her, seeing how tightly she clasped the wooden sheep he had carved for her.

'You will remember what Dada told you?' he asked anxiously. 'Should anyone come and stop us, you must run as hard as you can and hide. You must go as fast and as far as you can, not stopping to look back or to wait for me. You promise?'

'Yes, Dada, I promise.'

He climbed up beside her and stirred the little donkey between the shafts into reluctant action. It was a poor enough creature, but hard bargained for with all the old woman's possessions and few sticks of furniture. The cart he had fashioned from what lay about the farm.

'It will be a big adventure,' he said again as he saw her look back at the only place she remembered. 'It will be a lovely, kind lady who will look after you, always, I know, even if Dada cannot be with you. You understand?'

She nodded and sniffed, rubbing her nose with the back of her hand, and letting it creep to her eyes as she turned to look ahead.

'She will let me keep the donkey?' she asked. 'No one will take it away? It knows me.'

He shook his head. 'Now, once again, our game, my lovely girl. Show me how clever you are.'

'We have played it so many times, Dada, I know it by heart.'

'Just once more,' he coaxed, 'to show you are the cleverest, prettiest girl in all the world, and to make your old Dada proud. Where are we going, and why?'

'To the "Crown Inn", at Newton,' she said patiently, 'to Mistress Emily Randall. I am to say that my father, Elwyn Morris, puts me in her care. I am to tell the constable that the man he seeks is Hardee of . . .' she hesitated, 'Sker.'

'And?'

'If anyone else stops us, I am to run and leave you. If they catch me, I am to pretend I never knew you. You were taking me on the cart to see her, my aunt.'

'Yes, that is good,' he said, satisfied.

'But I will have to come back, Dada, for you and for the donkey,' she reminded him, smiling.

'No!' His voice was harsh, angry. She stared at him in puzzlement, teeth gnawing at her underlip, eyes anxious, as she closed her fist hard over her wooden sheep.

'No,' he repeated more gently, 'if you love us, Haulwen, you will do as I say, run and run, and not come back, you understand? Promise!'

Something in the urgency of his voice stirred answering fear in her, and it was no longer a game, although she did not know why it had changed.

'I promise.'

His hand slipped comfortingly over hers and he bent to kiss her dark head as the donkey trotted on, unknowing, towards the great adventure.

Joshua, seated at his table and eating frugally in order to offset the richness of Rebecca's party-fare, heard the hesitant knocking upon his door and arose at once to answer it. He was surprised to see the timid cadaverous figure of Walter Bevan standing awkwardly upon his doorstep, his mare fastened to the iron ring set in the wall.

'I have come with news of Elwyn Morris. Or, at least, I think it could be he.'

He resisted Joshua's urging to go within, pleading he had much hard riding to do, some to distant parts, which would occupy him into nightfall.

'You know, then, where Morris is?' Joshua prompted.

'A friend, a fellow overseer of the poor, in another parish, has told me of an old woman and child upon a remote farm, some five miles distant.'

'And Morris is there? He has seen him?'

He shook his head, saying regretfully, 'No, I fear not, but the old woman was sick and at the point of death. The child, he is sure, could not have tended her so carefully, nor worked with such strength and vigour upon the farm. Yet neither would admit to the presence of another. He has heard that the old woman, a former pauper, was buried yesterday, so he must return tomorrow to make arrangements for the child to be taken into the poorhouse. I have inscribed the name of the place, Hawksreach, and made a simple map for you, upon his advice.'

Joshua took it, thanking him sincerely for his trouble.

'No trouble, sir. My heart grieves for that poor child, and for Morris, too. He will never return to the workhouse, nor would he allow his child to be taken. I pray to

374

God that he will not be tempted into anything rash, for whoever seeks him would not baulk at killing a child.'

'I will leave as soon as I am able,' promised Joshua, 'and if there is any way I can offer them safety or shelter I shall spare no effort.'

Bevan nodded, his dark, intense eyes troubled. He turned to untether his mare, saying as he mounted, 'I pray to God, sir, that you will find them safe!'

Joshua, wasting no time, abandoned his unfinished meal and drink and, taking his pistol and stock from the safety of its drawer, with his ammunition, placed them carefully into the leather holder to strap upon the grey. Then, seeing that the fire was safely banked and the bailey door secured, he donned his helmet and set out for the stables of the 'Crown'.

Even as he was speaking to Walter Bevan, the travel-worn ass and the cart with its occupants had turned beneath the archway of the 'Crown'.

Ossie, emerging from the stables, and seeing the poor beast and the scarecrow occupants of the cart, was so taken aback that he actually halted upon the cobblestones then, recognising Elwyn Morris from Joshua's description of him, went resolutely forward to greet them. Morris was blue with cold and shivering, although whether with fear, Ossie could not be certain. The child was so thin and ill-nourished that beneath her father's tattered coat all that seemed visible were the dark, terrified eyes, set with bruised shadows.

'Well,' said Ossie, his voice rough and brusque, to hide his compassion, 'what have we here, then?'

The child had struggled down from the cart, hampered

by the heavy coat which fell below her hands and dragged almost to the ground about her. She stood fiercely in front of the donkey, arms outstretched to shield him, daring Ossie to approach nearer.

'A beautiful donkey,' he said admiringly, 'a king among beasts. Oh, how the others will like him! We must give him food and warm shelter. Will you not help me unloose him, and bring him with you?'

The child watched him, wide-eyed and suspicious, then dropped her arms and nodded.

Ossie looked up into the grateful, ravaged face of Elwyn Morris, and smiled understandingly. 'It would not do to say that there is no room at the inn,' he said gently, 'for any child. No, nor for any man, or beast.'

He called out to Emily Randall, and she came to the door of the coach house almost at once, and hurried down the stone steps to the cobbled yard.

'I have come to ask for your help,' said Elwyn Morris, 'if you will give it.'

Emily looked at him steadily, and then at the child standing rigid and defiant at the donkey's head, hair matted, small body tense under the too-big coat.

'It will give me the greatest pleasure, Elwyn, to return a fragment of the help and kindness you have given so willingly to others.'

He thought, not for the first time, what natural warmth and dignity Emily had, as he tried to thank her, feeling the tears of relief and gratitude filling his eyes, ashamed of his weakness.

Emily, turning, held out her arms wide to the child, who hesitated, then came uncertainly towards her. She stumbled over the hem of the long coat and Emily caught her and drew her impulsively to her breast, cradling her tenderly and smoothing the dark hair.

Ossie blinked rapidly, sniffing, then gently clearing his throat as he busied himself with the donkey. Any child, he thought, who could love such a paltry, moth-eaten beast, and seek to defend it, might even, in time, grow to appreciate an oddity such as me.

He led the donkey away, shoulders less bent, and whistling serenely through the gaps in his teeth.

Emily had scarcely time to settle Elwyn Morris and his daughter before her glowing fire to thaw the winter chill from their bones before Joshua came striding purposefully into the stable yard, gripping his pistol and stock, intent upon saddling his grey.

Ossie, recognising his footsteps upon the cobbles, left the donkey to the care of a delighted stable lad and hurried out to meet him.

'I trust it is not I whom you seek,' said Ossie, grinning broadly, 'for by the cut of your jib, you would as soon blow off my head as greet me civilly!'

'No. I heard news of Elwyn Morris.'

'So soon?' Ossie was mystified. 'I meant to come at once and warn you of his arrival.'

It was Joshua's turn to look mystified as Ossie, patiently beginning his explanation, took his friend's arm and guided him up the stone outer staircase to Emily's coach-loft.

Elwyn Morris, upon seeing Joshua's gun, grew pale and leapt to his feet in confusion, and Haulwen, frightened and bewildered, ran to him, fastening her arms about his waist and sobbing loudly. To add to the disorder she began shouting, between sobs, some garbled, incomprehensible tale about not knowing him, an aunt and a donkey . . . There followed a chorus of jumbled explanations and apologies, before peace was finally restored. Then, with admirable presence of mind, Emily wrapped the child warmly about with a pretty woollen shawl and, with a meaningful glance at Ossie, suggested that they all three go to enquire how well the donkey had settled in his new lodgings.

'What do you call him?' Emily asked conversationally of Haulwen as they left.

'He is too new, he has no name.'

'Then you had best choose one for him, else he will feel deprived,' said Ossie, kindly.

'What is your name, sir?' demanded Haulwen.

'Oswald, but I am known as Ossie the Ostler.'

'Oswald? Yes, I shall call him Oswald,' she said with certainty.

Ossie, meeting Emily's amused eyes, answered gravely with a bow, 'I thank you for the honour, ma'am. There is nothing on earth so well becomes a man as the good opinion of his friends.'

'Or a donkey,' added Emily, straight-faced.

Joshua placed his gun out of harm's way, upon a chest, and bade Morris seat himself by the warmth of the fire, taking a chair beside him.

'Now,' he said gently, 'you will tell me all you know of Jem's murder and the wreckers.'

'First, sir, I would tell you that my thought in fleeing was not to deprive you of a witness. It was ever my intention to return, as today,' he declared earnestly.

'Yes, I understand you fled in peril of your life, and to secure your daughter's future. But you know why Jem Crocutt was killed?'

'I do, sir, if you will bear with me. It is a strange and twisted story and some of it only what I learnt from him and others, like James Ploughman.'

Joshua nodded. 'Crocutt saw the wreckers, perhaps?'

'As did I, sir . . . for Jem crept out to meet me upon the night of the storm under the pretext of securing the animals.' Morris flushed. 'I awaited him in the barn, for we were set firm upon finding a hare or rabbit for the pot . . .' As Joshua made no comment, Morris continued. 'Well, we were deep into the dunes near Sker, when we saw the warning flare and hurried as best we could to the bay, for the storm was wild by then. We could scarce stand against the wind and rain and blowing sand . . .' He hesitated. 'There are many small paths known only to poachers . . .'

'You saw the shipwreck, then?'

'No, sir, the aftermath, for the ship was already aground.' His voice shook, thickened with tears and weakness. Joshua put a compassionate hand upon his shoulder, waiting until Morris had recovered himself.

'We gazed through a cleft in the dunes . . . and saw a most terrible sight – the wreck, and the dying and the dead dragged up on to the sand, their bodies mutilated and abused by the wreckers to steal their possessions . . .'

'Yes, I had feared as much.' Joshua's voice was low.

'Below where we stood, unseen, a huge, ungodly brute

of a man had dragged a woman ashore as she stumbled, half dead, to the sea's edge. She had thought he came to save her and, by the light of the lantern set into the sand, we saw the realisation, and the look of terror upon her face, as the man lifted a club to bludgeon her to the sand, wrenching the crucifix from her neck even as she begged for mercy in some foreign tongue. I was too frightened, sir, to show myself . . .'

'And Jem?'

'It seems he was incensed beyond reason, too maddened by what he had seen to be cautious. Upon an instant he had run to him and, as the man looked up from tearing off the rings upon her hands, Jem lifted a huge stone and brought it crashing down upon his face, felling him to the ground. Yet, even as he did so, he saw amongst the wreckers one he recognised. Even then, he could not leave the woman, lest there be some shred of life within her . . .'

'She was alive?' demanded Joshua sharply.

'No, thank God, for she would not long have remained so. Those few who reached the shore, barely alive, were cruelly and in cold blood murdered by the plunderers. Jem, crazed with shock and terror, stumbled to where I lay, our only thought to flee the carnage . . . We spoke not a word upon the way, for we were too sickened by horror and grief. It was not until we reached the farm that Jem found, still pressed tight in his palm, the crucifix he had torn from the murderer's grasp . . .'

'And then?'

'I could not leave, sir, for there was nowhere for me to go at that hour, so Jem came with me to the barn and let me settle there . . . bidding me flee when daylight came, lest the wreckers come searching.'

'As they did, indeed . . .'

'Yes, for he confided it to me upon the night of his death. They came as he worked alone in the fields – not once but many times, swearing him to silence by blows and threats . . . but not the villain Jem had struck down. It seems they did not know of the crucifix . . .'

'Yet they continued to come,' Joshua said.

'Yes. The last time, leading him away like an animal to brand a warning upon his raw flesh.'

'He told you of this?' asked Joshua, sickened.

'Yes, sir . . . and weeping, not for himself, but for the woman we had seen murdered. He declared that the look in her eyes was burned into his mind, deeper and more cruel than the brand upon his body. He would have come to you or the justice . . .'

'But they threatened him with death?'

'No, sir, for he could have borne that, for all he was a gentle, harmless man . . . They threatened to take his wife and brand her upon her bare flesh, as they had done to him, and to see his children dead. There is no man on earth who would take the risk of being the cause of that . . . He told me only because the fear of it, unspoken, had driven him to near madness . . .'

'And his death? You know of that?'

'I witnessed it.' Memory of the flesh skewered upon the down beam of the barn kept him silent.

'You were there . . . with him?' Joshua asked at last.

'Yes, for although I had done as he begged and left the farm after the wrecking my mind was not at ease. I laboured casually at other more distant farms and upon the roads, fearful to return. Yet the night of the fog, I made myself travel to the farm to seek Jem out, believing that since the inquest had declared the wrecking to be caused by the storm alone, and no man was blamed, then all had been forgot. It was then he told me of the branding, bidding me hide myself lest they came for me, too. Yet, so anguished and incapable had he become that I did not return to the workhouse, choosing to remain there, unseen, and watch over him, seeing to the safety and welfare of the animals if need arise, for the boy, Dafydd, was too young for such a burden . . .'

'It was a generous act,' murmured Joshua, but Morris shook his head.

'I heard Jem come into the barn where I was concealed behind a bale of hay. I would have spoken to him, called out, but the murderer came immediately, as if he had been awaiting him. I thought to stay there, listening, a witness should Jem have need of me.'

'You recall clearly what the man said?'

'He demanded the crucifix he had wrenched from the woman's throat. Jem said, "If I had it, I swear I would die before I put it into your filthy, ungodly hands! They are so stained with blood that all the waters in the sea could never cleanse them!" When the man lifted the pitchfork and pierced Jem through, I cried out and rose to my feet, and the villain turned towards me, the scar from the blow that Jem had dealt him still livid upon his skin. I fled past him and out into the yard, running and sobbing, leading him away from the house lest he harm the family within. I do not know how far, or even where,

I ran, but I know I finally fell exhausted and slept until early morn, grateful only for the fog which shrouded me. Then, hiding by day and walking by night, feeding upon what I could find in the hedgerows and fields, I made my way to Hawksreach. If you now demand that I bear witness to all that I have told you, to the justice or in a court of law, then I shall willingly do so. Haulwen is safe with Mistress Randall, and I have no fear upon my own account.'

'And Dai Bando?' Joshua demanded. 'He witnessed the wrecking, too?'

'No, he had but rested in some ruined pigsty upon the way, happy to escape the fury of the storm, and saw the wreckage the next morning only . . . or so I heard James Ploughman claim when he awakened Jem, the same morn, urging him to ride out that they might offer what aid they could to any who survived. Jem could not tell him there was none alive . . .'

'You saw Bando?'

'I did . . . for I ran at once to Ploughman's cot. James had confided to Jem that he had left the vagrant there, bidding him eat and drink his fill. It seems Dai Bando had gone early to Sker House, seeking a crust or work of any kind, only to be sent curtly upon his way. I knew then that when the wreckers learnt of it, his life, like ours, might well be forfeit. So I ran to warn him, sir.'

'You saw Dai Bando? Warned him?'

'No, sir, for there was a horseman already there, a rough, ill-spoken fellow, who drove Bando before him as if he were some beast upon the way, laying about him with a whip, and that poor old man so exhausted and ill-used, he scarce could speak for fear. I should have gone forward, sir, and spoken for him, but the rider was armed, you understand. I have regretted my cowardice many a day. It has been hard to live with.' Morris raised his eyes to Joshua's, face pale with anxiety and fatigue, to ask quietly, 'I beg you tell me he was unharmed . . . for I would wish to make it up to him somehow.'

There was no way for Joshua to cloak the truth of it. 'He is dead, murdered . . . beaten most brutally and thrown into the sea.'

'Dear God!' Morris's face was ashen. 'Is there no end to the hideousness of it?' He buried his face in his hands and wept without restraint, for Bando, for himself, and for Jem, and for all that was past and could not be forgot.

Heavy with pity, Joshua stretched out a hand to touch him, saying firmly, 'Yes, there will come an end, with your help . . . too late for those innocents who perished upon the shore. Yet it will save many more.'

Morris looked up at him bleakly and nodded. 'I shall be ready when you have need of me.'

'You will think this a strange question,' said Joshua hesitantly, 'but what role in this do the Tamworth pigs play?'

Morris smiled involuntarily. 'I know only what Jem told me. You did not question the swineherd at Sker?'

'No, I confess I did not, not knowing if he was in the wreckers' pay.'

'His was the face that Jem recognised upon the bay. He was a stupid, frightened creature, born and bred here in Nottage village . . . more sinned against than sinning, forced by Hardee to take the jewels from the dead, although he swore that he had not harmed a living soul.'

'And the Tamworths?'

'He came to Jem, believing him to be an honest man who would report all that he knew. He begged him to withhold his name, pleading that he had gone there on pain of death and took no part in the bloodshed, nor did he benefit. His wife would be destitute and his children starve were he sent to gaol. Jem, convinced it seems of his innocence, gave his word, whereupon, feeling himself beholden, the man entreated Jem to visit his brother at his poor holding near Candleston. Something of interest would await him there, neither gift nor bribe, but simple recognition of his kindness . . .'

'The Tamworth pigs!'

'It seems that with Hardee so often away, the swineherd took a piglet, unnoticed, from each farrowing sow, rearing a small herd of his own at his brother's isolated farm.'

'Well, I'll be damned,' cried Joshua, laughing, 'if the discovery of that would not incense Hardee more than our discovery of his own villainy! It will give me the purest pleasure to inform him of it . . . a casting down of pearls before swine!'

'Or,' corrected Elwyn Morris, smiling freely for the first time, 'perhaps casting down of a swine before pearls. Indeed, sir, jewels of any kind . . .'

Chapter Twenty-Three

Ossie had saddled and made ready Joshua's grey and stood patiently waiting upon the cobblestones for the young constable to mount. He seemed calm enough as he strapped his pistol-case upon the mare and set his boot into the stirrup, but the ostler had learnt to recognise the signs of that restless energy which surged within him, a quickening of blood and senses. Like an animal scenting danger, Ossie thought, fear and excitement pricking him alert! He watched him ride out under the arch, returned his salute, yet was unable to speak the words of caution which came to his mind. Perhaps they were best left unsaid; confidence is the talisman of the young – that and their eagerness. He hoped that it would be enough to protect him from what was to come.

Elwyn Morris had already left the 'Crown', secreted under a covering of sacks upon the wheelwright's cart. Hannah, Daniel's wife, would care for him well, knowing his story and impatient to build good flesh upon such gaunt, ill-covered bones. With Clatworthy and Emrys to guard him overnight, he would sleep safely in his bed, the nightmare fears gradually receding.

Haulwen, scrubbed, victualled and barely recognisable in a makeshift nightgown of one of Emily's lace-trimmed bodices, was already asleep in their shared bed, untangled hair spread darkly across the pillow. Her dream was a mixture of warmth, new faces and a mangy-furred donkey named Oswald, while Mistress Randall, vividly awake under the lamplight, restitched an old gown into a pretty new dress for her for the morrow.

The winter darkness was already closing about him as Joshua reached Tythegston Court with his news for the justice. He was surprised when Leyshon, who smilingly opened the door to him, was peremptorily brushed aside by his master with the barest apology, while he, in turn, was hustled impatiently into the library. Peter Rawlings, the exciseman, rose to his feet as they entered.

'A most opportune time to arrive,' approved Robert Knight, 'most opportune. I was about to dispatch a messenger to bring you here, Stradling. Well, be seated, the pair of you,' he ordered irritably, 'I find it distracting to have you standing there like a set of ill-matched vases!'

Joshua and Rawlings obediently took their chairs.

'Now, Stradling, Rawlings has just brought me an outstanding piece of news.' His florid, dark-jowled face was expectant. 'The jewels from the wreck of the *San Lorenzo* have been traced.'

'Here, sir? To Hardee?'

'No, not here, man! To London, where they had been taken to an intermediary, a dealer in stolen goods. But, yes, they can be traced directly to Hardee. There is no disputing it!'

'How did it come about, sir?'

'The usual way, Stradling, through hard work and application.'

'Yes, sir.'

'Mainly through the good offices of Sir Robert Peel's Metropolitan Police Force, although, to be fair,' Robert Knight glanced placatingly at Rawlings, 'the excisemen have played a not inconsiderable part in the affair.'

'The dealer has been apprehended, sir?' prompted Joshua.

'Indeed, and was eager to incriminate Hardee to save his own worthless neck. It seems they had done business upon other occasions, a fact long suspected by the excisemen in Cornwall, who believed him to be responsible for wreckings along the coast, yet lacked the proof to convict him.'

'There is no doubt that Hardee is the man?'

'None. He used an assumed name, of course, for his transactions, but the dealer, now held in protective custody, has identified a drawing of him which the excisemen were prudent enough to have retained.'

'And Mrs Hardee's connection, sir?'

'From what has been pieced together, tenuous to say the least. It seems that Hardee's interest in her was mercenary, her involvement accidental. They met when she was placed in the care of an aunt living in London who was to organise a "season" of social events and presentations for her, her own mother having died. Hardee's activities in Cornwall were already suspected and causing anxiety. As heiress to a considerable fortune, young and presumably innocent in the ways of the world and men, Hardee found her lure irresistible.'

'As she, regrettably, found his?'

'Indeed, and by all accounts she has bitterly lived to regret it.'

'And the link with Dr Elfed Thomas, sir?'

'That I have not yet been able to discover, but I swear that I will do so and bring him to justice for his perjured testimony at the inquest, and the part he played in the wrecking at Sker.' He looked at Rawlings intently. 'Well, sir, have you anything to add to my exposition?'

'No, sir, a most comprehensive account, impeccably rendered,' said Rawlings, face carefully expressionless as the justice scrutinised him through his gold-framed lenses.

'And you, Stradling? Have you anything to add?'

'Only what I came here to report, sir, that Elwyn Morris has been found. He witnessed Jem Crocutt's murder and will testify to you and in court as to the guilt of the wreckers.'

There was a moment of incredulous silence as the justice's protuberant, brown eyes grew fractionally wider, and Joshua felt the impact of Rawlings's toecap upon his riding boot.

'The murderer was one of Hardee's henchmen, then?'

'Yes, sir. The man who assaulted Ezra, and later died of his fall into the quarry. I believe that he might also have killed the vagrant, Bando, although there is no proof as yet.'

'Well,' said the justice drily, 'it seems that I am to congratulate you both upon your perseverance and industry, even if the results are somewhat tardy in coming to fruition. Since we cannot hope to take Hardee and his men under cover of darkness, we had best make our plans for dawn tomorrow. You will have need of a warrant, Stradling.'

'Yes, sir.'

'I will see that one is prepared. You will both have trustworthy men available, of course, and go well armed.'

Upon receiving their assent, he commanded irascibly, 'Well, let us waste no more time with superfluous pleasantries, let us plan our campaign and strategy. More battles are won upon the drawing-board than upon the field!'

Joshua stoically refrained from glancing at Rawlings as Robert Knight unfolded a meticulously drawn map of Sker Farm and its surroundings, and the exercise commenced with much argument, rebuttal and lively debate.

When all was agreed, Rawlings and Joshua began to blurt questions simultaneously to the justice, each pausing in embarrassment to let the other continue.

'You will require us to report to you, immediately after the prisoners have been transferred to Pyle?'

'You wish me to wait for the warrant?'

'I am delighted to see the exemplary eagerness with which you approach your task,' observed Robert Knight, eyes glinting with humour behind his lenses. 'The answer to both questions is the same. It will not be necessary. I will be there with you, doing battle! As a justice of the peace, I will see that the warrant is correctly served, and that Hardee complies with it.'

'And if he does not, sir?' asked Rawlings.

'Then, in my capacity as priest, I shall either seek to convert him through persuasion or, if all else fails, hope I may bring solace to the dying, and bury the dead. You understand?'

'Perfectly, sir,' said Rawlings, avoiding Joshua's eye.

Upon parting from Rawlings, on the friendliest terms after agreeing that it would be safer if they were not seen together that night, it was arranged that the two men would meet at the 'Ship Aground' upon the following eve to share a celebratory drink – bruises and events permitting.

The justice, who was dining at the quarry owner's house, had graciously agreed to request an hour's exemption from labour for Doonan and Emrys, confident both of his powers of persuasion and the ease of their victory. Now it only fell to Joshua to apprise Devereaux, Clatworthy, Daniel, the quarrymen, Illtyd and Ossie of their respective roles in the affair. Jeremiah, he considered, should be exempted from any active part in the battle because of his earlier grave illness, his age and his obligation to the Widow Cleat, although it would not do to tell him so! Instead, Joshua would plead that Elwyn Morris and Hannah might have need of protection from a murderous mob, and that it would take a man of rare courage and enterprise to provide it.

His preparations made, Joshua ate a solitary meal and, resisting the temptation to while away an hour at one of the inns, took himself to bed. He would need a clear head and all of his wits for the morrow's confrontation. He placed his uniform ready upon the wooden butler at his bedside, and his pistol and accessories upon the chest nearby. He lay down to sleep, leaving the candle guttering on the table beside him, but sleep would not come . . . His mind was filled with the images Elwyn Morris had evoked: the dying woman and the crucifix; the passengers upon the *San Lorenzo* struggling through the waves to be cold-bloodedly murdered upon the sand; Jem Crocutt transfixed upon a beam. Then the puzzles of Hardee's wife and Dr Elfed Thomas; the gold left for Jem Crocutt's widow; the torture and murder of Dai Bando; Jem Crocutt weeping and turning back, unable to face the horror of what he had seen . . .

Joshua was still awake when dawn's pale fingers clawed aside the darkness of night. He part dressed and washed himself in the icy water from the well in the bailey. Then he resolutely forced himself to eat some bread and oatcakes, with a little buttermilk, his stomach rebelling even as he did so. Finally he put on the rest of his uniform, donned his helmet and, taking his pistol and ammunition from the chest, walked out into the frosted winter air to fetch his grey.

By now, he was sure, his men and Rawlings's excisemen would have taken up their positions at the paths and tracks leading from Sker House. All would be covered, from the well-concealed poachers' ways to the clefts in the dunes, and the creeks and gullies upon the shore. Had they moved to take Hardee by force, as he and Rawlings favoured, they would have muffled their horses' hooves and thrown animal flesh, dowsed in some sleeping potion, to the hounds . . . Yet the justice's orders were explicit. He would attempt to serve the warrant and Hardee would be taken quietly, without need for gratuitous violence. God knows, there had been violence enough! Yet Joshua's hopes for Hardee's peaceful surrender were less sanguine than Robert Knight's; he could not imagine that a man so inured to bloodshed would submit meekly to his own incarceration and death upon a gibbet. The arrogant little coxcomb would surely fear death less than the threat of his lifeless flesh being set on public display, rotted by time and the weather, bones picked clean by carrion.

It was as well, Joshua thought, that his safe conduct to Tythegston Court did not depend upon silence, for the mare's hooves rang out, singular as church bells, upon the frosty ground, giving clear warning of his coming. As if in answer to his thought, Rawlings and the justice appeared in the griffon-topped entrance to the Court and, after a bare few words of greeting, they rode scarcely speaking through the tangle of lanes to Sker House.

The justice tolled upon the bell, to the fury of the unleashed dogs which hurled themselves at the gate, snarling and slavering, teeth bared. The justice's horse reared and backed away, and Joshua saw him struggle to control it, face blanched, before mopping himself agitatedly with a silk kerchief. Within minutes the ill-tempered kennel man had appeared from a hut nearby, his blustering and threats dying away as he recognised the justice. And harshly and not a little shamefaced, he called the curs to order and chained them.

Without a word, the justice entered the yard and, followed by Rawlings and Joshua, rode to the main door. The noise of the dogs and the sight of the armed riders had alerted those within for, before any one of them had time to dismount, a window was thrown open above and Hardee's languid, amused voice declared, 'It is an unconscionably early hour to be calling, sirs. Indeed, barely civilised. You will forgive the coolness of my welcome.'

Robert Knight urged his mount back, the better to see him. 'Descend at once, Hardee!' he ordered. 'I have here a warrant for your arrest upon charges of wrecking and murder.'

'And I, sir, have something for you.' A pistol shot glanced off the cobbled yard, and the justice's horse reared and threw him. He stumbled to his feet, dazed and humiliated, and remounted his horse which Rawlings had retrieved, to Hardee's mocking laughter.

'I allow you one more chance,' called the justice, anger and desperation raising his voice. 'Will you surrender yourself, sir, to this warrant? Answer, I say.'

Hardee's answer rattled in shot beside his mare's withers and, upon Joshua's shouted instructions, Robert Knight took cover behind a sea-washed boulder set into the earth, while Rawlings and the constable positioned themselves for a fight, first shouting and driving their mares to the safety of some farm outbuildings.

Within minutes, two of Hardee's armed men had run from the house and one from the stables, shouting wildly, their pistols raised, eyes searching for some vantage point. Rawlings winged one as he descended the steps and the man screamed out in pain, dropping his pistol as blood ran from his fingers. He retreated into the house, and one of the two remaining men fled to the cover of a laurel, firing wildly. The last man hesitated, throwing down his pistol, and ran blindly for the stables as shot erupted around him. Without thought or reason Robert Knight hurled himself from behind his rock in pursuit, corpulent body bouncing across the cobbles, jowls trembling, as he gave chase. For a moment it seemed as if the gunman behind the bush would wait until he drew level and shoot him at close range, but Joshua's involuntary shout lured the man into the open and Joshua, steadying pistol and stock, took aim. The wrecker staggered and fell, his face a mask of surprise as his leg buckled beneath him, pistol clattering harmlessly as the justice blundered past, throwing himself upon the second, still fleeing man. There was a groan as powerful and anguished as those of the wounded as Robert Knight's bulk knocked the air from his quarry's lungs. There was a partial revival, culminating in a flurry of most unclerical blows before the victor scrambled to his feet, dragging his terrified victim by his collar. His own eye was raw as a burn and rapidly closing, but there was a look of triumphant serenity upon his dark-stubbled face as Rawlings called out to Joshua in a laughter-choked voice, 'More battles are won upon the drawing-board than the field!' to Joshua's answering laughter and, to his credit, the justice's.

The first phase of the battle so effortlessly won, Joshua, suspicious of an ambush inside, cleared the yard to interrogate the man he had wounded. The fellow was taciturn and hostile but finally responded to Joshua's quietly delivered threat to shoot him where he lay.

'How many armed men within?' he demanded.

'None, save Hardee and Hayes, the man the exciseman wounded.'

'How so?'

'Three others fled across the dunes when they knew of your coming.' His response was surly.

'Upon whose orders?'

'Two fled to save their skins,' he spat contemptuously, 'the other to a craft in the bay, upon the master's orders, with gold and other things of value to be taken to a safe place where the master will join him.'

Joshua retrieved the man's fallen pistol and raced back with it to where Rawlings and the justice, with his prisoner, sheltered behind a massive outcrop of rock sunk deep into the bare earth. He saw that the captive's hands had been fastidiously tied with the justice's silk kerchief.

'We had best break into the house,' said Joshua. 'It seems that Hardee might have some way of escape, perhaps surfacing near the bay, where he has a craft waiting. I know there are underground cellars and passageways.'

'There has been no shooting from within of late,' conceded Rawlings. 'I had thought it a ruse to lure us into an ambush.'

'There are others with Hardee?' demanded the justice of his terrified prisoner.

'No, sir, none save the wounded man, the servants and Mrs Hardee.'

'Then we must act at once.' Robert Knight scrambled awkwardly to his feet, one eye grotesquely closed and darkening. Joshua silently offered him the pistol he had taken, but the justice shook his head, saying with conscious irony, 'No, Stradling, I am a man of God, a man of peace, but I will carry it with me, for there is more danger in leaving it here.'

Rawlings was already bracing himself to throw his weight upon the door in an attempt to force it, when it was unexpectedly opened for them by Edwards, the old liveried servant. He stood aside gravely to let them enter.

'Hardee?' Joshua demanded.

'In the cellars, sir. He has taken his wife at gun point, and the injured man, Hayes, is with them.'

He led them, unbidden, to the cellar door, where one of the serving maids guarded the two storm lanterns which had already been lit.

'Send someone immediately to bring Dr Elfed Thomas from Pyle,' Joshua commanded the girl. 'Tell him his services will be required at Sker House. Say the matter is of the utmost urgency.'

She went at once, eyes wide with apprehension, as Joshua prepared to descend.

'I will come with you, sir,' offered Edwards, 'for I know every twist and turn of these passageways. It will save you time, for I fear the mistress's life is at risk.'

Joshua nodded, and the old servant and the justice took a lantern each as Joshua and Rawlings, with pistols ready, entered the darkness below the house.

It seemed to Joshua that they scurried endlessly through passageways and vaulted chambers in a dark, entangled maze. Sometimes the voices and footsteps they heard appeared close at hand, then distant, and some but the disturbed echoes of their own cries and movements. Once a muffled shot rang out and the old man stopped, trembling in the lantern light, but quickly composed himself and hurried onwards. Rawlings had to steady him as he stumbled against something, the lantern crashing to the floor, catching in its light the lifeless, blood-splashed face of Hayes, the man whom Rawlings had earlier wounded. It seemed, then, that Mrs Hardee might still be alive.

It was with a jarring shock that they came upon them: Hardee sweating and wild-eyed in the beam of the candle-lantern which his wife clutched before her. Her face was pale, ravaged with pain and tears, and Hardee held a pistol hard against her temple. There was no languidness in his voice now and no amusement as he said, with cold deliberation, 'You have come at the right moment. My wife vows that she will go no further; her leg, it seems, makes movement too painful to bear.'

He cocked his pistol purposefully.

'In the name of God,' cried the justice, 'have pity, Hardee! It is your wife of whom you speak.'

The lantern she held aloft trembled in Mrs Hardee's hand, but her voice was steady as she said, 'He has no pity, sir, no love. I would as soon he shot me. It is the only escape I seek.'

'No!' the justice cried, voice anguished. 'I promise you, there is no despair too deep for God's comfort.'

'Then let Him prove it, if there is a God!' sneered Hardee.

In a confused movement Mrs Hardee had raised the lantern and stepped forward as the justice dropped his lantern and gun and held both hands outstretched towards her. Hardee, unnerved, fired blindly and his wife seemed untouched, even taking a few steps to clasp Robert Knight's hand before she and the lantern fell to the floor, a slow stain disfiguring the shoulder of her pale gown. In the reflected beams of light, Hardee paused, then fled into the blackness. Before Joshua or Rawlings could act, the old servant had taken the gun which the justice had forsaken, and fired. There was a stumbling and crashing in the darkness beyond and a wild, thin scream that seemed more animal than human in its anguish. When Joshua ran forward with the lantern, Hardee was already dying, unable even to speak, but his eyes looked at Joshua, so filled with terror and hurt that he took his hand and stayed with him until he knew, without doubt, that he was dead.

Chapter Twenty-Four

Joshua would long remember that eerie journey back through the dark passages and vaulted chambers, carrying in his arms the frail, almost lifeless body of Mrs Hardee, her blood staining the breast of his coat. Edwards no longer bore the lantern, yet he guided them unerringly by the pale light shed by those of Rawlings and the justice back to where they had entered. The old servant was weeping soundlessly as they went, stopping from time to time to chafe his mistress's cold hands or touch her cheek, and Joshua wondered at such devotion to a woman whom he himself had seen only as suspicious and cold. Once she opened her eyes and murmured something that Joshua had to bend low to hear. He caught the single word, 'Husband . . .'

'Dead,' replied Joshua gently, and she seemed to understand for she nodded and closed her eyes.

'Yes, he is dead, thank God!' declared the old man fervently, 'for He alone knows what she has been delivered from this day, and what she suffered at the hands of that evil filth! I would not dignify him by naming him an "animal", much less a man!'

'You know that you will be charged with his killing?'

Robert Knight's voice came low from the darkness, filled with compassion.

'Yes, and I would do it again, willingly, for her sake. Many is the time I have wanted to strike him down for the violence and humiliation he brought her, but I dared not, for then she would have been alone and friendless . . .'

'I will see that you have a good advocate, that Hardee's character will be made known in court. He will be revealed for the vicious, murdering brute that he was!' promised the justice. 'A common wrecker and plunderer of the dead!'

'And the living, sir. It would soil my lips to tell you of the wickedness and depravity she was forced to witness and tolerate, the men and women he brought here openly. But I shall never speak of it in court, or to anyone save you, for I would not have her grieved and humbled. Better she died than that should come to light.'

'I think there is every chance that she will not die,' said Joshua, to comfort him. 'I believe that it is but a flesh wound to her shoulder, dangerous certainly, yet one which can be treated. It is the shock and terror besides, and the loss of blood which weakens her so. Perhaps, when Dr Thomas comes . . .'

'Yes,' said the old man with satisfaction, 'he will help her. He is the only true friend she can count on. He would give his life for her.'

When they emerged finally into the light of the cellar room, Joshua's eyes were so dazzled by the unaccustomed brightness that for a moment he was blinded by it. When he became adjusted, and the vague forms resolved into clarity, he saw the dark, thickset figure of Dr Elfed Thomas as he moved forward to take Joshua's burden. He thought he had never seen such desolation and tragedy in a human face and he knew, without a word being spoken, that it was not friendship that Thomas offered Mrs Hardee, but love, deep and selfless enough to wipe away the horrors of the past.

It seemed to Joshua that it was not merely a day which had passed, but a lifetime, as he sat facing Rawlings across the tavern table of the 'Ship Aground'. He had never before felt so dispirited, and there was none of the usual fierce exhilaration and pride which came with a task well done. Rawlings appeared scarcely more euphoric as he supped his ale.

'What do you suppose will happen to Dr Elfed Thomas?' he demanded abruptly.

'He will stand trial, certainly, for his perjury at the inquest upon the victims of the *San Lorenzo*.'

'Yet, from the accounts of the wreckers taken prisoner, it would seem that he took no part in the massacre. Indeed, so sickened did he become that he tried desperately to halt the slaughter, suffering abuse and ill-treatment in his defence of the dying,' mused Rawlings. 'I cannot help but feel pity for him.'

'Yes. I have been wondering what I would have done, given the same circumstances. Hardee's wife was the hold over him, and his love for her. Thomas could not see her degraded further in mind and spirit. I do not know whether his silence was a weakness or a strength,' Joshua confessed. 'How do you weigh the torture of the woman you love against the lives of those shipwrecked, and those to come?'

'I would not like to be his judge,' admitted Rawlings. 'He knew how vicious and remorseless Hardee could be. What manner of man is it who would deliberately hunt down his own wife to cripple and disfigure her?'

'And having done so, continue to abuse her, calling upon a doctor to treat her wounds, then blackmailing him into silence by threatening to kill her unless he perjure himself about the dead?' Joshua shook his head despairingly. 'Yet in doing so, he betrayed not only them, but himself, becoming part of the crime . . .'

'As Hardee intended,' agreed Rawlings. 'At least it seems that his wife will recover. I confess, to my shame, Joshua, that I judged her cold and unfeeling. Yet how could she trust, or give of herself, fearing that someone might discover the humiliation she endured?'

'My own judgement was as ill-made,' admitted Joshua ruefully. 'I thought her treatment of Jem Crocutt's widow rude and patronising, until Edwards let fall to the justice that it was he who had visited the farm secretly on her behalf with a bag of gold coins for the widow and family. I assure you, it does nothing to raise my self-esteem!'

'Perhaps,' said Rawlings soberly, 'Dr Elfed Thomas will feel that whatever punishment he is called upon to endure cannot be greater than that which he and Mrs Hardee have shared this long time. With Hardee's death, they are free . . .' As Joshua looked at him questioningly, Rawlings added quietly, 'There are worse prisons than a convict's cell.'

'True,' agreed Joshua.

'Well, it is ended now,' declared Rawlings. 'At least our part in it. The wreckers were all taken at the house, or upon the shore.'

'Yes, ended indeed . . . for the wrecked upon the shore, and for Jem Crocutt,' agreed Joshua with bitterness. 'But, most of all, my pity is for that poor vagrant, Dai Bando, who stumbled unwittingly upon the aftermath of the crime, tortured and murdered for a knowledge he could not confess, knowing nothing . . . Justice will mean naught to him, for he knew it neither in life nor death.'

They sat there, soberly, in silence.

'At least the servant, Edwards, has identified that wretch who forced Dai Bando to Sker House,' offered Rawlings. 'Although, as you so rightly say, Joshua, God alone knows what agonies the poor creature was forced to endure in the months he was incarcerated there!' He paused, then added pityingly, 'It scarce bears thinking about! He was too honest and too simple a soul to lie to them.'

'An epitaph every whit as sorry as his life!' exclaimed Joshua. 'And with as little comfort.'

Rawlings nodded agreement, pondering aloud, 'I wonder what forced them to kill him when they did? Perhaps their viciousness finally went too far . . . or else they grew weary of him, believing that they would learn no more. Perhaps Bando even tried to escape their persecution. Well, we shall know soon enough, for they are a gutless, treacherous pack with no loyalty, save for their own worthless skins . . .'

'It will be small consolation for Jem Crocutt's

widow,' said Joshua with some vehemence, 'for the man who murdered her husband is already dead from his quarry fall . . . I could have wished him a crueller death, for all the suffering he inflicted.'

'But at least Ezra has a new apprentice and the pauper a new home, and both share those most excellent victuals from the "Crown",' remarked Rawlings, smiling in spite of himself, 'and no doubt he will continue to grow fatter and more odious at the expense of the vestry, hoping to keep them and the justice in ignorance.'

'I would not wager upon it,' declared Joshua, 'Believe me, there is little which escapes Robert Knight, even with his one remaining good eye!'

'How so?'

'His last question to me was, "By the way, Stradling, how is young Dafydd Crocutt faring?" I replied, "Well, sir, I believe . . ." "I had not his health in mind, Stradling," he declared tartly, "but that of the Tamworth pigs!" '

It was but days since the events at Sker House had so cruelly lacerated the lives of those involved, and yet it seemed already their cutting edge had been honed smooth, memory softening pain.

Joshua had paid a Christmas visit to Southerndown Court to present Rebecca with her gifts, so carefully and lovingly wrought by Ezra, and as lovingly offered and received. She had been enchanted with the love spoon with its emblem of devotion and constancy, and by the perfection of the little sewing table. In return, she announced, laughingly, she had bought Joshua a gift which she knew would please him greatly, but he must curb his impatience until Christmas Day, when there would be a small and intimate party for family and friends, which Joshua and Devereaux must attend.

Exuberant preparations had already been made by Louisa Crandle for the New Year party for all of Joshua's and Rebecca's friends from the three hamlets, thus their engagement would be celebrated in the presence of those they loved most dearly, and who had played so vital a part in their lives and loving.

Now, on the Eve of Christmas, Joshua was preparing for the midnight mass at the tiny parish church of St John the Baptist across the village green. The rector, Robert Knight, had declared most emphatically that Joshua was expected to attend. Indeed, it would seem from murmurings overheard in the inns that the parishioners had not so much been invited as commanded to be present. In addition, there were to be guests from beyond the hamlets, including the distinguished party from Southerndown Court: Sir Matthew, Dr Peate, Rebecca and Elizabeth Crandle.

Joshua dressed with special care in what Jeremiah termed 'his gentleman's clothes', allowing himself the luxury of his high silk hat. Upon arriving at the church porch he was handed a lighted taper to place in the holder in the pew, so that the church might be softly and fittingly illuminated.

In the flickering light Joshua could see the prettily garlanded windowsills and the soft greenery at the pew ends, and below the stone sculpted pulpit, the carved stable and nativity figures which Ezra had fashioned.

Ezra and his pauper friend were seated nearby, as were Rawlings and his excisemen, Dafydd and his mother, Elwyn Morris, Emily with Haulwen, and all Joshua's close friends and acquaintances from the parish and about. His pew had been carefully reserved for him, it seemed, for within minutes the party from Southerndown Court was being ushered in beside him, kneeling upon their embroidered hassocks to make their private communion before the service began.

The rector spoke gravely his traditional words of peace, his bruised eye vivid testimony to his efforts to sustain it. An irony, Joshua was sure, which had not escaped Rawlings.

Then, strangely, imperceptibly, the atmosphere of the church seemed to change, grow still, expectant.

'There is something I must do today,' Robert Knight began, 'a gift I have to bring. It is as precious and rare in its way as the gold, frankincense and myrrh which was brought, so many centuries ago, to that humble stable where lay the Christ Child. Like Christianity itself, and our salvation, it has been dearly bought with sacrifice and bloodshed.'

He looked compassionately at Jem Crocutt's widow and Dafydd. 'There was a man of this parish, a humble, ordinary farmer, who was prepared to give his own life to protect it, and what it meant to him. It was the innocent cause, too, of the death of a poor, bewildered vagrant, and of men, women and children who were the tragic victims of an evil man's insatiable and ungodly greed. Yet,' he paused, reflecting, his glance moving in turn on Joshua, Ezra, Rawlings and Elwyn Morris, 'there are those who, knowing the cost to themselves, fought selflessly to redeem it. Today, it is my privilege and joy to return it to its rightful owner, a gentleman of Italy whose wife was one of those innocents massacred in the unholy wreck of the *San Lorenzo*.'

Robert Knight descended from the pulpit and pulled across the vestry curtains to bring forward the bereaved man. Joshua felt Rebecca's hand slip gently into his, and Sir Matthew's hand firm upon his shoulder.

'From the people of the three hamlets, sir, I return to you this symbol of peace and love, so dearly bought.'

Robert Knight put his lips gently to the cross, and held it aloft in the flickering candlelight.

In the flame, its rubies shone red and deep as droplets of blood.

In Hac Cruce Salus.
In this Cross lies Salvation

Now read this extract from the third novel in the series of Welsh village life, following *The Running Tide* and *Upon Stormy Downs*:

A Wind From The Sea

by

Cynthia S Roberts

Rebecca was jerked from her shallow sleep by a frenzied shouting and the rocking of the coach as the coachman first whipped up the horses then brought them to a shuddering halt, the animals blundering and plunging into the snow, and the reserve pair stumbling into the rear of the coach, to the terrified cries of the man atop the luggage. Rebecca struggled to the window to enquire of the coachman what was amiss, believing that they might have met with some obstacle upon the highway or stopped to aid stranded travellers in distress. What she saw so surprised her that she could but stare in open-mouthed astonishment, soon to be replaced by a cold shaking rage. A highwayman sat astride a chestnut mare, face masked and screened by a silken kerchief, cocked pistol trained upon the coachman and guard.

'Stand and deliver!'

The highwayman stared with insolent coolness at the window of the coach, seeing Rebecca's flushed and handsome face, eyes furious and filled with contempt.

'Your servant, Mistress de Breos,' he said languidly, and there was no mistaking his amusement. 'I wager there is no jewel you carry to equal you, ma'am, but you will surrender them none the less . . .'